"Marry me, my sweet!"

Reana closed her eyes and shook her head. "Marriage is not for me, Ahnoud, it is a delusion and a snare. You are very lovable, but . . ."

"Darling," he said in a husky whisper, "that you love my kisses is something." Once more he bent his head above her, his lips meeting hers. Reana felt the strength of him against her, his magnetism engulfing her completely. Unreservedly she gave him her lips, her heart beating in thudding time with the passion of his own.

She was in another world . . . unhearing, unseeing, unaware of what went on about her . . . knowing nothing *until he decided that she should.*

Enchantment

Trix MacKenzie

WARNER BOOKS

A Warner Communications Company

WARNER BOOKS EDITION

Cover Art by James Griffin

Warner Books, Inc., 75 Rockefeller Plaza, New York, N.Y. 10019

A Warner Communications Company

Printed in the United States of America

First Printing: January, 1981

10 9 8 7 6 5 4 3 2 1

Enchantment

I

Somewhere in the semitropics is a town beside a blue bay. The place has a name and the bay has a name, but to many the town is known as Sun City. It lies enough to the south to be lazily warm in January and enough to the north to be pleasant in July.

Climate first attracted winter visitors to what had been only a fishing village forty years earlier. Some lingered, unable to say farewell to the beauty and charm of this peninsula. Others left but soon returned. Perhaps they were haunted into returning by vivid memories of the place.

Houses were built—simple ones, then those more pretentious. Gardens were cultivated, roads put through palmetto brush, and docks extended into the bay where luxury yachts soon came to anchor.

As the years passed, people said, in the accents of many states, "Here is our home." Millions of dollars from northern banks were lavished in improving the peninsula. It has been said that money made Sun City. Many know there is something else.

The town has a definite magnetism. Once gone, one dreams of its easy life, its flowers and winter sunshine. Those who have travelled away and returned, vowing never to leave again, are sure there is a beautiful enchantment in the very air of Sun City.

A gay winter season was at its height. The bay was behaving nicely for both fisherman and sailor, and the weather was showing off for tourists. Crowded hotels housed half the notables of the world and streamlined cars hugged the Boulevard. There was golf beneath the sun and dancing beneath the stars.

On a day toward the close of January's brilliant weeks, excitement shot along the palm-bordered avenues of Sun City. People paused in the midst of their hectic playing. Women shuddered, fascinated. Men swore futilely.

"Who is Ahnoud Bey Why the stir up over him?"

"Read your morning paper, silly. You're moss backed."

"You'd better say, 'Ask those who saw him last night at the Palm Club.' He had us glassy eyed."

"Oh well, who isn't glassy eyed by midnight at the Palm Club?"

"I don't mean stewed, youngster. I mean Bey performed magic tricks—*played* a piano with his mind—and did the women fall for it!"

"Then it's the Palm Club for us tonight. And I in my new Chanel gown—Egyptian red!"

II

Ahnoud Bey, youthful and simple of manner, only spectacular in the fame his intellect and mystical power had brought him, spent his evenings in a suite at the Bayside Hotel. Here he read a great deal and sat beside a window where the air was like spring and the scene below a constant source of enjoyment to his wondering eyes.

As a stranger suddenly walking hand in hand with beauty, Ahnoud resented the public work that kept him indoors at the Palm Club. He had not been very punctual for those performances lately, and his manager was raising all sorts of protests. Nor were these rebukes unwarranted.

Like the rest of Sun City, Ahnoud was

putting work second. His special point of distraction was a lighthouse that stood at Pelican Point, some ten miles down the Bay from Sun City.

Nearly every evening he drove out there, and in the deepening dusk he walked along the beach, hard and white, where pelicans came to be fed. Then, reluctantly Ahnoud returned to the club—to another night at the piano—another night of crowds, packed, standing, applauding . . .

By eleven o'clock the crowd had watched and wearied of Jado and Conchita, the dancing sensation of New York and, for three weeks before Bey came, the toast of Sun City.

By eleven, there was a distinct unrest among groups at the tables. Boredom seemed to have settled over champagne glasses and ashtrays.

Women's eyes, lovely but weary, glanced out open French windows. There was the garden—palms still in the mild air and flowers heavily sweet. In spite of it all, the audience was impatient, waiting for the thrill of Ahnoud Bey and his Mystic Melody.

"Where's the Egyptian dish, Ted?" someone asked, as Ted Maxime moved among the tables, greeting here, joking there as only he could. Ted knew everything about everybody, and no one could imagine Sun City without Maxime and his Palm Club.

"You can't make that boy understand we live by standard time in this part of the world," replied Maxime, resting his suntanned hands on a table near the center of the room.

"Isn't Bey late again?" someone else asked, and Ted nodded.

"Expect him when you see him. I can't do anything about it, but he's sure-fire. I understand he's kept audiences in London and New York waiting, so who are we to complain?

"You know, yesterday I said to him, 'Ahnoud, what's your secret, anyway?' He looked me through and through with those funny eyes and said, 'The universal mind.' And did I feel dumb!"

"He is right," agreed a French professor of psychology. "Ah, the universal mind! That is the answer to all things!"

Three tables away to the left a slightly inebriated gentleman tapped a fork on his plate and sang out, "*The* univershal *mind!* The—uni-*ver*-shal mind!"

"Ted," reproached the young and dark-eyed Sylvia Adams, "you promised to introduce Ahnoud to me—and then you didn't." Phil Pelham, across from Jim Adams' wife, caught Maxime's eye with a grimace. Ted understood and countered, "Sylvia, what are you doing, first-naming that heathen?"

"I like his Mystic Melody," she stated. A few tables back, Jado, the Spanish dancer, moodily repeated, "*Mystic Melody,*" as though in condemnation.

With Jado was a very beautiful woman whose intent stare was riveted on the low stage that stood between the French windows.

Now, with a whispered word, a waiter stepped up to the orchestra leader. The musicians finished a waltz and soon all chatter subsided in the Palm Club. This was Ahnoud Bey's prelude—silence.

"The great one," commented Jado, "late again!" The woman opposite him, she of the fair, impassive face and twilight eyes, sat motionless. Softly, she murmured, "At last!"

In the darkened room with a dim light upon him, and with the dark red floor under his feet, Ahnoud Bey stood before his audience. Bey was tall, with the athletic build of broad-shouldered youth. In the smooth lines of his white tuxedo and black trousers there was innate smartness. Here was Bond Street and Park Avenue, but in those meditative eyes under thick black lashes was Egypt, old and a little disillusioned.

This hint of the East was only a subtle one, the bold sketch of the picture being extremely modern. Dark hair was waved back from a widow's peak and Bey's hands were strong and supple. Clever fingers clasped easily over clever fingers and the gold of a watch band gleamed on one wrist. Ahnoud seemed deliberately to be waiting for something.

No one in that gathering, from princeling to divorcée, appeared to breathe. All eyes were on the impressive figure before them. And still Ahnoud waited.

Behind him was a French window, open wide and framing the tropical midnight sky. A setting moon hung within this oblong. Palm leaves cut its light, which fell across a hand-carved baby grand piano, beside which Bey stood.

The famous piano was golden in its shining entirety, except for the small black keys. These only accented the high gloss of those of deep yellow pearl.

Moonlight crossed the room and lay limp on a dozen or more tables. From one of these a woman rose to her feet—a woman almost unreal in the tranquil glow, so a part of it she seemed.

Her delicate pallor and slenderness, her clinging dress and smooth hair all seemed etched from the moonbeams' own remote mystery.

Ahnoud Bey drew in a quick breath. It was for this he had waited, tonight and the night before. Those eyes, calm as southern skies, rested on him for one long moment, went past Ahnoud to the piano, then returned.

Now Jado took her hand and urged her back to the chair beside him into which she sank with a smile sad and sweet as shadows of lonely pine trees.

Ahnoud received her message. He spoke now, in a low and pleasing voice.

"Good evening, my friends! I play tonight to the loveliness of a Golden Lady."

With a catlike step he reached the piano and seated himself on the tapestry-covered bench. He touched the Golden Keys with accustomed fingers in which keen psychic ability was blended with the musical.

What he played was the song of Sun City to which he had so recently come. It was a musical impression of the semitropics that Ahnoud's fingers drew from the piano. Through his touch, so strong yet so sensitive, the listener could envision blue shores where Maytime stayed year round.

Dominant chords crashed and one saw the fury of a hurricane. It abated perceptibly and the measures of light melody were as bright and fresh as the returning sun. Gaiety was in the fast dance tempo and one thought of Sun City's crowded avenues—the dash and color of her winter season.

Now Ahnoud Bey's fingers slowed to the lingering tones of a serenade. He lifted his head and faced the moon, playing gently and rather sadly of romance under Southern skies.

"Ah—he finishes—the master!" It was spoken so as to be barely audible, but a knowing person answered, "No, he's just beginning."

A hush fell over the supper club as Bey braced one foot on the floor and pushed his piano bench all of one yard from the instrument.

He sat very straight, with his feet against a low rung of the bench, fingers locked behind his back. His gaze centered on the baby grand piano. For a few seconds he remained absolutely still, his profile a silhouette in the moonlight that slanted across the stage.

Now the Golden Keys began to move. They played of their own accord, in Ahnoud's identical style. Every phrase, every harmonious bar, each deep beat of the music Bey had rendered was repeated with exact precision. This was the Mystic Melody—rung out as though by clear-voiced bells.

The audience was transfixed, with all eyes on the mentalist. Palm Club patrons felt the strain of Bey's concentration, realizing its force yet comprehending it only vaguely.

An electric current seemed to run through the room, for the music had made them all one. There was no individual mind nor person, only one great ensemble—the universal mind—in-tune with Ahnoud Bey and his Golden Keys.

III

After Ahnoud left the stage there was a stort pause, then the lights came up. The orchestra went into a rhumba, yet somehow no one felt like dancing. Many had peculiar shivers. Their voices sounded odd, their mirth too hollow.

"Why baby," one invited, "you're all white lipped after Bey's stunt. C'mon, havva drink. Warm you up." So drinks went round. Rouge compacts were opened and used, as women, gradually coming back, shakily laughed it off.

"How's it done, Ted? You don't expect us to believe our eyes and ears, do you?"

"Optical illusion—" This with a finality that was an attempt to say it all in a few words. Ted cut off that one with a swift retort.

"*Optical illusion?* Listen, don't you know

anything? Go to Egypt sometime and have a look at the fakirs on the streets. They're holy men and they're better than Bey. Of course some of them are fakes, but not so Ahnoud. *He's genuine!* That's been proven everywhere, whether you believe it or not."

"Holy man—eh?" A question came from the circle at a table for eight where Ted had dropped into a chair and was lighting a cigarette. "Not so holy, I'll say, if there's one grain of truth in New York gossip."

"Ahnoud's no fakir." Ted came back quickly. "Those boys are just Gandhi—with more clothes and no specs. Bey's half American, educated at Oxford—mah deah fellah—and all that!"

"Aw Ted—" protested someone else, "don't tell us there's no cord plugged in to make those piano keys go ta-ta-ta!"

"Look, Ted," said Sylvia, "I'm going to phone Ahnoud and invite him to a tea at my house, then you'll have to bring him, you meanie!" Ted affectionately patted Sylvia's shoulder but shook his head.

"Now honey." He remonstrated. "Bey's too queer a sort for you to entertain in that swell new villa. Jim's my pal, and while he's away on his jobs I'm in charge of you. And I say, *no Ahnoud Bey for you.* See?"

Throughout the room everyone had been deeply stirred by the Mystic Melody exhibition. Now cigarettes were *puff-puffed.* Glasses were *clink-clinked.* Talk was a jumble of dialects. There was doubt and discomfort. A newspaper publisher argued with a prince who had no country.

"But this young man is an enigma to Europe's psychoanalysts. Practical explanation of his act is impossible. Representatives of our local papers have made thorough investigations. They found only an exceptionally well made piano—and a mental wizard."

"Haven't your papers in Europe carried stories of Ahnoud Bey?" asked the prince. The publisher nodded, much interested.

"They certainly have," he replied. "He is young—not over thirty-five. In fact Ahnoud Bey is only starting. A few years from now—watch him! He'll be the greatest human wonder of our modern world."

A breeze from the bay swept in, a breeze as cool as the outside of a frosted silver goblet. It rustled magnolia leaves in the garden outside and billowed French window curtains. It sent tobacco smoke toward the ceiling and played with the curling hair of blonde and brunette.

Sylvia Adams, in her satin dress backless and black as her hair—Sylvia, of the beauty-contest-winning figure—went visiting. Denied Ahnoud by the unequivocal Ted, she took John Kingston as second choice.

"It's time you came to pay your respects," he said, laughing, as she sat down at his table. "You neglect me all evening and because you're alone a moment, over you come. That doesn't make me any the less glad to see you—looking swell, too! Say, Jim must be a model husband. How is he, anyhow?"

"Nice, rich, fatter than ever—and off on a construction job right now."

"Still think you picked a prize?"

Sylvia dubiously acquiesced. "Oh yes—no doubt about it—but," with a look of dissatisfaction, a slight frown, "J. L.'s away so much. Now here I am, begging Ted Maxime to introduce me to Ahnoud Bey. Ted merely tells me to roll a hoop, or something to that effect." She sighed in self-commiseration, meanwhile putting on more lipstick before a small square mirror.

Sylvia put up her compact and turned to John, sensing that he had been unusually quiet. He was staring across the room to a corner near the stage. He had a funny look—a sort of "seeing ghosts" look—on his face.

"Are you listening to that music," asked Sylvia, "or are you stricken by the beauty of my neighbor, who sits, where your eyes are glued, with that Spanish Jado?"

"Your neighbor?" Kingston was absorbed with this woman of whom he had just become aware.

"Okay," said Sylvia, "she can be a neighbor, can't she? The fact is she lives near us in Desdena subdivision. Jim built her place. I know her—but not well. Few folks here do. Five years ago she came to Sun City to live. She has a past, but what it is, who knows—and who cares? We all have them. I really think she's gorgeous. I wish I had been a blonde."

John Kingston missed the last wistful and foolish note in Sylvia's résumé of the Golden Lady. He was brooding on the passage of time. Sixteen years! How it could change a person! How it had changed her! If indeed, it was she. Only by chance John had heard someone call her name, then something in her face brought back the past vividly.

He was not at all certain, in fact he was wavering already from his first decision. That was ridiculous. This "Golden Lady"—this poised and worldly-wise young woman, with broken blossoms in her eyes—couldn't possibly be the girl he once knew.

Now she was bending over the table and scribbling on the menu card's margin. The dancer caught her moving hand and there was alarm in his face.

"Do not, dear, I beg you!" Jado entreated. "Ahnoud Bey is dangerous! Of course you do not know, but alas, I do! I am of his world—or rather the world to which he condescends—that of the entertainer. Do not let yourself slip into his power, *querida,* for dark regret will shadow your life, should Ahnoud Bey cast his cursed spell upon you."

The lovely lady in gold lamé was, however, unswayed. She smiled slightly, removed Jado's hand, held it in her own left hand, and continued writing. The dancer watched her as she swept the room with impersonal eyes. Finally she signaled a waiter. When he approached there was another protest from Jado.

"Take this to Ahnoud Bey," the lady said simply, placing a torn bit of menu card in the waiter's hand, along with a greenback. The dancer only glowered. From another table came his partner Conchita's laugh, mocking, jealous.

John Kingston half-rose to his feet. He must speak to this "Golden Lady" now—try to ascertain her identity—see if he found any happiness in those calculating eyes. This duty he owed a great friendship.

It was too late. She was wrapping her coat about her and rising as though to leave. Kingston resumed his seat, resolving that he would look her up next day, unless a telegram he expected early in the morning took him away from Sun City.

"Jado," the lady was saying, "don't be angry. The sedan is parked outside. Wait in it and ride home with me, won't you?" Her voice was full of intriguing inflections. It was the one voice in the world to harmonize with the expression in those sophisticated violet eyes.

"*Mother of God!* Do not go to him!" begged Jado in an intense whisper. She only smiled again, drawing the furry white folds of her coat closer.

"You're being melodramatic, my friend," she replied. Jado felt suddenly ill. She was so exquisite! White and gold—snowy coat, shimmering dress—arrogant in their simplicity! There was just a hint of the sun on that white skin—and her hair was gold mist. She was soft white, smooth gold, and reticent grace.

Now the lady left Jado and swayed away between the tables, seeing nothing as she passed, her real self withdrawn behind those thoughtful eyes.

The dancer slumped in his chair, all light gone from his face, while he ordered liquor, which to him was like a poison. With dark eyes he gazed across the ballroom. Again came Conchita's laugh and her malicious tone. "Fool!"

Then a sympathetic voice said, "Poor Harlequin—behind the eight ball." Jado was deaf to the jeers of those about him. His eyes were on a tall figure, a broad-shouldered figure in white tuxedo outside in the lobby.

Ahnoud Bey held in his hand a torn bit of menu card. His handsome, provocative profile was bent above the message, as with brows upraised and lips curved in pleasure, he read:

May I see you in the
Jasmine Dining Room?
The Golden Lady

IV

Ahnoud's hesitation as he hovered near the door of a private room was born of discretion, which for the moment had gained mastery over his real desires. He did not think it odd that she asked to meet him. It was the answer to his oft-repeated but unspoken wish.

Bey had felt this lovely woman watch him each time he played. The first night she came alone, though Maxime and Jado spent the evening at her table. Another time she appeared with a party of six, moving among the tables like a proud lady of the snows.

That night her dress seemed shaped from glittering crystals of ice, her wrap snatched from drifts of white flakes. That hair was like a cap of sunlight and into those eyes had surely been blown the smoke from distant forest fires.

Ahnoud had grown to regard her presence as a potent inspiration. He rather dreaded the day when he must perform without her silent approbation.

Tonight he had tried to convey to the Golden Lady his immediate need of her. This he effected by thought transference and by the dedication of his program to her. Here was her reply—a voluntary gesture. Bey read the note again, then opened the door marked "Jasmine."

She stood as he entered the room and they faced each other with a great deal of surprise—she that he had come and he at the delicacy of her beauty at close range. He was dazzled, as one is by a sparkling snow scene, and somewhat emotional over the response he saw in her face. He put out a hand in a rather hopeless way, for he longed to say, "I have loved you so long! I hoped—*I knew*—you would be like this." Instead of what was in his heart, he uttered only the brief and formal words that custom would have him use. He bent his head toward her, smiling and stating simply, "I am Ahnoud Bey."

"And I," she replied, "am Reana Robinson, or—as you flatter me—the Golden Lady." She laughed and took his hand. They sat down on the Chesterfield. Nearby a table was standing just as it had been cleared of a private dinner a short time before.

"You must know," said Reana, "that I like your playing immensely. I've been here every night."

"And I was just wondering," Ahnoud admitted, "what I shall do when you're not there to listen." Reana seemed astonished.

"You really noticed that I came every night?" she asked.

Ahnoud nodded. "That sort of thing doesn't happen often. When I expressed my appreciation to Ted Maxime he changed the subject."

Reana laughed again. "He was afraid I'd take you away from the Palm Club, where you certainly are a business asset right now."

Ahnoud's face brightened. "Please do," he begged. "I'm here for six weeks. People in Sun City act as though I were a freak. I find myself a bit lonely. Sometimes I visit that lighthouse way down on a tip of land. Have you been there?"

"Of course," she answered, "many times. We can go out together one day and I'll take you up to see the big light."

"Thank you. This means we're going to be friends?"

Reana was silent for a moment while dance music drifted in from the main dining room. Ahnoud was conscious of a fragrance that hung about her and recalled it as a very new perfume—exorbitantly tariffed—"Southern Night."

"You may think I'm crazy," Reana ventured, "but for two mornings at dawn, just as I was in that borderland between sleep and consciousness, I heard your music. It was not a radio, as I have none and my neighbors are not near. When I awakened fully I said to myself, 'I have heard the Golden Keys!' "

Ahnoud leaned toward her confidingly, his eyes odd and sober. "You heard my music," he replied with an unmistakable meaning in his words, "because I was awake—watching the dawn and thinking of you."

"It's too strange to be true," she objected, incredulity in her voice. She passed slender fingers over her eyes.

"You see, I was only half asleep and could dimly see things about my bedroom. It was all so queer. I must have been dreaming of the Golden Keys, having heard you play them so many times."

"No," Ahnoud assured her with peculiar finality, "you were not dreaming." Reana did not reply. She was amazed at Bey's statement that he had mentally communicated his music to her as she lay in bed.

The idea was fantastic, yet it rather fascinated her. She turned to face him. There was something of the confessional in her attitude.

"I am guilty," she said slowly, "of wanting the Golden Keys for my new music salon. Your piano is such a precious thing, with the song of harp and bells. Where can I find one like it?"

Ahnoud shook his head. "It was custom-made for East Indian royalty," he explained. "There is not another Golden Keys piano anywhere."

Reana was disappointed. "Oh I'm sorry," she replied, "and of course you're too attached to yours to sell it. I'd pay any price you asked."

Ahnoud measured her face with his indigo eyes. "*Any* price I ask?" he echoed. The emphasis he placed on the first word gave his question a double meaning.

"I want it so much," Reana assured him, "that I would not argue over the bargain."

Ahnoud regarded the Golden Lady in subtle contemplation, but with well-concealed admiration. What slender feet in those high-heeled, dainty slippers! What slim ankles—and a dress that clung to the feminine curves of her figure!

Hers was a dimpled chin, a romantic mouth, and the fairest hair that curled airily about her earrings. For all that, she could have Ahnoud Bey, he was sure, for the making or breaking.

"No," he said at last, "I cannot sell—but I might *give*—" Reana was at once pleased.

"You mean, naturally," she interrupted, "that you would consider exchanging the piano for some art treasure of mine?"

Again Bey smiled. *The American woman!* She was delightful, irresistible. She dressed and danced a daring role. She advertised her sophistication, yet missed an innuendo that the most naive European woman would grasp in an instant. However, he nodded politely.

"Good," agreed Reana eagerly, "then you'll drive out to Desdena and see my curios? I have a Taj Mahal tapestry, and a miniature of Westminster Abbey carved from a block of agate. Oh, I have lots of things that might interest you. I collected them on my travels here and there, before I found Sun City. I will be at home tomorrow afternoon. Come and look them over."

"Thank you for your invitation," Ahnoud replied evenly. "I will be happy to be there at five."

"For tea?" she asked.

"No, I'm not English."

"Then cocktails—or coffee," she suggested, taking from his hand the torn portion of the menu card that held her note. Under the scribbled words the Golden Lady pencilled her address and returned it to Ahnoud. He glanced at the parchment scrap, reading.

Reana Robinson,
2012 Desdena Way

"Ray-ah-nah," Ahnoud said aloud, supplying the missing French accents. "What a pretty name."

"It sounds right—and lovely—as you pronounce it," she commented. As she rose to go, Ahnoud stood also, noting that although she was slightly above average height for a woman, she appeared small when compared to him.

Now she paused by the door, her sunlight cap of hair barely grazing the word *Jasmine*. Ahnoud wrapped the white coat about her shoulders. He held her encircled, while he looked down into those twilight eyes, baffling eyes.

" 'Southern Night,' " he murmured, brushing his lips across her shining hair, sweet with that elusive perfume. "You came to me out of its darkness and I shall never let you vanish into it again."

"Yes," she answered very low, "the past is like a Southern night—heavy sweetness, soft darkness hiding tragedy."

"And the sun will never rise on it, Reana?" Ahnoud asked with some fear. "No one will come—to take you—back?"

The Golden Lady sighed and Bey thought

her hand felt cold as it touched his. She shook her head and then, as with a great effort, "No, Ahnoud, the sun will not rise and no one will come."

V

As they left the Jasmine Room and entered the foyer, a vacant stillness met them. There was an amber glow from the rust-iron chandelier overhead. Its light fell on an extravagant floor whose bright tiles shone like colored mirrors

Beyond an arched entranceway, past a stone terrace, a long sedan waited in the curving moonlit drive.

Ted Maxime loved the blare and crowd of early evenings at his Club, but after midnight things dulled a bit. This late crowd grew sentimental, grouping around several tables, generally in twos and fours, talking, dreaming, and dancing little.

Ted had formed the habit of leaving the Club about two o'clock, sometimes earlier. Tonight he was saying farewell until tomorrow to his friends. From the foyer one could see him moving from table to table.

It was not upon him, however, that Reana now fastened her eyes. She was watching a figure slouched against one of the twisted columns near the door of the café.

With a clutching terror in her throat, she tried to speak to Ahnoud—to warn him—but no words came. Her grasp on his wrist was barely quick enough.

Jado darted the length of the foyer and took a slide across the tiles. He caught at Ahnoud's arm, which still held Reana.

"*Dios!*" he cried. "You son of a disbeliever! Dealer in black magic! *Deny it*—if you can! Take your hands off her! If you try to take her from me—" His voice had risen steadily until it was a shrill cry. His right hand clapped against his red silk rhumba sash, gripping something hidden in its folds.

"No—no, Jado! You don't understand!" Reana rebuked. She turned in distress to Ahnoud. "He doesn't know what he's saying. He's mad drunk—" Bey put her behind him with a strong arm. She shuddered at the scowl on his face.

He held himself straight and aloof, but the sting of Jado's insults flamed through his proud being. Anger faded from the mystic's face as he laughed insolently. Slapping Jado's hand away from his sash front, Ahnoud jerked out a small knife. He threw the blade carelessly into a far corner of the foyer, where it clattered with sudden force on the tiles.

Bey said nothing, but Jado's talk grew

louder, his invective stronger. Finally Ahnoud caught the dancer's hands in an iron grip.

"Shut up, *you fool*—causing a scene like this!"

Already people were running out from the main dining room. Some grasped napkins in their hands, others held cocktail glasses or cigarettes.

They were amused and only mildly interested as they stood in groups around the twisted columns. None ventured word or action. In a moment Ted Maxime flung himself into the foyer.

"What's the matter? *What's the matter?* I can't have fighting in my Palm Club. C'mon now, you two—break it up!"

In a daze Jado saw Reana place a restraining hand on Bey's arm and heard her say in a low voice, "Ahnoud, don't hurt him."

The dancer felt relief as that bone-breaking grip on his wrists loosened, but Ahnoud Bey's haunting eyes still held Jado's fast. He grew dizzy as the Egyptian whispered, "No one lives long if he stand in *my* way." Then with a smile and louder, "Yes—*très bien*—I will deliver your apology to the lady."

Jado reeled back against Ted, covering his aching temples and blinded eyes with his hands. The dancer heard nothing but a discord that resounded in his ears. It was Bey's piano—the strange, half-human piano that played of its own accord.

Now the chords beat and jangled in crazing sequence. This was music of the Golden Keys, but now it was loud and distorted. It cut a line of torture through the dancer's head.

"*Mi Madre!*" he screamed, pressing his palms tighter against his throbbing forehead "The music he played on that piano—it's like a knife—there—driving me crazy!" He collapsed into Ted's arms and was taken to the Jasmine Room for first aid.

Bewildered, the crowd stood about. Some shrugged, attributing Jado's last words to his drunken condition.

"Poor kid! What a head he'll have in the morning! He'll be hearing the Bells of St. Mary's and the chimes of St. Andrews." Others, of keener discernment, stared at the figure of Ahnoud Bey and murmured, "They say he has the power to kill—*with his mind*—those whom he hates."

Ted soon emerged from the Jasmine Dining Room. His quiet ease reassured his patrons as he drew them back with him into the dancing room.

With a few tactful words and gay wisecracks he availed himself of Sylvia, and together they led off into a fox trot. Soon the floor was crowded, the incident forgotten. Thus was Ted's magic.

Back in the foyer Ahnoud turned to Reana and saw that she was visibly shaken.

"I'm sorry this happened," he said in a voice that had somehow never lost, throughout the melee, that low, balanced tone. "It was hard for you, I know. Blame me—then forgive me."

Reana laughed nervously, but taking his hand in hers she started toward the front entrance.

"Come along," she invited. "You're priceless. You're puzzling—" Then as her voice dropped lower, "You're sweet."

Reana's chauffeur, erect and uniformed, closed a famous mystic and Sun City's most charming lady into the sedan.

The chauffeur took his seat behind the wheel, and with scarcely a glance into the rear-view mirror above him, he threw in the clutch and touched the gas. The car rolled down Ted Maxime's driveway, through the Palm Club's garden, and out into the Boulevard.

To the left, toward town, lights in white globes edged the level concrete road. To the right, toward Desdena subdivision, was only a moon-silvered vista—weird, tropical foliage against a dusty blue sky—only the Southern night.

In this direction, down a deserted road, they drove. A silence had fallen over the two in the back seat. That she was courting danger in encouraging Ahnoud Bey Reana was sure, but it was this very danger that drew her against her will.

Her heart was pounding terribly and she placed one hand over it. Her face must have shown fear and discomfort, for Ahnoud immediately slid a hand beneath hers, holding his palm on the aching spot.

"Some say I have a knack of healing with my hands," he explained. "Are they right?" His face was near hers, his voice steady and low.

Reana leaned back, soothed by his warm touch that seemed to subdue the strange, painful heartbeats. "Oh thanks," she said, "that makes it better."

Something in her words melted Ahnoud Bey. He dropped his arm about her, saying, "Darling," in an emphatic way when there was no reason in the world for saying it.

Reana looked up into his face. Topped by thick dark hair, that face was modern in its coat of suntan, Eastern in its enigmatic aura, and Western in its lines of humorous expression.

"Ahnoud," she asked, "why are your eyes so blue? Real fakirs have black eyes and dreadful beards." An unhappy shadow passed over Bey's countenance when the question of that heritage of indigo eyes arose.

"Because my father was American," he replied. Just that, and a bit reluctantly. Reana touched his cheek with a light hand.

"Ahnoud," she said, "I think when you were a very small boy, Venus must have kissed you and left the shape of her lips on yours." Ahnoud smiled at the thought and bent his dark head nearer to the shining one.

"And after so long a time," he asked slowly, "she returns—for another kiss?" The car rushed on down the road into Desdena where yellow, blue, and green lanterns burned on the lampposts of that fairyland.

"Darling," Ahnoud said again, after a silence, "for that you may have my heart and soul—and the piano with Golden Keys."

VI

Peter was singing his morning song to a day that was young. As a matter of fact, he thought himself old, wise and gray feathered in contrast to the youthful sun that was sending horizontal rays across Desdena Shores. Peter had saluted so many dawns in this subdivision that he felt quite the veteran of bird greeters.

From his lofty perch on a pine branch he looked down on the flossy little red birds that rustled the leaves of a hibiscus bush. The golden-voiced mocker was particularly contemptuous, too, of the sparrows hopping about on the grass. Peter knew he was in a class by himself. He observed his contemporaries only to ape their calls with utter perfection.

Of course, there was a bird called the nightingale that sang very sweetly in England.

There was also the caged canary, whose captivity made his voice the more pathetic. Robins were talented too. They wintered frequently in these parts, as did the bluebird who spent every February at J. L. Adams' Desdena estate.

Peter was courteous but not too cordial to these visitors. They said goodbye as friends, but no one at the villa knew when they left. Peter kept on warbling, with uncanny accuracy, the songs of both robin and bluebird.

Now the sun climbed above tree tops, above the pine trees' highest branches. It cast a silver sheen on the waters of the bay some blocks to eastward. It slanted across red tile roofs, green tile roofs, across roman-striped awnings and the balcony canopies of lavender fringe with black.

The subdivision, flat with the sea level, gay with rainbow colors as far as the eye could reach, was at that hour quiet as the dead.

A few well-trained servants were stirring in the kitchens of the stucco villas, but the owners of those buff and delphinium-blue houses were wrapped in deep slumber. Dawn meant nothing to them. Eight o'clock was the middle of the night.

Near the electric-lighted archway that led into town, the telephone exchange was housed in a small building, pink as the oleanders that grew around it. At their switchboards two operators knit sports sweaters during the lull of early morning hours, read magazines, or merely gossiped.

In Desdena this was the hushed hour, when butlers stealthily entered living rooms and removed the remainders of night before parties.

It was the time when chauffeurs polished cars for mornings along the beach. At Jim Adams' villa it was the opportunity Sylvia's colored maid awaited. This was her chance to iron young Mrs. Adams' fine lingerie, washed the day before.

"Miss Sylvia," said Carrie Lou, "she is *so* fussy about these lace medallions. She will surely know if I don't press them face down. And the little ribbons—well—that *is* somethin'—"

Carrie Lou talked in the refined voice that she had acquired during many years of serving Sun City's critical ladies. Meanwhile she ironed tiny panties and a lace nightie with utmost care.

"Miss Ca' Lou," said the rotund cook who was always balancing a stalk of celery in his hands, "did you tell me one, or two eggs for Miss Sylvia's breakfast? I forgets numbers somehow when I hears yo' talk—like yo' been talking'—kinda sweet like." Carrie Lou laughed with much self-consciousness.

"Why Mr. Jackson, what things yo' go on! Now it was not even one egg for Miss Sylvia today. She said yesterday to make it a dish of bran instead. She has taken on two pounds and is worried."

At this the chef shook all over with merriment. "Two li'l pounds," he said to the mammoth Frigidaire. "Yessum—Miss Sylvia, she is *so fleshy* she have a sight uv worryin' to do 'bout two li'l pounds!"

The sun was growing warm and Peter moved over to a royal palm nearer the house. He seemed to know that it was high time for the household to be aroused and for the sleepy head in that awninged room to be awakened. He raised his voice exultantly.

The cheery notes of the mockingbird's song filled Sylvia's room. She came slowly out of her dream about a certain Ahnoud Bey. In her dream there had been no Reana Robinson, but here was reality again and Reana's house over there facing the Bay.

"Peter!" she cried with childish irritation, "no more opera, *please*, I want to sleep—" She turned and buried her cheek in a lace pillow. She could see Peter's cute little person out there, swinging against the blue sky.

He was on the mimosa tree now, flirting with sweet blossoms. She watched him through the bronze screen below half-lowered ivory Venetian blinds. He flitted about just beyond pale yellow curtains that draped the windows in graceful silken folds.

"What's the use of getting up," Sylvia went on drowsily. "Nothing new—same old crowd. Cocktails, wisecracks, and yacht parties! Mmm—sick of yacht parties! Now—*last night*—"

She closed her eyes on that memory while she twisted one of the dark curls that was tickling her chin. It was a curl just like this that Johnny had cut off with his pocket knife and tied to the ship's flagpole. A "pirate flag" they had called it—the sillies!

The mockingbird paused, then hearing no

sound within the room, he lifted his head and loosed another paean of song to the new day.

"Peter!" screamed Sylvia. She sat up and reached for a telegram lying on the table by her bed.

The wire had come the night before. She hadn't bothered to open the envelope, knowing well it only contained more of Jim's ramblings. He was the living personification of the slogan "don't write—telegraph." After many years of many wires, Sylvia imagined that J. L. Adams could not write, even were he so inclined.

In a hurried, half-awake glance, she read the message.

DEAR BABY WHAT ARE YOU DOING WITH YOUR SWEET LITTLE SELF ALL THIS TIME STOP HAVE A GOOD TIME AND DONT GET LONESOME STOP TELL TED THIS TOWN NEEDS A NIGHT SPOT NOTHING TO DO EVENINGS STOP NOT THAT IT MATTERS STOP WE ARE WORKING FIFTEEN MILES DOWN THE BAY SO GET IN TOWN MIGHTY SELDOM.

Sylvia curled her pretty lips over that "we are working." She sighed with something close to exasperation. It meant that her husband was overseeing a waterfront building job on the spot of construction, an entirely unnecessary proceeding.

His office—his building, rather—on Central Boulevard, with two hundred feet of glass window frontage and a huge neon sign that read "The James L. Adams Company" meant a little bit of nothing to Jim.

His idea of heaven was to go off on these

"jobs." He loved to mess around hot, new subdivisions and smelly harbors in sweaty working clothes, sometimes wearing nothing but pants and a pith helmet. Nor did these help the scenery, for what could be less exciting than a fat man in his forties without a shirt?

He was okay of course, to his Sun City friends. He practically *was* the Chamber of Commerce, the Yacht Club, and the Rotarians. No man on the peninsula was more popular than Jim Adams. There was no one who could play a faster game of poker nor a faster game of helping out a buddy in a pinch.

Jim had almost built that million-dollar pier himself, inch by inch. He had promoted Desdena Shores from palmetto scrub brush to a veritable Garden of Eden.

What he really liked, however, was to pal around with his workmen—those boys he had picked up and to whom he had handed twenty-five-a-week jobs.

J. L. liked to eat hamburgers "all the way" and laugh with his men over somewhat broad jokes. He had even wanted to bring some of the boys home to the villa once, but how Sylvia had put her foot down on that—*how!*

VII

Young Mrs. Adams pushed an electric buzzer beside her bed. A couple of minutes later she sleepily greeted Carrie Lou.

"Miss Sylvia, you lookin' mighty well this mawnin'." The maid came smiling into the room, her arms laden with laundered underthings. She carefully put them away in their special drawers. Sylvia sat on the side of her bed, watching the neat, pleasant servant.

Pondering several things, J. L.'s wife saw her perfect maid as more than perfect this forenoon. Last night, as on many other nights, Carrie Lou had been up waiting for Sylvia when she came in, a little uncertainly, just before daybreak.

She thought how different was this "waiting up" from that of her mean old stepmother back home in Arkansas.

"Young lady, the next time you stay out till after midnight," she had once warned, "don't come in at all. You're going to perdition, yes, perdition—"

One night Sylvia had danced until morning. She didn't go home to the tumbledown house but to a girl friend's flat—and *from there?* If Jim Adams' villa were perdition, it was a very nice layout. In this setting, one was loved, allowed to be modern and lighthearted.

"Carrie Lou, you wouldn't leave me, would you?"

A rising inflection ran through the honeyed voice in reply. "Why Miss Sylvia, 'cos I wouldn't. Why you ask me?"

Mrs. Adams bounced across the room, tapping her feet in dance steps—those feet in tiny gold leather mules. Dark curls shook about her shoulders as she stopped before a full-length mirror.

"Oh, no reason," she answered. "Only—I need you, we get on. If there's anything else you want—higher wages, more of my clothes, or anything—just let me know. Will you, Carrie Lou?"

The maid appeared in the bathroom doorway. She was reverently opening a bottle of blue bath salts. She grinned engagingly.

"I'm jus' satisfied, Miss Sylvia," she testified. "You are the sweetest, most very generous young lady I ever served—an' I boun' I will serve you long as you want me for yoah maid."

Sylvia heard with only half her mind. The other half was studying her reflection in the mirror. Her figure, in tea-rose pajamas, was showing the slightest signs of heaviness. This was the result of much good living and not enough exercise.

She was exactly five feet two. That height was padded firmly with smooth young flesh in the correct places. Her hands and feet were small and restless. There was a pleasing slenderness in wrists, waist, and ankles. There were lovely curves at hips and bosom.

With common sense overbalancing vanity, Sylvia knew that where there had been only piquancy in her lines, there was now a hint of maturity. It was a symmetrical ripeness that would surely change to bulging grossness, unless she were smart enough to tap, swim, and bicycle steadily.

Sylvia sighed again. Work and diet, those two things and nothing else could regain for her that elfin grace that had been her fortune—that with her doll-like face and curls.

This brought on a train of retrospection. She was unusually quiet during her bath and over her breakfast tray.

Three years before Sylvia had been seventeen and poverty stricken. She knew no other home but that battered Arkansas house and hated the place. She despised her father, who drank to excess and the slatternly stepmother, who in turn loathed the girl.

When Sylvia was sixteen she found work in the local ten-cent store. There the world began to pay homage to her beauty. Men fell before her, offered her their all, but this wasn't enough. Sylvia burned with one ambition. She was determined to marry wealth and flee from the ghastly poverty of her home.

As the girl felt her power and realized what it could do for her, she began to defy her stepmother. Finally Sylvia left the leaking family roof forever. She took a room with a chum who had a small terrace flat. One day this friend begged, "Sylvia, enter the bathing beauty contest! If you win over all the other Arkansas girls, you'll go to Galveston. Imagine! What a chance!"

"Mmm," Sylvia replied. Her dark eyes grew scheming. "Galveston? A hot tip, honey! *Galveston*—where rich suckers hold their conventions!"

In a forty-nine-cent red bathing suit and borrowed scarlet sandals, Sylvia took the Arkansas beauty crown easily. She was photographed and interviewed. She made front pages over the state.

At seventeen, life started for her in Galveston. She did not win the Miss America title, but she caught and held the eye of James L. Adams, land promoter and home builder from the much-publicized Sun City.

"Boy oh boy!" he cried, mopping a sunburned brow. "She's the prettiest little thing in the whole mess of pretty gals and she ought to have been Miss America. I'm gonna marry her if she'll have me. I'm gonna give her anything on earth—if she'll let me!"

That night at dinner in Galveston's best hotel Sylvia sat opposite J. L. Adams. He feasted his eyes upon her. She wore a simple white dress she had made herself, but she knew that a swell home, a Packard, and a yacht were not far away.

"Got any folks, baby?" Jim had asked. She soon grew accustomed to his bluff, "never meet a stranger" manner.

"No," she answered, looking pitiful, "not any that I want to claim. I haven't any home—no mother—"

Adams grew serious. Reaching over, he took her hand.

"Like me, kid." He sympathized. "My paw kicked me out to make a living when I was twelve. I know what it is to be hungry and alone!

"I know too, baby, I'm not much to look at—I'm fat and past forty—but I've plenty of dough. It's all yours if you'll have it. I fell for you at the first look. You can't go back to that tank town, you with those wonderful eyes. I'll do anything to make you happy if you'll marry me—*will you?* Say tomorrow?"

Sylvia caught her breath and caught his hands. Her eyes gleamed with flashes of light. A terrible tension snapped within her. She wanted to cry but instead laughed bravely.

"Oh, you're a darling—*Jim.* How can I say no? Of course, if you want me, I'll make it tomorrow."

They were married at the Grand Ball given for beauty contestants. Newspaper cameras clicked and people crowded about curiously.

Sylvia, in the most costly outfit of clothes Galveston could supply—Sylvia with her feet on the first rung of the social ladder—smiled and smiled. She kissed Jim thankfully, as though he were Romeo and a fairy godfather rolled into one.

They took a train at once for New York. Theirs was not a stuffy day coach like the one on which Sylvia had jolted to the bathing-girl parade, but a compartment filled with flowers, candy, and presents from Jim's friends.

It was a gala departure for the youngster who had arrived so poorly dressed and badly frightened. It was a real triumph for little Sylvia from Arkansas!

In New York they saw what sights one can see in midsummer. When Mr. and Mrs. Adams left for Sun City, Jim shipped ahead three trunks of his wife's new clothes. Adams' Packard carried the couple from their train to J. L.'s redecorated suite at the Bayside Hotel.

Sylvia was soon a sensation in a town dulled to sensations. Ted Maxime was the first enslaved. He gave a dinner at his Palm Club in her honor and remarked several times during the evening, "J. L., you certainly picked a beauty! She's a honey with her Ah-kan-sah accent—a doll all right—you lucky old plutocrat!"

From that night on, no one danced with such swinging *joie de vivre* as young Mrs. Adams. Incessantly her light feet skimmed the polished Palm Club floor. At first she divided her fox trots between Ted and a rich, personable fellow named Johnny, but lately Phil Pelham had taken every dance. He and Sylvia floated through waltzes and laughed hilariously through rhumbas. Sylvia, the bacchante, with curls that rang like bells.

"And," said Sun City's night-clubbers dryly, "with a husband who can't dance one step."

VIII

For one prismatic year Sylvia and J. L. lived at the Bayside Hotel, then Adams built in Desdena Shores, which he was promoting. This new subdivision, a dream spot out west of town, was locked in an elbow of the Bay. A hotel and a country club were already completed. Houses were fast spreading over a wide, carefully developed area.

Every home in Desdena was a small estate, with garden, wall, and a gate where bells tinkled when visitors arrived. Each house bore some individuality, whether it be coquina rock or pastel stucco. Each was a contrast to its neighbor.

There were many walks of faience tile and street lights were varicolored lanterns on wrought-iron posts. Over it all climbed a moon, mellow as the lanterns. In that glow lovers strolled down lanes, around circles, and over to the waterfront. Here they wrote their names on sandy paths of the park and heard the *purr-rush* of motors tearing beachward.

"It's like a fairy-tale picture, Jim darling!" cried Sylvia. "I think I'm away here, far from all the mean, ugly things of the world! Why not live life this way—*why not?*"

Sylvia knew that she was on the second rung of the ladder when she opened her own villa in Desdena Shores.

This meant a big party for the friends she had met during the last year. Crashers came too, but young Mrs. Adams did not resent that. She was most hospitable with food, drink, and music. Beaming, J. L. went around back-slapping and swapping land price yarns for doubtful jokes.

Sylvia, however, was the center of attention, a smartly gowned, cordial hostess in her own home. It all served to dull her memory of that tumbledown Arkansas house, a hateful stepmother, and a life on poverty street.

When Sylvia recalled such things, fat J. L. Adams became the archangel Gabriel in person. At other times she began to feel a definite lack in her glorified life. After the first intoxication of wealth and social success wore off, the woman within her wakened and asked for something more—romance.

"Sylvia," Ted Maxime said one night, "J. L. stays away on these business trips entirely too much. You come dancing to my Club with your blond lad night after night."

Sylvia's lips smiled over her wine glass.

She touched Ted on the arm. "Don't break up his trips, Teddy, they're his life. As for me, you know *I'm* not lonely—" Here she glanced across the table at a slim, correctly-tailored young man, whose presence with Sylvia was now an accepted thing.

Phillip Pelham, impoverished scion of an aristocratic family and salesman for Auburn-Duesenberg cars, was not romance alone to Sylvia. He was also background and intellect. With his low voice and easy manner, he offered Sylvia an atmosphere of culture that she lacked and keenly desired. Phil was the third rung on her ladder.

"Phil—*my Phil*—" she was saying as she sat before her vanity mirror. "He brought me home last night, Carrie Lou."

"Yes'm," replied the maid, smiling to herself, as she fastened copper-colored beach sandals on Sylvia's feet. "An' he gave me a dollar!" There were more white-toothed smiles. Sylvia shrugged.

"My money," she reproached, "but no matter . . . Get the Western Union on the phone, Carrie Lou."

"Yes'm—"

In a few moments she dictated a telegram that made girls at the office uptown stare, then shrug in jealous despair.

"Dear Daddy," Mrs. J. L. Adams began, "I am lonesome. The house is so ladylike without you. Did you know, king promoter, that our Packard is in the shop? I have nothing but the old roadster and it's so casual. The Packard is creaking in the joints but it has a swell trade-in value. Please, Pop, let me buy the Duesenberg—"

Sylvia stopped short, then rushed on, correcting, "No, change that last line to, *'I am buying the Duesenberg!'* "

IX

Phil Pelham turned the bonnet of an Auburn phaeton into Central Boulevard. Taking the road to Desdena at ten o'clock in the morning like a playboy, piloting a top-class car and wearing two hundred dollars worth of smart clothes, Pelham ironically enough had only sixty cents to his name.

"Phil," the manager of the Bayside Hotel had said an hour before, "I hate to mention that bill of yours again, but they're on my neck about it."

"Oh, of course," replied the boy, nonchalantly sorting his morning mail, "how much is it, anyway?"

"One hundred fifty," Mr. Deane, the manager, answered, scanning a sheet in his hand.

"This notice, Phil, says 'must' by tonight. I'm sorry, kid."

"By tonight? Okay, I'll take care of it." Pelham raised his brows and smiled as though the amount were a mere writing of the check.

A little dry in his throat, he reached the office of his automobile agency. There he found calls from two potential customers, Mrs. Nicholas and Sylvia Adams. Phil took long steps out to the phaeton and hopefully headed for Desdena.

He stepped on noiseless brakes as he paused for the red light. He gestured with a smile to a customer who turned the corner in an Auburn bought from Pelham two months ago.

And where the hell is that commission now? thought Phil. Gone, like the others—spent keeping up a front I must have if I sell anything to socialites.

Mrs. Nicholas, he continued to muse, Lord—even she sounded good this morning—*even she*—fat, dark, and a foolish forty-odd!

Nella Nicholas, wife of a Greek restaurant chain owner, was an old story to Pelham. He knew she wanted him more than any automobile. With the shrewdness of her nationality, she had been holding off her purchase until she was sure she was getting Phil with the car.

It was really amusing how he had run from her. Mrs. Nicholas could not say she was snubbed, since Phil only kept her from having a private word with him. She had cornered him one night at a beach party and said a few indiscreet things.

After that Phil avoided her like the plague, though not on account of moral scruples. Pelham merely wanted to stay in Sun City alive. Nick was a great, black-browed, knife-carrying Greek, and regarding wives, wholly without the Anglo-Saxon sense of humor.

This morning, though, with sixty cents in his pocket and a hotel bill overdue, Mrs. Nicholas seemed a heaven-sent benefactress. As Phil turned into lovely Desdena Shores, he saw her home on a conspicuous corner.

It was the only house in the subdivision that was Greek to the smallest detail. Nick had called in Weinberger, the foremost architect in Sun City, and with much hand-waving, the café owner had made Weinberger understand that he must design a Greek house.

Because the Greek had so much money and Weinberger, like Phil, needed some just then, the architect created something of surpassing beauty. Here before Pelham's eyes were white columns, huge blue urns, and cedars that might have come from Ithaca itself. The house had very cleverly been placed on a manmade hill. From this eminence, the whole arm of the Bay was visible.

Pelham had seen the place in passing a hundred times, but this morning it appeared to be a fairy castle wherein good fortune was waiting. Nella had said over the phone that she was ready to buy a Cord car. It was evident that she fancied a new model that he had recently demonstrated for her and two friends.

This phone call of Mrs. Nick's meant either a sale for Phil or a ruse to get him to her house. He would soon find out and waste little time doing so.

Nella's heart beat high in her ample bosom as she watched the slender blond youth leave the phaeton and enter her portico.

"Ah," she said, "for the first time—*welcome!*" She took his lean, tanned hands in both her fat, ringed ones, drawing him into an interior that made Pelham decide to shake the Nicholas bank account for the highest f.o.b. his agency boasted.

They chatted about one thing then another until Mrs. Nicholas came over and sat beside him on the divan. She rested one hand on his, displaying a pudgy finger ornamented by a diamond of at least five carats.

"Dear boy," she said intimately, "I have made the decision. I want the little sleek Cord! You, with your gentleness, with your strange ways of not speaking too much of what you sell, have proved to me that there is only one car for us."

"Well fine!" responded Phil. "You appreciate a good motor as well as a classy body. Few women do. I'm sure you'll enjoy driving one of our new models."

"And you?" asked Mrs. Nicholas, looking up into the boy's English-blue eyes. "You'll drive with me—often? Oh let us go together picnicking, down to the lighthouse. Just we two—alone—and nights, when Nick's working—" Phil cleared his throat uncomfortably. Taking out his kerchief, he dabbed it on a brow suddenly grown moist.

There was a steam of vitality and perfume

exuding from Mrs. Nicholas as she leaned toward Pelham, her plump shoulder heavy against his arm. That arm he gingerly patted now. He swallowed with some difficulty as he thought first of his own financial plight, then of the knife-wielding Nick.

"Yes," Phil agreed slowly, "you may be sure I'll teach you the ways of the Cord. And now, shall we sign it all up—you know, business first—"

"*And pleasure later,*" Mrs. Nicholas finished with a giggle that shook the pearls around her neck. Finally she settled, with much preening of feathers, at a desk in the large library. She produced a checkbook and began to write. Phil held his breath.

"I'll pay for it in cash," she said. "You know it's Mr. Nicholas' rule never to buy anything on credit or time payments." Phil, watching, listening, and murmuring salesman suavities, felt as though he could shout for joy.

Blessings on the Greeks! He never knew they were so generous! Cash—paying cash—and a Nicholas check was good as gold bullion! Pelham tried hard to keep his hands from trembling as he reached for the precious slip.

"Thank you," he said aloud. "We're glad to have you in our Auburn-Cord family. I'll rush the order." Phil spoke as though checks like this were a part of every day's work, still he reverently took the chubby hand that could honestly write a check that size. He folded her hands together and in his gratitude kissed them—thus leaving behind him a radiant Mrs. Nicholas with her twenty-three hundred dollars' worth of ecstasy.

X

Covering the blocks to Jim Adams' villa, Phil's spirits rose steadily. With that check in his billfold he felt strong and courageous once more. Money made people feel that way—money or liquor, but Phil had not taken one drink that morning and none the night before.

He had been cold sober all evening while on that yacht fiesta, part of him worrying over his economic status, the other part going mad over Sylvia.

Those were the two big issues in his life at present. Yesterday when he felt rather frantic, with his hotel bill mounting like a taxi meter, he should have known that sooner or later someone would say, "Sure Phil, I'll take the Cord," or better still, "I'm ready to order the Duesenberg.

The trouble was that no one had said either of those things lately. Pelham had really worked hard, drumming up trade in his own way, a way that had proven successful the past year. He seldom talked automobiles outright to prospects. Instead he discussed motors and trade-in values with the men, bodies and Shakespeare with the women.

This system had kept him in good standing at the clubs and the Bayside for nearly a year and a half. Today it worked again.

Everyone knew Phil was a polished addition to any representative Sun City gathering. Everyone knew that he sold cars for the biggest agency in town, yet Phil never used hot pursuit nor high pressure. His sway was subtle persuasion.

There came to be a general feeling among the moneyed men of Sun City that unless one bought from Pelham one was excluded from a sort of honorary club. Automobile owners began to cast an eye of discontent on their cars purchased from other agencies. It was the style, indeed almost etiquette, to trade with Phil.

Women had another reason. She who bought a car from Pelham annexed him as a regular at all her dinners and bridge teas. What a prize he was, with his good looks, the right clothes, and the smooth manners!

But in spite of all this prestige, Phil still lived by his wits. He was genuine in everything except that air of vast wealth—accustomed affluence—that seemed to travel with him. Keeping up a front was hard, with his own abilities the only backing.

His, however, was a growing power. He felt sure that in another year, with good management, he would be well established. If he then took an agency of his own, many satisfied customers would go along with him.

Right now Pelham's business career was in a ticklish spot. Recently he had been taken into the Junior Chamber of Commerce. Following this, when he should have done everything just so, he had slipped and fallen in love with the wife of Sun City's most popular citizen.

As he turned his car into Sylvia's street, he slowed down and rolled along the curving lane, sensing the danger of temptation. In his financial panic of early morning, he forgot Sylvia for a time. Now, with his money matters adjusted, her image was vivid once more in his mind—the desire for her filling his heart.

Perhaps if Phil were slaving at a job with hours, his money being earned at the end of a plodding week, he could have passed up this adorable baby. As things stood, she knew only too well that he was hers. Who was he to turn away from this Paradise of dancing sun shadows and perfume of gardenias? One wish was in his heart—to go on and give whatever she asked, even though it might be his eventual ruin.

With a low-swung sneak and a throaty growl, the phaeton circled the Adams' drive. As Pelham entered through a side garden he heard Peter singing in the mimosa tree. God, those blossoms were sweet! That bird, too, was a symbol of the Southland Phil had known so briefly, yet loved strangely.

The Connecticut boy paused a moment in

the sunroom, with the modern aluminum chairs and tables surrounding him. The blue of their leather upholstery was the exact shade of that sky beyond the trees and flower bushes that were massed outside encircling the windows. Winter sunshine lay in spokes across the room, as the moonlight had lain last night when he brought her home.

Phil turned away from that thought and drew up as he heard her sandal heels coming down the hall stairs. Another moment and Sylvia stood in the doorway. He saw at a glance that her petite figure was clad in a Maywine bathing suit and jacket as she faced him with a challenging expression on her young face.

Sylvia didn't say good morning, nor pass any formalities of greeting. She came into his arms, her own arms locking about his neck. She buried her face on his broad, tweedy shoulder, the tiny sandals tiptoeing, for Phil was tall.

He dared not speak. With a quiet intensity, he turned her face up to his, kissing her lovely mouth with slow tenderness.

Sylvia did not speak, but clung to him with a sort of desperation. She held him tightly, then swung out of his arms, clutching one of his hands in hers.

"Oh honey," she said at last, "if only this could all be yours and not his. Oh, if you could stay forever, and he—never come back! If the blue chairs and mimosa blooms and Peter were mine—and yours—alone—"

Phil's heart went leaden. She had said just what he was wishing too! They couldn't go on this way! He gripped her hand, asking, "You sent for me, sweet. Anything special?" That was better. He called back the old manner, the light, flirtatious manner in which he felt safest. Sylvia responded likewise, essaying her smart little smile and handing him a cigarette from a small table.

She took a smoke herself and puffed once or twice, till her cheeks were cooler, her brain clearer. Then, herself again, she bantered, "That was a business call, darling. I am a customer and you are an expert car salesman. I want the best you have, sir—a Duesenberg, if you please!"

XI

The morning, golden on Desdena, with a tang of Indian summer in the air, was glossed with success for Phil. In his wallet were two perfectly good checks and an order for a Duesenberg, the first one he had ever sold. Beside him on the phaeton's front seat was Sylvia, her dark curls blowing back from the quaint wine-colored cap.

"How in the world," Phil queried, "do you keep that pill box on your head?"

Sylvia laughed. "Silly boy, it stretches."

"Well anyway." He shrugged. "That outfit looks darn cute on you. New?"

The girl nodded, opening her eyes very wide. "Yes suh, thankyuh suh, first time I've worn it!"

"I know." Pelham smiled, his eyes wrinkling up at the corners into twinkles of amusement. "I see a thing in Raymond's window and think, What a fiendish color—no woman on earth could wear it! I come out here next day —*you have it on*—and—"

Sylvia lifted an eyebrow in suspicion. "And?" she repeated.

Phil bowed his head toward her. "Why my dear, I immediately reverse my first opinion to—no woman but Sylvia."

Pelham turned the phaeton into Desdena Way, a boulevard hardly as wide as the main artery but appearing so because it fronted the Bay. They sped past Reana Robinson's mysterious coquina villa and in turn skirted the green edges of a golf course. Adjacent to this was the Desdena Hotel, a Moorish affair, where one paid astonishing rates and was permitted to look into the court's wishing well.

On this street, as along others in the subdivision, the houses were set in large gardens. These were even more exotic than the waterfront park of palm trees, winding paths, and lily pools.

There to the right of Phil and Sylvia was the limpid bay, still as a mirror for the tide was low. Only tiny ripples followed the pink flamingoes that waded out to catch small fish.

Midmorning quietude held everything in a spell. Here was water without a boat, a level road without a car, and apparently houses without occupants.

That, thought Phil, was one of the charms of Sun City. In the residential sections there were what he chose to call "deserted hours," when human beings disappeared completely from the scene.

The beauty they had built and the beauty nature gave this more than blessed peninsula remained at such times silent. There was only the whisper of pine needles, a gentle lap of an incoming tide, or the wild cries of winging seagulls.

Now with one of these deserted hours about him, with the green vista spread out before him, Phil caught his breath, fighting his love for her, fighting the turmoil that rose in his heart, choking the air from his throat. He remained to all intents grimly preoccupied. He stepped on the gas and the motor roared to forty, forty-five, then a rushing fifty. The salt wind blew hard against them. They had a sense of adventure, of escape.

Ahead the road widened and merged into a new causeway bridge that led across Desdena Bay to the beach. Slowing down, Phil turned in between white stone posts. Each was topped by a blue spotlight, which at night could be seen miles away.

Pelham remembered somewhat wearily the weeks of talk that preceded the building of this causeway, replacing an old wooden bridge.

The Adams office of course got the commission for the work. Details of cost and civic value, along with proposed toll rates, were discussed freely over Chamber of Commerce and Ad Club luncheons.

At these masculine affairs, big Nick alternately hovered behind chairs at the long table, listening eagerly, then waving both hands at his waiters as signal for more mashed potatoes and lemon pie.

Nick was a good sport at heart and proud of his position in the community. His gift had been the revolving lights at either end of the causeway. They cost him plenty, but his reward was watching them on dark nights from the Athenian villa's master bedroom windows.

There had also been a great opening when Phil drove the first car across the new bridge. It was another Auburn phaeton, open to the sun. In it lounged the mayor and his wife, with a couple of councilmen. Rival motor dealers called it a fix-up, and secretly they burned with jealousy.

The mayor, quite red-faced from too many highballs, forgot most of his speech. Standing unsteadily in the car, he exhorted, "Proshperity ish returning to our city 'n may thish beau-ti-ful new bridge 'naugerate a new era. I'm happy t' b' here t' day an' christen our new caush-way. Hope ev'rybody else's happy. Are y' happy, folks? Well then, le's all sing, '*Happy Days Are Here Again'!*"

So they sang and lustily—the entire motorcade, led by the Auburn—all the way across to the beach where a barbecue was waiting.

To Phil it seemed a sort of Gilbert and Sullivan opera, an unreal farce. He was new to Sun City—he with his northern conservatism. To him the sky was too blue, the flowers too red and purple. Awnings were likewise zebra striped and the natives' enthusiasm mere playacting.

Today things were different, for his viewpoint had changed. Now he was no longer "Mr.

Pelham from Connecticut." He was "Phil," who sold cars to everyone worthwhile. Pelham was used to it all and one with it all. He only asked to keep making good and stay in Paradise.

XII

Slowing down to forty as he passed the toll house, Phil snatched up a metal disc that bore a number. This indicated the bearer had paid in advance for so many rides across Sun City's new bridge.

He extended his left hand, which held the tag, as he passed the toll collector who waited before a small office. The young man nodded and Phil shot the car faster along a smooth as silk roadway. When the Auburn's motor was some distance away, another man in the toll house called to the youth on the bridge, "Who's that a goin' so fast?"

"Phil Pelham a doin' fifty."

There was a snarl from inside. "Him an' his high-powered cars! Ain't no use to report him

—with them rich friends ready to pay his fines an' go his bond."

The lad outside was gazing sulkily down the causeway on which the phaeton now appeared to be a diminishing toy. A broken speed law was an insignificant thing to the youth in the khaki suit. He had seen Sylvia's curls blowing in the wind. He had seen her wine cap and daring smile.

Envy, absurd as it was useless, distended the boy's lower lip into a full-fledged pout. "He's got Jim Adams' wife with him again," he called out in a sloughing, cracker dialect.

There came a curt rejoinder from the cynic within the toll office. "Well—*when ain't he?*"

Five minutes later Phil pulled the Auburn into the Tennis and Bath Club's driveway.

A spacious white-frame, green-shuttered building recalled many happy times he and Sylvia had shared in the past month or so. They had danced on the long veranda overlooking the ocean. Often they had been alone, swaying to informal music on the radio. Sylvia's fluffy skirts swirled about her while the moon transformed her curls into silver filigree.

Phil turned now, slipping one hand flat against Sylvia's throat, those curls tickling his fingers.

"Look sweet, I'll leave you here—have to go back to the office and get off these orders."

"Okay honey," she agreed. "I'm having lunch with Trudy and the bunch."

They were both quiet for a few moments. On the dunes salt cedars were swaying in the breeze. Beyond them was the water, a restless aqua dotted here and there with swimmers.

From the courts came the rhythmical *Bop, Bop* of returned tennis balls and the called scores of "Love–2," "Love–4." Cries of pleasure came from the beach—vague, lazy sounds that the wind whisked around the Club House and off again.

A delicate fragrance sifted down and over the phaeton. Glancing up, Phil saw that they were under a blooming mimosa tree. Sylvia reached out and picked one of the fluffball flowers, sniffed it, then fastened it in Phil's lapel.

"Dinner tonight—at my house?" she invited. He grasped both her hands, dwelling on dark-lashed eyes and the oval contour of her face with its pointed chin.

"If you want me—" he said by way of acceptance.

At this a play of expression went over the face under the wine-red cap. A sort of adoration filled Sylvia's eyes with tears. She ducked her head uneasily.

"*If* I want you—*if* I want you—" Her lips were warm against his hands, then Mercurylike she was out of the car, waving a gallant little hand back at him. She ran along the dune path—cute and who knew how brave—with her maywine costume, high-heeled sandals, and bare legs.

As she reached the dunes' edge, she squared her shoulders and wigwagged one hand in salute to someone below. There were cries of "Sylvia," "Sylvia—darling," as she tap-danced down the stone steps and vanished from Phil's sight.

He sat there in the phaeton, his hands resting on the wheel and Sylvia's last avowal with him like the mimosa perfume.

Now Phil turned slightly cold as his business success and his popularity in Sun City took on the light of things perfect but short lived.

With memberships at this and other clubs, with a room at the Bayside, orders in his pocket that meant real money, and a high-powered car under his hand, he was lucky. The breaks had been phenomenal, yet twice today Sylvia's eyes had been full of tears. Twice his own throat had choked with a nothing-else-matters ache.

Phil snapped on his engine. As he circled the drive, friendly hands waved to him and he saw cars he had sold parked here and there. Deftly guiding the phaeton out into the open road, there was still one thing that went through and through his mind. At last he said it aloud, in a frightened tone: "*'Whom the gods would destroy—they first favor!'*"

XIII

In front of her cabana tent Sylvia was surrounded by a group of friends. There was an unfaithful young matron or two and a collection of youngsters who stalked Mrs. Adams' heels whenever she darkened the doors of the Tennis and Bath Club.

Dressed in every sort of swimming attire, from scant trunks to loud print bathrobes, these playmates hailed their pet pal with wisecracks, lunatic gyrations, and teasing verbal slams that showed their great devotion.

"Now just look at that cap, boys," shouted one youth, tall and strong enough to be a lifeguard. He laid his hands on Sylvia's shoulders, turning her about to meet the wry faces of the others. "Isn't that the craziest cap you ever saw?"

"Yeah—nuts!" another howled.

"Crazy as the girl in it! She never did know how to dress, anyway, jus' a li'l western cracker girl."

Then, from the handsome brute, "C'mon honey an' cry on my shoulder! Cannon loves you even if you are a washout!"

Sylvia shook herself loose and made for the door of her cabana. "Phooey on you all," she said sharply, "and shut up, I can't hear what Trudy's saying." With this she took a blonde girl by the arm and they vanished into the striped tent.

"Oh Sylvia," cried Trudy, "they're just awful! Honestly, Tiny and I've spent a miserable morning. I mean these clucks have simply *tormented* us!"

"Yes," echoed Tiny, pretending to be furious, "first they played handies and got one about rich Mrs. Williamson coming home lit. Mrs. W. simply sailed across the beach and bawled out the whole crowd of us."

"Then," continued Trudy, "they caught a lobster—from goodness knows where—and put it in my makeup kit. When I reached down to get my suntan oil that horrid thing came crawling up. My screams brought everybody in the Club House out here."

Sylvia had slipped off her flannel jacket and skirt and stood before them in her maywine bathing suit. She viewed judicially the semicircle of outcast youngsters.

One boy was a thin, knock-kneed monkey, another had buck teeth. Number three had laughing Irish eyes and a turned-up, freckled nose. The fourth was a good-looking brunette

—a devil after midnight in a two-seater. Number five had a social register name, a dumb, amiable face, and a dad with millions. The last one was Bill, the big boy, who should have been a lifeguard or halfback.

"Boys," Sylvia said sternly, "I'm ashamed of you."

"Yes teacher," in mock penitence from the semicircle. Sylvia reached into a carryall zipper bag and pulled out a lady bug pin, a small round trinket with blue enamelled wings and gold feet. She fastened this thing on the halter of her suit, then faced the boys again.

"As I said—you've been bad," she continued. "I ought to throw you out." The boys were deaf to this threat. Their eyes were on the pin, recently attached to Sylvia's halter. An elbow nudge went round the group.

"Teacher," they demanded in unison, "we want to recite." In a concerted falsetto they prattled, fingers pointing to the metal insect:

Lady bug, lady bug—fly away home,
Your house is on fire, your children will
burn!

Trudy giggled, Tiny giggled, but Sylvia looked pained.

"Listen, freshies," she advised, "the liquor's over there on the open-up table. You'll find the portable, with spank new records, in that corner. Now if you're going to stay here—*scram*—let us talk in peace!" There was a dive for the entertainment. Soon a top band was blaring a fox trot.

"We'll dance with them—okay, Jean?" asked Tiny, conscience stricken. "They look right pitiful . . . You folks can talk." Gertrude and Sylvia stretched out in canvas chairs, one beside the other.

"What did Don say last night when you told him?" inquired Sylvia, making up her face.

Trudy chuckled. "He shouted, 'Whoopee—blessed event! We'll name them Dafoe and Dionne for good luck and hope for more next time!' "

"He's a kidder." Sylvia smiled. "I'll bet he's thrilled—he with his father complex."

"He—not I." Trudy shrugged. "Though what's it matter—all in a lifetime." She paused, musing, then asked alertly, "Been with Phil again today, haven't you?"

Sylvia averted her face, betraying nothing. "I'm buying a Duesenberg," she replied tersely.

"A Duesenberg!" cried Tiny. "Gosh but your old man must be coining it!"

Sylvia opened a box of cigarettes and handed them round. "I wanted a Duesenberg," she said, "and I usually get what I want."

"You've got Phil, all rightie," Trudy murmured. "He's dropped all his girl friends and they're furious." With their cigarettes lighted, the tent rapidly filled with smoke as well as music.

"Say, honey," Trudy went on, "did you know Ahnoud Bey's going to give his piano with the Golden Keys to Reana Robinson? They say he's mad about her. His cabana's just six down the beach from yours. He was in the water a while ago. He's a grand swimmer! Why he went out to the sand bar!"

Sylvia listened to Trudy's chatter. She watched the boys doing rhumbas and generally making fools of themselves over Tiny and Jean, visiting girls, pert and fancy free.

Trudy and the bunch were evidently talking about Pelham and Jim Adams' wife—saying, no doubt, behind their backs, far more than was really true.

Somehow, Sylvia thought, she must stop this gossip before it came back to J. L. He and Phil were friends. As long as there were numbers, Jim excused, laughed off her light affairs. "Kids," he called them, for those she liked seemed so young to him.

Were her husband faced, though, with one real rival for her love the situation might grow ghastly. She knew it would not be advisable to try J. L. that far.

Sylvia was still a bit shaky from the emotion that had almost overwhelmed her this morning. Even a thought of Phil went like an electric shock down her spine and crisscrossed her heart. That was a danger signal. To save herself—to stem this talk—she must appear to have someone else, a new interest, a second fiddle.

She rose quickly from her deck chair, took another cigarette and, tapping its unlighted end on her hand, announced to Trudy, "Ahnoud Bey's my friend as well as Reana Robinson's. I'm so glad you told me he was here. 'Scuse a minute, while I step over and see the new Egyptian heart, will you?"

A few brisk steps and she stopped before Bey's cabana. Sylvia groped for courage to lift the tent flap and go in. The blood was pounding in her cheeks and her heart was fairly turning over.

Damnit! she thought. Why this schoolgirl act? I've only met the man once, at a party. Their introduction had been crowd stifled. Ahnoud, however, was famous on two continents, as mystic and mind reader. What could Sylvia Adams say to this player of the Golden Keys?

While she stood there in such a state the tent flaps before her eyes parted. There in the doorway of his cabana stood Ahnoud Bey, half-smiling and extending to her the hand of welcome.

XIV

"I had no idea," said Sylvia, when she found her voice, "that you would remember me." The Egyptian stared at her in that sort of way that makes the most self-confident woman blush.

"I never forget a *pretty* face," he answered. "Sit down and let me light your cigarette."

Sylvia stared absently at the cigarette she held between two fingers. It seemed to her a million miles away. She regarded it as a discovery, considered her hand as something just acquired. She was still partially numb. When Bey had opened that cabana flap as Sylvia stood debating entrance the girl was astonished.

"Of course, and thanks," she managed, as he held his lighter first to her cigarette, then to his own. Sylvia took a puff or two, then stepped forward, a question on her lips. "Look here, Mr. World's Wonder—did you *happen* to open the door of your tent a minute ago, or did you know I was outside, grappling with a case of celebrity fright?"

Ahnoud Bey lifted a leatherbound volume from the table beside him. The book had been placed half open, face down. Bey indicated a couch behind him, covered with an East Indian blanket of bright colors.

"I was resting after my swim—and reading," he related. "I found that I could not concentrate. I was swept with exhilaration and felt very famous, beyond the reach of humble folk."

Sylvia shivered. "My God!" she gasped. "I was thinking those very things about you!"

"Certainly," Bey vouched. "It has happened before, when someone wished to meet me and stopped shyly the other side of my dressing room door. In this case, the door was a tent flap—so—*voilà!*"

Ahnoud made an expressive motion with one hand. He smiled at the wonderment in Sylvia's eyes. Reaching over, he caught her fingers in his.

"I'm glad you came," he said with only the slightest foreign accent in his Oxford-polished English. "May we be friends?"

Sylvia, who could handle six times her weight in college boys, was now at a loss for words. They seemed hard to put together correctly. She searched for her poise. "That's swell," she finally replied, brightening, "if my friendship will mean anything in your life. You must think I'm dumb but really I'm only scared. I know one thing though—your piano act is marvelous! I've watched it so often I know the music by heart."

"I'm glad you have enjoyed it," Bey responded. "We closed our engagement at the Palm Club last night, you know."

Sylvia laughed nervously. "Yes, and Ted's going to have the devil of a time filling his tables without you. After six weeks Ahnoud Bey is a habit with us. Where do you go from here?"

He gazed off, then bringing himself back caught her question, answering indifferently, "Oh, New York I suppose. I think my manager has me booked there next and on to Europe, in the spring—London, Paris, the same places I've played a dozen times."

Sylvia's eyes danced. She leaned back in the canvas chair. "London! Paris!" she repeated. "I've never been across, though J. L. says we'll go next summer."

"You are fortunate," Ahnoud replied. "To you it is all new, but to me—" He shrugged and his smile grew cynical.

With the fatalism of the East in his eyes, with the shadow of old Egypt on his face, Ahnoud Bey was yet the thoroughly modernized European as he sat opposite Sylvia.

No vestige remained today of the colorful Arabian costume in which he had appeared at his Sun City farewell. Not one hint of the theatrical was visible. Bey's white flannel suit was the last word in tailoring and his dark shirt nicely matched his American blue eyes.

Ahnoud's grooming, even to the indigo kerchief and Hamilton wristwatch, was exemplary. He might have been the best-dressed man at a Mayfair tea.

With his quiet manners and cultured way of speaking, Ahnoud was something rare and delightful to Sylvia. She thought of the crowd of half-clad nitwits she had left tearing round her cabana. After their senseless effervescence, Bey's repose was a relief.

There was, too, at close range a world-weary sadness about him. No one would have suspected this lay beneath the surface of the masterful performer spotlighted at the Palm Club.

"I think you don't want to leave Sun City," Sylvia accused.

Ahnoud smiled again. "You are right," he agreed. "I should like to live here, were I free, but who among us is free to do the heart's bidding?"

Sylvia's eyes sobered and darkened. The mystic knew his words had struck home. "That's it," she cried, "freedom's only a word—for most of us."

Bey saw and regretted that he had stirred the girl so deeply. His face changed with that illusive light that was peculiarly his.

"But my dear child, I am boring you—" he apologized. "It is merely my mood today. I find leaving this place difficult, to say the least. I have been revealing to you these feelings of mine. Forgive me."

Sylvia rose and took Bey's hand. "You're the most interesting man I ever met," she said. "Not one of the others ever knew I was outside his door and let me in before I knocked." She moved to go, for guests were waiting in her cabana, she remembered.

"Here's wishing you loads of fame and don't forget to come back."

"Thank you." Bey's eyes were admiring. "I will come back. You must stay as lovely as you are, and—" lifting his brows and casting a glance at the pin on her halter "please save the lady bug for me—as a souvenir of our first meeting."

They laughed together. As Sylvia turned to go, the tent flaps parted and in the canvas doorway stood Reana Robinson.

XV

There was no mistaking the look in Ahnoud Bey's eyes as he caught sight of the orchid and gold vision in his cabana entranceway. It was the sort of look that said, "You know I love you. We understand—no one else can. It's a grand secret between us." Instead Bey was saying, "Miss Robinson—Mrs. Adams—Reana, this is a young lady who came in to pay her respects, as I am leaving town."

The Golden Lady stepped forward into the tent. She smiled sweetly on young Mrs. Adams. "Isn't this 'Sylvia'?" she asked, taking the girl's hand. "We're neighbors though we've never met."

"That's true," the little one replied. "They all call me Sylvia. 'Mrs. Adams' sounds odd."

"You know," Reana added pleasantly,

"your husband's company dug the coquina rock for my house. That was how I met him."

Sylvia smiled. "I think J. L. knows everybody around here." She saw that Ahnoud's eyes were fastened on Reana. He seemed unable to turn from that picture before him—the slender woman with sunlit hair framed by a hat as orchid as her eyes.

Sylvia had heard much of Reana's beauty. She had seen the Golden Lady at a distance in various clubs and dancing places. Jim Adams' wife knew that those who talked of Reana in superlatives were right. This close-up made their compliments almost an injustice.

Miss Robinson was wearing a classic white dress, too, something rare in this setting where near nudity was the accepted thing.

A dress! thought Sylvia. Of all things! She longed wildly for her skirt and jacket. The contest-winning legs and the balance of her suntanned body seemed now very plump and bare.

"I was just leaving," she said in discomfort. "I'm so glad to have met you." She felt her cheeks flaming with embarrassment at the thought of turning her shoulders and back as she left.

Afraid to try her usual wisecrack that was the expected final salute in her own set, Mrs. Adams said something she well knew was commonplace but all right. Reana took the tent flap from Sylvia's fumbling fingers, holding it open until the girl made a grateful departure.

"She felt rather undressed," Reana observed. "Just a child—and such a pretty one."

"I only wish you were jealous," Ahnoud commented.

The Golden Lady turned a surprised face up to him. "Jealous?" she asked coolly. "Of Sylvia? Why she's eating her heart out over young Phil Pelham, didn't you know? Too bad —her husband is so fond of her."

Ahnoud drew Reana to him, caressing the slim shoulders with his strong hands.

"This is our last day together," he said softly. "How am I going to leave you? That's what I've been thinking all morning. I've been wishing the waves would drown me, wishing I might do anything but tell you goodbye."

"You will come back," Reana reminded. "They all do. The magnet of the winter sun draws them—"

Ahnoud held her to him and half-closed his eyes. "Of course," he whispered, "I will return soon, maybe on a flying trip in the spring, between engagements."

"In the spring," echoed Reana, "cypress trees that you call gray ghosts are feathery green. Warm clouds pile up like puffballs in the sky."

They were silent while Ahnoud closed his eyes, envisioning swamp cypress trees dressed as he had never seen them, in dainty green, and counting the clouds in that summer sky. He had seen those skies in Egypt and over great silences of the desert.

"We still have today." Reana was speaking with a promise in her voice. "We're going down the Bay and along the coast for all afternoon and evening, just you and I, as you like it—*alone*."

Ahnoud centered his gaze on her face as she spoke—on her violet eyes and the coral curve of her mouth. His desire was to kiss her again and again, to add hundreds of rapturous moments to those he had known during the span of weeks past! To wait, though, was better. There would be time enough when they were on the yacht, out on the Bay where noisy people could not annoy nor intrude.

The Egyptian dropped his hands from her shoulders, his eyes going a puzzling opaque. "I am ready to go," he said. "Shall we?"

Back in town at the Yacht Club Reana and Ahnoud inquired for weather reports and the reply was optimistic. "No storm in sight—westerly winds and fair skies."

They stood in the lobby of the Club and through half-open doors saw folks lunching early out on the terrace. There was laughter and music. Many eyes instantly spotted Reana and the mentalist.

"There's Ahnoud Bey from the Palm Club—and Reana Robinson."

"Yes, isn't he good looking? I heard he was going to give her his piano."

"Not the one he plays with his mind? What a gift! He must have it badly!"

And then someone said the same old thing. "How he can sit and make that piano play, without even touching it with his hands, is past me—"

"Shall we eat in here before we go?" Reana asked.

Bey seemed dubious. "As far as I'm concerned, no. I breakfasted late."

Reana took his arm. "Then let's eat at San Rafael. They serve Spanish food there and no one knows us in the whole town."

Bey acquiesced, locking her fingers in those of his left hand. They ducked out a side door, crossed the glary docks, and boarded a long white yacht. A ruddy-faced sailor waited to haul up the anchor. He tipped his cap to Reana. "Yes ma'm, any others a comin' aboard?"

Reana shook her head. "No, Jess. You have only two passengers today, so take off right away."

The lean, sun-reddened Jess bowed to the lady. He lifted the plank and shut the gate, calling meanwhile to other sailors in distant parts of the boat.

One of these boys, the pilot, more experienced than the others, came down the deck to greet Reana. "Madame," he said with great importance, "the Hawaiian musicians came half an hour ago. They are down in the salon."

"Have they had lunch?" asked Reana.

"No, Madame."

"Then have cook feed them," she rebuked. "Where is your hospitality?"

"Waiting for Madame's orders," replied the pilot respectfully.

"We're leaving right away for San Rafael, Edward," Reana directed. "You know the place —thirty miles due south down the coast."

"Yes, Madame, it's on our log. We've been there often. As you say, we leave at once. Anything else, Madame?"

Reana shook her head and the pilot hastened to his cabin room and wheel, calling orders along the way. As his step died on the polished floors of the deck Reana leaned against the rail.

The yacht, loosed from its moorings, began to sway and presently there was the vibration of the engine. Reana took off her hat. The cool wind ruffled her short hair and blew back her lavender coat until the white dress clung like wet silk to the outline of her body.

Ahnoud stood behind her. With both hands he pressed her shoulders back against his chest, tenderly laying his cheek on hers.

"To San Rafael," he said in that meaning baritone, "alone together."

"To San Rafael," repeated Reana, caught in his magic, "where cathedral bells ring and life is old and slow, where brown-eyed boys play steel guitars and sing 'Cielito Lindo'—San Rafael, where the sweetest orange blossoms in the world are blooming."

XVI

Sun City's bay was gently rounded as the pearl drop from a lady's earring. The sea came roaring in between Pelican and Angelo points and with the sea came its salt, its white caps, and its sharks. With all its depth and temperament, the Bay held a flaunting beauty and definite charm.

Other towns around its shores were attractive, if not as captivating as Sun City. In the latter life swirled along at seventy in streamline motors and as the seasons changed the population shifted with them.

The other towns were more of one piece. Their citizens were older for the most part, settled home owners and retired businessmen living in the pleasant haze of quiet tropical days. They fished a little, motored a little, dreamed in the sun, and rested well each night, with salt wind rustling palm leaves beyond the windows.

The same things every day, the same friends each evening, and the peace of easy-flowing years all spelled life in those other towns. Their lights winked across the Bay to Sun City as though to say, "You're too gay for us old dogs over here!"

A blue and red neon blaze, dulling the stars, called back, "Come here and find your youth—find your lost laughter—learn to play again."

The Bay, bringing its damp air and fish that made such delicious meals, washed the sands of each town impartially. It took to ride on its swaying back their boats, from rough, flat-bottom dinghies to glossy yachts manned by uniformed sailors.

In summer the same bay slugged and sulked under a torrid sun. At night the stars were all ten-carat diamonds, hanging near enough for one to snatch a handful. In the sultry dusk every sound could be heard blocks away. Only the chimes kept a lazy, musical catalogue of the slow hours.

In winter all was different. The air was wine, the Bay sparkling champagne, mirroring in moving transparency the bright turquoise of an overhanging sky.

There were crisp days when sunbeams danced with palm and magnolia leaves. The nights were a glittering chrysolite, a darkness shot through with the glowing string of waterfront lights—dance roof lights, a swift, long stab of auto headlights, and the dazzle of diamonds and ermine.

Reana had seen many of these winter nights, had filled many a season with her blonde beauty. She had ridden the January-February crest and there were men to whom she was only a figment of playland.

After they returned to northern cities, she became to them a sort of legendary Aphrodite. She was one with the opal waves of Sun City's bay, one with its night and music.

However, Reana had not always lived this carefree life. She had come to the popular resort several years before, ill and sad, broken by heartache and afraid of the future.

Reclining in her deck chair as the afternoon sun crossed the dark head of Ahnoud Bey who sat beside her, Reana thought of her first lone pilgrimage to Sun City.

She had just asked the Hawaiian musicians seated at the ship's bow to "play something American" and now they were beginning Victor Herbert's "Sweet Mystery of Life."

It was sympathetically done, in a twanging harmony, and it brought a host of memories to Reana Robinson. She looked off across the sunlit water where motorboats were streaking the waves behind them into ostrich plumes, then said with a sigh, "Ten years ago I came to Sun City and heard that song of Herbert's the first night I was here."

Ahnoud was immediately attentive. "You came for your health, I believe?"

"I went to my doctor one March afternoon," Reana answered. "It was raining. I was coughing and didn't care whether I lived or died. I had mushed around in so much snow I felt like an Eskimo. There were parties, night and day—dinners, dances, teas. A few I considered obligations, others just diversion.

"You see, Ahnoud, I was trying to outrun something. I thought a hurt heart would grow well in the company of other hurt hearts. In short, I was running from myself and that, Ahnoud, is a very silly thing to try because it can't be done."

The ship was in A-one order and the water placid. The two on deck found that their appetites arrived before San Rafael, so Reana ordered a snack, which now stood between them on a small table. The mystic munched a sandwich and Reana took a canapé, handing Ahnoud an olive, which he accepted with a bow and smile.

"I recall seeing you in New York in those days," he said as he ate the olive. "You were charming in black."

"Yes, I had on very smart black that day and wondered if they would bury me in it. I was that low," she went on. "I thought I was ill but my doctor knew better. Oh, he was a wise doctor, as few are. He recognized heartbreak. He knew what life in New York was doing to me!

"That good man, that calm, gray-haired man I had known half my life, listened to my symptoms. It was the third time in a month he had heard them. I felt sure he was worn out with it all. He sat down at his desk and wrote what I supposed to be another prescription. He handed me the slip of paper. Can you guess what was on it, Ahnoud—only two words—*Sun City!*"

XVII

"As you said," reminded Ahnoud, "he was a wise doctor."

"Oh very!" answered Reana, leaning forward in her chair, eyes shining. "No better man ever lived. When I asked him what he meant by this new prescription, he smiled indulgently. 'You need sunshine on that pale skin,' he warned, 'and plenty of sleep to drive away those dark shadows round your eyes, my dear. Leave for Sun City as soon as you can.'

"Then I objected, 'But doctor, the season is closing down there. This is March the twenty-first.' He folded his strong hands and consulted the calendar, as if to say he had been so busy caring for the sick he didn't know about spring on the way, then he turned to me.

"'The healing qualities of the sun's rays

and sea air have no seasons, Reana,' he advised. 'You should have quiet. With your set gone from Sun City you can rest and renew the vitality that a winter in New York impairs.

" 'Register at a seaside hotel and become a beachcomber. Forget your fine clothes. Knock around in fisherman's togs, put your feet on the ground, in the warm sands and—' this with a finger shake, 'do not forget—to bed at nine and *positively* no liquor or cigarettes.'

"The next day I met Aunt Emaline at the station. She had been in Baton Rouge the whole winter. She was spry and rejuvenated. After she kissed me and said that I should have come with her, Auntie gave me a worried look from her keen eyes.

" 'Goldylocks,' she said, 'you don't look well. What on earth's the matter?'

" 'Doctor Marlowe's ordered me to Sun City.' I replied, 'I'm leaving tomorrow. I'm going to be a beachcomber.' Our car went out into the crowded Avenue. We turned into that street in the East Sixties where Aunt Emaline and I lived. The old house has been hers since she drove up to it in a hansom cab. Again she scanned me in that quizzical way of hers.

"She took in my silk dress, French-heeled slippers, my chiffon hose and pearl necklace. Laughing, she squeezed my hand.

" '*You,*' she said, '*a beachcomber!* Sam Marlowe is one man in a million to have you going south out of season. But don't mind me—go on! You need it, goodness only knows! Sam should be kissed for this—yes, he *should be kissed!*' "

Reana raised her eyes to the blue vista.

They were nearing the Inlet now. Over to the right was Pelican Point, where the tall brick lighthouse was like a pink finger at land's edge. Reana knew it all so well she could scarcely believe it could ever have been new.

"And so I came." She picked up her story slowly. "Only Madeleine was with me. We took rooms at an old frame hotel here on the waterfront. The recently built Bayside was closing for the season but the manager of my hotel told me it stayed open all year.

"That night I said to Madeleine, 'We're alone at the end of the world.' She, poor girl, couldn't deny the lonesome feeling that depressed us both.

"Not that I cared much. Had I found the end I should have jumped off. I was sick and unhappy. My memories had followed me, as they always do.

"I sat beside my window most of the night. About eleven o'clock there was an orchestra playing somewhere below, possibly in a dance hall.

"I listened in the darkness to 'Sweet Mystery of Life' and Ahnoud, it was solace to a tortured heart. I had heard the composition many times, but never like this, away from everybody—everything—with a wide bay out there and twinkling lights all around it.

"The words held a new meaning for me. *'It's love and love alone the world is seeking'*. I had been doing just that—feverishly seeking and failing to find love—again. I had been in the self-conscious life of Manhattan all winter, where we magnified our troubles and cried, dramatizing them over nightclub tables.

"Now I seemed to lose myself in spaces of sea and sky, in the presence of something greater than my petty world. It came to me that love meant so many things—harmony of thought, forgiveness, kindness to others—all bringing sweet peace to one who knew only regret and discontent."

She paused, her voice dying away on the breeze. Bey, observing her intently from his chair, asked, "And you regained your health?"

"In a short time, Ahnoud. Sun City healed my spirit as well as my body. I went back to New York in June, a new person. After that, the sand was in my shoes. I was not satisfied, so I came down every winter, staying for months. At last I settled here year round and built the coquina villa that you know so well."

"What about Aunt Emaline?" asked Ahnoud, a twinkle in his eyes.

"Sometimes Aunt Emaline came with me," replied Reana, "but more often she preferred to stay in Manhattan. She loves the winters there—the social life, musicals and such—where she is a privileged character."

"You, with your beauty, must have brightened that old house in the East Sixties," Bey said, a light in his eyes. He had heard her speak of this aunt, a witty little lady with netted gray curls, a velvet ribbon round her throat, and a diamond broach on the bosom of her black lace dress.

Ahnoud could picture Reana, also in black, hair shining under ancestral chandeliers, white hands pouring tea before the drawing-room fire. Aunt Emaline doubtless kept them laughing with her sage and snappy comments on

New York society, about which she could write a racy fifty-year history.

"Aunt Emaline was very ill that cold winter of thirty-two, thirty-three," Reana was saying. "I flew back from Sun City to be with her. Doctor Marlowe and I had given her up to die. One night when the snow was deep, we sat up with Aunt Emaline.

"We were both sad, the doctor and I, for sadness was in the air. People were ringing bells and begging bread. Men walked the streets with no overcoats. Want and suffering were everywhere and of the future—we did not know.

"In the middle of the night, Auntie called me to her bedside. I thought she was going to bid me goodbye. Instead she spoke in a weak voice, 'Reana, when I get on my feet again, we're going south and we'll take the yacht out of dry dock. If I die now, promise me to take that boat out and enjoy it. Give parties on it, spend money on the ship, go on pleasure trips!

" 'A depression doesn't mean the end of civilization is coming—bah, I've seen them before. They pass, yes indeed they pass, and this one will too! That ship's yours, anyway. I want you to take it, and if I live we'll all have fun together—certainly we will, child.'

"Doctor Marlowe couldn't help smiling. It was so characteristic of dear Auntie. I cried with joy, for I knew if she felt that way she was going to live. And live she did! We took this yacht out of dry dock the next winter. Aunt Emaline gave it to me with the request that I enjoy it—"

"She must love you," concluded Ahnoud,

"as I do." He drew his chair near Reana's, and reaching over clasped her hand in his. His warm, lithe fingers locked in hers. His strong arm lay alongside the inside of her arm. They sat very still, while the yacht nosed south and the real sea began to break in foam bubbles on its sides.

XVIII

San Rafael's port was seldom visited by yachts as large as Reana's and waterfront boys came running down the dock as the Robinson craft dropped anchor. These boys were of varying ages from ten to twenty and able to amuse or guide tourists, as the case may be. The lads were dark, bright eyed, and Spanish as La Paloma; yet they spoke fluent English, thought fifty cents a fortune, and a dollar all the money in the world.

"Let us guide you, lady," and

"We'll show you the old fort," or

"I'll play for you and Juan here will dance—" came from young throats, as Reana and Ahnoud walked up the dock toward shore.

"Guide you—lady," persisted one, and an

older boy said in a breathless way, "Beautiful lady!"

Reana smiled at them and as she drew her lavender coat about her replied, "You may come with us, play for us, and show us where we can get a nice hot Spanish meal." The boys were glad to tag along, one dancing a sort of improvised rhumba as he went, another plunking the strings of an ancient guitar hung round his neck.

San Rafael was old and its waterfront smelled of fish and of wet driftwood. The main street had stores of distinctly Spanish design, dark, moldering buildings where curios were hidden. Side streets were narrow and cobblestoned, with built-over-the-street roof or balcony shadowing each crooked thoroughfare.

Some residences were large frame houses of early southern style with wide verandas. Others were forbidding, bare-walled villas flush with the street. These had secret patios beyond locked gates. Ahnoud and Reana stopped at the pier's edge and surveyed the town.

"This place is so quaint! It is old wine aged in bond—Cuba speaking English!" remarked the Egyptian.

"These people came here from Cuba originally," explained Reana. "They intermarried with Americans and built that large fort we saw on the way down as protection against enemies. Now it is an American town, but scratch the surface and you find everything Cuban—food, dark-eyed people, the love of music and the hot temper."

"Lady, lady," one of the boys was calling, "do you want to ride? Here is the donkey cart, ready to take you anywhere. The donkey is so very gentle. His name is Pedro, see—he lets me pull his ears. He really likes to have his ears pulled, see—*he shuts his eyes*—"

Ahnoud and Reana laughed aloud at this demonstration. As they climbed into the light wicker wagon, Bey divided some coins among the boys.

"There's not room for you all," he said. "Two may come—you, with the guitar, and that tall one, the guide."

"Yes sir," replied the favored ones, "and we'll sit on the back and hang our feet off. We can tell you anything you want to know about the town."

The boys, with riches in their pockets, took up their precarious position on the back of the trap. As the driver whistled to Pedro and they lurched away, the young guide waved a boastful goodbye to the remaining greeters left behind.

"Didn't I tell you?" asked Reana as they jogged through the old streets. Ahnoud called to the boys, "Where shall we go—for lunch?"

At once there was a dispute but it was too swift for American ears to follow. For the sake of business they compromised, giving orders to the driver. He, like his good-natured donkey, seemed totally without the bouncing pep and commercial knack of the young guides.

After bumping up one picturesque street and down another, they drew up before one of the old plaster walls. Evidently it had seen more prosperous days, and since the economic crisis was forced to hang out a sign that read:

SAN RAFAEL TEA ROOM

SPANISH DINNERS

Reana and Ahnoud pushed open the blue wooden gate. As they did so a bell rang.

Once in the secluded patio they found an open-air tea room, hidden from the street by walls and shaded by several trees. There were striped canopies over the tables. A fountain was playing and from within the villa came pungent aromas that testified to the culinary ability of the hostess.

In a moment a stout, dark-haired woman came out. She wore a clean apron tied about her orange cotton dress.

"Are we too late for lunch?" asked Bey.

"Oh, no sir. I have plenty—chili, tamales, frijoles—anything you want, Mexican or Cuban." She added with a grin, "You came on the lovely yacht? Ah—lovely—like a gull!"

They ordered Spanish dinners, and while they ate little birds fluttered down and begged for crumbs. Ahnoud and Reana threw pieces of bread on the old tiling and watched the greedy, chirping mites fight over them.

The food was excellent, the service cheerful, and from outside in the wagon the boys serenaded with one song after another.

"I've never eaten a better Spanish dinner," said Ahnoud as he paid the stout woman and tipped her heavily. She beamed back at this handsome stranger with an air of the world about him, with the gloss of travel and experience like a polish on his manners and speech.

She smiled too at the quiet woman in a coat of wild orchid color and with a face as haunting as a blonde Madonna.

"Do you like orange blossoms?" the tea room hostess asked as she carefully folded her money and tucked it away in a pocket under her apron. "Through that blue gate on the far side of the court is our grove. It is now full of bloom. Maybe you could not smell the perfume, for my dinner cooking. If you like you can go through the gate. So pretty now—all white and sweet."

"We'd love to," assured Reana. Presently she and Ahnoud were standing alone in a cloud of blossoms that reached as far as they could see.

A late sun was shooting golden lances among the leaves and patterning the moist earth with odd arabesques. This sweetness was unbelievable—hanging in cool air, sifting away on the breeze, now returning to enchant.

"Ah," exclaimed Ahnoud, "you did not tell me it was like this—a poem, and you in the poem—" He took her hand and they walked down the lanes as in a wonderland, his dark head touching the blooms on low twigs. Through it all came the music of a steel guitar playing "Estrellita."

XIX

There were long moments in the orange grove. Reana sat beside Bey on the old iron bench they had found. His arm was about her shoulders and now he drew the orchid coat closer at her throat, for the sun was sinking and a chill night was near.

Reana, still in a dream, leaned her head on Ahnoud's broad shoulder. She saw orange blossoms swaying in a white mist above her and Ahnoud's face—the darkness of his hair, the red curve of his lips. Reana touched his cheek gently. "You are looking so well today," she observed. "I think Sun City agrees with you."

Without a word Bey bent his head and kissed her with slow deliberation, then, still holding her close to his heart, "Marry me, my sweet. I'm asking again though you may be tired of my request."

Reana closed her eyes and shook her head. "Not for me, Ahnoud. Marriage is a delusion and a snare. You are very lovable, but—"

"You do not really love me," he accused.

"As a friend, dear," she countered, "even—at times—as a sweetheart. But beyond that, I can't say—"

"I should not ask more," replied the Egyptian, "only—that if I may not have you, no one else shall. I am first?"

"You are first, Ahnoud," Reana declared. "I am a slave to the strangeness of your face, that mysterious beauty of the Nile under starlight. I am chained to your mind behind the face, the mind that is so understanding. There is no one like you, Ahnoud, *no one*—" She laid her fingertips on his lips.

He took the hand and kissed it gravely. "Darling," he said in a husky whisper, "I am grateful for what you wish to give me. That you love my kisses is something—" Once more he bent his head above her, his lips meeting hers, his hand smoothing the soft gold of her hair.

Reana felt the strength of him against her, his magnetism engulfing her completely. Unreservedly she gave him her lips, her heart beating in thudding time with the passion of his own.

For awhile there were no orange trees, no tea room, nor even guitar music to her ears. All drifted off into the beyond. She was as one in another era, of great silence, of great ecstasy.

She was in a spell, seeing only Ahnoud's face, hearing his soft voice, feeling his lips on hers.

At last she pulled herself free of his encircling arms and standing up uncertainly, threw one hand to her head. The fragrance of orange blossoms and the music of a steel guitar had returned with a force that made her dizzy. Her pulse was pounding and she knew that something peculiar had happened to her.

"Ahnoud," she ventured, rather shaken, "it's getting late. They will think we're lost."

These ordinary words, spoken disjointedly with scarcely a thought behind them, were to her merely proof that she was still able to frame a sentence, to use her voice. After them Reana was quiet again, studying Ahnoud with troubled eyes.

Had it been his physical charm alone that put her out mentally those few moments, or another power—his greatest—that had wiped away her whole world in that space of time? Certainly his will had been dominant, her will nothing. She neither heard, saw, nor felt things about her *until he decided that she should!*

Belying what had passed between them, Bey now addressed her as with only a simple devotion, "You—among these trees! It is a picture I shall never forget."

Reana felt better. She attributed it to the evening air, the chill that had come over her. "Look—" she said, "the sun has gone and the blossoms are so pale."

"It is already twilight," replied Ahnoud. He held her hand as they started back to the blue gate.

Lights were on in the villa. Lanterns hung

from trees illumined the patio with glowing yellow squares. People were drifting in for early supper.

Hushed as the trees in a gray dusk that they had left behind, Reana and Ahnoud climbed into the hack. As they rattled away the air was filled with the peaceful sound of cathedral bells marking the close of day. Gradually they grew louder. Before Reana was aware, the wicker wagon was in front of a church, an ancient and crenellated building with open stone court and tall towers.

The driver stopped his cart, crossing himself reverently. The two boys jumped off the trap's back end and ran into the court, for coming down the church steps they saw the new father who had been there only a short time. He was already beloved for his good deeds and kind words.

The boys ran up to him, kneeling one on each side of the black-gowned figure. One had kissed the father's left hand, the other his right.

When this occurred, the priest was halfway down the court's front walk, very near the street and the hack. As their mentor smiled on his boys and blessed them, Reana bent forward, one hand outstretched as though to the holy father.

"Oh!" she cried, stepping out of the trap and hurrying to the priest. "Oh, Father Couperin, *Father Couperin*, don't you know me?"

The boys stood aside and the priest took Reana's proferred hands, his dark eyes lighting, a sort of half recognition on his face. Reana's eyes searched that face, so familiar to her even though the thick hair was now snowy white.

Breathlessly she spoke in French, "Father, it is I—" she explained, calling a name of her youth, "don't you recall, Paris—the Cathedral of Notre Dame?"

Now the priest seemed to grasp who she was and he answered in rapid French, "Why my child, of course I remember. It has been so long—the years between—and I—I am growing old, as you see."

"Not your heart, ever," contradicted Reana, shaking her head. "But how long have you been here, Father, and why are you so far from your native France?"

"I came to this church about six months ago," the priest was saying in his soothing voice. "We are called, you know, many times far afield on mission duty. In my last years I find this little town peaceful, its people simple hearted and full of God's love." Then with a movement toward the church, "Come into my study here at the side, my daughter, and let us talk, if you can spare the time."

"Oh surely," responded Reana, and she waved a hand to Ahnoud Bey, who sat, puzzled, in the wagon. He only nodded his agreement to her but he felt much worried, as the dusk came thicker and Reana vanished into the gloomy building.

XX

Behind that door in the cloistered seclusion of Father Couperin's study, Reana dropped into a chair and the past came vividly back to her. The priest lighted a swinging lamp, then sat down in the great chair.

"My daughter," he asked so gently, "what of your life and your happiness; what of—" and he called a name that made Reana realize how the years had passed since she had seen the priest.

"That happiness is no more, Father," she replied shakily in a low voice. "You see—" and as she talked she saw the old sorrow of her own heart reflected in the priest's face.

"I am sorry," he said. "It grieves me to know that."

"I, too, Father," she answered, still in

French. "I look back so often on the days at the convent school and then later, when you were our kind counselor. I'm afraid I've wandered far from your teachings. I am of the world now, Father. Pray for me—will you?"

Reana's eyes were filled with tears and she lowered her lashes, swallowing hard. Those memories that rushed in were almost overwhelming, but she must not go to pieces like this. She must do something for Father Couperin. Maybe money would help, that was all she could give—now.

She looked round the study. The furniture was old and in need of repair. The religious books, worn with much reading, were losing torn pages. The carpet was frayed in spots and there was a break in the stained glass window above the priest's head.

It was a poor church—of a poor community—but the parishioners had good hearts and loved their new father, as evidenced by the impulsive gesture of the boys.

Reana reached into the deep pocket of her coat and gladly took out her checkbook.

"Have you a pen and ink, Father?" she asked and when he produced them she wrote out a check and handed it over to him.

"That's in memory of a great love," she said.

"Oh, thank you, my daughter," exclaimed Father Couperin, "thank you with all my heart. I have so many calls from the needy. This will help greatly—"

"It's nothing," said Reana, rising with a sigh. "I would stay longer, Father, and talk of the old days, but you know I live in Sun City and we must go back tonight."

As Father Couperin ushered Reana from out of the dusky sanctuary of the past into the reality of her present life, he saw Ahnoud coming up the walk to meet her. Bey appeared somewhat apprehensive and Reana, introducing him to the priest, said by way of explanation, "Father, this is my friend Ahnoud Bey, a famous mystic from Egypt. Ahnoud, this is Father Couperin, who gave me my First Communion when I was thirteen."

Father Couperin scanned the handsome face before him with curiosity. He recognized that reticent hint of the East in Bey's manner, that restraint and lost look in the eyes.

"I am glad to meet you, my son," said the priest kindly. "Are you a Mohammedan?"

Ahnoud shook his head and lifted dark brows, his mouth drawing into a smile. He replied in easy French. "No Father, I am not. I was educated in England."

"Then you are a Christian?" asked the priest, but again Bey's face expressed the negative. "I am afraid not. I neither believe nor disbelieve."

Father Couperin's eyes now rested upon Ahnoud with great compassion, and he touched the white-coated arm. "Come back to see me, my son," he invited, "and let me talk with you. I was in a mission in Egypt for several years. I know your people and your country. Come again, will you not?"

Bey bowed politely out of it, then grasped Reana by the arm. As they went down the walk and entered the wicker wagon—Reana so moved she could not talk, Ahnoud in a haze of doubt—Father Couperin stood in the dusk, watching them depart.

The priest's head was bare, his gold cross gleamed on his black gown, and behind him rose the weathered towers of the old church where bells rang at dawn and nightfall.

From where he stood Father Couperin could look down and see a white yacht at anchor in the bay and, winding toward the docks, a donkey cart.

He thought of this convent-bred child as she had once been, then as she was today with the heartbreak of life in her eyes. He recalled a June day years ago and a girl with fair curls who carried a missal against her heart. He thought sadly of today and of the unhappy woman who wrote a check and went away with a Mohammedan.

Father Couperin loved people and understood them. As darkness closed over the Spanish town and lights flickered along the waterfront, Reana's words came back to him and he knew that they were very true. "Father—pray for me—I am now of the world."

XXI

Twenty minutes after the yacht left San Rafael, Reana was still in her bedroom. Ahnoud had walked a restless mile or two round the deck, then coming below had circled from the salon into the guest room and back again.

This salon seemed large and rather lonely without the several cosmopolites who usually sparked its confines with their conversation. Without them and the glow of Reana's presence, the room was leathery and metallic. There were water trophies on the walls and tables. Huge tobacco-brown chairs seemed to harbor ghosts of many nautical-minded Robinsons.

But Bey knew the fault was with him. He was a bit too sensitized at the moment. This place was in good taste, he knew. It was essentially traditional, the sort of place where tall tales could be told. Here, adventures on the brine might be relived by those whose hobby rather than profession was seafaring.

To be frank with himself, Ahnoud was sure that kind of pleasure appealed to him hardly at all. The fact that many an amateur seaman had held forth in this room compensated little for Reana's absence.

The mystic sat down and listened, but no sound came from the walnut-panelled door at his right. He frowned, stuck a cigarette between his lips, and forgot to light it. He leaned back and with troubled eyes surveyed the heavily beamed ceiling. No sound except the engine's throb, a distant rush of wind, and the *slap-slap* of breakers on the ship's hull met his anxious ears.

Bey was not always the mental master of situations. In fact, his private life would have been smoother had he possessed such a faculty. Instead he was just a young man with a superior intellect. With that intellect his turbulent emotions were constantly warring. Now they had the best of him.

The cathedral incident had left him shaken, for since her visit with Father Couperin Reana had been sad and remote. She went off to the blue region behind her eyes. She was deaf to the Egyptian's words, quite unaware of him when the boat had left San Rafael harbor.

It was evident that this French priest was linked with the Golden Lady's past. How unfortunate now to have those memories surface, after that sweet rapture in the orange grove! What an end to such a happy day—no harsh words, merely a silent barrier between Ahnoud and Reana, as intangible as it was effective.

Bey's nerves were quieting as he reached for a pile of magazines and papers and began to leaf through them—*Cosmopolitan, Yachting, Town and Country*. The smartness of their covers stared back at him. Among the magazines was Sun City's *Tribune* of the day before, which carried a Palm Club ad:

LAST PERFORMANCE

AHNOUD BEY AND HIS MYSTIC MELODY

Ahnoud started a little and regarded the ad steadily. Here was the man who could solve his problems of tonight. Here was a real showman, one who had used an incredible power to the delight and wonderment of audiences on three continents. Was this the same Ahnoud Bey who was now thwarted by the sudden reserve in a lovely women's manner?

As Bey drew the contrast, he felt foolish and angry with himself. To be upset thus, to be shaken by a barrier of thought was alien to him. Certainly it was only that, and if it were?

The storm within his heart was abating as his restless hands lay against the magazines. His eyes were concentrating on the multicolored jackets.

There was red and canary, with a bolt of russet, green of early leaves and a girl's scarlet smile; and names and letters, modernly angular or curved—*Cosmo, Town and, Yacht, Politan,*

Country— The words were blurring now. Colors crossed, rose and fell, rose again, and then retreated.

The titles were no longer registering as such in his brain. They were symbols—a round *C*, a sharp *T*, and the bolt of russet, the girl's lips meaning nothing, not even color, not even femininity. While his eyes saw, the mystic's brain shut out the definition of colors, shut out the formation of all words except those by which he was mentally speaking to Reana.

"My dear, have you forgotten poor Ahnoud, who is waiting here in the salon? We are living in the present, you and I, living a love of today. Let the past go back—*back*—dimmer and *dimmer* . . .

"It is dead—no power over you now, no appeal for you . . . Memories mean unhappiness, memories are specters . . .

"Forget them and think of us as we were in the orange grove a short while ago, a few heartbeats ago . . . Nothing has happened since then, *nothing*. I am here, waiting as before, *waiting—to love you* . . .

As Ahnoud lingered in his chair before the walnut-panelled door, there was a slight stir from within Reana's room.

She sat at her dressing table with head bent over souvenirs of the past—a letter and pictures, and a ring. Reana slowly lifted her eyes to the clock. It was busily ticking, and all at once she thought, *Ahnoud Bey is waiting for me!*

When again she sought her keepsakes, they had lost their significance. It was silly, she reflected, to care for such things—to weep over them. They were useless relics of a dead past—of a broken faith. Reana put them into a tiny cedar chest, locked the chest, and replaced it in a dresser drawer.

She viewed herself in the mirror and was surprised that her eyelashes were wet. She wiped them dry and ran a comb through her fair hair until the curls wisped up prettily.

Ahnoud liked those curls, the Golden Lady was thinking as she powdered her nose. Ahnoud liked that rounded chin, too. He had told her so—in the fragrant orange grove. She could smell those blossoms now! She could feel Ahnoud's brooding eyes upon her—hear his pleading voice! Reana stepped to the door and, opening it, called, "Forgive me, Ahnoud, have I been very long?"

She came into the saloon and stood before Bey. She was so graceful in the classic dress as she smiled a beg-pardon-excuse-me smile. Her hand was extended to the mystic.

Bey rose from the leather chair and the immobility of his countenance broke. His somber eyes lighted and in the briefest space of time he was standing beside Reana, wrapping the orchid coat about her.

"Reading?" she asked, and he shrugged, replying truthfully, "Covers—perhaps." He took the two ends of her coat collar, one in either hand, and held them a minute before buttoning them close about her throat. His eyes searched her face and he saw that the sad and chilling cloud was gone. The Egyptian reached for his own coat and heard Reana say as they walked up the companionway, "After all, Ahnoud, we can only live today. And what a day it's been—you and I, *and the white orange grove . . .*"

XXII

They found the deck bright, for what had been a paper half moon in the evening sky was now, in full darkness, glowing with a strong platinum light. It seemed to move and ride with the fall and rise of the water. The illumination was everywhere, throwing queer shadows and giving the deck floor a silvery appearance.

Reana and Ahnoud chose the afterdeck because at night the wind there was less noticeable. Up in the bow the Hawaiian musicians were singing their songs—the songs that merged, as though having no beginning nor end. Now the boys were playing a chanson of the sea. They swayed to and fro with their music, no doubt dreaming of breakers that crashed on another shore—a distant western shore.

The lilt of their melodies was carried on the breeze to Reana and Ahnoud who had settled in chairs on the afterdeck. They sat side by side, with comfortable pillows at their backs, and listened to the music that came to them softly as the undertone of a sea, rushing on and on just below them.

They were covered by the shadow of the cabin's roof, and in the semidarkness Ahnoud's huge white polo coat blanched the scene strangely. It was vastly becoming, that coat, with the collar turned up in sharp contrast to his black hair.

With magnificent indolence Bey had stretched out his great length in the chair. Even like this, at rest—speechless, shadowed—he was tremendously magnetic. One felt drawn to him curiously definitely.

It may have been Ahnoud's mind or it may have been his profile. On this people differed in their opinions. Some used the word *charm,* but the word was too thin and superficial. Others said "sex appeal," but that was far too cheap and gross a term. What the public could not define, it let go at that, so Bey continued to be a mystifying quantity.

Reana wondered now where his thoughts were as he lay there next to her, his eyes looking off into the night. She hoped they were with Egypt and his early life of which she longed to hear.

"Ahnoud," she said lazily.

"Yes, my darling," he replied without moving his head an inch.

"You promised to tell me about the Golden Keys," she went on in a persuasive tone.

"Chérie," he half-chuckled, "to tell you of the piano is to bore you with my own life."

"It wouldn't bore me," answered Reana. "I want to hear it, really, all about your life, even the smallest things."

Ahnoud gestured lightly with one hand. "Can you bear a story of three generations?" he asked. "What happened before I was born is, in this case, the point, but—my own—why should you care what went on in the turbulent Egypt of thirty-seven years ago?"

"Go on, tell me," she persisted. "Your grandfather was—?"

Ahnoud settled back, folded his hands, and sighed with resignation. "He was a Turk, as stern and narrow an old Moslem as ever lived. For years he made his home in Cairo and amassed a great fortune.

"His most valued treasure was a young daughter who embodied all the proud beauty of her native Egypt. She was like her mother, queenly and reserved, with that erect carriage and small-boned limbs that are peculiar to the Egyptian aristocrat.

"Like her father, though, she was willful, but to him her will was subservient, at least apparently. Being young, Zyra favored the new English regime. She welcomed the social reforms with secret excitement. Everything about the Anglo-Egyptian status intrigued her immensely, including the English themselves.

"My mother's one thought was to escape from Turkish parental vigilance. To an aunt, her confidante, Zyra murmured of balls and silken gowns, of wine and Anglo-Saxon men. That was the modern Cairo she knew, a whirl of dazzling nightlife—a society banned from the old-fashioned villa in which she was practically a prisoner.

"Zyra plotted, and an American—*Allah forbid*—was in her plot!"

Reana thought Ahnoud's voice had become somewhat detached, his words dispassionate. He hesitated, afraid to dramatize; he dared not voice his own feelings lest he make himself ridiculous to his listener.

"An American," said Reana meditatively, "your father?"

Ahnoud very slowly nodded his head, his eyes still seaward, his profile toward Reana.

"He was a friend of an English lad who served the Crown in Cairo. How the sheltered child of a tyrannical Bey made her dash for freedom, how she attended the dances and receptions of international society, heaven only knows!

"It was a miracle that my grandfather did not find out until too late. It was a miracle when Zyra, daughter of ancient Egypt, tore off her veil to kiss an American boy, begging with soulful conviction, to be made part of his world.

"At any rate, he and the young Britisher, through much scheming and bribing, finally managed to call on Zyra. I suppose they all sat stiffly in the long parlor in my mother's private palace within the confines of the Bey estate. My great aunt also lived as chaperone in this little villa."

With his jokes and sunny personality the American boy penetrated this atmosphere of the suspicion-bound East. He played the piano in that musty foreign parlor for Zyra and her aunt.

They had never heard the music of "Swannee River," "My Old Kentucky Home" nor the lighter songs of musical comedy. The American played, in the broken rhythm of that day, many ragtime classics.

Ahnoud then told of the daring girl's constant and clandestine meetings with the blond American. The aunt, partially under the Yankee's influence herself, failed to play the proper part of chaperone. Her only love affair had been blocked years before by her dominating brother. Now she shut eyes and ears to much that her niece was doing. One day Zyra was missing. A note lay on the silken cushion of her couch.

Fearfully the aunt took this note to the lord of the manor. His fury was awesome.

"Marrying out of her faith—" he screamed, "marrying at her age—of seventeen—a man from the United States—a *Christian!* "Where have you been, my sister? Why have you allowed this blight, this tragedy, to fall upon our household?"

"Put me out of your house, brother," she answered bravely, "but I have seen a great love born, seen it grow into a glorious thing. The young man loves Zyra. He is fine and good, courageous and tender hearted.

"He and she will face the scorn of Islam for their love. Fate has ordained such a union —what more can you ask?"

The old man's eyes flashed with hatred as he clenched his teeth behind hard lips. "Woman —*fool*—" he shrieked, "go from my presence forever! You have allowed my pearl, my white dove, be taken off by an unbeliever!

"But be sure I will have her back—and soon—before many muezzin calls have sounded on the desert air. Send me Motec! I will have Cairo combed from one end to the other and every departing steamer thoroughly searched. Ah, my little princess! What have I done that Allah should put this curse upon me?"

For three weeks the dragnet was thrown. Every policeman was watching for the proud, disobedient Zyra, whose wealthy father was going mad with sorrow and rage.

Twenty-two days after her elopement, Zyra was back in her father's villa. She stood before his judgment, the throne of his wrath.

"Your marriage was not a marriage under the laws of our Moslem fathers," he said brutally. "I have had it—such as it was—annulled."

The girl's chin went up defiantly. Her eyes smouldered with the hurt pride of the captive. "Where have you taken my husband?" she demanded. "Was it not enough to tear him from my arms? You cannot keep us apart. We love each other! I will appeal to the English!"

The old man's eyes were darkly cruel as he retorted, "Guard your tongue! This is no affair for British meddlers!"

"But it was legal," she maintained, "under the English laws of today. We were married and blessed by a missionary. He prayed to the

Christian God—Bill's God—to make our union a sacred and happy one."

Zyra's eyes were brimming with tears that she tried to hold back, but the old man, unmoved, looked off and away. His face was a study in the bitter prejudice of East against West.

"*Missionary!*" he said scornfully. "*Christian God!* You have lost your reason! You have had no marriage that I, your father and still your guardian, can acknowledge. You have sinned with an unbeliever and I have forgiven you, taking you back into my home again. Your —er—lover left today on the steamer for America. You shall never see him again."

XXIII

As Ahnoud stopped speaking, the yacht was entering the bay, leaving the rougher waters of a night sea for the easy run of a smooth cove.

With the exact precision of oiled machinery, the ship turned in between two lonely shores that formed an inlet. On Angelo Point to the right were the jigsaw lights of an amusement park. The ferris wheel was turning over and over, its latticework outlined in neon. Tents lined a midway and the barkers' singsong drifted on the breeze, along with a hurdy-gurdy sort of music.

To the left was a scene as useful as the other was nonessential. Across the depth of waves that swirled and surged between the yacht and the land, Pelican Point lighthouse played a constant and powerful beam of light.

All night long—every night year round—the huge lamp steadily revolved. On dark and rough nights, the light was a beam of guidance to ships in distress.

"Romantic," observed Ahnoud, indicating the tall pink tower against a moon-bright sky. They passed within hailing distance.

"Our rendezvous," whispered Reana, and Bey touched her hand. "Always," as moonbeams crept over the top of the cabin and slanted a triangle across their deck chairs.

"But your story," reminded Reana, "what of poor little Zyra?"

"Zyra," said Ahnoud briefly, "was submissive, as women of the East must be. I should have hated my grandfather for it all. Strangely I did not. He was devoted to me as long as he lived, granting me my every wish. Often, though, he turned from the sight of my heathen blue eyes, as though they were too much for him.

"My mother did not live long. I remember her as an exotic figure, with bangle bracelets on her wrists and a weblike veil across her nose whenever she left the villa. Unsmiling, yet with a great love, she moved sadly through my early days and then went away.

"In those young years, those impressionable years, I grew very fond of my grandfather. I took his name and was made his sole heir. When I later learned the whole story from my great-aunt I could not completely condemn the man who had caused my mother's sorrow."

Bey continued talking in his low, expressive voice, and Reana could envision a picture of his past.

As a boy Ahnoud was allowed a freedom that his mother had been denied. Until he approached his teens a tutor came every day to the old villa and made clear to a bright but restless lad the intricacies of the three "*R*"s.

Just before Ahnoud was fourteen, he began teasing to go to school in London. Perhaps somewhat cynically, the elder Bey saw that Western civilization was drawing the boy as it had drawn his mother. Now the call was stronger, surer. America was the birthright of this child, although much to the old Turk's dismay.

This sense of justice, however, could not have caused the Moslem patriarch to give his grandson to England nine months of every year. Defiance must have prompted such a decision on the part of Bey Senior. He gambled with the fealty of a half-American boy and in his blind conceit believed that Ahnoud would always come back to him unchanged.

"After that," said Ahnoud, "my life was very different. My dream was realized. I saw Dover's Cliffs, London Bridge, Big Ben, and, strangely, it was home.

"I soon learned to speak a language that to me had only been primer-book words and sentences. I learned to love the drabness of the English countryside in winter. I grew accustomed to the cold climate and weird fogs.

"London was a never-ending source of adventure and its people seemed in a sense to be my people. They were free spoken and fair minded. Their religion was kept for Sundays, seldom talked of at other times, and was far from being an obsession.

"My grandfather had done a dangerous thing in sending me to England. He was switching me, yearly, between two worlds as though daring me to take my choice. He never lived to know that I did not choose Egypt."

Ahnoud took from his pocket a jade cigarette case and opened it. He stopped talking as he offered Reana a smoke, lighting both his and hers from a single match in his cupped hand.

"And when," asked Reana, "did you discover you were a mental marvel?"

Bey lifted an eyebrow and bent his head toward her. "My, what flattery!" he said with a short laugh. "Were I as you make me in your compliments, I should be great indeed. As to the power that I have commercialized into a rather spectacular act, I realized it for the first time when I was seventeen.

"During my last year at Eton, the news came to me of my grandfather's illness. The message was not one to cause much concern on my part, yet I was utterly unable to read my lessons that afternoon. The dark, impassive face of my grandfather kept coming before my mind's eye. On his face was the shadow of death."

Finally, Ahnoud conferred with the Housemaster.

"You must let me go to my grandfather," Bey demanded. "He is very ill."

"But Ahnoud," countered the Housemaster, "you showed me the cable you received yesterday. It was not an urgent message."

"He is worse," stated the boy with some impatience.

"Have you heard again?" persisted the Housemaster.

Bey was exasperated. "Yes sir," he lied, "a cablegram. He's dying. I have booked passage for Egypt. Give me leave, sir. I have no time to lose."

After a fast trip, Ahnoud reached Cairo. The faithful carriage driver met the younger Bey at the docks and said in Arabic in an awed voice, "Seigneur, your revered grandfather will soon be with the Holy Prophet. How did you know? We could not reach you by cable. You had already gone."

"I received that message," replied Ahnoud tersely, "long before you tried to cable me."

The lad was barely in time. His grandfather, after hovering at the point of death for four days, succumbed, leaving his all to Ahnoud, child of Zyra the beloved.

"I was very sad," continued Bey, "but I returned to Eton, encountering along the way more and more psychic experiences. I took them for granted and my friends soon began coming to me with their problems. When it turned out that I could solve a few, they urged that I prepare to do this sort of thing professionally. I only laughed at the idea.

"Another cigarette—to digress a bit?" asked Ahnoud, offering Reana the open case. She shook her head. "Nor shall I," he said, closing the green cover. He stood up, taking his chair in one hand and placing his other hand on the back of Reana's.

"Let's move around the corner," he proposed, "out of this wind."

"Surely," agreed the Golden Lady. Soon they were settled on the more narrow but warmer deck. The moonlight here was not in their eyes, the gale was entirely blocked. Their backs were against the cabin wall and their feet on the chairs' footrests, near the canvas-covered railing.

"Much better," Reana said.

Bey lay back gazing at her face, which was very close. "Ah, indeed much better," he replied. "I can see your lovely eyes without blinking at the wind." Reaching over, he took her hand, clasped it in his, and put both into the capacious pocket of his greatcoat.

"Later, after winning my degree at Oxford," Ahnoud continued, "—and in order to pursue further musical study at the University, I took a townhouse in London.

"I felt myself to be quite a man of the world, with my retinue of Egyptian servants. I constantly played host to London's artistic crowd, many of the visitors twenty years my senior. I fed them and let them talk about themselves, so—" he grimaced, "I was vastly popular."

Again Reana could visualize the young Ahnoud Bey, tall, handsome, and with an authoritative manner, freely spending the money left him by a doting grandfather.

Perhaps that had been Ahnoud's method of avenging the heartache his mother suffered. Thus the old Moslem had paid heavily for his unkindness to his favorite daughter. He lived long enough to regret that his grandson had become a polished member of the Anglo-Saxon world.

"There was an actress," Ahnoud related with a reminiscent smile, "and though she was five years my elder, I imagined myself deeply in love with her. We were together on many diverting evenings, but there was a Lord who wanted to marry her. She debated long whether to accept an English title or an Egyptian fortune.

"It was necessary for me to return home that summer in order to dispose of certain local property that came to me under my grandfather's will. I was in love and loathe to leave London. It was only with the girl's promise to follow me to Cairo during June that I at last tore myself away.

"I greeted my native friends in the best English I had yet spoken, for when you have made love in a language its words and inflections are impressed on your heart as well as your mind."

Those first weeks at home were distracted ones for Ahnoud. Everything in Egypt seemed alien to him and his every thought was in England. For diversion he threw himself into intensive piano practice. The old keyboard rang with Chopin and Beethoven, played remarkably well for one so young. His father's musical ability was in Bey's fingers, no doubt of that, but his grandfather's love of horses was in Ahnoud too.

He had an Arabian stallion that was light stepping and quick tempered and when not at the piano the boy rode daily.

"My favorite excursion," said Bey, "was a commonplace one—to the pyramids. I took a short but ragged route, one known only to natives, thereby outdistancing the hordes of tourists.

"One day I went forth with the pleasant feeling that it would not be many days until my sweetheart would be in Cairo; then, as I rode over the sandy trail and the desert began to open up before me, I had a feeling that my girl was not coming south.

"My spirits began to sink. By the time I reached the pyramids and the evening sky was green and mauve above yellow sands, I knew one thing for a fact—my love had married her Lord.

"This was the last thing I wanted to believe but the impression was too strong to doubt. With a heavy heart I rode home. That night I sent a cablegram of congratulations. One week later I received a letter from her. That very afternoon while I was visiting the pyramids, my sweetheart and her Lord had been married."

XXIV

The wind had swung round from west to east. It was growing colder on the afterdeck as the pilot came and stood beside Reana, his cap in hand, his manner respectful.

"Madame," he said, "we are heading due northwest for Sun City. Is that correct?"

"Yes, Edward, and where are we now?"

"In midchannel, Madame," he answered, "one mile off the peninsula's coast between Pelican Point and Porte Sebastian."

"When shall we see the lights of Sun City?" asked Reana.

The uniformed pilot glanced at his wristwatch. "In about half an hour, Madame." Reana strained her eyes ahead but the bay was only lighted by moonlight, far as she could see.

"Any other orders, Madame?" asked the pilot.

"None," Reana replied.

"Now," said Reana to Ahnoud, "I am again your ready listener."

"I went on living my pleasant life," Bey continued, dividing my summers between London, Paris, and the Riviera. In each place I had friends and it was in the home of one that I first tried the piano experiment. This woman lived near me in Mayfair. One evening when a congenial crowd was gathered in her drawing room, and I at her request had been playing, she asked whether I had ever tried the power of my mind on inanimate objects—the piano, for instance? She wondered if I could make it play without touching the keys.

"One of the men, a typical Englishman, snorted, 'My deah lady, are you mad? My word, *the ideah!*' "

Ahnoud, unshaken, took the dare. He remained at the piano until all was very quiet in the room. He played a few bars of a serenata, then dropped his hands from the keys and sat perfectly still, his eyes on the ivories. Presently there was a movement of the keys and the serenade began faintly, haltingly.

A gasp went around the room. Every eye stared in amazement. The melody went on uncertainly, missing bars here and there, tinkling in a music-box way, without Ahnoud's skillful touch. The drawing-room audience was petrified. Women's faces went white. Men's throats were dry.

The Mystic Melody lasted only a moment or two, then stopped. Ahnoud snapped from his rigid posture, slumping his shoulders and covering his face with both hands.

He was overcome by what he had done, but by the time the crowd reached him he was once more calm, imperturbable. His acclaim by the Mayfair circle was genuine and tremendous. A man with theatrical interests offered the boy one thousand pounds a week to do this same thing before great audiences.

"I laughed at his offer," said Ahnoud, "I scorned the career of a stage wizard. That year I was enjoying my freedom from studies, from Egypt, and was spending my inheritance recklessly. It was two years later, with my finances somewhat impaired and my Egyptian interests depreciating, that I reconsidered the stage offer.

"Purely for social purposes, I had perfected my Mystic Melody exhibition. It was just then that I needed—and found—the Golden Keys."

When Ahnoud Bey had decided to give public performances, he asked himself where there could be found a piano suitable for the act he planned to perform. To be sure, London was full of pianos. Theaters were cluttered with every kind, from concert grands down to a red midget upright.

None of these would do, Ahnoud decided. He must have an instrument of his own, one more ornate than the conventional mahogany baby grand in his London townhouse.

Bey went the rounds of music stores. He was told that he could give an order for the most elaborate piano cabinet and have his order filled in every detail. Ahnoud was still unsatisfied. A bit discouraged, he walked home to his house in Mayfair.

As he walked down one street and then another, he noticed that just ahead of him stood a certain stone mansion on the corner. He had a feeling that in this house there was a piano to fill his needs.

When Bey came to the mansion he was gripped with a desire to go up and lift the brass knocker. He scoffed at this unfounded impulse and went on his way. That night at a dinner party he asked a friend next to him, "Do you know who lives at Number three—— Street, two blocks from my place?"

"Why yes," replied the lady. "That's the London home of an East Indian prince. I forget his name—there's so much to it—but if you called him 'Your Highness,' I am sure his vanity would be touched." The woman's husband, seated across the gleaming table, chimed in with an informative, "The Prince is leaving for India in a few days. All the furnishings in that house are to be sold at auction tomorrow."

"*Auction?*" echoed Bey.

The gentleman nodded. "Exactly. The Prince has some real treasures. It might be worth our while to stop by there and bring home a thing or two."

Ahnoud listened, absorbed. "Has the Prince a piano?" he asked.

"I rather fancy he has, but—why not go and see?"

"Richard," his wife cut in, "why is the Prince selling out and returning to India?"

Her husband essayed a taut smile and his blue eyes were blasé. "An *affair de coeur*, my dear, hadn't you heard? A girl who does something on the stage, I believe, has lived for a long time at Number Three——Street. Now that she has gone, the Prince sells off as worthless his other precious things."

Early next morning Ahnoud was at the auction. There he met his friends of the evening before.

"Have you discovered a piano anywhere?" inquired the woman, as the auctioneer's strident voice was filling the drawing room. One priceless piece of furniture or bric-a-brac after another was falling to a sale under the hammer.

"No," replied Ahnoud, "but I shall hunt for it right now."

The house was open to the public. Ahnoud wandered about until he came to a French music room whose shining centerpiece was a golden baby grand piano.

"Ah!" Bey cried softly. "There it is—my ideal!" Reverently he took a seat on the velvet-covered bench and touched the keys with eager fingers.

He played and the tones were like ringing bells. Ahnoud had never heard such vibrant harmony in another piano. Musician that he was, Bey was lost to everything but the sheer loveliness of this melody on the Golden Keys.

Presently he looked up and saw a thin, dark young man standing by the piano. The lad looked ill and dissipated. His burning eyes were red rimmed as though from tears.

"You play so well, I hate to let it go," he commented.

Ahnoud was on his feet at once. "Your Highness," he begged, bowing slightly, "set your price and I will pay it."

"Money," replied the Prince, "is nothing to me. I have too much now. I should like to spare this instrument the ignominy of the auction gavel. The piano cost me an absurd amount a year ago. It was made on order by the most skilled cabinet carver in the world. It was bought as a birthday present for—*someone*—"

His face clouded and his eyes shone with unshed tears. There seemed to be something that cut his heart so sharply he could scarcely endure the pain. At last he spoke again.

"Oh, I do not care. Take it at your own price. What are material possessions when the soul of the house has fled?" Ahnoud named a figure and the Prince agreed.

"It is yours," he stated, accepting Ahnoud's cash banknotes, "and, my friend, I trust that it may bring you more happiness than it has brought me. Doubtless when I am far away in India, I shall hear in my mind the ringing melody of the Golden Keys.

"It is like that—the piano—you shall see. I have asked myself a thousand times if there were not an evil fate within the cabinet of this instrument, if the music of its tones were not, after all, the song of heartbreak."

"And that piano," Ahnoud concluded, "has not brought me the ill fate of which the East

Indian prince warned. It has given me fame, money, and—most to be desired—*you.*"

"But Ahnoud," asked Reana, "would you be able to do your mental playing on another piano?"

"Of course." He laughed. "I have, you see, many times. You are to keep the original Golden Keys. I shall travel with its copy, which has been made to my order and is now waiting for me in New York. So, your conscience need not worry you." He put his arm around her and drew her head over on his shoulder.

"I would give you the world were it mine. I would give you my life if you should ask. The story I have just told was only a prelude to our meeting. I have waited—through the years—*for you*—"

His low voice paused and quiet fell between them. The ship cut along sharply, and ahead there was a semicircle of vivid yellow on the dusky horizon.

"Look Ahnoud, the lights—" murmured Reana, "we are almost home."

Ahnoud smiled cryptically over the top of her head. "Home," he repeated, "and a surprise awaits you. But do not guess now—"

"Darling, I won't," promised Reana, sitting up and laughing, "but you know about the curiosity of the cat—and the woman." She stood and took his hand in hers. "Come, let's go up to the bow where we can watch the lights."

Gradually the yacht was turning westward to the brightest illumination in the night sky. Now the skyline of Sun City was just ahead—its pier dance hall, its yacht club, and hotel roofs with their twinkling lights. Up into the sky flashed red and blue neon signs, on and off, off and on—symbols of another gay evening begun, symbols of youth recaptured and lost laughter found.

XXV

Reana left Ahnoud at the Bayside Hotel with his promise to be out at Villa Robinson for dinner. Ten minutes later, Jado the dancer dropped into a chair at Nick's café.

The boss himself came over to Jado's table, with a menu in his hand and a smile on his face.

"Good evening," he greeted the dancer. "Glad to see you. What you have tonight?"

"Oh hello Nick," answered Jado, taking the menu. "What's good? I feel rotten. My appetite's gone, *yes gone!*"

The big Greek moued up his full lips and drew his beetle brows together in a frown of sympathy. "Too bad, too bad," he said quickly, "but look—I make you hungry. How 'bout some nice broiled pompano—fresh caught this afternoon? How 'bout lobster Newburg or fine ice-cold oyster cocktail, with my rich tomato-Tabasco sauce—uh?"

"The pompano'll do." Jado decided, laying down the menu. "And fry some potatoes with it, but—*dios*—bring me a Manhattan cocktail first. My spirits—they are gasping!"

Nick waved a hand to one of the waiters, who came running. After relaying the order the Greek took a seat opposite Jado.

"Now whats-a-matter with you?" Nick queried, taking a mammoth cigar from the pocket of his vest, across which a gold watch chain was strung.

"Oh lots the matter," answered the dancer. "My partner, Conchita, for one thing. We do not speak, yet I must kiss her in our rhumba each night. She says, 'Just wait till we are back in New York, Jado, you will have no partner—fool!' "

"Umm." Nick grunted. "Jealous?"

"Righto," agreed Jado, "of one blonde lady who does not know I live." The cocktail came and he sipped its contents with gratitude if not enthusiasm. He had tasted better Manhattans.

Light wines and beer were in the front window, behind a broad expanse of plate glass over which a tubular run of neon red stated:

NATIONAL CAFÉ—SEA FOODS
SPAGHETTI—WINE AND BEER
STEAKS—OPEN ALL NIGHT

Every Nicholas Café—and there were fifty over the country—was designed and run on much the same pattern. They all had bright lights and porcelain-topped tables, and tile wainscotting halfway up the walls.

In this Sun City restaurant Nick played the democratic role of manager. Nick was just past fifty and he liked the restaurant business. He had been at it since he was sixteen, when he had served as a hotel waiter in the old country. He was more than twenty when he came to America. For years his road had been one of endless work.

Nick had slaved and sacrificed, purchasing one café after another, usually living up over each one while doing most of the work himself with the help of his faithful wife.

They had climbed together—he and Nella—raising two fine boys, who now ran "National" restaurants in other parts of the country. It had not been easy for Nick, reaching the idyllic place that he and his wife now enjoyed. They had built that columned Athenian villa with the sweat of their brows and the labor of life's best years.

As for him he was still old "Nick the Greek," caring for nothing much beside his home, his family, and his restaurants. From force of habit he hung out at this one most of the time and wanted folks to make this their meeting place. He wanted everyone to call him Nick and use his café as a banquet hall.

"Ah—*women!*" exclaimed the Greek, waving a hand and slamming it palm down on the table. "We love 'em, but—golly—they funny!"

Jado stared grimly ahead, unstirred by Nick's explosive words. They helped the dancer, somehow. This was like life in the foreign quarter of New York where he had spent ten lively years. "Golly—they *are* funny!" he chimed in. "Take this Reana Robinson. You know—beautiful from head to foot, just swell!"

"Oh sure." Nick smiled. "She live near us in Desdena. You her good friend?"

Jado drank the last of his drink and set the glass down firmly. "Who wants to be a friend to one that beautiful? *Sabe Dios!*" There was a sullen, downward tilt to the corners of his mouth. Black eyes brooded with an unspoken hurt.

"Until that damned heathen, Ahnoud Bey, set foot in the Palm Club, all was a sweet, sweet story. *Now*—" The dancer drew up his shoulders and gestured fatally with one hand. She no longer sees Jado—sees none but Allah, Allah, in person!"

"Oh ho!" cried Nick with a hearty and somewhat misplaced humor, "he cut you out! Oh ho! Now I know why you sad—why you not eat my good food!"

Jado took this jocularity without irritation. "Yeah," he replied. "Poor Jado, the fool, is dumped. She feels silly, maybe, because she noticed a rhumba dancer. I went out to that villa of hers one day. I told her I would die of loving her and was ill because she had passed me by. *Madre!* What did she say— 'Jado, I hold nothing against you. Can we not be friends?' "

The dinner came and Jado attacked the pompano with a vicious quietude. He drank a cup of strong coffee with his meal.

Nick sat smoking and bowing to various patrons who entered or left the café. "Everything okay?" he asked. "More tartar sauce?

Here—" Nick clapped his chubby palms and signaled a waiter.

"Another order of tartar sauce—and more coffee for the gentleman."

Jado's mood of gloom was such that he barely tasted what was set before him.

"I wish I never come to Sun City," he declared angrily. "I wish I never saw the Palm Club or heard of Ted Maxime. He's to blame, making us acquainted three weeks before the Great Bey rolled in, with his private car and his fake English accent." Jado stuck out his long chin.

"My life is ruined, Nick," he went on despondently. "I'm dead in love with her, God knows! If I stay here she will surely snub me, yet I can't make myself go. Conchita's up in the air too. What would you do, Nick? I'm nuts about Reana—she's so swell—Maria—but not for Jado!"

"Oh that just how you feel now," Nick consoled. "You young and good looking. There be other girls nice too. You wait and see."

Jado shook his head miserably. "Reana's got class and she knows it. Why then must she trifle with a nightclub dancer? Because she's cold and cruel—no heart at all. But Nick, I love her just the same. Oh, Paradise it is to be with her—but how she let me down!"

For awhile the dancer sat and smoked with Nick. They talked in that monosyllabic way that two men call a visit.

"You dancing at the Palm Club tonight?" asked Nick.

"No, thank goodness," Jado shot back. "I danced my finale there last night. Conchita, she went and told the manager of Desdena Hotel we will dance there tonight and what a head I have now!"

"How soon you got to be out there?" asked Nick. "I goin' home soon. I take you in my car."

"Thanks, Nick," Jado answered consulting his wristwatch. "Not till nine-thirty. It will perhaps be ten when—alas—we go on, and me with that Conchita who can't say one polite word. *Dios!* I wish I never have to dance another step. I wish I never live another day, for that matter."

The Greek made a pushover movement with his right hand toward Jado. Rising to his feet with a weighty grunt, Nick said: "Aw, you too sad. Look—I get somethin' to cheer you up!" He went over to the counter and took a bottle from the glass showcase. He carefully read the label, then with a bear walk returned to the table, ordering cracked ice as he sat down again.

"Oh me," said Nick hospitable, pouring the liquor into their glasses.

The hour hand of the Western Union clock up on the white wall went round the timepiece's bland face from eight to nine. The café owner's car drew up to the curb outside.

In another moment the Greek chauffeur was in the restaurant chatting with the pretty cashier. Nick came up to the counter and gave the girl a few instructions for the night.

Jado's sallow cheeks were flushed by the liquor's warmth—a liquor he should never have tasted with an exacting rhumba ahead.

Nick was merely jovial, his aspect kindly,

his outlook on humanity generous. They sat together in the back seat of the car which spun away out the Boulevard to Desdena.

"Nick," said Jado after a silence, a cunning silence, "I'm going by Reana's house. If I find Bey there maybe I punch him in the nose."

Nick chuckled—a deep, bearish chuckle. "That the thing!" he cried, slapping Jado on the knee. "Go see her—maybe she still love you!"

The dancer was intoxicated mostly by a sense of bravado. He was still sober enough to know that Nick's words were untrue. Reana had never loved anyone, he figured. She didn't know what love meant, but Jado wanted her and he had no idea of giving her away to a piano-playing Arab.

Reana was out there in her house by the sea—alone, the dancer hoped. She couldn't throw him out this way, ruin his life, *she couldn't—couldn't . . .*

The words seemed to beat up and through his head, from the constant throb of the car's motor. Ahead, past pink gateposts, was Desdena and Reana's yellow coquina house.

XXVI

When Reana had arrived home an hour and a half earlier, Madeleine was waiting in the villa's hallway.

"Madame," requested the maid, clasping her hands together over the front of her apron, a trick she employed in moments of delight, "look into the music room. Something is there for you."

Reana stopped short and faced Madeleine, then she swung round to an arched doorway. "Madeleine!" she reproved. "Don't frighten me that way. What is it?"

"Oh Madame," assured the girl, "something nice—really." Reana was now in the music room and she snapped on the wall switch.

With curious eyes she scanned the circular

salon. There were, just as she had left them, the black Chesterfield, the deep armchairs, and a teakwood table set with pearl inlay. There were also gold net curtains at three windows. The polished floor was still partially covered by two rugs of solid turquoise blue.

On the only wide expanse of wall, to her left, hung a large tapestry of the Taj Mahal, woven with glittering threads. All these things Reana catalogued in an instant, then she glanced beyond them to a far corner of the salon.

That corner was an alcove. Its floor was a raised platform to which three shallow steps led. On each side of these steps a sliding door jutted out a few inches from the wall. This semicircular wall was set with high small-paned windows. On the dais Reana saw the "piano with Golden Keys."

"Madeleine!" she called aloud, rushing over toward the instrument. "When did he send it? I have never believed he was going to give it to me."

"Nor I, Madame," replied the maid with some scepticism, "but it arrived this afternoon while you were gone. There was no word—no card—nothing. I told them to put it here on the dais."

Reana was standing beside the piano now. She felt the carving of its cabinet and smoothed her hand over the velvet of the bench cushion. She peered under the piano's upraised top where harp strings were stretched.

"Oh Madeleine!" she cried. "He said I would find a surprise when I came home, but I really never dreamed—! Oh Madeleine, have you ever seen anything like it?"

"Never Madame," replied the maid.

"But you should hear its tone!" Reana settled on the bench and touched the keys that were a smooth pearl overlay. Madeleine came close and stood by the piano.

"Please play something, Madame," she begged.

Reana shook her head, rising hastily from the bench. "I haven't an hour to bathe and dress. Ahnoud Bey will be out for dinner. Hurry, hurry!" She whisked out of the music room and upstairs, Madeleine anxiously behind her.

When the Egyptian arrived at the villa, he was greeted by the music of the Golden Keys. Reana met him at the door and took his hands in hers, her eyes glowing with joy.

"Darling, how can I thank you?" she asked. "The answer is, I can't. You have given me your prized piano, the instrument that has been a part of you all these years. I am unworthy. No gratitude I could express would be enough."

Ahnoud's eyes dwelled long upon her. What a picture she was, in that powder-blue evening dress with the silver girdle! There was a silver star in her hair, too, and curling bangs on her forehead.

"Forget the 'thank you's' " he said at last, "and let us see how my old friend likes your music salon." They spent a half hour in the music room, and when dinner was served were slow to leave the Golden Keys.

The dining room was just across the hall.

Here they sat at an oblong table with a blue mirrored top. A bowl of yellow roses was in the center and candlelight cast a romantic glow, making Reana's face a study in pastels.

After dinner they returned to the music room and Reana, once more seeing her gift, turned to Ahnoud hopelessly.

"It is so costly, so famous!" She rejoiced. "I can't believe it's mine."

"My dear," said the mystic, "another woman of your beauty would take such a gift as merely her just due. It is unfortunate that gratitude, in women, is an old-fashioned virtue. Perhaps, after all, it is just a matter of breeding."

"They taught me," said Reana, "in my convent school to express thanks for even trifles. I hope I shall never forget their lessons in graciousness."

Ahnoud took her hand as they sat side by side on the divan. The butler brought demitasse coffee, which they sipped slowly, and Reana's eyes often strayed to her new treasure. She was thinking about its history, about Ahnoud's past.

Reana thought of the unhappy prince of India who had great wealth and no happiness, of Ahnoud's finding the piano and playing it on the stage all across Europe and America,—playing it, maybe, on the Ile de France in midocean.

"But I gotta see Miss Robinson—no foolin' now, I'm gonna see her! No matter about my name!"

These words, in Jado's unmistakable voice, cleft the quiet of the night with an imperative ring that reached easily from terrace to music room. Reana's thoughts were abruptly cut short. She rose and took a step toward the door. As she did so, Jado was standing in that door. Ahnoud set down his coffee and jumped to his feet.

"What are you doing," he asked, "forcing your way into this house?"

"I got the right here much as you have, replied Jado. "I gotta talk to Reana—you can scram!"

"You're drunk and cannot talk with her alone! What you have to say, say now before me, and then go." Bey stood, tall and fearless. His face was scowling but his voice was modulated.

He knew well that Jado generally carried either a stiletto or pistol and had the reputation in New York of using both at times. The idea of fear, however, never entered the Egyptian's head.

"Ahnoud," Reana begged, "let me speak to him." She advanced toward the dancer. "Jado, why must you come here like this? I told you the last time I saw you that we could still be friends."

Jado snapped up her words almost before she had finished speaking. "*Friends! Dios!* Yeah, that's what you say now, but not once you said it before he came. Not once you said 'friends' when you were pulling your stuff on me, when you were just kidding a nightclub hoofer that way!

"Got him crazy, like hell, then gave him the air—put the skids under him! Just so far, then the skids! But you're not the same. *He's* got you goofy. But Jado loves you—God, Reana, see how I suffer!"

The dancer rested his head against the door's archway and gripped his brow with one hand. Reana came closer to him, seeing with concern his tortured eyes.

"Jado, I'm terribly sorry. We were just friends. I didn't suppose you'd take it seriously. I didn't intend to hurt you, poor boy—"

He knew then that she was innocent of the wrong she had done him. Jado now realized that it was he who had been wrong. He had thought she was cold, heartless but who could doubt her sincerity? The goodness of her was in her sorrowful face!

As she stopped speaking, Bey said in his imperious way, "Reana, *dear*—" He motioned her back beside him, behind his powerful figure. She cast her eyes down and turned away from the dancer, retreating to the divan as though she had dropped the matter for all time.

"Now," said Ahnoud to Jado, "you may talk." The situation was at once plain to the Spaniard. He thrashed out at Bey with stinging words.

"All right!" Jado's voice was hoarse with emotion. "Okay, Reana, I'll give you the works on him! Ahnoud Bey thinks—and you think. He speaks and you move. Get me? People say he's only amusing—maybe a fake—but Ahnoud Bey's no fake. God in Heaven! 'Tis too true—he's the real McCoy!"

"Shut up!" demanded Ahnoud. His voice was raised a little but Jado's rose higher. He

seemed to be half sober, yet his eyes stared wildly and his hands shook frightfully.

"You can't shut me up!" he yelled. "She's hypnotized and can't get away! It's time somebody squealed about it—about your black art! Yeah! I'll get out! If I shoved you to hell, the devil and you'd shake hands! Just buddies—you and the devil—that's what you are! Yeah, Jado will go, but he can *talk!*

"He'll spread the dirty news that Reana Robinson is in the power of a black Moslem! She's Ahnoud Bey's slave! *Get it—his slave!*"

Having shrieked those last words, Jado raced out of the house.

Back in the music salon, Ahnoud stood amidst the wreckage Jado had left, but he spoke bravely to Reana in a perfectly balanced tone, "I think Jado was quite drunk. We shall forget what he said."

In a meaningless way Reana repeated, "Yes, he was drunk. We shall forget it." Nevertheless, as she sat there in her blue dress with the star in her hair she was far from forgetting Jado's words. They seared through her mind like a branding iron.

"A slave?" Was the piano with Golden Keys, then, only her keeper?

XXVII

All was very quiet in the yard of James L. Adams' estancia. Peter was sleeping on a leafy bough of the giant live oak he chose to call home. His bed was of soft gray moss. He had retired with the dark, that he might be alert when the moon was descending westward.

It was the negro chef who was singing now as he washed dinner dishes. His melodious voice floated from the kitchen into the side yard.

Somehow Cook's singing was soothing. It made one deliciously sleepy as does a lullaby, although there was no one in the moonlit spaces of the back yard to hear or grow drowsy.

The chef's song did not carry through to the front garden, nor the living room. Here stillness hung, as in a deserted castle. Sylvia's laugh broke the silence and Phil appeared startled.

"Now what?" he asked.

"Nothing," she answered, "only I was thinking of Trudy and the lobster in her make-up kit."

Phil knit his brows in mock solemnity. "I wonder," he said, holding his chin, "if that could have been one of the same lobsters we had for dinner tonight." Sylvia giggled.

"It might have been," he went on, "the poor lobster developed such an inferiority complex from being caught in Trudy's bag that it was unable to resist being caught by the first fisherman. This is the question we must decide—the psychological problem we must work out—how digestible is a lobster with an inferiority complex?"

They were lolling in a tête-à-tête love seat. Sylvia, convulsed with laughter, rumpled Phil's blond hair with her hand.

"And where are we going tonight, Mr. Duesenberg Pelham? You don't aim to sit here in the pahlah all evening, a la gay nineties, do you?"

"I envy the men of the gay nineties," Phil stated with great conviction. "They could sit all evening, not only in comfort but with due respect, in the homes of their girl friends. They could rest in peace after days of strife and labor.

"And what labor have you done today?" asked Sylvia. "Selling two cars with a word or two and a few slick smiles?"

"Today?" echoed Phil. "Oh this has been a terrible day! You and Mrs. Nicholas yanked me from the precipice. I *almost* didn't pay my overdue hotel bill. I *almost* couldn't go back and sleep at the Bayside tonight. I'm still catching my breath and my heart's skipping beats!"

Sylvia affected a pout, putting up her chin. "If your heart does any beat skipping, young man, it must be over me."

Pelham's eyes twinkled. "That's just it—I want to sit here all evening and look at you. It's really such a fascinating picture, with those gardenias on your shoulder."

Sylvia wrinkled up her nose. "And not even play Monopoly?"

Phil moved over and kissed her red lips. "Not even Monopoly," he whispered, "but where shall we dance? It would be a cardinal sin to keep you from the world—the way you look tonight."

"We could walk over to the Desdena Hotel," said Sylvia. "They're having a program of New York entertainers. Al Benton's there with his radio broadcast orchestra and, if we look in the wishing well—"

"And see this moon reflected there—" finished Pelham.

Just then a car backed out of the driveway and Jim Adams came in the front door.

"Hi baby! Where are you?" he called, and Sylvia stepped hastily to the living-room door.

"Why Jim, you burglar, how come?" J. L. kissed his wife with a resounding smack, then patted her cheeks and pinched her chin.

"Pretty as a little doll," he observed," but listen kid—I flew home and took a taxi from the field. A man's coming out tonight to talk a deal. He's only in town one day, gotta be back in New York Monday."

Sylvia set her lips in disapproval. She saw Jim's worn sneakers, his ancient and grease-stained slacks bay-windowing out in front. She saw his shirt—a horrid checked one he adored—open at the throat to a sunburned neck. Worst of all, he had on that old leather jacket that looked as if a lion had clawed it and a horse slept on it.

"You flew home that way?" she asked coldly, but J. L.'s florid face only shone the more.

"Sure," he replied blithely, "everybody knows me round these diggins!" He hustled over to the living room and took a peek inside. "Who's in there?"

"Phil," said Sylvia, "but you can't come in till you're properly dressed for the evening." She stood in the doorway, her arms sidewise across the portal, her hands on the opposite door jambs.

"Hey Phil." shouted J. L.

"Hello Jim," Pelham saluted. "How's the new subdivision?"

"Fine," Adams returned, "but what's all this about a new addition to my family?" Sylvia turned beet red and Phil started.

"The Duesenberg—ha ha!" Jim laughed aloud and his stomach shook. The color drained from Sylvia's face and her eyes narrowed with irritation.

Phil breathed more easily and, reaching for a cigarette, came back nonchalantly, "You'll like the Duesy, Jim. It's the car for you."

J. L. tried to duck under Sylvia's arm, but

she stopped him sternly. "Go up and dress," she commanded. "You can't come in here till you do."

"See how the baby bosses me, Phil?" J. L. called out, and he made for the stairway.

"Have you had dinner, Daddy?" asked Sylvia as Adams went upstairs. "Or shall I have them fix something for you?"

"No time to eat, baby," J. L. objected noisily from his bedroom as he stripped off his clothes. "The man's coming in fifteen minutes. I'm not hungry. I had a swell hamburger at the field."

Sylvia released her sentry at the door and walked back into the room. She opened her eyes wide and waved her hands as if to say—"That's how he is."

"I've been married to him four years," complained Sylvia, "and every time he's ever come into this house he's 'just had a hamburger.' "

"What about my being here?" asked Phil, a trifle apprehensive.

"Don't be silly." Sylvia laughed. "Hasn't he found you here a dozen times? He likes you—thinks you're a smart boy."

"And you think?" Phil went on, catching her in his arms.

"I think you're a big mess—" Sylvia accused, "—the biggest mess I ever saw!"

"May the big, bad mess take you dancing?"

"Wait," said Sylvia, and she ran out into the hall, calling up to Jim who was splashing in the bathtub—splashing so fiercely that she knew the bathroom door must be open.

"Daddy," Sylvia ventured, "Phil and I are going dancing. Do you mind?"

"No, baby," J. L. shouted back. "I'm going to be busy at the office for an hour or more. Go on, have a good time."

"Well bye, Daddykins," Sylvia called meekly as Phil helped her into her velvet evening wrap.

Together they left the house and soon were lost in the enchantment of Desdena under moonlight. Phil took Sylvia's hand, and with scarcely a word spoken they walked the three blocks to the hotel grounds.

As Phil and Sylvia entered the Moorish court of the hotel, sweet music drifted out to them. They stopped beside the wishing well, and, gazing down, they saw the moon reflected in the black water—the clear image of a silver crescent. That meant a wish would soon come true.

XXVIII

To the dining and dancing rooms of the Desdena Hotel had come a late-winter crowd of sun worshipers. There were nut-brown pleasure seekers, up from weeks in warmer points south and those pale, tired faces just down from the ice-locked north.

There were heirs of wealthy families and European titles, the latter invariably accepting bounty from the former. There were divorcées, fresh from Reno and giddy with new freedom. All seemed to have that acquaintance that exists between travelers who meet here and there at resorts around the seasons' clock.

Kidding each other between drinks were the broker down from Wall Street on a secret trip and the bookie who talked horses with a slangy fervency. Near them was a somewhat sulky prize fighter who bigged around beside his pint-sized manager.

The people dancing in Desdena's Moorish hotel were here tonight and gone tomorrow. Time meant money to some of them. Others considered too many hours in one resort wearisome. So they flew a lot, spent half their lives taking planes. They were always rushing—arriving here, going back to New York at short notice on Pullman ships, and returning to Sun City later in the season.

Because the Desdena Hotel was nearest the airport, it remained the choice of this particular crowd. They could fly in for a night or a weekend and be back in Manhattan for any business or social appointment by Monday forenoon.

There, bending an elbow at the chromium bar, was a playwright who had just melted the snows in New York with his hit play. Near his bespectacled face was one of the ten best-dressed women in the world, though no one here singled her out for special notice.

Celebrities glamorized the setting at the bar, in the more sedate dining room, and on the dance floor. Here Ted Maxime was taking a busman's holiday and it seemed that he knew everyone. He was a fine dancer, and now he danced with a debutante, then an actress, and finally an ex-princess whose prince had cost her a quarter-million when she bought him and a half-million when she returned him to circulation.

It was with the ex-princess that Ted wandered out into the walkway. There he saw Sylvia and Phil looking into the wishing well.

Maxime swore under his breath. *Phil again!* Where was J. L.? Where were his eyes?

Ted and the princess sat down on the tiled steps that led up to the balcony. Above was a door leading into other corridors and private dining rooms. These rooms in turn opened onto another Spanish balcony that circled the dance floor.

The princess was confiding wistfully that she still loved the expensive prince, but Ted, only half-listening, threw his cigarette onto the titles and smashed its ashes with one foot. Well, Sylvia was young—too young for J. L. She was a sweet lass. Who could blame her for anything? Ted surely couldn't. He was her faithful pal, do what she may, and she often did plenty.

Ted had never told on Sylvia. Why should he worry J. L., who was as happy as a puppy with an old shoe? There was time enough for talk. Ted would still paint Sylvia the innocent child, keep Jim's home together as long as possible.

Maxime wondered why he had come out here tonight. He really liked this place very little and had told Jim Adams so the night it opened a few years before. It was too Moorish. The moon cast such queer shadows in the court and the sun was never any too bright around that mouldy wishing well.

The Desdena Hotel had a spooky atmosphere that Ted felt even now, when it was filled with people. Perhaps Maxime had had too much to drink at the bar. He stood up for a couple was heading toward the steps.

"Well hello, hello!" he greeted as Ahnoud

Bey and Reana approached. "Here's my mystic from the Palm Club, no longer punching my time clock."

Bey smiled in his enigmatic way and shook his head. "No," he replied, "tonight is my own."

"And Reana!" exclaimed Ted, taking her hand and introducing her to the ex-princess, "You look bea-u-ti-ful! If I didn't know it was my golden-haired Reana, I'd think you were just the dream of an old man in his second childhood."

"Who said you were old?" Reana reproved. She went up the steps and Ahnoud followed, but she was struck by a look in the eyes of Ted's partner as she saw the Egyptian mystic.

That this princess knew Bey was undeniable. That she had been hurt by him was almost a surety. That she sought his favor in spite of it all was evident. Young girls were like that, Reana thought. Their faces always gave them away.

Ted glanced up to where Reana stood at the head of the stairs. She wore silver sandals tonight. They were small and high heeled, barely visible under the blue skirt that billowed round her feet. Those were gay, dancing feet before Bey came.

"Better go down and dance, Reana," Ted advised. "Al's got a swell band, just up from two months at the Royal Plaza."

"Thanks, Ted." She shook her head. "We're tired, so all we plan to do is watch and listen."

Tired of yachting for two? thought Maxime. He knew that Reana, wrapped in a coat silver as the moon, was vanishing inside one of the balcony doors. He turned to the princess and caught her rapt expression.

"Oh," she said breathlessly, "I didn't know *he* was here." In her simple words Ted grasped both regret and hope. He stood up and stared across the court. Phil and Sylvia still pressed against the wishing well's stone ledge, oblivious to all else.

"Let's dance," said Ted, taking the princess by the hand and pulling her up from the steps. "This place is haunted. It'll get you. Safer in there with the lights and folks."

Ted and the princess mixed with the crowd on the floor and danced a fox trot.

"Great music, Al," Ted said as he passed the maestro. He and his accomplished boys were rendering about the smoothest music south of New York.

"Glad you're enjoying it," responded the blond Al.

Ted danced closer to the slender leader. "Look, Al," he said, "how about playing 'Sylvia' next?"

The lad nodded. "As you like it," he agreed. Five minutes later he lifted his baton on the first romantic bars of Oley Speaks' "Sylvia," just as young Mrs. Adams and Phil entered the room.

She stood under the arches that upheld the balcony and felt many admiring eyes upon her. Year-round residents, as well as tourists, were at Desdena. They all knew Sylvia—little Mrs. Adams—with the curls that rang like bells. Tonight they weren't ringing but were waved back into a glossy coiffure. Across the regimented curls were white gardenias.

Sylvia looked around the room and saw everyone she knew. They were quietly smiling. Her cheeks began to redden and she tapped one toe on the shiny floor.

"Ted did this," she said. "Look at him over there—the snoop dragon. I saw him out in the court." Phil did not answer. He took her into his arms and danced off with her. For all he cared, no one else existed.

Sylvia rested her cheek on his shoulder. No one danced like Phil, she was thinking. He had smoothness and perfect timing. She never tired of fox-trotting with him. She even liked a rhumba—but a waltz? Why, waltzing with Phil was like heaven—nothing this side of it—*nothing!*

XXIX

Al stood facing his dancing audience. He held his stilled baton in one hand as he sang with the gentle simplicity of the times. In like manner the orchestra behind him was toned down with the soft swing of muted horns.

And the touch of Sylvia's hand
Is as light as milkweed down—

Al's tenor was clear and his listeners hummed with him, walking amorously through the waltz. Each girl was a "Sylvia" to her partner, but only to Phil was given a real-life one.

His chin brushed her dark head and he smelled again the fragrance of gardenias in her hair, that perfume he always associated with her. To Phil, they were dancing on the rim of the moon.

Al sang as the colorful crowd swayed and lingered before him. Skirts of tulle frothed like sea foam around gold heels, and satin glowed with the coronation shades of the season—crimson, orange, and purple.

Each charming head became a picture. Here was one with quaint flowers in the hair, violet, daisy, or mignonette. There was a real jasmine, white, with living sweetness, breath of the Sun City garden from whence it came.

Such blossoms were in Sylvia's hair, on the sleek curls. As Phil dreamed with her against his heart she lifted her head and spoke, "Al may be a big shot, but he needn't think he can play my song the way Neil King does." Phil came down from the moon's rim.

"King's music," Sylvia went on, "always makes me feel that something grand is going to happen to me—and soon!"

Phil smiled. "In other words," he added, "it's a sort of paean of returning prosperity?"

"That's it!" the girl in his arms agreed. "Remember way back in 1932—what Neil did with 'Night and Day' and 'Play Fiddle Play'? Something more than keen—it was magic!"

Phil's eyes clouded a bit. His mind reached back over several years. "Neil came up from the black pit of the depression, with his dynamic piano and golden horns," Phil said at last, "and, I think, some sort of courage—a gallant sort! We caught this from his music and so we carried on, *else*—"

He shrugged expressively. Sylvia felt his implication. She thought of herself, a poor girl in that battered Arkansas house with nothing but a small radio set—a cherished radio, with Neil King's music coming through.

As the music stopped, Phil and Sylvia dropped down at one of the tables. A negro waiter came running, a grin on his face for "Mistah Pelham," whose tips were always ample.

"Yessuh, *yessuh,* what y'all gonna have?" Phil, undecided, studied the menu, and then Sylvia, raising his eyebrows in query.

"Order for me—you know what I like," she replied, powdering her face from a small compact. Phil ordered with the fine sense of selection that made dining with him a pleasure.

Now Sylvia absently looked out over the dance floor, then up to the balcony that entirely circled the two-story room.

There, leaning on the carved balustrade, watching the crowd below, she saw a blonde in blue with a silver star in her hair. Beside her stood a dark young man, tall and meditative, possessed of a magnetism that was palpable even at this distance.

"I see Ahnoud Bey being exclusive up there on the balcony," said Sylvia, "and with him of course is Miss Robinson. She caught me in Ahnoud's cabana this morning on the beach and I felt like a fool. She's as gorgeous by daylight as she is right now."

The dance floor was completely clear of people now. In its center was a rather obnoxious little man who never stopped talking a minute, while everyone was laughing, half at him and half with him.

"What is that M.C. trying to say?" asked Phil.

"He's saying," translated Sylvia, "in the long-tailed way of M.C.s who love to hear themselves talk, that Jado and Conchita are going to dance."

"Their rhumba, do you suppose, which we know so well?" Phil inquired.

As he spoke, Jado and Conchita appeared. Lights dimmed to a purplish dusk, and a spot of amber followed the dancers as they threw themselves with wild abandon into the Spanish dance.

Al and his boys had played before for this team. If Al sensed a reckless lack of sureness in Jado's steps tonight, the maestro merely made a greater effort to time his music exactly and to merge it with this new capriciousness of the dancers.

"Like the Palm Club," someone commented, "with Bey watching from the balcony. Is he on the program tonight?" Someone else, staring up at the mystic's dark face, replied, "No, not officially."

Beneath the staccato of the rhumba was the eccentric beat of the maraca. To this savage symphony, Jado and Conchita danced as they had never danced before, Conchita with insolent scorn of her partner. Her black lace skirt swirled round red slippers. Her taunting dark head flung insult after insult at Jado.

He was the devil himself tonight, but uncertain in his steps—his face ghost white under mascara and rouge, his black eyes sullen and deep in their sockets. The stamp and swing of his feet kept perfect time to the madness in his brain.

Now the audience ceased to talk, even to

move, for the climax of the dance was imminent. Jado and Conchita were circling away from each other and back again, the most difficult feature of their rhumba.

The marimba was going strong and again was that maraca beat, thudding, *thudding*. The smile had left Al's face as he watched the dancers and led his band at the same time. Something was wrong—Jado was dancing too long, too many bars. Maybe now, though, they did it longer. *Maybe*—

Gonglike tones of the marimba, roll of the rhumba, and Jado went whirling out to the center of the floor—round and round—with a frantic Conchita improvising and whispering hurried instructions under her breath.

On and on Jado spun, with the ends of his red sash flying. All at once he clapped one hand against his head, then a cry came from his dry lips. Those agile legs gave way under him. The room went to blackness as he fell unconscious on the floor.

In the crowd that rushed to Jado was a doctor. He bent over the prostrate dancer for a few seconds, then announced in his professional way that Jado had died from heart failure.

Conchita screamed and they led her off the floor into a private room where she collapsed in hysterics. As they took Jado out a pall fell upon the room. Al was white as a sheet. He could scarcely lift his baton, but at a signal from the manager he continued his music.

Sylvia's face had a sudden ill look as people pushed and milled past their table.

"Jado's dead!" they cried.

"He fell as he was dancing!"

"Jado's dead—heart failure, the doctor said."

"Oh *terrible*—poor fellow!"

Alarm was in Phil's face. He rose swiftly from the table. "Let's get out of here," he said.

As he stood beside Sylvia, his hand on her shoulder, she cried out very low, "Look!" Phil followed her glance up to the balcony. There Ahnoud Bey was still standing, his eyes centered on the scene below. His hands rested on the carved wood balustrade.

The Egyptian's air of concentration was evident. He lifted his hands from where they had been resting and passed them over his eyes; then, quite observant again, he turned to a shocked Reana, spoke to her, and took her arm as if to go.

In the bedlam, in the crush of excitement, other faces besides Phil's were lifted to the balcony. Pelham, with a strange comprehension, felt an undercurrent of suspicion surging about him. Was it heart failure?

XXX

Without a word Reana had left the hotel. Once away from the scene of tragedy and out in the brisk air, she felt strengthened and revived. When Jado fell, things had swayed before her crazily but now in the clear moonlight they were steadied.

She and Bey walked back to Villa Robinson. Then something seemed to snap. She sank down weakly on the divan in the music salon. Ahnoud rang for one of the servants and Madeleine hastened to the front.

"Bring Madame a drink," he ordered in French. "There was an accident at the hotel and she is badly unnerved.

The maid hurried into the corridor and soon returned with brandy in a tiny goblet. She stood by her mistress while Reana swallowed the stimulant. Madeleine smoothed the fair, curly bangs away from a damp forehead. "Oh Madame," she rejoiced when Reana smiled again, "you are better now?"

The Golden Lady seemed embarrassed. "Yes, Madeleine. I hate to cause so much fuss. I'm just a bit shaken, that's all. It was Jado, Madeleine! He dropped dead on the ballroom floor—while dancing!"

The maid was horrified. "M'sieur Jado, Madame?" she gasped. "Not he who came to this house scarce two hours ago?"

Reana nodded. "It was a ghastly shock, following the scene he caused here."

"He was drunk," Ahnoud put in quickly. "No doubt too much liquor caused his heart to stop."

There was a note in his voice that made Madeleine turn and regard Ahnoud Bey with mistrust in her dark eyes.

"That's all now, Madeleine," Reana said. "If I need anything else I will ring." She had seen Madeleine's look. The Golden Lady knew that she and her maid were thinking the same thing, wondering, speculating. Reana turned to Ahnoud, summoning an expression of calm that she was far from feeling.

"Darling," she begged, "play for me, please? I shall sit here and rest, and listen." Ahnoud kissed her hand lightly, then went to the piano.

When his back was turned and he began running his fingers over the Golden Keys, Reana closed her eyes. Her brows drew together and her face changed into a mask of pain and horror. She slumped a little on the black Chesterfield. One thought filled her mind; *Ahnoud Bey has murdered Jado!*

It was a dreadful accusation to bring against anyone or even to keep in the dark recesses of her mind. Surely though, Reana thought, if Jado had not rushed into Villa Robinson and quarreled with Ahnoud Bey, the dancer would still be living.

Had Ahnoud known that Jado was dancing at the Desdena Hotel? Was that why the Egyptian proposed that they go there? Had he proposed it after all? She didn't know. Her mind was filled with one obsession—*Ahnoud Bey was a murderer!*

Reana opened her eyes and stared at the mystic with a sort of morbid fascination. She watched him as he sat playing, his profile dimly outlined, for no lights were on above the dais. The piano keys shone with their own pearly glow. Ahnoud knew them so well that he could have played in pitch darkness.

Moonlight came down through high, paned windows and cast a beam across Bey's dark, well-shaped head. How expressive were those long fingers!

She listened now to the bell-like tones of the piano. Those gifted fingers were lingering in soul-reaching minor measures of Chopin. Reana's perturbation lessened and peace stole into her heart.

That black thought—that verdict—of recent moments now became almost absurd. She had been overwrought by Jado's death. Of course it was true he had been drinking. As a dancer, he was unused to liquor, which often affected the heart and caused an untimely end.

Reana recalled how the doctor had bent over Jado, then pronounced him dead from "heart failure." That doctor knew—*doctors always knew.*

Reana leaned back and breathed deeply and her eyes on Ahnoud were tender. His playing had touched her heart. The harplike Golden Keys were speaking to her as the mystic lifted his face to the moonlight. He had done that one evening at the Palm Club—the night she met him. He had promised her the piano then and had made good that promise, giving her also an unequaled devotion.

She was sorry now for that black thought! How natural it was that Jado should have died of heart failure! It was best, perhaps, that he—wretched soul—should go.

Reana rose and went over to the piano, standing behind Ahnoud. She laid her hands on his strong shoulders. "That's wonderful," she assured him. He played on as he replied, "Not as wonderful as our love. That is my fate. If it should end, so shall I . . ."

Reana was held in the spell of his music and his soothing voice as he continued, "The Golden Keys and I are one. We are yours. In spirit I will remain here, with you and the piano. But—if you ever cease to care—" His voice broke and he stopped playing. He reached up and took Reana's hands in his, without moving other than that, without turning. He looked up once more to the moonlight.

Slowly and with a definite finality, Ahnoud

spoke in Arabic—in that language of the desert, the blue Nile, and the tombs of kings, of the East and all its shadowed mysteries.

The words were crisp and brief. Unable to understand them, Reana somehow grasped their meaning. She knew as she stood there, her hands in his, that Ahnoud had made a vow in Arabic. In that vow lay not only her captivity, but his—*love, death, and the Golden Keys.*

XXXI

One January morning almost two years later, Jules Courtney's schooner docked at Sun City.

After registering and attending to matters at the Yacht Club, Jules walked across the street to the Bayside Hotel and up its palm-bordered driveway.

Courtney wore an informal outfit—dark blue jacket, white flannel slacks, and tennis sneakers. A "cruising pipe" was stuck in one corner of his mouth. He was hatless and sunshine fell on his thick brown hair.

Beside Jules, was huge Chris, First Mate of the schooner that had just docked. Chris was as tough as the Barbery Coast, and he looked it. He carried Courtney's hand luggage, which included several airline suitcases, each bearing the conventional red stripe on tan and the name "J. C. Courtney."

The pair entered the Bayside's lobby and if doubtful glances were accorded the oddly matched duo, Jules cared little. He stopped by the black and white marble desk.

"I am Mr. Courtney from New York. How about my reservations?"

The clerk was at once alert. "Yes, Mr. Courtney," he replied politely, reaching for his card index, "you wired for a suite and chauffeur's room." He took a dubious glance at Chris, trusting that one like this would not be lodged within the confines of the exclusive Bayside. "Do you need a single or double chauffeur's room, Mr. Courtney?"

"Single," answered Jules casually. "This man stays on the ship. My chauffeur is driving the car down. I'm expecting him here within the next three or four days."

"Then your rooms are waiting," the clerk went on urbanely.

While Jules registered and Chris reluctantly gave over the luggage to a bellhop, the clerk picked up a phone and called the manager's office.

"Mr. Deane," he said, "Mr. Courtney from New York has just arrived . . . Yes, sir." He hung up and addressed Jules.

"Can you wait a moment? Mr. Deane wants to see you."

Jules appeared pleased. He had met Deane sometime ago in New York and liked him very much.

"Sure," the guest agreed, sorting his mail,

which had come on ahead and which he had just received from the clerk.

"How *do* you *do*, Mr. Courtney," Deane exclaimed. "I'm so glad to see you again. We've been expecting you for days. You came down on your yacht?"

Jules laughed. "It's really an old schooner. Think it will disgrace your swank Yacht Club?"

"You'll be the envy of every man here," voiced the manager. "Our seagoing is too polished for the average man's taste. You'll be overrun with guests if you have one of those wear-what-you-please, cook-your-own-meals, fish-all-day schooners."

"That's exactly the sort of tub mine is," said Jules. "How is the fishing here, by the way?"

The manager's eyes brightened. "Fine right now, if you go out half a mile and drop anchor—nice bass, trout, tarpon, oh most anything, even a gentle barracuda, if you want one—"

Jules put up an interrupting hand. "No-oo thanks," he cut in, "none of those babies! One came a little too near making a meal of me once!"

They walked to the elevator, and as Courtney boarded it with the baggage-laden bellhop behind him the manager added genially, "Make yourself at home and if everything's not okay—phone me."

Jules' suite was a pleasant one, with the most cheerful furnishings he had ever seen in a hotel room. Everything was well appointed and in good taste. At the three living room windows were lowered venetian blinds. Courtney ran up one of these, looking out on the scene below.

This was the fifth floor. His rooms faced east, as did the hotel. Out there lay the Bay, blue and still in the light of a winking winter sun. There was the Yacht Club, near which his schooner was anchored.

It was a large, expensive ship with thoroughbred lines and tall masts. Jules had called it an old schooner," as though the floor were rotting, the hatches caving in, and rats holding carnival in the hold.

"Some view," said Jules to himself, "sweeter than ever." He turned from the window and went to take his shower, thinking meanwhile of the town that lay out there below him.

He had been away from Sun City for seven years, for the depression held noses to the grindstone and ruled out midwinter vacations. The ship he kept at Bermuda most of the time. Now and then he ran down there for a weekend or fortnight.

The intrepid Chris lived in Bermuda and took care of the boat, earning what Courtney thought a meager salary. Chris had stuck through the dark years, until better times came. Otherwise Jules would have sold the boat, missing those cruises and schooner parties on his trips to the island.

"How in the world," his friends had asked him a dozen times, "can you endure that horny-handed Chris? He seems to consider everyone guilty unless proven innocent."

"Yep," added another, "Chris popped that

weather-stung, nutcracker face of his into my stateroom at midnight and I swore it was a nightmare."

"But why do you keep him, Jules?" this or that guest persisted. "I should think he'd steal everything on the ship."

"Not a chance," Courtney had replied. "Chris is honest as the day is long and faithful as a good dog. He's my schooner's best insurance against storms, thieves, and such. Chris would give his life for that boat—or I'm a bad guesser."

Jules, in dressing gown and slippers, came back refreshed into the bedroom now. He felt more respectable than when he had arrived. Whistling, he unpacked his clothes from the suitcases.

It was great how these airline trunks kept suits so well pressed, even when folded—well, at least the tweed and nubby kind. The others were not in such a happy state. To the hotel pressers they must go.

When he was dressed Courtney went into the living room and by twilight sat reading his mail. Three wires—about airplane designs—were from New York. A fine way, he thought, to treat a fellow, meeting him on his vacation with telegrams about a business that he came south to forget!

Jules put the wires aside and began opening the letters. He had half-expected these—signed "Gloria," "Patricia," and "Jean." They were all missing him—wishing they were there—all promising to come down during the month.

How they knew he would be in Sun City was more than Courtney could imagine. No doubt John Kingston had told.

John can't keep his mouth shut, Jules thought, and now the whole gushing bunch will be here in no time!

They were all very charming, but Courtney was fed up with women, New York, and nightclubs. A man had to get away and rough it once in a while.

Jules stopped and cast his eyes around the room, then laughed shortly. What a far cry this was from roughing it! He was only kidding himself! Anyway he hoped that Gloria and the crowd wouldn't come down too soon.

Women were out of Courtney's vacation picture, at least New York women were. He knew them too well and cared for them so little. That was the trouble, or he was just lucky. Love was a dangerous thing, a painful thing, and yet—

Jules laid his letters on the table and walked over to the windows. He watched the lights come on below along the Boulevard, the Pier, the Yacht Club, and Hotel gardens.

To Courtney, the balmy air and blooming flowers were miraculous. He had left behind a city working like mad to get snow off its streets, as new snow and sleet fell upon the old.

Sun City was a knockout, all right! Seven years had enhanced what then was a new, if interesting aspect. Those little houses were recently built—and honeys—those off on the South Shore where banana trees grew and friendly lights shone from the windows.

Now as Jules looked down at them he felt very weary and very lonely. He wanted never to go back to that life in New York. All he longed for was to live in one of those colored stucco houses—to live peacefully in the sun, to know a great love.

That night Courtney dreamed of the little houses. The next morning sunlight flooded his bedroom and he wakened to the glorious reality of Sun City.

XXXII

Chris greeted his captain with a cheery, "Good mornin' sir," and Courtney found everything on the schooner shipshape.

Jules pottered around the boat, hunting out his fishing tackle and wicker basket for catch. When he found them and made sure he was equipped with all the necessary aids for deep-sea fishing, he called to Chris to get going.

"Aye aye sir," returned the lusty gob. With a tough line of sea jargon and an air of insufferable authority, Chris yelled orders to a couple of sailors who had recently been hired to help keep the schooner in sea-going form.

When the schooner pulled out from the Yacht Club dock, Jules was at its wheel. He

"Hello, Emerald Eyes. Like fish, do you?" For the cat had found the wicker basket. With its paws on the hamper's sides, it set up a regular full-moon, back-fence wail.

Jules laughed, and taking out his pocket knife, he cut off a few dead fish heads and threw them to the importunate guest.

Once more quiet reigned and Jules went back to his fishing. Only the cat's low growls broke the stillness. Courtney took a look and chuckled to himself. The kitty, fish bones all mixed up with long white whiskers, finished the luscious meal and licked his chops happily.

Catching the eyes of his new friend, the cat went over to Jules. Kittenlike, he rubbed to and fro across Courtney's back, then tunneled under one arm and crouched on Jules' knee. Here he purred, with the sweet smell of dead fish in his nostrils, and at last went to sleep.

It was all of noon when Jules carried the basket of fish below to the galley where Chris waited to prepare lunch. Courtney leisurely went into his stateroom and changed his old shirt and frayed slacks for black trunks, then went back up on deck for a sun bath.

He might have been a tall, bronzed god of old as he lay there, firm and fit. His figure was splendidly and fashionably proportioned. His legs were fine as a Greek runner's. Jules' shoulders were like a discus thrower's, and the Courtney arms rounded in muscles hard as a heavyweight champion's.

Jules thought of nothing much as the sun's rays went down beneath his skin easing nerves that had been so tense and overworked. A laziness engulfed him. He wondered why the kitty did not come over beside him where it was sunny, but chose instead a dank and windy spot under the shadow of a lifeboat.

Courtney must have lain there an hour before the aroma of broiling fish began to drift up from below. That was too much for a husky man who had been in the salt air all morning. Jules got up, hungry but loathe to leave the pleasant deck.

Stretching his arms and slapping his smooth brown chest, he walked over to where the cat was curled in a complete circle under the lifeboat.

"Come on, shiny eyes, you mean to tell me that you don't know the smell of fish when it's *cooked?* That means dinner—yes, in your language as well as mine!"

XXXIII

Mr. Deane was killing some time at the Yacht Club when Courtney's schooner docked about four that afternoon.

After a few instructions to Chris, Jules left the boat and walked along the pier, then across a plot of grass to the Club House. As Courtney approached a side door of this popular retreat, he heard voices inside and saw Deane coming toward him. Jules groaned. He was by no means properly clad for the tea and cocktail hour.

"Hello," Deane welcomed, holding open the screen door. "Come in and meet some grand folks. How was the fishing?"

"Swell!" Courtney responded, brightening at the memory of his day on the Bay.

They walked together into the wide

lounge room with its red leather armchairs, nautical emblems, and framed pictures of regattas. There was an English-style fireplace, where real logs burned on bronze andirons, for in Sun City a chill came with winter evenings.

Jules' attention was soon drawn to a group in front of the fireplace. With this group of three men Courtney saw a striking brunette girl in a suit yellow as the sun had been at high noon. She was laughing with red-lipped spontaneity. Bending over her was a young fellow in tweeds who looked decidedly English.

"Sylvia," Mr. Deane said, "I want you to meet my friend Mr. Courtney. He's down here from New York on a much needed vacation and he intends to join our Yacht Club.

"She's Mrs. Adams to you, Courtney," he explained to Jules, "though we all call her Sylvia." The girl extended her hand in a friendly gesture. Jules smiled and shook Sylvia's small hand warmly, then Deane proceeded with the introductions.

"Ted, J. L., Phil—this is Mr. Courtney. Jules—these are three of my best friends and Sun City's leading citizens. Mr. Maxime here runs our leading night spot, Mr. Adams promotes our subdivisions, and Mr. Pelham sells us automobiles—*painlessly!*"

They all laughed now and, following Sylvia's example, shook hands with their guest.

"You must excuse my appearance," Courtney begged. "I look as if I'd been manning my own ship, which is just what I *have* been doing all day, and catching half the fish in your bay."

"Okay, *okay!*" Adams waved aside Jules'

idea of formality. "Don't mind us. We're just home folks!"

Phil sat on the arm of Sylvia's chair and looked at Jules with admiration. What a figure he was—tall, brawny, with his short-sleeved polo shirt, a blue jacket over one arm, and a pipe cupped in his left hand! What a fine, strong mouth lay below that close-cropped mustache!

Phil liked men of Courtney's age—men around forty. He, much younger, found them humorous, tolerant, and all in all, good sports. They were usually of the *pater familias* type and took love or passion pretty much for granted. Most of them had long since adopted a "*Well the illusions are gone, but life is still good*" philosophy.

The lad thought about all this as he subtly watched Jules. Finally Phil spoke in that calm New England way, "What a beautiful schooner you have, Mr. Courtney! We haven't seen the likes of her in a blue moon. She makes me think of sea chanteys, the Southern Cross, and Joseph Conrad."

Jules was evidently pleased. "Thanks," he replied. "She is a pretty good old tub. Come aboard and see her sometime."

"How did you leave New York, Mr. Courtney—the weather, I mean?" Sylvia asked.

"Cold as the devil," he answered.

"But gay as the devil too, I'll bet," Sylvia ventured, to which Jules shrugged.

"Oh sure, plenty of that all right, but snow? Honestly, I haven't seen the sidewalk in front of my apartment for six weeks. They're seriously debating buying a fur coat for the Statue of Liberty."

"The cold wouldn't bother me," Sylvia went on, undaunted. "I'm dying to see some of those hit plays."

"Listen to the child," said Ted, "talking big about zero weather."

J. L. laughed with great indulgence at his little Sylvia. "She's just a sun baby," he said lovingly. Jules couldn't miss the devotion in J. L.'s eyes and voice.

Courtney also saw how Phil covertly dropped an arm around Sylvia, saying in his clever way, with a double meaning, "Why she doesn't even *know how* to be cold."

The conversation was swift, casual. Jules took the invitations he received with a grain of salt. He sat in a deep armchair, and hearing the screen door open, lifted his eyes to the entranceway.

Someone there held the stare of the dark Courtney eyes—those tired, cynical eyes. They followed, from door to desk, the willowy movements of a lovely blonde. She was in a party of three and she seemed to know the man behind the desk to whom she talked. One could see he was her ardent admirer.

As Jules watched her something made him feel queer and sad at heart. How pretty she was in her fuzzy pink sweater and white pleated skirt! It was short enough to show lovely legs and trim ankles. Her hair was real gold—the color a fairy godmother would have to bestow at birth! It was brushed back into upcurling ends like cobwebs of spun amber about that even profile. Questioningly, Jules turned to Deane.

"That's Reana Robinson," Deane said in answer to what he knew was in Jules' mind.

Courtney's expression at once became inexplicably immobile. "Robinson?" he asked, his eyes narrowing.

"Yes," continued Deane," from New York originally, I believe. One of our year-round residents and home owners."

"She's our neighbor," put in Sylvia, and Phil added, "She's a mystery—and down here we grow too lazy to solve them."

Now the ebullient Ted caught Reana's eye. She waved to him and he waved back, beckoning her to come over. "Who says 'mystery,'" he scoffed. "I know Reana better than any of you. She's a sweet li'l gal."

Courtney heard heels lightly tapping the floor behind him. He heard Ted Maxime's heavy tread meet that airy one, then both coming—*coming*—Jules' throat went dry. When he stood his knees were weak, for no sensible reason. Then Maxime said, "Miss Robinson, I want you to meet Mr. Courtney—"

Jules murmured something formal of which he had no recollection thereafter. In that first instant he was stricken dumb by the Golden Lady's sheer physical beauty. He saw a strange light in those misty eyes as they were directed toward him.

There was astonishment and wistfulness, too, in their depths as those eyes covered every curve and angle of Jules' face, every hair of his head, even those that were gray. There was something oddly familiar in the way she looked at him, in how their eyes met. All this was like the effect of ripples on a sunlit stream and as instantly passing. Once more Reana's countenance became a mask; eyes veiled in sophistication. She put her head slightly to one side, bowing in acknowledgment.

"This is a pleasure," she said graciously. "Our ships have come in together and are docked beside one another! Does that mean we shall be friends?"

"I hope so." Jules was more at ease now, his eyes twinkling. "I'll do my part." But even as he spoke he stared fixedly on that bright head, thinking, for hair like that, ships have been launched, thrones have fallen, and souls been lost! What chance have I against the examples of history? Not one? *Not one!*

XXXIV

That evening Deane knocked on Courtney's door at about six-thirty.

"Come up on the roof," the manager invited. "We dine and dance there; you'll like it."

"Thanks," said Jules as he buttoned a white dinner shirt and adjusted his tie before the mirror. "Won't you come in?" Deane, his head poked in the door, seemed in a hurry.

"Haven't time now," he answered. "I'll see you later on the roof," and he was gone.

Courtney finished dressing. After scanning his mirrored image with some approval, he snapped out the lights, locked his door, and went whistling down the hall to the elevator.

The lift stopped at the seventh floor and Phil Pelham got on, slender and handsome in his dinner suit. The severity of its black and white accentuated Phil's light hair and smooth, suntanned skin. After two years in the south the youth still had the high color of New England.

"Hello, Mr. Courtney!" Phil greeted Jules with a salute of his right hand and that flattering manner of correctly remembering one's name.

"Hello," replied Courtney, "are you dining on the roof, bachelor fashion, also?"

"Right," Phil said, "though I'm due at some sort of shindig later."

The elevator stopped and the uniformed boy pulled back bronze doors. Jules and Phil emerged into the glamour of the Bayside Hotel Roof, a glamour new to Jules but old stuff to the initiated Pelham.

Courtney's New York eyes were dulled by the clubs and roofs of Manhattan, but somehow he found a new attraction here. This roof, evidently a recent addition to the hotel which had been built all of a decade ago, was done in the most unique design Jules had ever seen.

The room, glassed in on two sides with the far end open to a dancing terrace, was a picture in cream and orchid. The walls and curtains were plain cream, against them blooming potted lilacs. The tables filled half the room where one entered from the elevator foyer. Their tops were orchid mirrors and their chairs upholstered in boxlike cushions of cream leather.

Tonight these tables were all filled, the room a gay scene of men and women dancing to the music of a New York orchestra.

Because the place was S.R.O., as one

usually found it on any January evening, the ropes were up. They only came down to let in the favored few. Jules and Phil joined the waiting crowd. With every elevator stop it was growing larger, adding parties of five to fifteen, or couples with dreamy eyes.

"Let's eat together," suggested Jules. Pelham signaled the head waiter, who came up to the rope. The roof's potentate, in tails and white tie—the man with menus in one hand but people's numbers in his mind—caught Phil's eye of all the eyes that besought him.

Pelham held up two fingers and the head waiter darted back to take a look across the room. As he did so, a couple left a table. At once he hurried over, catching the Pelham eye again, lifting two fingers to him and unhooking the lilac cord to admit a pair of bachelors "who belonged."

"Say, you must have a rabbit's foot," remarked Jules with a short laugh as he and Phil left the envious crowd and were ushered up front to a ringside table for two.

"Satisfied customer," replied Phil as they sat down.

"You mean you sold the *head waiter* a car?"

Phil's face expressed the affirmative. "Yes. He thinks it's the best one in the world and that I made it specially for him and handed it to him, gratis."

Jules laughed. "You *are* a salesman! How can I doubt what you say when I saw that fellow take us in ahead of all the others? They had been there cooling their heels long before we came. In New York you'd have to represent more than a seat in the Stock Exchange, a penthouse, and a flock of polo ponies to get a break like that."

Phil shrugged and smiled. "I know," he replied, "but remember this is a little pond and, cater though we all do to the tourists, the year-round boy is given preference every time. It seems that the plain Sun City man who sells them cars is considered quite a big frog. Funny, isn't it?"

"Listen kid," said Jules, leaning forward after the waiter had taken their orders, "why don't you come to New York and sell cars? This place is too small for you."

Phil slowly shook his head, lowering his eyes thoughtfully to the orchid goblet he turned with finger and thumb. He gazed down at the cocktail, peculiar to this roof, with a cherry in the bottom. It was red, like Sylvia's lips. She loved these tiny, bittersweet specialties.

Pelham raised his eyes to Jules' dark, intent scrutiny. "Not a chance," he said. "I can't even recall New York and New England, Broadway and Yale, first nights and football games, snow and blizzards until you believe there'll never be another summer!" Phil paused, his eyes again on the goblet.

Lilac! She had worn lilac only a few days before—satin lounging pajamas—one day when he dropped into her house unexpectedly, one rainy afternoon when J. L. was away. Again Pelham raised his eyes to the listening Jules. This time Phil shook his head.

"No, Mr. Courtney, I shall never go back. When I came down here they told me about the enchantment of Sun City. 'Stay a year, then try to leave,' they warned. I laughed at them. I stayed a year, and—" Phil lifted the lilac goblet.

"Mr. Courtney, perhaps this is the only Paradise we shall ever know. Let's drink to it! Let's drink to Sun City! To the warmth of its winter sunshine and its flowers that bloom in January. To a life that is sparkling with the gloss of today. To friends who forget faults and remember virtues—to Sun City, Mr. Courtney—*and the romance that goes with it!*"

Jules reached for his own goblet automatically, his eyes still on Pelham, then he returned the boy's smile. They drank their cocktails, leaving a lonely cherry in each lavender glass—cherries gone begging in Sylvia's absence.

XXXV

Now if Reana had not entered the Bayside Roof that night wearing orchid, if she had not matched her dress to the flowers and the table tops and dramatized them all, if she had not been quite so ethereal and devastating in her blonde loveliness—things might have ended differently.

As it was, havoc began when she sat down at her table with a party of six. Other women went unnoticed, for Reana was the cynosure of all male eyes. She appeared not to see anyone beyond her own table, nor did she care for those who stared when they dared and talked freely, with much behind their words. The general tenor of their comments went something like this:

"Who's she—the beauty in orchid?"

"Reana Robinson."

"Where'd she come from?"

"She lives here. You know Ahnoud Bey, the mystic?"

"Uh huh. What about him?"

"Nothing—only the vision in violet's Bey's heart."

"Yeah?"

"Yeah. He gave her the original Golden Keys piano."

"Humph—I'd give her one with *diamond* keys!"

Reana rose from her seat and the man beside her stood also. She put her hand on his shoulder and with ineffable grace danced out across the floor.

Reana danced to the modern music but her mousseline dress was like old English lavender, scattered to blow and drift through the room.

Jules Courtney watched her as he ate his third course. Conversation at the table for two lagged. Phil, conscious of this, came through with a provocative question.

"Do you recognize her as the lady you met this afternoon at the Yacht Club?"

"Yep," Jules replied, his voice husky, his eyes narrowed as though trying to unravel a mystery, "that's true, I only met her today, but she's the sort of woman you've loved all your life. She's the first love you never got over."

With extreme absorption Courtney still stared at the Golden Lady, at her white and fragile profile, silhouetted against a black tux shoulder. Now he saw that the shoulder belonged to manager Deane.

The music stopped and Reana said something to her partner, motioning to the open terrace doors. She touched her temple as though entreating, "Please, I should like a breath of air—*alone*."

She crossed the dance floor and paused between the wide-flung French doors, lifting her face to the starlit night outside.

Jules' eyes were stardusted. He ventured no word to Pelham, lest the sound break some sort of spell. At length Phil said in his understanding way, " 'She walks in beauty, like the night, of cloudless climes and starry skies—' "

In the dark Courtney eyes Phil saw a glow of Byron's immortal words reflected. Jules took a cigarette, tapped it on the table, forgot to light it, and, neglecting his third course, spoke absently to Phil.

"You'll excuse me? I shan't be long." With Phil's nod, Jules was gone. He crossed the floor with the resolute Courtney walk and vanished into the darkness of the terrace.

"Hello," he said, coming up behind Reana as she stood beside the parapet. "I didn't suppose I'd see you again so soon."

With some surprise Reana faced Jules, replying, with a smile, "Nor did I, and it's exciting—for me, anyway."

"For me too," Jules was quick to answer. "We had no time to get acquainted this afternoon."

A momentary silence fell between them and tango music drifted out, its ardor cooled on the chilly terrace. Jules glanced about him at the pretty tiles that glistened in the half light and marble love seats along the railing.

"Gee, this is the top of the world!" he exclaimed almost boyishly and with approval. "I'm new to it all. Tonight's the first time I've ever set foot up here."

Reana watched him and her smile was a Mona Lisa one as she took his hand. "Come over closer to the ledge," she invited. "Now, *look down—*"

Jules folded his arms on the stone railing, bent massive shoulders, and squinted.

Under the pale light of the moon, Sun City lay below. The hotel topped the town in height. Other buildings seemed tiny by comparison. Streets were wide and most of them lined with trees. On these boulevards cars moved constantly, north and south, stopping to let out or take in passengers. Reana motioned to the left where a thick block of olive-green trees was strung with lights.

"That's the Municipal Park where they play shuffleboard and quoits," she said, "and out there where the cars are going is the new Casino." Her hand came up eastward as it indicated a long pier to the far left of their view. Along this wide water highway, lighted by many frosted globes, cars came and went, their headlights moving like lazy glowworms.

From pier to Yacht Club, a waterfront park edged the Bay and glorified the midnight-blue vista of restless water. In this park royal palms and banana trees grew amid a magnificent design of sand walks, benches, oleander bushes, and lily pools. These caught and threw back the light as though they were artificial ponds.

Between this park and the Bayside Gardens ran a smooth, paved boulevard. The private hotel grounds were a shade more cultivated than the public ones across the highway. At the Bayside flowers of rare varieties were blooming and the lawn was dotted with little tea tables under varicolored striped umbrellas.

"And there's the Yacht Club." Reana directed Jules' attention to the far right, where short piers extended into the bay, where yachts were taking off for evening parties or, berthed and dark, awaited the whims of their owners.

"Well, there's the old tub all right." Jules laughed. "She looks as though she has a coating of ice on her masts."

"It's this silver light," explained Reana. "Sometimes the road ahead of your car will seem snow covered."

"That schooner knows how the crack of the ice hatchet feels," Jules went on. "I bought her one summer when I was in Nova Scotia and had her renovated—all but the parrot, who refused to be reformed. He curses with a cockney accent and sings 'God Save the King.' "

Reana's eyes shone and she asked impulsively, "Take me to see the parrot, please?"

Jules lifted an objecting hand, a strong hand with a signet ring on the small finger. "Nothing doing—you're too nice to meet Bobo. He's tough, I tell you. Why, he could be sued for libel for his comments."

Reana was more diverted than she had been in a long time. Now joy was in her eyes. She regarded the masted schooner lovingly. One hand caught and twisted the plain gold cross that hung around her neck on a slight chain.

"I've never been on a real schooner. Our yacht's so slick. I've never handled the wheel."

"Well you shall," promised Jules. "Tomorrow you're coming aboard and you'll learn to pilot a schooner. Is it a date?"

Reana looked full into Courtney's eyes. "It is," she replied, "and thank you." As she held Jules' eyes with hers, he grasped her shoulders with both hands, searching her face—seeking something that tantalized and eluded him. Was it possible that they had met before? He seemed to be taken back in time as their eyes met.

"What's the matter?" Reana asked. Would he now say something, would he now realize?

Jules merely dropped his hands and, wheeling about again, stationed himself by the parapet. "Nothing," he said briefly, "I only thought—but of course not—"

Reana drew in her breath and set her lips together firmly. She smoothed her palms one on the other and felt that they were damp and trembling.

When Jules spoke again, his voice was composed. "What's that way out there like a gray plume?" he asked, pointing to a line of blue smoke that was traveling down from the extreme northeast toward town.

"That's the Sun City Special," explained Reana. "It arrives—plumed—at midnight."

Jules was silent, brooding, his thoughts a medley of all that had happened in the last two days. Plumed trains! Midnight, and chimes that rang the hour of twelve! Beauty, a haunting beauty of violet eyes, and a voice like music! He took Reana's hands in his.

"Look," he asked, "what do you say to this? Let's go back and finish our dinner and then go to a movie?"

If he had suggested that they go out to Angelo Point and she ride the roller coaster in her lilac mousseline, Reana could not have been more amused.

"But," she objected. Then catching herself, she finished, "—of course. My crowd won't miss me—and you?"

"I'm really alone," Jules explained as they walked back to the French doors, "though Mr. Pelham has been a splendid dinner partner. He's a nice lad, isn't he?"

With a handgrasp they left each other for their respective tables. Half an hour later, Jules stood behind Reana's chair, helping her on with her short fur wrap.

"We're going to the movies," he said to Deane and the others.

"*To the movies?*" they chorused in disbelief.

"Yeah," Jules replied, "Why not? There's a theater three blocks away." Then there was a laugh and another laugh.

"Nobody here goes to the movies," someone said. The news circulated to other tables.

"He's taking her to the movies! *Imagine!*"

"Where does he think he is, back in New York with the Paramount organ?"

"When a moon's over Sun City, he takes that lovely to a show!"

As Reana rose the men at the table also stood. She smiled up at Jules with a look that said, "this is the first time I've had any fun in so long," and Deane remarked, "Mr. Courtney,

I'm afraid you won't find our theaters much after New York. You see there's so much else to do here we seldom go—"

"No—" one of the guests cut in solemnly, as though it were some kind of sacred vow, "we *never* go to the movies!"

"Then," Jules said decisively, taking Reana's arm and tossing his words back over his shoulder, "we'll break precedent and give the movies a new deal!"

XXXVI

Blithely Reana and Jules made their exit through a side door of the Bayside Hotel as though they were twenty and carefree.

"There's my car," she said as a uniformed chauffeur straightened beside a long shiny limousine and tipped his visored cap. "But let's walk," she added. "It's only three blocks."

"Good," agreed Jules, drawing her hand through his arm. They paced along evenly, heads up, lips smiling.

"We're Mr. and Mrs. America," Courtney went on, "going to the show on Saturday night. We live in one of those pink and yellow houses among the banana trees. Today I got a raise, so tonight we're extra happy."

"Oh yes—" replied Reana, with a new

meaning in her words that was not wholly play-acting, "—extra happy!"

They made their way along the wide sidewalk, and ahead of them burned the red and blue neon signals of "town"— shops, drug stores, and a theater.

Darling," said Jules, stopping and swinging around to face Reana, "do you realize the Frigidaire is paid for and with three more payments the car'll be ours? Think of it! Are we good—or *are we good?*"

Reana laughed, then her face clouded to suit the occasion. "Honey, what shall I do? I left the east living room window open. Suppose it should rain—and do you think Mrs. Mason will be good to the baby while we're gone? She offered to keep him, but I'm not happy over it. I still owe her one cup of sugar, a bowl of flour, two eggs, and a loaf of bread."

Now Jules laughed and showed the deep indentations that some called dimples on either side of his mouth.

"Never mind," he coaxed, "we'll ransom the baby. Surely he's worth some cake ingredients and a loaf of bread."

They covered one block as with wings on their heels. They entered the second block and Reana continued the farce.

"Darling," she wailed, "I left the key in the mailbox and told Junior he could find it there when he came home from the Scout meeting. What if a burglar saw me put it there? Let's go home and see if everything's all right."

"Nonsense," replied Courtney, "no one was

around when you put that key in the box. Think of something pleasant—" Again he faced her.

"Look in the window," he demanded, indicating a shop ahead. "There's the dress you wanted—six ninety five! Get it, honey, it'll be swell on you!"

"Oh but Daddy—" reminded Reana, "the roast for tomorrow's dinner! We haven't bought the roast!"

"Does a roast cost six ninety five?" Jules tried hard to keep a straight face. Reana drew down her mouth corners, opened her eyes innocently, and twisted a kerchief.

"No, but you see honey, I got some shoes on Tuesday and a new hat on Thursday and I—er—charged them. I was just sure you'd get the raise."

"So you charged them did you—like that," cried Courtney in mock fury, "and didn't tell me? What about that pillbox you bought and called a hat two weeks ago? Whadda you think I am—Rockefeller or somebody? Anyway, come to think of it, that's a nice dress you have on! What's the matter with it?"

Reana was now overcome with the fun of it all. Her eyes glistened and she smiled up at Jules who caught the contagion of her amusement. He broke into chuckles that he had with difficulty held back during his last emphatic speech.

"Nothing's wrong with this," said Reana breathlessly, fluttering a hand on the orchid mousseline skirt. "A dressmaker named Lanvin made it! Don't you think it's a good job for two and a quarter?"

Jules' heart did a flipflop and he caught Reana to him in a sudden embrace. He forgot that they were on a street where cars and people passed frequently.

"This," he said, his voice tender, "isn't playacting. You're divine in that dress. It pays the French war debt!"

"Jules dear," Reana answered gratefully, "neither is this acting. I had forgotten how it felt to laugh—*and laugh*—" Her voice dropped lower. "I had forgotten how to be happy like this—really, truly happy!"

Down the next block were benches on the broad sidewalk. This had been for years a feature of Sun City's hospitality. With a grace that was its chief charm, the town provided that its visitors, if weary, might rest anywhere on the main street and watch the crowd go by.

Tonight in the liveliness of shops open late, in the glow from theater, hotel lobbies, and drug stores, elderly ones whose steps were slowing sat here and there on the friendly benches.

Ladies with white hair, with pale pink or blue dresses were beside their husbands, those find old gentlemen in Palm Beach suits who smoked pipes and now and then dozed peacefully.

These couples talked little, but doubtless they thought of other winters in Pennsylvania or Illinois. They were younger then and working like beavers for the chance to enjoy this very ease in the warm sun and balmy air.

Tonight as they occupied their favorite green benches they saw a couple approaching with winged pace. The girl's face was joyous and her tall escort very gallant. They were hand in hand, these two, and the man was good looking and dark eyed with teeth that flashed when he smiled.

"Dearie," said one of the white-haired ladies in a pink knit dress, "we were like that—fifty years ago." She touched her husband's arm with a loving pat. He started from a cat nap, setting his spectacles up on his nose and peering through them at Jules and Reana.

"Yes, yes," he replied reminiscently, "we were like that—in love." His wife took the wrinkled hand, saying, "And we still are, dearie."

"Yes, mamma," he answered, bending his gray head. "We're still like that in our hearts—young and in love."

With indulgent smiles the couples watched Reana and Jules come on, running a gamut of kindly glances. A silver-haired lady dropped her knitting and whispered to the old gentleman beside her, "Papa, don't look now, but that lilac dress is just like one I wore in the nineties! How the old styles have come back. Mousseline de soie—it was *so stylish* in my day!" Her husband leaned forward, removing a cigar from his mouth.

"Yes, that was how you looked," he said jovially, "when I knelt down on one knee and asked you to be mine. Well, I didn't make a mistake, my dear, no indeed—and you?" His wife shook her head. Tears were in her eyes. "No mistake for me either. We've been very happy, haven't we, Papa?"

At the corner at the last of the benches

was the movie house. Breathing hard after their hurried walk, Jules and Reana came in front of the box office. Their conversation, lilted to their own gay mood, was overheard by the occupants of the end benches.

After their tickets were bought and the couple disappeared into the theater, a little lady in a pansy dress on the last bench asked her husband, "Dickey, did you ever hear of such a thing as sun jewels on the Bay here? Is it a legend? And did you ever hear of one person's inviting another one to be her breakfast guest every morning, when those jewels were on the water?"

Her husband, with his wavy, pompadoured hair and natty navy jacket, patted the soft hand on his arm, laughing hearitly.

"My dear," he said, "there may be sun jewels on the Bay, but only for the eyes of youth to see. We couldn't find them should we try, but to young love, dancing sunbeams become diamonds with a thousand promises radiant as the dawn."

XXXVII

For twenty mornings there were sun jewels on the Bay. For twenty successive nights, Jules Courtney reached the marble registry desk of the Bayside Hotel when the clock's hands were somewhere between midnight and two o'clock.

"Shall we call you at seven, Mr. Courtney?" had become the clerk's repeated question, to which Jules always answered, "Unless it's raining and that, I gather, doesn't happen here during the season."

Every morning Jules snatched at a ringing phone beside his bed and curtly demanded ice water. The burst of sunlight flooding over his room seemed exceedingly cheerful and fresh. It was a rebuke to his sleepy eyes, tousled hair, and wrinkled pajamas.

Regularly a rising sun set its level beams into the two bedroom windows, and just so regularly Jules left his bed, sleepily but with an appreciation of the scene below. Sunshine was like a benediction on him as he recalled hearing the local say, "The mildest winter in years, like summer!" Yes, it was like summer—a June of one's youth—and out there were those dazzling sun jewels.

They might have been diamonds dumped helter skelter on the wide-flung Bay. They sparkled and tossed on blue hills, scattering down white valleys and up again, cresting new waves.

From all this Jules turned away, to ice water and a waking shower. One late January morning, however, something outside caught and held his interest longer than usual.

To the right of Courtney's suite and within a yard or two of his own bedroom there was a balcony. This morning there was life on that balcony—someone moving, talking, the voice of a man.

Curious, Jules leaned close to the bronze screen and now he could easily see the whole of an attractive Spanish balcony. There, under a striped canopy, amid the flowering plants and canvas chairs was a dark man, his face lifted to the east. He was an impressive figure in white silk lounge pajamas and matching robe. On his feet were odd sandals of white kid.

"Oh, yeah," Jules murmured to himself as he remembered something Deane had said the night before.

"You're going to have a famous neighbor, Mr. Courtney," the manager had divulged, and there was something queer in his look as he said it. "A private car was side tracked at the station yards tonight. Ahnoud Bey, celebrated mentalist, is with us again."

Jules had been blissfully ignorant of the significance of this. Now he regarded Bey merely as one might any sort of person in the public eye.

Ahnoud's lips were moving as he looked off across the tops of coconut palms to the glowing horizon. Jules pressed against his window screen and listened. On the still air the mystic's words were clearly audible. They struck hard on the heart of Jules Courtney.

"To you, my Golden Lady of the morning, I speak," the velvety voice was saying intently. "You came to me out of blue mist—your eyes like the sea, your hair so sunny.

"You did not know as you slept last night that I had come again to our enchanted city, come again to play you a love song on the piano with Golden Keys. Now, as you still sleep, I greet you once more. I stand beside your bed, touching the curls on your cheek. In thought I kiss your lips, as in reality I shall kiss them tonight—beloved."

Ahnoud hesitated a moment and in that moment his wide shoulders squared, his strong figure tensed. The restrained simplicity in the smartly cut lines of that gleaming white pajama robe was at variance with the Egyptian's own dark complexities.

"When the sun is high," he continued, "meet me at the lighthouse, reunion at our rendezvous. *The lighthouse—when the sun is high—meet me there!*"

Half an hour later Courtney crossed Reana's terrace and took the hall steps two at a time. To his knock on her bedroom door she answered an airy, "Come."

"Reana," Jules asked, searching her tranquil eyes with his troubled ones, "are you okay? No trouble? No bad news? Everything okay?"

"Why darling," she cried, "what's the matter. You look ill. Not a thing has happened since I left you last night. Wait, I'll have Madeleine get you some coffee." She stepped to the room door, calling, "Madeleine—"

Jules felt a little foolish, as one does after a nightmare. He sat down on the window-seat alongside yellow roses in bowls on the sill.

There was a tang of salt from the Bay beyond Desdena Park and fragrance from blooming trees in the yard.

"It's nothing. I'm crazy, that's all!" he confessed when Reana returned. "I broke laws aplenty driving out here." His voice grew a shade suspicious as he asked, "What about your piano—called the Golden Keys? Is there some history to it?"

Reana shook back her hair and smiled with relief. "Is it only that?" she countered. "Of course the piano has a history! It belonged to a prince of India—land of mystery—land of a bird that rose from its ashes."

Jules' brows lifted a bit. "India, eh?" he asked pointedly. "Did you *buy* it from the Prince? Or was it a gift?"

The smile died from Reana's lips. She withdrew behind long lashes, her eyes expressionless. "So what? Am I on trial for murder? Are you the district attorney?"

"I'm sorry! I'm sorry!" Jules apologized, taking her hands. "It's none of my business if you have half a dozen bewitched pianos. I'm an old nosey." He put his arm around Reana and lifted her face to his. "Forgiven?" he whispered, and her gentle answer made Courtney's eyes sober with penitence. "For a thousand sins, my darling."

The notes of a Chinese gong ringing below stairs broke the tableau in Reana's bedroom. Once more there was breakfast on the canopy-shaded terrace. Jules told Reana's maid that the coffee was perfect, as were the waffles and toast. Madeleine bowed and thanked him in her quaint French way.

When breakfast was over the table was cleared of linen cloth and pottery dishes. Jules set it again, this time with charts, pencils, papers, and what not—all his battered, much used implements of plane designing. This was his work time, when the first glare of morning had burned itself out, leaving the terrace cooled by a breeze from the Bay.

Reana was busy overseeing Madeleine and attending to those household duties that call a hostess during the forenoon hours. Courtney sat alone, hair mussed, eyes absorbed in concentration, the conversation of an hour before banished from his mind.

He was knee deep in visions, in actual designing. Just now nothing but the work he loved counted. He was creating the plane of his career.

He must have worked all of two hours in

the quiet of the morning, broken only by a drone of bees that dipped into flower blooms. The gardener's feet pattered on sandy paths and Madeleine's scissors clipped yellow roses for the upstairs window vases.

Reana softly opened the screen door and stood in the doorway until Jules became aware of her presence. While she waited there, while the car slid around front along the curving drive, a clock inside was chiming eleven-thirty.

"Well, are you running off and leaving your guest?" Courtney queried as she came across the terrace. What a slim picture of elegance she was in the white linen suit! What was it they called that panama perched on her curly head? Town Topper? He extended a brawny arm toward her.

"You're not a guest," she replied, "and I'm not leaving you."

"Then why the trotting togs, my deah?" Jules hugged the slender figure with one arm, glancing up from his chair before the table. Reana viewed his sketches with pleasure.

"A good morning's work," she observed, "and you must keep at it till I come back. I'm going on an errand and I'll return before you have a chance to be lonesome—or hungry for luncheon." Jules tapped the hamper that Reana carried on one arm.

"You're not, by any chance, going berry picking down by the Yacht Club are you little girl?"

Reana laughed. "Silly! This basket carries goodies and quilt scraps for Mrs. Counihan—things she can't afford. Yes darling, there're still women who patch quilts and Auntie Counihan is one of them. I'm running out to pay her a tiny visit."

"But," objected Jules, "it's so hot this time of day. Why not send William with the stuff?"

"Hot?" asked Reana vaguely. "Why hardly, just nice, with a high sun." Jules was startled. He rose in some alarm.

"I'll go with you."

She pushed him back into the chair. "No dear, no," this nervously. "There's no need. I shan't be gone twenty minutes. Bye—'" She was on the terrace steps and the "high sun" beyond the canopy caught in her hair beneath the "Town Topper." Courtney, still uneasy, called to her, "Where does this Aunt Counihan live?" and Reana called back ever so lightly, "Why, don't you know, Jules? Her husband is the lighthouse keeper out at Pelican Point."

XXXVIII

Ahnoud Bey had walked the beach for half an hour. Under his feet the sand was dry and packed. He had seen this undeveloped beach when carpeted by a storm-swept mass of seaweed, shells, and rotted spars, as gray waves churned back from the dunes. Today the gods had smiled. The place was blessed with that mild and innocent beauty that only tropic shores may claim.

The water was running far out with a gentle tenor in its liquid blueness. Into this low tide waded a dozen or more pelicans from which the Point took its name. They were ugly and brown, but bright-eyed personages, each sporting a hungry-looking food pouch. They were all quite tame and given to showing off for the tourists. No one who visited this deserted finger of land failed to humor and feed the pet pelicans.

For the first time Bey gave no attention to the birds, as his mind was elsewhere than on shifting dunes and eddying sea. One question filled his thoughts—*Reana*—had she received his message? The sun was now high. Would she meet him at the lighthouse?

Ahnoud still felt rather dizzy from his rapid trip south. Two weeks before insomnia had overtaken him. Through those wakeful nights Reana was continually on his mind. He saw her plainly, and someone was always beside her—a man whose arms were about her, his lips on hers.

Nor was this a mere figment of fancy on Bey's part. Reana's letters had stopped. Of course there had been other times when she wrote only at intervals, but now Ahnoud felt a certain blankness between them. No word had come from 2012 Desdena Way for more than a month.

Often on those nights, Ahnoud had reached for the phone by his bed. Each time he replaced the instrument without calling Sun City. After all, that was not the best way! He knew that he must go in person.

"You'll have to cancel those dates in Buffalo and Toronto," he told his manager next day. "I'm going down to Sun City for two weeks." The manager, Mike Burgman, hit the ceiling.

"Sun City? Are you nuts? Now listen, Ahnoud, you can't walk out on engagements like this. You wanta get the black eye at the agencies? You want me, as your manager, to get laughed out of every bookin' office in this town? *Sun City!* I wish you'd never laid eyes on that dame!"

Instead of replying Bey stuck a cigarette between his lips and clapped his hands in signal to the Arabian valet. "Yussef," he said to the dark youth who came in from the bedroom, "pack clothes for a fortnight in the south. We're going to Sun City tomorrow."

Again the manager exploded.

"Now look, Ahnoud," he argued in a frenzy, "if you'll just wait two weeks—fill the Buffalo and Toronto dates—then you can go down there and lookit that woman the rest of the season! Cantcha wait just two weeks?" Bey puffed his smoke, regarding the fussy Mike with a calm but determined eye, then he spoke in a monotone, "Two more weeks—and I need not go at all."

Ahnoud was seized by a gripping fatigue during the trip south. Perhaps the relaxation made him realize his weariness. He slept and read a great deal, hardly touching the imitation Golden Keys—a white and gold baby grand—that traveled with him in his private car.

All the way he was debating something in his mind. Bey paid small heed to the landscape that flashed past outside the windows. In his thoughts was an eternal balance—scales—with either side going up or down. Ahnoud asked himself over and over, "Against him—what chance have I? And yet, what can he do—*against me?*"

Bey was unsure of himself—with the balance still swinging—when his car had been side tracked at the yards the night before. At last he had talked with Deane—discreet Deane, who spoke ill of no one and had never betrayed secrets.

"No, Ahnoud," he said thoughtfully as he sat on the side of Bey's bed, "I have not mentioned you to him. I doubt if anyone else has done so. You know folks are funny that way—men are, at least—and Courtney's a swell fellow."

The Egyptian leaned back against the pillow and gripped the coverlet with both hands. Something like a knife turned in his heart. A red glow of anger mounted his cheeks as he asked, "You like him, don't you?"

The hotel manager shrugged uncomfortably. "Well, yes, Ahnoud—I do. Everybody here likes Jules. He's been nice to us all, a good mixer, a good sport."

Bey's hot jealousy over Deane's compliment to Jules Courtney abated. Ahnoud stared at the little blue leather folding clock on a table by his bed. He saw that in ten minutes a new day would begin.

Mentally Bey condemned himself. He had acted like a child. Deane was his friend. When Ahnoud had registered earlier in the evening the manager had been out, but after Bey retired Deane came in with a cheery greeting.

Ahnoud reached for a box of monogrammed cigarettes and carelessly put them on the bed before his guest. They lighted two on a match—not unluckily—silently, in that way men have of keeping quiet in the midst of a storm, something women never learn. Bey was the first to speak, following his subject tenaciously.

"What do they do—together?" he asked, his voice toneless and painful with envy.

"Oh they have fun, mostly," Deane answered. "Courtney's a great kidder and Reana laughs at him a lot. You know, I always thought she was too sad and serious, but—" he waved away the thought, "you should see her now. They're like a couple of kids—just that happy."

Ahnoud dwelt on this for a short time then smiled in his ingratiating way. Now he knew this worry had been unfounded. Two people did not laugh much nor have a great amount of fun in public, for the world to observe, when they were actually in love. At least in Bey's European point of view that was true. As he saw and believed the situation, so he reacted to it.

Almost at once his self-confidence returned. With this passing affair of Reana's brushed aside as a mere nothing Ahnoud had slept soundly. He wakened with the early light and spoke from his Bayside balcony to the Golden Lady, asleep in her coquina villa.

Now, as Bey reviewed his emotions of the past few days, he swung on a pivot and started up the dunes toward the lighthouse. He passed along with an easy stride. A soft south wind—a fair-weather wind—was in his face.

He came closer to the lighthouse, covering with his eyes its every detail. Mr. Counihan, who lived with a lantern in his hand, had planted a nice garden around the circular red brick base of the tower.

Ahnoud, knowing nothing of such things, wondered how the lightkeeper managed to grow anything in such sand, even blackened as it was by imported fertilizer. There they were, neat rows of green and, flanking the front door, two oleander bushes in full bloom. There was Counihan now—the old sea lover—prowling around the place, in his hand the ever ready lantern. As Ahnoud reached the neat yard Counihan waved the light and called through his tobacco quid; "Shure an' you're a stranger in this port—or is it me eyes that's foolin' me?"

Bey climbed the firm stone stairway to the dune's plateau. There, in the center of its cultivated space, the lighthouse stood, enormous from this range and with crisp, ruffled curtains at the lower windows.

"It is good to see you again, Uncle Counihan," Ahnoud said. "I came down for a vacation and I have visited your good wife already. How have you been?

The old sailor walked over nearer to Ahnoud Bey. Wind-bitten eyes scrutinized the guest rigidly.

"Faith an' I'm doin' right well, s'help me, only a bit of rheumatism. But 'tis true a man can't be a mast climbin' monkey all his life—now can he?" The lightkeeper laughed and Ahnoud laughed with him, then Bey inquired about the health of the garden, which appeared flourishing.

The mystic did not hear, however, half of what the amusing Irishman was saying for a streamlined car was coming down the white road. It circled a crushed-shell drive and stopped before the front door of the lighthouse.

As Reana left the car Bey watched, but she seemed not to see him. On one arm she carried a basket and seemed to be intent on her mission. She went into the house, glancing neither to the right nor left.

When Ahnoud looked back at the garden, he thought the green vegetables were the most delightful things he had ever seen. Old Counihan's scrappy voice, too, became music indeed. *She had come!* Reana had received his message! Here again they were—where they had met so often in the past!

Bey's heart was pounding as he excused himself from the lightkeeper. With a few steps Ahnoud was around the tower, pausing near the front door.

His white sneakers made no sound on the stone steps. He swung the screen door noiselessly. Bey stood within the half light of the old-fashioned sitting room. He felt like an eavesdropper, for Aunt Counihan was saying, "Why dearie, bless the heart of you! Shure an' 'tis the prettiest basket of goodies a body ever saw. An' quilt scraps, silk ones, why darlin'—"

Aunt Counihan, who was seated facing the door, glanced up with an inpulsive motion of her head and hands in Irish enthusiasm. She saw Ahnoud standing in the doorway.

"Come in, lad," she invited. "By all the saints, 'tis me birthday—or Christmas. First *you* bring me a real silk dress from New Yorrk, then—" She stopped, for Reana had seen Bey and mechanically rising she went toward him.

"Why Ahnoud!" she cried. The tall figure stood very still, silhouetted against the light as a lone Bedouin might be on a desert hill at sunset.

He was momentarily inarticulate, reading

so much in the lovely face before him. There was that new aspect and carriage of youth, in the shorter hair, the set of boyish shoulders, and a soft light in those violet eyes. The whole was enhanced by a subtle something that happiness alone can bring.

"Well hello, Ahnoud," Reana said again. This time there was a forced welcome in her voice. "When did you come?" Bey, his heart like lead, knew that she wanted with all her soul to say, "Oh—*why* did you have to come—*now?*"

XXXIX

How many times they had met here, Ahnoud was thinking. How many times they had come into Aunt Counihan's quaint living room—sometimes hand in hand, often first one, then the other. The genial Irish biddy usually served them hot chocolate or iced tea and once in a while a dinner of her own delicious cooking.

Mrs. Counihan was at heart a romantic. She loved lovers. She understood that when a boy and girl called on her, they really visited the lighthouse to snatch a few words alone together. Auntie was so clever about this that they believed her well-planned subterfuge.

After she had chatted with her visitors a few minutes, she mentioned some work in the kitchen or yard that must have her immediate attention. It was so cheerful and easy, the way she took herself off, Ahnoud now thought. She had just served them tea and cookies and then departed to tend to a nice-smelling hen in the oven.

Reana and Ahnoud sat side by side on the gay-nineties sofa with crocheted tidies on back and arms.

"Do you recall the first time we came here? It was a stormy afternoon—gusty and gray."

"Surely," replied Reana, "we had been walking and the rain had caught us. I introduced you to Aunt Counihan while my teeth chattered with cold. My hair was soaked and I must have looked like an orphan of the storm."

Ahnoud rested his eyes on the bright head. "It was wet," he said, "but still curly. It fluffed up as we sat over there beside the heater, on the floor. Aunt Counihan brought us very hot tea." Reana's eyes were half-closed. It all came back so plainly now—*that afternoon.*

"Rain beat on the window panes," she went on. "Uncle Counihan came through telling us that hurricane warnings were posted along the coast."

"But we did not care," Ahnoud added with a tender laugh. "The rain was melody on the panes. It could have gone on till eternity."

Reana said nothing for awhile, then very slowly, "And you—you hold me in your arms, as we sat on the floor drying our clothes before the heater. The flames were in your eyes too—" She broke off and stood up suddenly, swallowing hard, making a frantic grasp for her dispassionate poise of an hour ago.

"Ahnoud," she reproved, "I must be back home for luncheon. I have a guest." She reached for her "Town Topper," which was lying on the sofa, but Ahnoud caught her hand before it could take the hat. He rose and stood by Reana, his arms around her.

"Chérie," he objected, "think how long it has been since I have seen you—three endless months! Phone your guest. I will not let you go!" Reana looked down, avoiding Bey's eyes. She seemed troubled. She tried to pull away from him, but strong arms held her fast.

"Oh, but I couldn't phone—" she stammered, "you don't understand. *I must go—*" Ahnoud breathed easier. This was better. Gently he touched her chin, raising her face until those violet eyes were on his.

"Look at me," he ordered, "and say that you wish to go. Do not consider my feelings but speak your own. Do you *want* to leave me?"

Reana's eyes went over the handsome face above her—that oval face with shadows of sadness around the eyes. In those eyes she saw her own face, saw herself in shining blue depths, away back in that peculiar world where Ahnoud Bey lived.

Yes, there she was, in *his world.* She wasn't in Sun City. She wasn't even in the lighthouse, but off there with him. All the time she had been there, when she thought she had escaped. Why had she sought escape? What was there more than this? His arms were about her. His dark face bent above her, his voice spoke to her so softly.

"No, darling, no!" she cried, her arms going up about his neck. "I don't want to go, I was only trying— Hold me close to you, Ahnoud. You stayed away—so long—" Reana buried her face on his warm throat and closed her eyes to all else.

Without a word Ahnoud held her firmly against him, caressing the tumbled light hair, the smooth cheek, feeling the rise and fall of her breast upon his heart.

Somehow this submission was more than he had hoped. Past the power of speech, he bit his lower lip, for tears were very near his eyes. The ache of three months' torment was in his throat—now, when everything was all right. That slenderness of Reana was in his arms—and willingly—her delicate perfume around him.

Ahnoud tried once more to speak, but as he did so he heard Uncle Counihan pottering in the dining room very near to the open living-room door. The old man was setting the table and calling back and forth to Auntie, who was in the kitchen. All at once Counihan boomed out in a strident voice, "Sure an' you young folks must stay for dinner. I'm thinkin' it won't be long now—with the smell of that fowl a roastin'!"

These words from the sailor brought Reana and Ahnoud back to earth. The Golden Lady lifted her head responsively, saying, "Oh yes, Uncle Counihan—we'll stay, thank you."

Ahnoud spoke at last, in soft-toned wonderment, "Shall we go up into the tower while we wait for luncheon? It has been quite a while since we were there. It may be that the big light has missed us."

XL

"Wait," replied Reana, as she stepped to the phone, placed on a table in the tiny round hallway from which circular steps went up. She called her home, then as she heard the French maid's balanced answer, "Madeleine, I'm out at Aunt Counihan's. She insists I stay for lunch and I hate to refuse. Serve Mr. Courtney his luncheon and explain to him—will you, Madeleine?"

"Yes Madame," came the dubious but dutiful voice from The Robinson villa. The maid sensed something had come up that Reana did not care to discuss over the wire. Madeleine finished, as for effect, in a louder voice, "We were waiting luncheon for you, Madame, but I told Mr. Courtney that Mrs. Counihan would certainly keep you."

Ahnoud stood behind Reana, his manner detached, his hand on the iron railing of the staircase. Bey's lips were compressed, his eyes veiled by dark lashes. He betrayed none of the uneasiness that seized him as Courtney's name was spoken.

He, then, was the guest to whom Reana must return? It was a disquieting thought. Ahnoud was not surprised after what he had heard since he arrived the night before. Courtney, they said, was at Villa Robinson for breakfast every morning. It was not as bad as it sounded, but bad enough, at that.

Now, even now, after the scene of a moment ago, some concern was in Reana's voice as she made her excuses to Madeleine, who would in turn make them to this arrogant, demanding "guest."

"Madeleine," Reana was saying now, "whom do you suppose I met out here? Ahnoud Bey!" His heart lifted as she smiled at him, but the maid was rather horrified.

"*No*—Madame?" she asked.

"Yes—" Reana went on, "he came down unexpectedly on a vacation. I want a chance to talk with him. This is strictly entre nous, Madeleine—you understand?"

Back at the villa, the maid could look through the music room windows out to the terrace. There sat Mr. Courtney, and, she thought, a finer, more straightforward American never lived.

He was sitting there working, knowing nothing of it all. M'sieur Jules had such sparkling brown eyes and dark hair that shook down over his forehead like a bad boy's. As Madeleine pondered over the strong outline of Courtney's face, the capable hands of skill and precision at the drawing board, a clammy chill went over her.

Why, better that M'sieur Jules had never come, she thought, than for him to step into this situation. Now they were all caught in it: Mr. Courtney, blind with dangerous ignorance; Reana, not herself at all; she, Madeleine, unable to warn M'sieur Jules because of loyalty to her half-hypnotized mistress. All the maid could reply was a frightened, "Oh yes, Madame, I understand," but as she stood there looking through at Courtney, she thought of how Reana had said one night not so long ago, "Madeleine—Jado dropped dead, while he was dancing—"

Single file they climbed the circular staircase—Ahnoud ahead, his hand holding Reana's as she followed. The ascent was steep and their steps echoed in ghostly fashion through the tower. If they glanced up or down they had the queer sensation of being in a narrow well of height.

When they reached the top, Reana threw her hand to her head. The room was spinning, for she had come up too quickly, unused as she was to the many turns.

"Darling, catch me, I'm dizzy!" she begged. Instantly Ahnoud circled her with his arm and led her over to a rough pine bench.

"Sit down," he said. "The air will do you good but don't look out just yet." He dropped on the bench beside her, his arm still around her. He drew her head over on his shoulder and laid gentle fingers across her eyes.

"Close them," he directed, "and soon the room will be still." They sat quietly for a time. He felt no ill effects from the hasty climb for his was a good sense of equilibrium.

Presently Reana opened her eyes and there before her, stationary now, was the same room—the round room with the big light.

No wonder lovers came here to sit on the benches and dream. This was land's end. The colorful boulevards and swank foibles of Sun City were a million miles away.

Here was only the essential, the vital. A huge light lived a useful life upstairs and a couple below was even more useful. Uncle and Auntie Counihan's one thought was that of every lighthouse keeper since a tallow candle touched the wick of a giant lantern—"keep the light burning."

Reana lifted her head and brushed back her mussed hair.

"I'm all right now," she said, surveying the room. "Looks natural, doesn't it? Uncle keeps it much the same—day and night, year in and year out. Sun City shifts and changes, but this is something real and permanent."

Ahnoud nodded and rested one arm on the window sill beside him.

"The sky is such a vivid blue today," he said, "and I think those clouds are deceiving us. They must be ships from dreamland."

Reana leaned over across Ahnoud, her hand touching his arm on the window ledge.

Her face brightened, for she loved the scene below.

"Oh it's lovely, isn't it—the cloud ships and all?"

"Yes," replied Ahnoud moodily, "but I've been thinking what it would be without you—"

"Certainly not a breath less beautiful," Reana answered, but Bey countered, "Certainly chaos for me."

Reana took her hand from his arm and laid it on his cheek, turning his face round to hers.

"Don't talk that way," she admonished. Ahnoud put his arm around Reana, drawing her close to him. Her head was on his shoulder again and one of her smooth hands lay against his cheek. Ahnoud's eyes were thoughtful as he kissed Reana on her upturned mouth.

"Not for so long," he whispered, "not for months, for so many sleepless nights." Deliberately he kissed her a second time, then as she closed her eyes he held her to him, staring over her head out the front window and off into the horizon.

"When I am away," he said slowly, "your flirtations are—just that? Nothing more serious?"

Reana heard her voice speaking as though it were another's voice. It said with sure emphasis, "Nothing but friends."

Ahnoud's eyes were inscrutable. So this one was a "friend." He didn't like that word—too much began with it.

"And if one of these—*friends*—were to love you, as, my darling, several have," Bey continued, "then—no matter who he might be—you close the affair? It is ended? *He must go?*"

As Ahnoud repeated the last three words he thought of Courtney. Reana too thought of Jules and into her mind came many things she had forgotten long ago.

Jules Courtney appeared to her in a new light—an unfavorable light—as she sat there with her head on Ahnoud's shoulder and the sea breeze in her hair. Now memories, unhappy ones, came and a great bitterness filled her heart.

Reana was sure she had forgiven, but no—some hurts, some cuts were too deep for the healing of forgiveness. What about retaliation? Was there any satisfaction in "getting even?" There must be. It would at least compensate, in part, that and *this love.*

Now Reana sat up and opened her eyes. In the stillness of the tower her voice sounded again in that odd way as she replied, "Yes Ahnoud, *he must go.*"

XLI

With January nearly over and the winter season at its peak, three daytime clerks at the Bayside's desk barely handled record crowds.

One clerk spent eight hours telling people over the phone that the hotel was full. Another registered the rush of new guests who peppered the air with questions like gattling gun bullets. A third clerk handled reservations. He was the final arbiter and could say to someone bluffing his way into a hotel where rooms in January were priceless, "We have no reservation wire from you on file."

Taking his cue from this, the registry clerk would add, "We can accommodate only those whose wires we received before December fifteenth."

All day long they came—from planes,

trains, and boats, from cars parked in the hotel's side drive. All day the clerk said, "No rooms—sorry," or "Yes, we have your rooms reserved" to a fortunate few whose wires had come early in December. Those lucky ones breathed sighs of satisfaction as bellhops escorted them to elevators.

Twelve day-time hours the spacious lobby of the Bayside was a criss-crossing and checkered pattern of vacationers. People entered the front door wearing anything from yacht captains' suits, and shorts to pin-striped trousers, dark coats, spats, and black derbys.

When they left the crowded elevators as those green and silver doors opened or slammed shut, the apparel was more typical of Sun City.

There were men carrying every known variety of golf bag and every imaginable make of fishing tackle. There were plain women and chic women, with all shades of hair and all kinds of rainbow-splashed clothes.

One wore slacks and halter that displayed a sunburned back. Another flaunted a pink lastex bathing suit, revealing a length of symmetrical legs. A third was correctly dressed in Mainbocher's last word for winter resorts. No one paid the slightest attention to any of it.

Anything went here. The place was impossible to shock, for the crowd at the season's height was a fish-eyed one, largely from New York. Everyone was out for himself in this stampede to the sun. The seasoned visitor knew the secret was, "Bring your crowd with you," for friends and acquaintances made overnight often proved wolves in sheep's clothing.

Tourists would lie to take reserved rooms, bribe the head waiters to give them tables someone else wanted, grab choice cabanas, or steal a yacht berth unless its occupant docked before sundown.

Milling about the lobby they grouped here and there to gush, "Darling, imagine finding you here," when really they were thinking, Getting here first—the cat!

They piled around the registry desk, waving wild hands and screaming at the clerk, "But you don't know who I *am!* If I can't get a room down here, who *can?* I ain't gonna sleep in my automobile—*I ain't!*"

To which the clerk, who was a paragon of tact and patience, would reply, "I'm sorry, your wire came only a week ago. By February fifteenth we may have a vacancy." This date, nearly three weeks ahead, when quoted threw the tourist into a near spasm. He shuddered and held his head, pushing the air with convulsed hands.

"By February fifteenth I gotta be back in N'Yawk," he protested, "*I gotta!*"

At four switchboards in a small room near the registry desk the regular drama was much the same. A skilled operator sat at each switchboard, handling calls from the north and local ones also.

"Bayside Hotel," each girl answered a thousand times every day. Now the same routine was going on.

"Sun City, Bayside Hotel. Mr. Courtney is out—no, I do not."

"Sun City . . . Bayside Hotel . . . no vacant rooms . . . our reservation files are full . . . I am sorry we cannot take your reservation . . . I will let you speak with the manager . . ."

The much used plug went into the hole and a phone rang on Deane's desk in his glass-enclosed office nearby. At the switchboards insistent buzzes and pleas for rooms went on.

"Sun City . . . Bayside Hotel . . . Mr. Courtney is out . . . I can ring his room . . ."

"Bayside Hotel . . . Mr. Pelham is out, but will be back . . . I can ring his room . . ."

"Sun City . . . Bayside Hotel . . . no vacant rooms . . . we cannot take any more reservations—" Then, as the voice from New York grew rather fresh and annoying, a stream of words the operator had bottled up broke out—"Lissen, this hotel's just so big. We can't stretch it to make room for you or the President or even movie stars. Take my tip, mister, and ride down in a trailer if you *hav't* come to Sun City."

She looked round cautiously after that, but the girl friend next to her was only snickering. In the Main Exchange, from which they came to this job, an operator would have been fired for such talk, but Mr. Deane was human—a good sport. He knew a girl just had to blow up and hand a little back talk to some of those smart guys who took up time on a busy day.

"Bayside Hotel . . . I will see if he's in . . ." Again the plug to Jules' room and the strong Courtney voice answering a hurried, "Yes."

"New York is calling, Mr. Courtney," the operator replied, "please hold the line . . . Hello New York . . . Here's Mr. Courtney . . . All right, go ahead, he is on the line . . . *Go ahead* New York."

"Hello Jules," greeted the cheerful voice of John Kingston from Manhattan. Courtney's face broke into a smile at the sound of his buddy's salutation.

"Well hello yourself," he shot back. "What in the world do you want with me? I'm on a vacation, you old killjoy! How are you, anyway—still trying to learn to fly a plane?"

"See here, you bum," John retorted, "I've been busy trying to fly the tin junk you design. Do they know down there how crazy you are?"

"Oh I shouldn't be surprised." Jules laughed. "Only I'm sane compared to the ones who have fits ten times a day at the registry desk downstairs. The clerk says, 'No rooms,' and they go nuts."

"So you're full up?" asked John. "I know what that mob's like—wouldn't be there for anything."

"Oh it's fun," Jules corrected. "This is the worst week in the year. After this, they all go off to Havana, get drunk, and forget about Sun City."

"Oh yeah?" John cut in sceptically. "Well I've been there in *February* when they were pulling each other's hair and dropping bridgework to get tables in a restaurant."

"Now *that,*" added Jules, "as anybody but a dimwit like you ought to know, was just after a bomb had been thrown in Havana!"

XLII

"Well look, playboy—" John Kingston continued over long distance, "you're not by any chance working on those three designs you showed me before you left? Howard-Rolf Company is cooling its heels impatiently. Bernie Rolf still thinks you're the only designer in the business, but I can't keep him thinking that indefinitely."

"Sure," replied Courtney with a good deal of spirit, "those ships are on paper—believe it or not. I've accomplished the remarkable feat of *working* in Sun City."

"Okay!" responded John, evidently pleased. "Send them up!"

"Keep your shirt on," Jules warned. "They're not finished yet."

"I thought there was a trick to it." John sighed heavily.

"The trick is," Jules answered, "I'm here on a vacation and I'm doing no rush work, not even for a customer as good as Bernie Rolf."

"Sez you?" John came back. "You talk like that because your customers think you're a genius, but I know better. I think you're a loafer." Then, with a more confidential and slightly envious tone, "Sa-ay, how's the fishing there?"

"Swell!" Courtney boomed and John could almost see Jules laughing as he boasted, "If all the fish I've caught were placed head to tail and—"

"I know, I know," John interrupted, "they'd have fish dinner at every tourist camp between Sun City and New York. But seriously Jules, *when* are you coming back?"

"In a few weeks," Jules promised vaguely. "I can't say now."

"About those designs—can't I tell Bernie you'll have them here by the first?"

Kingston's effort to pin the errant Jules down to business proved hopeless. With only generalities and wisecracks from Courtney, John replaced his phone and drew a deep breath.

If he had not been genuinely fond of Jules, Kingston would have been provoked. He knew, too, that Courtney was tops in plane designing and must be humored. John sat still for a time thinking of his absent friend.

Kingston had known Courtney since they were together in France, youthful buddies in the war. Jules was an impulsive kid, hot headed but smart as the devil—*and courageous?* Good Lord! Too much so!

Courtney had been anxious to get into the big fight. He enlisted in the summer of '17 when he was only seventeen. He told a whopper about his age and then went and confessed it to the priest—but not to a superior officer.

Jules had changed a lot as had this century that paralleled his life. He never confessed anything now. He rarely darkened a cathedral's door and apparently was pretty much the cynic about everything.

John understood Courtney and thought he could handle him better than anyone else might. It was a wonder that Jules had not been ruined long ago. Women went wild over Courtney's build-up of brawn and sinew, his panther walk and take-me-or-leave-me air.

The eccentric thing about Jules was that he designed planes but seldom flew unless his work made it necessary. Some said that he disliked planes. Others said he would surely quit the whole business one day, staying on the schooner he loved. With those two devils, Chris and Bobo, aboard, Jules would fish, sunbathe, and hang around tropical harbors to his heart's content.

There was now nothing to do but wait on the well-known Courtney humor. Some fine morning Jules might blow in, brown as a Spaniard, showing white teeth and dimples that he despised in a grin. He might even hand John Kingston a design that would astound the entire aircraft trade.

Kingston noticed that Jules juggled the

idea of returning to New York. Something seemed to be holding him in Sun City. John pondered how much Courtney meant by this evasiveness. Maybe nothing, as when his eyes squinted out over other people's heads.

At such times John speculated on what Jules saw out there. Was it the ghost of memory or vision of things to come? Was it the lure of a dear face—*one face?* In all their years of friendship, John Kingston had never learned that secret.

It was natural that women should trail Jules Courtney to Sun City. He was comparatively rich, good looking, and at present unattached. He had never lost the pep and enthusiasm of Chicago, from whence he migrated east, though never to become an easterner.

The women who knew Jules found him fair minded, a good spender, and a real lover of fun. Underneath all that, however, there was something hard as nails, into which every woman ran sooner or later. Men never struck this armor. The women knew, and debated what was behind it—what grudge Jules guarded so fiercely in his heart.

One could only have the superficial, good-humored Jules Courtney, as Gloria, Patricia, and Jean had long since discovered. They were reconciled to this partial conquest, but, with a fine sense of feminine optimism, pursued him still.

His company afforded them much diversion. There was always the hope that someday the hidden Jules Courtney—that self he never revealed—might by a miracle come to light.

"Three women out of every ten have asked for Mr. Courtney today," observed one of the Bayside's desk clerks wearily.

"And wires!" cut in one of the other clerks.

"They're easier," answered the first young man. He was almost lifeless after the exhausting day. "A telegram can be put into a key box and that's the end of it."

Those wires were not all about business by any means. They were signed, for the most part, "Gloria," "Patricia," or "Jean," without the incriminating last name. Husbands were not supposed to hear the cry of the hour, "*Jules Courtney's at Sun City—let's go there!*"

Usually the messages asked for replies. They were all opened, chuckled over, and stuffed inside Courtney's jacket pocket and forgotten.

A few days before, the girls had begun arriving in Sun City and congesting traffic at the Bayside's registry desk. It so happened that Jules was out when they called in person. Gloria, with the self-assurance and aplomb of the recently divorced and the perennially lucky, wrote on the back of her visiting card:

> Hello Jules—Escape me never!
> I'm out at the Desdena Hotel for
> two weeks. Will ring you around
> ten in the morning. Gloria.

This morning, at the prescribed hour, Jules was at Villa Robinson when the blithe voice from the Desdena Hotel called. It was met with a discouraging, "Mr. Courtney is out. I do not—"

Now in the dusk of late afternoon, with

the lobby somewhat cleared, one of the clerks mumbled to another, "My God! There's that woman again!" As he spoke, Jules stepped from the elevator, crossed the lobby, and caught Gloria's hands in both his own.

Together they walked through the garden and settled at a table under a black and orange umbrella. Jules ordered cocktails and took the time to be most engaging. He laid his hand over Gloria's and she imagined that he was saying love words. In fact he was only enthusing over "this swell place" and giving her a sure tip on a horse to win in tomorrow's races.

"You know that night I had dinner with you—the last time—a week before I came down here?" Jules rambled on, telling something about Kingston to identify the date, but Gloria sighed joyously to herself, "He remembers!"

Likewise, she thrilled when he laughed over one of her funny stories. He still had dimples! In that rugged, bronzed face there was a smile for Gloria. There were those darling dimples she had loved a month—a year—ago! All was well with the world!

XLIII

That evening Reana gave a small clam dinner on her ship. It was an informal gathering of a few well-chosen friends. While Jules was guest of honor, he actually enjoyed himself very little.

This was one of those sinister nights in the dark of the moon that sailors fear. Chris had looked at Jules askance when the latter came aboard the schooner before leaving on the Robinson yacht for the evening.

"Bad luck, sir," Chris croaked. "Water tonight bad luck. Better stay at dock. Evil spirits a walkin' th' water an' ain't no moon seein' nuthin'. Hell night, sir, bloody night—with bubbles a comin' up through th' water from 'tween th' teeth uv men what's been in Davy

Jones' locker for twelve moons—for a hunnerd moons!"

Here Chris cast a glance at "Emerald Eyes," who purred and rubbed his ebon self back and forth against Jules' trouser cuffs.

"An' us—" the wry-faced one finished, "with a black cat on deck!"

"Shut up!" cried Jules. "Attend to what I'm telling you." Chris listened glumly to orders for the next day, but he had a distinct feeling that he was not going to see his captain again for some time. The sailor brooded over this, as a starless night brooded over the water and land. There was nothing healthy in that, Chris reasoned with a sailor's superstition-drenched reasoning.

"Mr. Courtney, sir," asked Chris, as Jules swung on his heel to leave the cabin, "you ain't goin' far out on the bay tonight?"

Jules stood irresolute, one foot on the companionway stairs. He didn't like to submit to the ridiculous fears of Chris, but somehow they were contagious tonight. Courtney looked down at the cat singing around his shoes, then he faced the anxious sailor.

"Quit worrying about me," Jules said, but his words carried small conviction. The green parrot, marching on its perch, chimed in with Chris' own accent, "Helluva cat—bat without wings from bad place—blamed if it ain't one-legged smuggler Sam's ghost come to haunt me—" Jules laughed now heartily and Chris laughed too, grudgingly.

"Well hello!" said Courtney. "So that's what you think? You haven't talked today. I thought Emerald Eyes had your tongue."

The bird rolled its wicked eyes, clawed its perch, and squawked out a maniacal laugh in which there was well-aimed raillery.

"He's with her night and day—night and day—ha!ha! He don't know nuthin'—it's the devil of a crime—him not knowin'—nobody tellin' him—b-rrr! She's a beaut all right—with her yella hair—a beaut—Gawd! How's it gonna end—he don't know—ha!ha!" Jules' agile figure grew suddenly rigid and his smile died. He shot a quick, mean glance at Chris.

"What's he talking about?" Courtney asked, holding the sailor with hard eyes.

"Nothin' sir!" Chris' whole manner was one of apology. "Nothin' sir—believe me—jus' somethin' th' cook wuz reading—" He swallowed and pointed a stubby finger toward the galley.

"*You see,* sir—he—th' cook—reads out loud—*True Confessions,* sir, *yes sir*—an' th' bird—*he jus'*—" Jules scanned his wristwatch, then frowned at Chris.

"I'll see you about this tomorrow," Courtney said in a threatening tone. With that, he disappeared up the companionway and into the evil night.

To Jules, the clam dinner was a fiasco. Nothing directly unpleasant happened, but there was about the whole thing a stiff air impossible to dissipate. It might have been Courtney's imagination but he felt as though the whole crowd was against him. He sensed that everyone else knew something that no one dared tell.

Jules and Reana rode out to the Villa in his car after the evening on the yacht. He saw that she was in a somewhat uncommunicative mood, reaction from her extreme hilarity on the ship. They sat together on the back seat while Antoine drove and Jules took the Golden Lady's hand.

"Honey, it's hurting us both—going on this way. We love each other—let's admit it," he begged.

Reana only sat and stared straight ahead. Her voice was very sad when she spoke. "Oh yes, Jules," she confessed. "I do love you—with all my heart. Remember that, darling, will you —*with all my heart!*"

Jules held the slim hand tightly as they drove through the lantern-lighted streets of Desdena.

"And I too, dear," he said, deep and sincere emotion in his voice. "Finding you has not been like finding a new love, but one I treasured and lost long ago. I have wanted to tell you—*wanted to ask you*—"

"Our love is something complete," murmured Reana, "something that cannot be broken, no matter what may happen—" After that they rode along in silence until they reached Desdena Way. Gazing into the blackness of the bay view, conscious of a change in the weather, Reana commented; "I'm afraid there will be no jewels on the water tomorrow morning."

The music room was warm when they entered. A heavy rose perfume drifted in through open windows. The darkness of the night seemed to have settled here as everywhere else. Shadows were upon the Taj Mahal tapestry, hanging on the east wall, and upon the agate carving of Westminster Abbey.

The Golden Keys piano stood on its majestic dais, lighted by two high and eerie Mazdas under each window. Reana as one mesmerized moved to this, her most valued possession.

She played a few chords and somehow tonight this clear, ringing music depressed Jules. He took a drink and a cigarette. He walked restlessly around the small room.

When Reana stopped playing, left the dais, and came to stand before him, he drew her down on the divan. Courtney lighted her cigarette for her, then, studying the lovely face meditatively, spoke slowly, "Do you know—once on the boat tonight, when your hair blew round your cheeks and the lipstick was off your mouth, I thought of France—of chestnut trees. Were you ever there, or am I nuts?"

Reana leaned back, long lashes veiling her smoky eyes. "*France,*" she echoed. "Shall I tell you my memories of France?"

"By all means," Jules replied. The pulse at his wrist was *tick-tacking* like a trip hammer.

"Well," said Reana, "they began with a French convent, which turned me out a well-behaved *jeune fille* in white organdy. I was pretty, but didn't know it, and pitifully sentimental. There was a young man—an American—and it was Paris, *in the spring*—"

XLIV

There was a subdued air in that music salon. Outside infrequent motor horns honked and cars of joy riders cut the darkness with shouts.

"You, a kid—under those chestnut trees." Courtney ruminated. "Go on."

"Picture a romance, Jules!" Reana's eyes shone. "Picture a boy and girl, Americans of course, for to them alone is 'April in Paris' a magic time!

"He was so glad to be alive after facing the big guns. All France was in renaissance with him, but I—I lived for the first time.

"I wore at last grown-up clothes instead of convent pinafores and heelless slippers. I pinned up my curls. Just think, Jules, at sixteen I had long curls to pin up—" Reana's color rose in her ivory cheeks. Courtney tapped the ends of her bob.

"Let them grow again," he entreated.

"Oh I lived in a daze," she continued, "all about me was a mist of sunbeams, that which glorifies everything, everyone. I was lost in the dream of first love." Jules seemed sad now. He gazed far away—far back and away.

"Nothing ever like first love," he admitted, with a catch in his voice. Why was what she was saying having this effect upon him? It was as though he had been with her, then. Was it possible? "It only comes once and its memory is sweet." Reana drew in a breath, then asked in a beseeching way, "'*Sweet*,' Jules? Is *that* what you think?"

He nodded without a word. He was not seeing the walls of Reana's music room, nor Ahnoud Bey's Golden Keys. *France—chestnut trees in bloom!* No—it couldn't be, Courtney thought, not this way—from out of the gray years—since that time long ago.

Reana picked up her cigarette and puffed a bit to ease that sharp pain in her throat, to veil her tear-filled eyes with smoke.

"The rest of the story, Jules, is not a story. It is life," she went on as though with a great effort. "The boy and the girl became man and wife. That consummation of their love was a precious thing, but just here, Jules, learn this if you do not already know it. The world hates to see two people happy together.

"My soldier boy and I were too happy—that was all! Forces began working. Rumors and lies were spread. I was painted as unfaithful to the one who was my life."

"Unfaithful?" said Courtney. "Did they use that Victorian word as recently as the early twenties?"

"Yes, and it meant something to me then," she insisted sadly. "My very innocence, my singleminded devotion sunk me. With more knowledge of the world and less love for him, I might have conquered the situation. As it stood, I was bewildered, then panic stricken by doubting looks, questions, finally outright accusations from him.

"Even our friends lined up against us. At last came a letter from one of these—an insinuating, unsigned letter. A horrible scene ensued and with it the end of our home and our love. Oh Jules, my soldier boy should have known that letter was untrue! He should have known my heart was loyal to him alone!"

Reana's eyes had turned from violet to steel blue now, as though the story had imbued her whole being with cruelty. Courtney was at a loss for words. He sat watching the fast-burning cigarette between his fingers.

"On such an occasion," Reana finished, "a European woman flings her body into the nearest river. An American woman finds the other way to kill herself—in the divorce court."

Subconsciously Jules heard the phone ring in the corridor. He heard Madeleine as she answered it, then approached the music salon's door.

"Reana—" Courtney cried, clutching her hands, "it can't be that—" The all observant maid was now standing in the doorway.

Madeleine swept the room before her with calculating eyes. There was the alcove with high windows above the yellow lights, that gleam of piano keys, a sheath of pale silk along a black Chesterfield, graceful arms, one bent close to a dark man. Madeleine's eyes met Jules' and she felt as though her throat would close. Making a great effort, she announced, "*Madame—the telephone.*"

With a slight excuse, Reana left the room. Madeleine stood in the doorway, still resting worried eyes on Jules. The maid knew that Ahnoud Bey was on the other end of that phone wire.

Inwardly Madeleine was distraught. Every fiber of her body was twitching. No one but she knew it all. She was alone now with this situation, and in which direction could she turn for help? Should she speak now to M'sieur Jules? It was the last chance—*should she?*

"Oh Mr. Courtney," she said, stretching out one hand toward him. As Jules' eyes met hers, Madeleine hastily improvised. "Your chauffeur, Antoine, asked me to tell you that your car is in the side drive. He is waiting for you there."

Courtney answered abstractedly, "Oh yes, Madeleine—thank you." As the maid went down the corridor with fear-filled eyes and fingers clasping and unclasping, she knew she was not strong enough to fight the power that ruled this household. M'sieur Jules would have to make his own way out. Madeleine was no help, none at all! It was with *Le Bon Dieu,* she thought, and may He take care of M'sieur Jules.

XLV

Jules Courtney sat in the music salon after Madeleine had gone, listening to Reana's voice as she talked over the phone. He could not distinguish the words, however. Now the call seemed to be over. The one-sided conversation ceased and he heard her steps on the stairs, then in her bedroom overhead.

Jules lighted another cigarette, but its friendly taste failed to soothe his nerves. Nerves? Silly idea! He didn't know what they were. The man who flew couldn't have nerves!

Courtney heard a distant drone as a plane took off from the airport three miles away. In a few minutes the trimotored giant was roaring over Desdena—over Reana's villa. Jules knew the ceiling was low by the throaty cry of those engines. They were husking loudly against the elements—a storm ahead.

Courtney looked at his watch. Yep, that was the midnight plane, heading for points north. Kid Ricks flew that ship. At least he had been flying it two weeks before when Jules talked with him out at the field.

Ricks had seemed impressed on meeting Jules. Even though the boy knew a whale of a lot about aviation and the mechanism of different ships, he was still a youngster and thought J. C. Courtney, the designer, was somebody.

Jules smiled to himself now at this recollection, then he heard a clock striking twelve. Thoughts of Kid Ricks and his ship faded before another scene, with which tonight was closely linked.

"France—chestnut trees in bloom—" Jules recounted with a sigh. In sadness and some dismay, he saw again that yesterday that Reana had resurrected.

It was twelve o'clock—high noon—of an April day in postwar Paris. In historic Notre Dame Cathedral the aristocracy of a great city was gathered. There were wealthy Americans, titled Britons, and the best names of Parisian society.

"Ah—*exquis, exquis!*" the latter whispered, sympathetic because they were French.

"*Mom Dieu! La belle Claire!*" they exclaimed and "Jules Courtney? Handsome? *Mais oui!*"

"Claire—*chérie!*" murmured the men, and the women answered, equally despairing, "Jules—*chérie!*"

They were glad, piteous, and curious in one breath. They turned eyes of admiration on the young bride, who walked with the dignity of a princess.

She carried lilies of the valley and her white slippered feet trod a carpet snowy with rose petals. She reached the altar and knelt before Father Couperin. The French priest stood, tall and distinguished, in his white surplice, a gold cross gleaming on his breast. His fine face was alight with happiness as he read with solemnity the marriage service.

Long streams of sunlight pointed down through stained-glass windows. They crossed the altar and fell upon Claire's soft cornsilk hair held by transparent lace veiling.

To the impressionable crowd, the golden beams formed an aureole of purity and goodness. To Jules Courtney, then only twenty, but twice that from experience in a war-torn world, this was a happy omen.

Jules listened to the ritual that Father Couperin was intoning so musically. The lad knew the kindly priest was praying in his heart, "Blessed Mother, may he be good to this child whom we have loved and guided all these years!"

Young Courtney, meeting those dark eyes, answered in spirit, "Holy Father, do not fear. I will love and protect her—always."

Actually he only repeated marriage vows. When he faced his bride, her beauty reduced him to a sort of reverence. Claire, pure as her satin gown and orange blossoms, lifted her face to a gold crucifix above the chancel—just for a fleeting moment—before she smiled at Jules, with sunshine about her.

She held a missal against her heart earnestly, devoutly. Over the other hand showered clusters of valley lilies. The violet eyes settled on Jules. In them was love inestimable—the love he had doubted, cast away.

Now, thought Courtney, she had been dead ten years. He heard it through various channels on a trip to France in 1931. An old friend talked with him in the Ritz Bar.

"The last I heard of Claire," he said, "she was in seclusion on the Riviera with her folks. Later, someone told me she had passed away. Was it from a broken heart, Jules?"

Courtney had ordered more drinks in reply. Next day he tried to locate his former wife's relatives. The search was useless. There had been an aunt, for whom he had a great liking. She had married a second time and was living in New York, but under what name he could not discover. Along the Cote d'Azur, he was told, "The family hasn't been here in years. The daughter died a few years ago."

Now Jules rose and paced the floor in a state of utter distraction. Claire was gone, but the spirit of her lived on—surely that must be true. If only she knew, tonight, of his remorse—how he had loved her through the years. If only she might come back, just long enough for him to say, "I'm sorry."

"Claire," said Courtney, covering his eyes with one hand. "Little Claire, forgive me! It was the madness of youth, my doubting you. Claire—wherever you are, whoseever you are, whether you may be in this world or happy with the saints—come back, dear! Return to me now, Claire—*if only to forgive.*"

Faint as a whisper there was a stir on the dais. Jules fastened his eyes on the Golden Keys, for close to the piano stood a slender girl in wedding veil and white satin dress. A gold-crossed missal she held to her heart, while over the other hand floated the petals of showering valley lilies.

Yellow glow filtered down from high window lights. It touched the cornsilk hair that fluffed beneath a band of orange blossoms. It fell about the lovely, tranquil face—the very face of *jeune fille Claire.*

"*Good God!*" It was a hoarse cry, for Jules Courtney's throat had gone dry and his eyes stared in disbelief. At length with a trembling hand he crossed himself, then drew back stealthily.

"I called her," he gasped, "and there she is, *there she is*—little Claire!" A cold fear seized him now, for the vision before him moved. She advanced a step nearer and Jules withdrew to the side wall, grasping the Taj Mahal tapestry for tangible support.

As his hand touched the red and gold threaded material, as he felt that the world was still about him, his aplomb returned. Jules now saw that the lace veiling, orange blossoms, missal, and sun-gloried hair all belonged to the little bride of years ago, but the eyes resting upon him were the sophisticated violets that lived behind the misty lashes of Sun City's Golden Lady.

"Claire! *Reana!*" he cried, stepping forward and extending one hand. "Oh, my God, it *is* true then! Since that first afternoon, I've wondered. You were so familiar, yet so different. I must have known, that was why—*oh that was why I loved you*—even though I wasn't quite sure!" She stood before him inarticulate, expressionless. Her eyes seemed to be of cold steel.

Jules felt a sudden oppression, perhaps from the heat and rose perfume. The music room seemed miles square and he alone in it. Was he here, at a villa in Desdena, or had he too passed over into that other world? No, Reana—alive and too beautiful—was on that dais, and she had been his war bride, Claire! He essayed a brave smile as he went closer to her, but his knees were leaden.

"I'm sorry for the past, Reana," he said simply. His eyes were burning strangely. "It's not too late to forgive and forget—not too late to love again."

As one devil dominated, Reana retreated from Jules' outstretched hand. Her eyes grew scornful and dark with hatred; then, from opposite sides of the archway that separated the dais from the music salon two black mango doors slid out. They slammed together in Courtney's very face. They clicked as with a lock and Reana was behind them.

Simultaneously the lights went out—every light in the villa—as far as Jules could see. He was left in pitch darkness. He hurled himself forward and beat against the massive panels of the twin doors.

"Reana, Reana!" he called. "Where are you? What's happened? *Answer me!*"

When he stopped speaking, silence blanketed all— a silence thick and ominous. Now in his dilemma Jules recalled a sentence or two he had overheard at the Yacht Club only a few nights ago.

"Courtney? He is with her night and day?"

"And doesn't he know?"

"About Reana, you mean—and her '*L'adieu noir*'?"

Now Jules understood what they had meant. "Black farewell!" The heavy perfume of tropical flowers coming in was like a cloying funeral wreath. On all sides of him was an inky chasm.

"Damn this darkness!" Courtney called out, his nerves on edge. He banged his hand against a wall and stumbled over a chair. "The door—*hell!* Isn't there a door somewhere, leading out? There, *the knob—*"

Afterward Jules could not remember what he did during those wretched moments. He fumbled crazily with the knob, opening the door that led into a corridor equally dark. Then he heard from behind those closed doors the music of the Golden Keys.

That exultant melody cleft the midnight of the house, resounding upon ceiling and windows. It followed Courtney as he reeled from the place, hurrying across the tiled terrace and out into the driveway.

"Antoine, *Antoine!*" It seemed to Jules he would never reach the two tiny sparks of hope in all this sickening pall—the parking lights of his waiting Cadillac. Presently a firm hand grasped his. Anxiety was on the chauffeur's face.

"What is the matter, sir?" he asked. "You came from a house in darkness. What has happened?"

"Not now," said Jules hoarsely, "just let's get out of here!" He crept into the far corner of the tonneau, slamming the door as though to exclude a dreaded memory.

"Take the highway north, Antoine, and don't stop at all!" ordered Courtney. And a mighty Cadillac roared through the starless night, that evil night, in the dark of the moon, going northward—*ever northward.*

XLVI

Manhattan was in the grip of winter's icy hand. His avaricious fingers strove to catch that smart crowd that went south once the holly and mistletoe of Christmas had withered.

Each January these restless ones tumbled expensive luggage, pedigreed dogs, and able chauffeurs into high-powered cars, then swung away down the highway that led to summer.

Along this highway, as the snow grew thinner and birds began to sing in trees that were still green, tourists passed a long Cadillac making for the north in a kind of unfriendly haste.

"A Cadillac going north at this season?" asked the occupants of the other cars, cautiously according half the road to a flash of streamlined motor that evidently had not a second to lose.

Passing them going the opposite way, Jules Courtney felt, for the first time in his correctly traveled life, a sense of being considered quite "wrong." Already he was feeling sorry that he had fled from Sun City. However, it might be better this way. He would never visit the place again—at least not for many seasons. The job before Courtney was the hard one of forgetting it all. He was rather good at that, though.

His old life in Manhattan was sure to absorb him completely. Airplane designs must be finished and work would harness his thoughts for hours each day. There were many friends in New York, too, at Jules' club and the office. Several women might be more than glad to welcome him back.

Could all this pay for missing sunshine and coral beaches, for the lost Reana, the newly found Claire, both down the road that led to Paradise? "Black farewell"—and now back to an ice-locked city!

Courtney shivered involuntarily, for in his sulky preoccupation he had grown cold, and outside the window a light snow was falling.

Antoine pulled the Cadillac under the shed of a filling station. Jules got out, dragging from the front seat a fur coat, which by the merest coincidence happened to be in the car that night they left Sun City.

Gratefully he slid into the wrap, fastening it savagely about him. His moody eyes contemplated the skyline of a Maryland town in the distance.

"That town," Courtney said to himself, "and another, still another, then the biggest one in the world—that magnificent line of towers—New York! No, it won't be long now."

Jules had wired Martin, his housekeeper-valet, to have things in order for this arrival. He hoped Martin received the wire. Jules decided to phone somewhere along the way. He wondered too if Jean and Patricia were back in town, then laughed at such an idea. They had left calls for him at the Bayside just two days before. He hadn't bothered to answer either one.

A great discontent rather than happiness rode with the Cadillac as it burned up snowy roads, cut towns in half, and finally, conquering an ice storm, entered the gray canyons of New York.

"Home," Jules remarked, and he felt better as he handed Antoine some money. "Go out and buy yourself an overcoat," he urged, but the chauffeur declined.

"Thank you sir, but I have the fur-trimmed uniform overcoat here. I took only the light one south."

Jules found his apartment in perfect order, with Martin waiting to welcome him home. Everything Courtney needed was there, but somehow it seemed empty—barren of one presence, which had become the cornerstone of his spirit.

It was too late to go to the office, so Jules spent a colorless hour or two. He called John

Kingston, but he was out of town for the weekend—up at Lake Placid—with that fluff of a girl who was learning to ski.

With darkness and the subtle stimulation of night lights, Jules' mood brightened. He settled into a deep chair, the phone in one hand. First there was Dorothy. It had been all of a month since her last letter arrived at the Bayside.

"Is Mrs. McDaniel in?" Jules asked quickly into the phone.

"Nope," replied Dot's brother, "she's gone to Sun City."

From another number Jules received the same answer. It was piteously apparent that he was caught in town out of season. Everyone he knew—well, not everyone, but the majority—was in the South. Should he risk one more call and then hoot at himself?

"Gloria!" He rejoiced into the telephone. "I thought you were in Sun City. Did I talk with your double that afternoon at the Bayside?"

"I heard you had left," she admitted, "and I flew back to New York. I think we're two babes lost in the cold, cold woods!" Courtney was pleased. He talked half an hour, concluding with an enthusiastic, "Here's a kiss—on your kissable hands. I'll see you at eight. We'll go out and explore the frozen Main Stem."

It was all of three A.M. when Jules returned to his apartment. He felt very tired as he crossed the living room, took off his fur coat, and threw it over a bedroom chair. He undressed and warmed his hands now and then at the radiator. Shivering a little, he reached for the silk pajamas folded at the foot of his bed.

"I was a fool to run away from Sun City," he reflected aloud. "After Reana, who cares for the others?" Courtney leaned near a narrow window beside the radiator. With one hand he looped back the curtain beyond which he could see the city lights, blurred by a brisk snow.

Already fresh flakes gleamed on ledges and sills. The winter night was not a picture that might cheer a lonely heart. There were few answering lights from the close-ranged windows across the court.

This was deadly cold, Jules thought, and somehow he couldn't get warm. How different from those balmy nights in Sun City. There was always music drifting down from this roof or that one! The stars were amazingly large and bright. Morning came in so fast, with singing birds.

Courtney yawned again and his eyes were dispassionate. He and Gloria had trotted around town, beginning with a hotel dinner and followed by a show that cost six sixty a seat and wasn't worth the sixty cents.

The streets were slushy, too. Gloria's white rubber boots, topped in bunny fur, didn't stay white very long. They had mushed in and out of the Cadillac, doing up the clubs.

Jules and Gloria took in a private party, then one more night spot where a torch singer who had never seen the Mississippi sang that old chestnut, "My River Home." Another girl trucked all over the place, till the tables shook.

Rounding up at Reubens, the crowd that Gloria and Courtney had collected grew sad, crying into black coffee and talking about "wassa use, anyway."

XLVII

"Same old bunch," Jules complained, lighting a cigarette and throwing back the counterpane, "still mooching on me—or anyone. Gloria's a good sort—fun and all that." Courtney settled in bed and picked up a magazine from the small table nearby.

Now he began to feel shaky, as he imagined one felt when coming to from a dope shot. Tonight he had made a big show of forgetting the Sun City incident. The pain was not cured, only dulled. All at once it was coming back. What to do?

It was hard to believe, even after days of knowing it, that Claire was living down there where the roses were blooming. If this were only a bad dream, Jules could laugh it off, but facts were in the way. He had loved Reana without knowing why. Jules had not even recognized his little Claire, the years had changed her so. Time, though, had glamorized her appeal.

And now, thought Courtney, I've lost her a second time. Tonight—and all the others—without her.

He paged through the magazine, paying small heed to its contents, then with a short, "I'm a damned fool!" he snapped out the light, buried his dark head in the pillow, hunched up his great shoulders, and found a welcome oblivion in sleep.

Jules' dreams were confused, but just before dawn lighted the snowy sky he lay in that soothed state between sleep and consciousness. Into this peaceful haze, into his bedroom, came the sound of music—the clear tones of a piano played by a master's hands.

The whole world became twilight through which notes of the Golden Keys cascaded like stars, then semidarkness closed in. With it came the fragrance of those too sweet yellow roses. About Jules were objects bitterly familiar. There was the tinsel-threaded Taj Mahal tapestry, the black of a Chesterfield, and, over there on the dais, under soft lights—

Twilight returned, still unrevealing! The music came closer. He might have put out his hand and touched the piano—Reana's piano.

"Claire, *Claire!*" Wide awake the next second. Jules sat bolt upright in bed. He was calling that name over and over.

A sickly light of early day crept round the velvet window drapes. Beyond them all was quiet. Windows across the court were dark, radios long since turned off. There was no sound in Courtney's rooms except for the ticking of his bedside clock.

Jules lighted a cigarette and sat back against his pillow.

"What the devil!" he exploded. He had lain there only half asleep and heard the music of Reana's piano, which was hundreds of miles away. As Courtney had snapped to a wide-awake condition, the music stopped. He felt as though he had been struggling, beating his hands on those black mango doors.

He remembered now a crazy tale they told in Sun City. Any man who loved Reana and lost her was haunted the rest of his life by the music of the Golden Keys.

Because Reana's answer to Jules' questions about the piano had been equivocal, fear now struck him. He might believe as very truth inferences that had reached him in Sun City. One man, they said, fled as far as China to escape this tormenting melody of the Golden Keys. Another one lost his reason.

There was even a dancer whose untimely death was very mysterious. He had loved Reana hopelessly. Always lurking in these snatches of hearsay was the name "Ahnoud Bey."

"Oh I'm nuts all right!" Jules decided. "I've got to get over this thing!" He hurtled out of bed, calling for Martin. Obsequiously the valet hurried in.

"It's very cold this morning, sir," he observed. "I brought out your eiderdown robe; and I shall hurry the coffee."

The dressing gown was comforting, a bath still more so. By the time Courtney was midway through breakfast, he was himself once more. He was even brave enough to call Sun City on long distance.

"Get the Bayside Hotel," he told Martin. The valet calmly obeyed and presently handed Jules the phone.

"Hello, is that you, Deane?" asked Courtney. "Well Deane, I was called away by a wire. Had to leave without getting my things.... Yeah, I came north in the car—darned cold here too.... No, I don't expect to be back anytime soon—business is going to keep me here. ... What's my bill? Let me know now." Then a pause.

"Okay, I'll wire you the money today. And say, Deane, will you please ship our stuff—clothes and mail, Antoine's and mine—to this address." Jules gave his New York apartment number while the Bayside manager carefully took it down.

"Thanks, Deane," Courtney continued, "and one more thing—tell Chris to wait there for any instructions, will you? Well much obliged—and say, I'm sorry I had to go.... Yep—you're an A-one host, Deane, *no place like the Bayside.*"

Jules left the phone and went back to the dining room. He finished his breakfast thoughtfully. Martin placed cigarettes and matches by Courtney's plate.

"You came home rather—er—unexpectedly—Mr. Courtney," the valet observed discreetly.

Jules smiled sourly. "Mmmm—you put it mildly, Martin. I fled from a ghost of the past."

"A real ghost, sir?" queried Martin, and his eyes grew very round.

"No," Jules shot back bluntly, "a woman."

Martin was relieved. "Oh of course sir, that's usual, isn't it?"

"This is *unusual*," said Jules as he went into his bedroom to change into street clothes. "What would you do, Martin, if your ex-wife were to appear? Would you think her a live woman or a ghost?"

The valet was standing in the doorway of a cedar closet, balancing a suit of clothes, a hat box, and shoes with perfect equanimity.

"Well sir," he replied slowly, "much as I dislike the supernatural, I, like any normal man, would hope she were a ghost. A ghost never accuses, nor recriminates, never demands overdue mercenary compensation, as it were."

Jules had pulled on the smart eel-gray trousers and garnet shirt. He tied a slate tie just so and slid his arms into the gray jacket that Martin held.

"Nice job," Courtney commented, scrutinizing the new suit in a full-length mirror. "That tailor was good to fit me with this order while I was away."

"Yours is not a hard figure to fit, sir," complimented Martin, who was small and slight. "It is the ideal one—tall, with football shoulders." Jules put on his hat and fur coat, picked up his gloves, and walked out into the living room.

"Call down for the car," he told the valet.

"Antoine was to have it cleaned this morning. If it's not ready I'll take a taxi."

"It's ready, sir," said Martin quickly. "Antoine phoned while you were at breakfast."

"Okay then, and I left you a check—enough? I'm having six guests to dinner tonight, Martin." The housekeeper-valet bowed and smoothed his hands together.

"Very good sir. I will tell the cook to order champagne. Anything special, sir?"

"No, nothing special. Just grub and drinks—that's all they want." He opened the front door and flung over his shoulder a last-minute thought.

"If Gloria calls, tell her I'm dancing with her at luncheon today, as arranged. If she's not there, then I shall dance with someone else."

With this he swung out—a leopard's stride in an alien fur—and Martin, going back to his duties, said aloud, "He didn't want her to be a ghost. He still loves her."

XLVIII

Sun City had been good to Phil Pelham. He arrived there with practically no friends and very little money. At once people began to help him. They suggested ways in which he might make the ample income one needed to live on in Sun City. Someone sent Phil to the Auburn agency with the information that the Cord was going back on the market and that he'd be the one to sell it.

Pelham never forgot that first week of work. He sold two cars and moved over to the Bayside Hotel upon which his heart had been set since he first saw the place.

Staying there was another thing. The car business was not yet up to an all-time high, especially the sale of luxury cars, which he was handling. Sometimes the commissions rolled in and Phil grandly paid his hotel bill. After this he dined on the roof, entertaining a party of six or more, and bought himself newer, smarter clothes.

Again he would go for weeks without making a sale. During these discouraging times he used his credit at Nick's restaurant. He also put off Deane as long as he could do so and remain at the Bayside.

Now those days of worry were over. He had his own automobile agency, representing three popular-priced cars. His building was modern, with plate-glass windows on two sides of a prominent corner. Those show windows held the most impressive car display in town. Beside his spread the other agencies were shoddy, for Pelham had the trade!

Sometimes the work of managing such a large concern was almost too much for Phil, as it had been today—phone calls, letters, and salesmen coming in with their various problems.

Pelham sat now at his wide, chromium-topped desk. He signed letters and talked into two phones at the same time.

"Yes," he said, "of course I'll be at the barbecue tonight," and, "The sedan came, Doc, instead of the coupe, but your car will be here in three days. I have a wire from the factory. They've shipped your coupe." As he tried to sign three more letters, one of the phones buzzed insistently.

"Yes," he answered, "oh yes, Mrs. Nicholas, how are you?" "I'm afraid I can't come tonight," Phil demurred. "You see, I'm due at the barbecue they're having out on the North

Shore this evening. You had forgotten? Yes, some other night. Well, I'll see you and Nick at the barbecue, yes—and thanks."

Phil put down the phone, smoothed back his hair, and noticed that his secretary was standing at the other side of his desk.

"Mr. Pelham, Mrs. Adams is outside in her car." Instantly Phil was all attention. An electric energy charged his whole being as he advised, "Tell her I shan't be more than five minutes, will you please, Miss Nelson?"

"Yes, Mr. Pelham," replied the secretary evenly as she left the room. The door of Phil's office opened and shut. He heard a girl in the next room say, "When I get my millionaire I'm going to have a car like *that* one out at the curb."

Phil smiled to himself. She meant the Duesenberg—still holding up admirably after two years of punishment under Sylvia's constant driving. *Sylvia!* Her face, with those brown eyes, came before his mind's eye. He shuffled some papers on his desk, then put them into a drawer.

"They can wait until tomorrow," Phil decided. He was tired. He had to get out of the office.

Phil snapped out his desk light. The wintry dusk came through jade venetian blinds. It fell on furniture in green and bronze and a deep-piled rug of olive blocked squares. On the wall was a framed photo of Sylvia's Duesenberg.

Phil remembered a day two years ago when he had sold that car and also one to Mrs.

Nicholas. Since the panic of that morning he had come a long way financially. Where Sylvia was concerned, things were much the same as they had been one forenoon when she came down in her maywine bathing suit and met him in the sun room.

There was still an exquisite thrill in the clasp of their hands, the touch of their cheeks. Both hearts caught flame with their kisses and a danger signal was over them like the Sword of Damocles. Phil was sure that things couldn't go on this way.

The jitters had caught up with him lately. In consequence he smoked too much, worked too hard, and, when with J. L. Adams, laughed too much to hide acute nervousness.

In three minutes Pelham was getting into the Duesenberg, slipping into the driver's seat. As he sent the powerful car off down the Boulevard, he whispered to Sylvia, "Been busy today, sweet?"

"Uh huh," she replied, "and I bet you have. Honey, you look worn out." Phil expertly put the great car into high gear, then dropped one hand over Sylvia's.

"I was," he said. "Where to now?"

"We're going home," said Sylvia, "and have a snack, then somewhere and dance, then to the barbecue."

Phil lifted his hand from hers and made a salute of approval. "You are judge and jury," he stated, "but if those are our plans, may I stop at the hotel and change my clothes?"

Sylvia giggled. "And maybe I'll see Ahnoud Bey—goody!"

They were now within a half block of the Bayside's luxuriant grounds. Phil steered the "Duesy" into the crescent-shaped driveway.

"You flatter yourself, my dear," Pelham taunted, giving Sylvia a sidelong glance, "if you think Ahnoud will see you. He is concentrating on the usual blonde."

Phil knowingly took the car on past the Bayside's front entrance, around the hotel, and down a side drive where parking was permitted.

Sylvia sat alone in the Duesenberg under palm trees whose leaves rusted in a breeze from the rising bay tide.

Life was teeming all about her. Voices floated out from nearby rooms of the hotel. Folks were going back and forth, leaving or taking out parked cars. To Sylvia nothing mattered but Phil. Soon he'd be here beside her again, and for hours.

She put her hand across on the steering wheel. Phil's fingers had just rested there! The wheel was still warm from his touch. Sylvia's eyes glinted and she said to herself slowly and with determination, "*Barbecue!* We're not going to any old barbecue *tonight!*"

XLIX

It was still daylight, but trees and bushes were blurring into dusk as Phil and Sylvia left her car in the drive and walked around to the front door of Adams' villa.

They lingered on the terrace for there was a zephyr softness in the air, a mild sweetness from the south. Summer was in that breeze, or the last days of a gently departing spring. In this hour, half-forgotten ecstasy stirred and lived again. Somehow it tugged mightily at the heart strings.

"This air is heavenly," said Phil, breathing deeply of the perfume sifting in from oleander and acacia flowers. "On a day like this at home we would see apple trees in bloom and clover blossoms on every hillside. In short, it would be May, not February." He pressed his hand on Sylvia's arm.

"By the way," he went on, "is this February, or is it a lovely dream? Shall I wake to the snows of Connecticut?"

"Not if I can keep you dreaming," Sylvia replied, ringing the doorbell.

"Please keep me," begged Phil. "I never liked those Connecticut winter mornings."

Carrie Lou opened the door of the deserted house and seemed glad to see Mrs. Adams.

"Oh Miss Sylvia!" she cried, "I didn't know that was you, even though I was jes' sure I heard yoah car in the drive."

"Is Mr. Adams here, Carrie Lou?" asked Sylvia as she and Phil entered the reception hall.

"No'm, Mistah Jim still out. Nobody heah but Cook an' me. I hadn't ever turned on the lights. Me and Cook was jes' talkin' 'bout the barbecue tonight."

"Are the colored folks having one too, Carrie Lou?" queried Sylvia as the maid took young Mrs. Adams' gloves and bag. Carrie Lou beamed a white-toothed grin.

"Yassum, we has our's ovah on that sandy lot right up a little way from the white folks grounds, near the Bay. Miss Sylvia, you and Mistah Jim—yo'all aren't havin' dinnah at home tonight? Or that's what Cook, he say."

J. L.'s wife laughed shortly. "Carrie Lou, that barbecue couldn't open without my husband. Which one ever did?"

"Well Miss Sylvia," asked the maid carefully, "you reckin cud Cook and me get off f' the evenin'? We mighty like to go to the barbecue."

Sylvia waved a hand of unlimited permission. "That's all right," she said generously. "Go as soon as you like, but—" this emphatically, "leave some stuff for us to eat—all fixed, you know."

"Yessum, thank you." answered the maid. "Cook, he had fixed some nice potato salad an stuffed eggs, an' in the Frigidaire you will find some good ham an' chicken, ready to slice for yoah sandwichs."

With this Carrie Lou departed to the back of the house, carrying the good news to Cook.

Sylvia stepped into the living room. Carrie Lou had forgotten to turn on the lights and the room was dim in the twilight. All the things Sylvia loved were now in somber formation, each taking on a different personality with the day's departure.

Sylvia reached for the light switch, but Phil caught her hand and held it, taking her into his arms.

"Don't turn it on," he whispered. "It's nicer this way." He locked his arms about Sylvia and kissed her lips in that quick way he reserved for ticklish moments. J. L. would be in any minute and Phil had no intention of letting himself go.

"Where've you been the last few days?" he asked. Sylvia saw his face above her, the eyes full of unspoken feeling, the strong chin with its slight cleft plainly etched.

"Jim's been home." She apologized. She saw Pelham's face darken with jealousy and his lips twist into a cynical smile. He seemed to say, "What to do about it?" Sylvia slipped her arm around him as they crossed the room to the Chesterfield.

"Darling," she advised, "skip it."

"As if I could do anything else," he answered. They dropped into the divan and his hands clasped Sylvia's. They sat there in silence, a sort of hopeless apathy having fallen upon them, their spirits gone gray as the light beyond the four windows.

"Forgive me, sweet," Pelham said at last, "if I seem dull tonight." He half-closed his eyes. "What a day I've had at the office!" He gestured feebly but expressively.

Sylvia rose and picked up a satin cushion, puffing it up and piling it with three others on the Chesterfield's end.

"Look, honey," she invited, "lie down and take a nap, hear? It's nice and quiet—no one to disturb you."

Phil squeezed the hand he held. "That's all off the Romeo pattern, isn't it?" he jested.

"You're no Romeo—at this moment," Sylvia was quick to reply. "You're a tired car dealer who wishes there never had been an automobile made. Now rest, be good, and we'll have a snappy evening." He kissed her fingers and sat looking up at her.

"At the barbecue?" he asked, in a tone that showed small anticipation.

"Not if I can help it," confided Sylvia. Her brown eyes danced with mischief even in this half darkness, then she was gone up the stairs, calling back about some things that *must* have her attention.

Phil stretched himself the length of the divan. Velvet cushions came up to take him to their soft hearts. This Chesterfield, Pelham thought gratefully, was long enough for all his six feet.

Pelham closed his eyes. Everything was so still that he could hear his own heart beating. How that balmy air swelled the curtains! It was like a caress on his face. Somewhere a mockingbird was singing in a drowsy way, as though he were sorting over his repertoire before retiring.

Soon he was asleep.

L

Almost an hour later Sylvia came downstairs and tiptoed to the living-room door. She was a picture as she stood there in her pink evening dress with the billowing skirt that swayed into a million flounces and folds as she walked.

Her smooth shoulders were bare, with flower straps across them holding up ruffled sleeves that fell down over her arms. On one wrist was a wide, old, gold bracelet set with an oval of delicate cloisonné, on which was painted a miniature of Sylvia herself.

One could see the tiny face with its tilted nose and chin. One could see it clearly as Sylvia balanced in the doorway, her right hand resting on the white panels of the jamb, her head lifted to a questioning angle. Around those thick curls, as in the miniature, was a dainty pink ribbon.

Now she tiptoed into the room, dark but for a streak of light from the hall door. She watched Phil as he slept like a little boy. His fair hair had shaken loose and lay in short, wavy strands across her best satin pillow.

"Boy Blue," whispered Sylvia. Young—*young*—Phil appeared as he lay there. One lean, boyish hand locked its fingers around the cushion's edge. Those satirical lips were relaxed and curved. Far indeed was the sardonic smile, the clever quip!

Impulsively Sylvia dropped on her knees beside the Chesterfield. Holding her breath, she touched the short waves of honey-colored hair and the strong shoulder barely moving in time with Phil's breathing.

Sylvia touched his hand. The fingers curled under the pillow's edge. It was a hand that should hold a shepherd's horn, not the wheel of a Duesenberg. If those eyes were to open they should look on meadow and haystack, not the artificial gloss of life in Sun City.

"Boy Blue," Sylvia said again. In the silent room even her whisper sounded too loud. She slid her arm under Phil's head and drew him to her, cradling his face against her heart.

Pelham stirred, and then for the space of a split second his eyes opened. He saw where he was and closed them quickly again. He pretended to breathe very deeply, but his hand somehow found its way up against the flower strand that crossed Sylvia's left shoulder. Even in the half darkness, however, Sylvia did not miss that pointed smile on Phil's lips.

"You're awake," she accused, but Phil only clung to her, closing his eyes the tighter and maintaining, "No, really I'm not!" Sylvia dropped him back unceremoniously on the divan pillows. She rose to her feet and her cheeks were hot. Phil lay there regarding her as she smoothed the folds of her crushed skirt and fluffed out the bodice ruffles where the fair hair had lain.

Sylvia saw the twinkle in Pelham's eyes, as with them he possessively covered her face, her curls, and the pink dress.

Boy Blue indeed! she thought. She was silly to have pretended even to herself that an embrace between her and Phil was anything at all. After two years of loving him, she was playing the schoolgirl.

"In a hundred lives, my dear," said Phil at last, "I'll be trying to understand you. Is love given me while I'm asleep—love?" Sylvia shook her head. Her eyes were melancholy.

"No dear, no," she answered. "It isn't love. It was just a little something I stole when—when the piracy wouldn't hurt any of us, except me."

Pelham sat up now, his face going serious, the old desire again filling his eyes. He took the girl's small hand and drew her close to his side.

"Sylvia," he implored.

"Hush!" she cried, drawing away, two fingers at her lips, "Jim's coming!" There were heavy steps on the terrace, a clear whistle, then the doorbell rang.

With thistledown swiftness, Sylvia crossed the living room and switched on the lights. As she stepped to the front door all emotion was gone from her face. Her eyes danced and the gay lilt was in her voice as she said in welcome, "Hello, hello, Daddy, Ted, Johnny! Come in you three bad boys. Phil and I were just getting bored with each other."

Ted glanced at Johnny and Johnny gave Sylvia a "shame on you" look, which she pretended not to comprehend. Instead she was watching her husband warily, but J. L., booming into his home, called out, "I'm glad Phil's here, baby! I want to see that boy."

A wide-awake, well-groomed Phil came through the drawing-room doorway. Adams added, "Hello, Pelham—where've you been keeping yourself lately? Say, I want to talk to you about those trucks you shipped down to us for that Point Crystal job." Phil made some light rejoinder, and with Adams' hand on his arm, he walked into the room of recent romance.

Sylvia took a step as though to follow them, but paused, following the pair with her eyes. Then she took the hand of each guest cordially.

"Ted! Johnny!" she exclaimed. "It's good to see you! Let's go out to the kitchen. This is Cook's night off!" Young Mrs. Adams turned her dark loveliness upon them—the flash of bright eyes, clustered curls, and scarlet lips, along with the certain allure of a pink dress.

"Sylvia's willing slaves! Right, Johnny?" and Johnny answered a ready and convincing, "*Right!*"

LI

Again there was a moon over Sun City. Across Desdena shadows were clear and blue—shadows of pine and palm. These grew to tall dignity against a bright night sky through which silver planes took their passengers close to studded constellations.

Dance music seemed to circle the Moorish hotel grounds on all sides, but it was discreet, muted horn music, as was all else in Desdena. Melodies were tempered to merge with the atmosphere of the subdivision.

Life here in midwinter was every bit as mad as in Sun City proper, but it was a madness traveling on more cylinders. Reveling was muffled by green distances of garden and walled estancia.

Lantern-lighted sidewalks were peaceful,

even at the season's height. From a glance down one or more decorous lanes, there was no imagining the trysts, the love scenes that those yellow-eyed lanterns had witnessed. To know such things one must live in Desdena.

Just north of sweeping avenues, jewel-box civilization suddenly ceased. The vast jungle lay for miles under a wizard moon. Through the matted gloom of palmetto trees, vines with octopus tentacles, and lush undergrowth, there ran a concrete road, smooth and hard as polished marble.

Speed maniacs loved this road. Sylvia and Phil loved the jungle as they drove it tonight.

"To eighty!" urged Sylvia, snuggling up to Phil, who was at the wheel. "What's eighty to a Duesenberg?"

The hand of the big speedometer went to seventy-five, to seventy-eight, then past eighty, and Sylvia squealed with delight.

Phil's enjoyment was as keen as that of the girl beside him. Celebrating escape from the barbecue—that was it! They had taken J. L. and the boys there, stopping to let them out, for J. L. had to open the thing. Phil and Sylvia intended to return later.

Later? Perhaps, but this night—and a Duesenberg on perfect roads—was too much for a man who loved fine cars. The barbecue might begin and end, sans the Pelham presence.

Phil thought along those lines as the wind tore through his hair. The tremendous power of the car throbbed under his hands and the sweet warmth of Sylvia was next to him.

Now he slacked the speed to fifty, then forty. The highway began to grow uninteresting. It swerved eastward, merging with one of lesser smoothness. This in turn entered the confines of a town where traffic cops were very technical about the speed limit.

Phil turned into a narrow and seldom used road that would take them to the waterfront highway, three miles to the west on a parallel.

Pelham drove the lonely trail slowly, one hand on the wheel, the other arm around Sylvia. He liked it that she talked scarcely at all when they rode together.

Just being beside each other in the intimacy of a car seat was enough. To be honest, Phil and Sylvia were afraid of words at times like this when the moon rode high. Words were flames that might burn out these patches of happiness.

Around them the jungle seethed with the fundamental impulse. Wild things slipped from the roadside as the Duesenberg's headlights came on and on. Giant flowers, white and sweet, unfolded to the night. Phil could hear the jungle scoffing at his and Sylvia's civilization—at conventions that kept them apart.

Phil swung round a corner into the waterfront highway. There—a welcome sight—spread the Jungle Club. It was brightly lighted and many cars were parked in the drive that half-circled the green lawn and gardens.

The Duesenberg and its occupants found instant recognition from their place on the road. Hands waved from the veranda of the Club.

"Yoo hoo, Sylvia!" someone called and Phil answered, "Yoo hoo, yourself!" He turned to the girl by him. "Want to go in?" he asked. Sylvia wrinkled her nose with distaste.

"Drive on, James," she ordered. "They just want a drink from my little bar back there. I'm not opening up house for *that* crowd."

"In other words," Phil stated as he shifted gear and went on, "Madame regrets she's not at home in the Duesenberg tonight?"

Sylvia thought jealously of the little bar that opened up into the car's rear compartment.

"Already," she complained, "they've broken three sets of bubble glasses. They just like to say they've been riding—and drinking—in a Duesenberg."

Phil was secretly glad to have Sylvia to himself. "You don't tell me," he replied incredulously. "Well, my sweet, the next time I sell you a car, let's make it a popular-priced one. Then we can enjoy it without all this show business."

Sylvia murmured something in accord with that idea and Phil sent the car faster now, both hands dutifully on the wheel. They were silent again—moonstruck maybe—with the platinum light blanching the car's hood, refracting rays from its windshield, pouring magic on magic in pale tides all about them.

Their road went alongside the water, winding snakily with the shoreline. To their right was a narrow arm of the Bay.

Now hibiscus bushes dotted the roadside with a wealth of pink bloom. By this sign Desdena and Sun City were not far away. Phil breathed more easily. At last he steered the Duesenberg under that stucco archway where neon letters said.

WELCOME TO DESDENA

Here were the gay villas once more, idyllic streets, the Desdena Hotel to which half the world came. Ahead of the Duesenberg fell blue light as arcs swept the scene from their bridge posts' mounting. The moon dimmed Nick's pet spots tonight, Phil thought, as he and Sylvia drove upon the azure-lighted causeway and headed for the beach.

Soon they were parked in the back yard of the Tennis and Bath Club, where only four other cars stood. They heard the low roar and crash of ocean waves. With the glossy expanse of the veranda under their feet, Phil and Sylvia found themselves lone lovers on a moonlit plateau.

LII

"Look, Sylvia," Phil rejoiced, "the place is ours. Empty chairs, empty beach, and—" He peeped through the wide window, "—only a crowd of past-fifty bridge fiends, engrossed in three tables of betting, back there in the second parlor."

"But where is everybody?" Sylvia asked, looking about her. The porch rockers were pushed up to the wall of the wide veranda that ran the length of the Club House.

"It's late," Phil said reflectively, "they all must be at—" Sylvia spun on her heel and flung herself lightly against Pelham, her fingers on his lips.

"Don't say it," she warned, "because we're not going. Why should we, with this floor and this moonlight? Phil—the radio!"

In reply Pelham squeezed her hand, then stepped inside the front door to the console radio. Soon he was back on the porch, taking Sylvia into his arms. As they walked off in a fox trot he heard her say, "Oh swell!" in answer to the announcement, "—bringing you the music of Neil King and his orchestra—"

"That's music of the gods," Phil stated solemnly. "I tuned in on Olympus. There's nothing like that in New York, nor on this planet, for that matter." Sylvia sighed and her curls were ringing like bells.

"Maybe it's broadcast from the planet Venus," she ventured. "Listen!"

Phil and Sylvia danced down the length of the veranda. Phil's chin was on the curly head, his eyes almost unseeing in a world of moon mist about them.

Phil and Sylvia were lost. They danced with a native intensity. The barbaric harmony coursed through them like an intoxicant.

No longer was the Club floor under their feet and the crash of ocean waves down below. They were rhumba dancing to music played by a master of the tango and rhumba. The aroma and color of Spanish America were around them.

Sylvia laughed hysterically. Her pink skirts whirled out and about her as she stamped and swung. Phil bent her back and kissed her.

They leaned against the broad balustrade, catching their breaths.

As he took the girl's hand that rested on his arm, he noted the bracelet with its miniature on cloisonné.

"Little Sylvia," he said absently. "I think I

love her most of all when we're dancing." Sylvia was past hearing his voice. Her eyes were half closed as she swayed to a waltz that her feet were too tired to follow.

Phil could feel the thrill too, for this music seemed one with the moonlight in time with the ocean's surge. Then, breaking his thoughts, the announcer spoke. "By special request, Neil King will play that fine old favorite, 'Sylvia.' "

"Darling!" cried the original of the miniature. She came to life, tingling to her fingertips as they danced off. Neil's piano was speaking clearly, "—*dum*-dum-*dum*-dum—*Syl*—vi—ah—" Here horns and violins came in, interlocking like gold mesh over velvet, lifting the melody up, up—until Sylvia said with awe, "*The piano* is singing 'Sylvia'!"

As they covered the veranda with light steps Phil held her close and added, "I think when we die, if we've been very, *very* good, we may go where Neil King broadcasts every night."

Phil held the girl closer in his arms. No one could ever rob them of this moment. Here was fantasy of the highest order. They were not dancing on this Club veranda. They were dancing out there over the water, up near the moon, on a golden platform that moved through night skies.

LIII

It must have been all of four-thirty the next afternoon when Sylvia and Phil turned their horses into the road leading to Pelican Point, for a winter sun was red in the western sky. Sylvia called over her shoulder, "I'll race you to the lighthouse, dude easterner." Phil took her dare, knowing well he would lose to the girl whose riding, born of youthful days in Arkansas, was really competitive.

Their horses' hoofs clattered on down the white shell road, the lonely road. Ahead of them was a red finger of brick, at an end of this land that grew more narrow as they approached.

The horses were panting and Sylvia laughing as they reined to a stop before the lighthouse, Sylvia a little before Phil.

"Tenderfoot," said the girl, slipping off her brown mount before Pelham could help her. "You let me beat you."

"I deny that," Phil replied, tying up the horses to a gnarled salt cedar nearby. "Can I outride a hard-riding cowgirl?"

"You're kidding me," Sylvia protested. "Ted told me you jumped hurdles with him one day at the polo field."

"Well I never knew Ted was such a liar, or maybe he took a drink of that Palm Club vermouth after losing on the races."

Sylvia smiled and tucked her white sweater more securely into her brown jodhpurs. Her head was bare and she shook the blown sand from her curls a couple of brisk times.

"I wonder if Aunt Counihan's home," she said.

"We haven't been here in quite a while," Pelham reminded. "I wonder, does Uncle still carry that lantern?"

"I'm hungry," Sylvia declared as she rang the doorbell. "I hope Aunt Counihan—" Then the stout and cheery Mrs. Counihan opened the door and beamed at her "two children" who had been away so long—all of three weeks.

"Come in, Phil and Sylvia, come in," she invited, ushering them through the door, then, indicating a swarthy well-dressed woman inside on the sofa, "an' shure 'tis Mrs. Nicholas that's here. Both of ye know her."

Something inside of Sylvia froze at the sight of Nella—black-eyed, Greek Nella—greatly reduced and with a better command of English than of yore.

"Oh yes," young Mrs. Adams said coolly. "Hello, Mrs. Nicholas." Sylvia tried to say something to dear Auntie, who knew nothing of it all, but from the corner of one eye she saw Phil greet the restaurant owner's wife.

Pelham acted as though Nella were a long-lost sweetheart, grasping both her hands in his and covering her diamond rings with too friendly fingers.

"My dear boy," Mrs. Nick was saying in that endearing, accented English. "The weeks go by, and I do not see you." Phil still held her hands. Sylvia stood quite still in speechless fury.

"Oh, I've been terribly busy," Phil said as excuse, as though he had to make excuses to Nella Nicholas for neglecting her.

"You were not at the barbecue last night," she added, and the disappointment of missing him was keen in her eyes.

"I wasn't there long," Pelham said. "How've you been, anyway, and how's the new car running? You certainly *look* stunning!"

He continued to ignore Sylvia's presence. Auntie became troubled. Sylvia longed to stamp her foot and scream. Her face burned like fire.

"Aunt Counihan," she stammered with some effort and very low, "excuse me, please. I'm going up in the tower." With a sort of slapped feeling, Sylvia ran up the circular staircase. When she reached the room at the top, she dropped down on a bench and stared out the window.

Sylvia boiled with humiliation as she sat looking out the window. The sunset scene below—rose and gold in the sky and sea—failed to soften or brighten her outlook. Presently she heard Pelham's firm tread on the staircase, then he was at the door, saying, "Girl deserts boy."

Sylvia did not move. She sat with her face away from Phil and toward the window. Her profile was insultingly self-sufficient. Phil frowned and went to her.

"What's the matter, sweet?" he asked, and Sylvia snapped back, "*Sweet*—that's a good one!"

"It's a good one when you're suddenly cross with me," Phil replied. "What have I done now?"

Sylvia jumped to her feet, standing against the window sill facing Phil with blazing eyes.

"You stay down there holding her hands and I don't exist! I'm just *not*—that's all!"

"Oh, baby," Phil objected, much hurt, "it's not that way at all. You have it wrong. Mrs. Nicholas is a good customer. I'm nice to all my customers—my business depends on them."

Sylvia laughed a hard laugh and shook her head. She folded her arms boyishly, gripping those arms with her fingertips.

"Not *that* nice, my friend," she mocked. "For fear of losing the sale of that next car Nella buys, I advise you to go downstairs and listen to the Greek words for it a while longer!"

Pelham drew back, something within him stiffening at Sylvia's well-aimed irony. "Sylvia," he said, "I'm not going to quarrel with you." He shook his head, smiling in that one-sided way. "You're a child and I forgive what you say and think. Let's go home and forget this nonsense."

Sylvia set her lips and turned her back squarely on Phil. "Go on," she said, "but I'm staying here. Don't wait for me. I'll watch the light all night before I'll ride home with you."

At these words Phil's temper was sorely tried. His first impulse was to go over and shake those pretty shoulders until those pearly teeth rattled. He remembered his position, however. If Sylvia went crying to her husband, Pelham's life wouldn't be worth a Chinese coin.

He tried to speak but there was a bad lump in his throat. He extended one hand in supplication, as if to say, "Oh honey, forget this. Let's be sweethearts again." The hurt grew painful in his heart. He knew the odds were against him. Dropping his hand helplessly, his eyes stinging, he left the room.

Without a word he descended the winding steps and opened the front door. His horse's hoofs clattered on the shell road then were lost in the distance.

Sylvia listened and all was quiet. As she realized that Phil had really gone, a great sadness filled her heart.

Mrs. Nicholas, the Greek storm center, had departed and Aunt Counihan had settled in her favorite rocker. She put down her knitting as she heard Sylvia's steps on the stairs.

Something was wrong—yes, Auntie knew something was badly wrong between these two friends of hers. Phil strode out a few moments before, without saying a word to anyone.

"Now what about Sylvia?" Mrs. Counihan thought. "Maybe she's had hard words with him, silly colleen!"

"Well dearie," Auntie said aloud looking

up to the alcove door in which young Mrs. Adams stood irresolute on the last step. One small hand was on the balustrade, curls were mussed, and the figure in brushed-wool sweater and jodhpurs looked dejected.

"Why dearie!" exclaimed Aunt Counihan again. "Whativer's th' matter?" for Sylvia had flung herself down beside the older woman's chair and hid her face in the comforting folds of Auntie's gingham apron.

Mrs. Counihan smoothed back the tumbled curls and put a motherly arm about the motherless girl as Sylvia stammered jerkily, "Oh, Auntie, *I love him*. And he's *gone!* What must I do?"

LIV

The triumph of the moment was all Ahnoud Bey's. The interference of a reappearing ex-husband had been easily removed. Not more than a week before Ahnoud had questioned Reana as though oblivious of Jules Courtney's very existence.

"So Mr. Courtney returned to New York?" Reana shot back, with some defiance, "*You* ask me? Why you must have known it last night as soon as his car left Desdena."

Ahnoud opened his eyes and lifted his brows, feigning complete ignorance. "No, chérie," he answered in his cool way, "perhaps I was not concentrating on the matter last night. After I phoned you I found a book that interested me very much. I suppose it held my thoughts the rest of the evening."

"Then," said Reana, with a catch in her voice, "since you are all I have left, make me happy! Help me, Ahnoud, out of this foggy valley in which I seem to be lost and wandering." She rose from where she had been sitting beside him on the music salon's divan. She motioned with irritation to her surroundings.

"Let's get out of this house!" she cried. "It is haunted by a strong step and a stronger laugh, and—" her voice fell badly, "—a work table on the terrace, where brave planes were designed." In answer Ahnoud had wrapped the white fur coat about Reana, kissed her lips, and noticed her unhappy eyes.

"Come," he invited, "and we shall be so carefree this evening. There is nothing one cannot forget on a midwinter night in Sun City!"

"Yes," agreed Reana hopefully, "that's true. Let's go where the lights are brightest, the music loudest, the cocktails strongest. Let us be gay, Ahnoud!"

They had been gay the past five days, Ahnoud thought as he dressed for dinner in his bedroom at the Bayside Hotel. If one husky specter still trailed Reana, she spoke of him not at all. Her laughter had grown only a bit hectic and her eyes were gone back somewhat into their sockets. Hers was a sort of reckless and dazzling beauty now.

Ahnoud wished he might stay longer in Sun City, but his manager was phoning almost daily. Finally he announced that he had booked Bey for ten solid weeks, beginning in a New York nightclub the next Monday. Now Saturday night had come. Ahnoud's bags were standing all round him, packed and ready to be taken down to the car.

"What time does the train leave, Yussef?" Bey asked of the valet who was helping him dress.

"At a quarter to eleven, Monseigneur," replied the Arabian, holding a white dinner jacket while Ahnoud slipped his arms into it.

"What an hour!" demurred Bey as he squared his shoulders into the coat, adjusted his cuffs smartly, and fastened the white buttons. "The middle of the evening! Why couldn't we have gone after midnight?"

"That was the only train today that could take the private car," Yussef explained a little dogmatically. He glanced down at the seven pieces of matching blond luggage. "Shall I take these down now, sir? You're leaving direct from the dining roof?" Bey nodded.

"Righto," he ordered, "and take everything. I'm going down to pay my bill. After that I shall attend a party on the roof, which must break up at a ridiculously early hour, due to the railroad's obstinacy in regard to private cars." There was a knock at the door and a bellhop entered.

"Mr. Ahnoud Bey—checking out?" he asked, seeing the suitcases.

"Yes," Ahnoud said. "Take these downstairs and call a taxi. I will see you in the lobby." Thirty minutes later Bey entered the Bayside roof garden with Reana and a few other friends.

"There's no need of your coming way out to Desdena," she had said late that afternoon as they left her yacht. "I can easily go by and pick up the Harrisons. We will meet you in the hotel lobby."

It would have pleased Bey more had he and Reana spent those last hours in Sun City alone, together. However, he yielded to the lady's plans and expressed appreciation of the party she was giving in honor of his departure.

As a celebrity he was the center of around sixteen of the most entertaining and representative people in Sun City. They were Desdena home and yacht owners. Reana knew Ahnoud had found them all amusing during his many visits to the winter resort.

The roof was crowded tonight with a shifting sea of colors. Women were wearing both jewel shades, with rhinestones, sequins, gold slippers, and diamond bracelets. The large floor was packed with couples. An orchestra beat out a rhumba then swung into a waltz.

Voices mingled and moved in a steady undertone, now and then ascending sharply to crash through the music. There was a babel of greetings and running conversation, punctuated by explosions of laughter and the tinkle of cocktail glasses.

With February barely introduced, crowds packed behind the ropes—red-faced people back from Havana, white-faced ones down from the north. Now the elevator disgorged more and more people. Still undisputed potentate of it all was the head waiter, menus in hand, tails flying, and fingers, two, three, or more constantly upflung.

Deane, making his way through the mob, spoke a word to this autocrat, who at once became assiduous.

"Yes sir," he smiled, unlocking the rope, "reserved table for sixteen. Right over here." The head waiter ushered Reana and her party into a quiet yet choice part of the room. Here was a long table, covered with an Irish lace cloth and set with bowls of real lilacs and lavender candles.

"Do you like it?" Reana asked Ahnoud as soon as they were all seated. He took her hand under the table and clasped it tightly as he looked into her eyes. Before he could answer, Reana saw something new to her in the tasteful decoration, every detail of which she had carefully planned.

"What is this?" she asked and, "Well what *is* this?" was echoed up and down the table's festive length.

Beside each plate of imported china was a small square box bearing the name of a prominent Sun City jeweler. Reana stared at the boxes in a puzzled way, then opened her own. From it she lifted a gold cigarette case, diamond set. Likewise each guest was taking out a similar case and exulting over its quality and workmanship.

"I knew nothing of this." Reana spoke to the table. "Really I didn't! Someone has been so charming, and big hearted—" She looked from one guest to another in quest of the donor, then to Deane, but he was obviously delighted as the rest with his case.

At last Reana's eyes rested on Ahnoud's face—Ahnoud, who had no cigarette case but who seemed satisfied as a cat that has just swallowed a very fat canary.

"You did this," she accused, touching his arm lightly with one hand. "How did you get such lovely favors at the last minute?"

Bey smiled now. "You think they're pretty?"

"Pretty? Why they're *gorgeous!*" came an enthusiastic voice. Diagonally across the table from him, Bey saw Sylvia, red lipped and piquant. One of her hands held the new toy against her tailored jacket of gold sequins.

"They might have been bought to match," she observed. Then the first course was served. When Sylvia had played long enough with the idea of eating, Ted Maxime took her off to dance, saying, "Come on, baby, with your gold tobacco box, armor plate on your shoulders, and wings on your heels!"

LV

"Where's J. L.?" Maxime asked as he and Sylvia circled and recircled the shining floor.

"Went back this morning to the Point Crystal job," she replied, and her voice was dull.

"Well, what's wrong with you and Phil?" Ted went on probing and Sylvia could have screamed.

"If you talk about him we'll just go back and eat," she answered tersely, but Maxime overrode the sharp cut-off.

"Deane says Phil's been down in his room all evening. Wasn't he invited to this dinner party?"

"No," said Sylvia emphatically as the dance ended and she returned with Ted to their table, "Mr. and Mrs. Adams were invited." When she was once more seated and eating her second course, Sylvia heard Trudy, next to her, whisper, "Honey, where's Sir Galahad tonight?" Sylvia laid down her fork and confided to the blonde girl beside her;

"Trudy, we had an awful fuss this afternoon and I could die I'm so low." The other girl appeared sincerely distressed.

"How could you have quarreled with Phil?" she answered ruefully. "But I'm still mad," she added, setting her lips and returning to her food. "I'm never going to make up." Trudy chuckled and patted her friend's arm.

"Listen, hon, Don and I said that a dozen times! Now look at us, with a darling baby."

Just then an interruption came in the form of Johnny's imperative hand on Sylvia's curls and Johnny's voice saying, "Sylvia, darling, what is a rhumba without you in my arms?" As he swept her off and lilac lights played down upon the swaying couples, Johnny asked, "Are you broken hearted?"

"How did you know?" Sylvia replied with a question.

"Oh," said Johnny widely, "I just read your sad eyes, that's all."

The evening passed in that easy, impersonal style for which Reana had hoped when she planned Ahnoud Bey's farewell dinner. The food was delicious, the company congenial, the conversation clever. That was all as she would have it—Ahnoud's last evening a diverting one, with friends seeing him off, wishing him well.

Reana had keenly dreaded this final night

with Ahnoud, dreaded the feeling that seemed to sweep them both when they were alone. In his own passion she was always caught, whether she wished it or not.

Reana feared the Egyptian as she feared to grasp a red flame in her hand, yet she drew near and even nearer to that flame. She was magnetized by a deadly power she hardly understood and dared not try to analyze.

Sometimes Reana thought she could not let Bey go so far away again. After this came the chill rush of misery over Jules' departure—over that thing she knew to be fine and true, which she had blasted with her own hand. At these times, which were frequent enough, she longed for Ahnoud to go and leave her to her own unhappiness.

Now Reana sat at the colorful table on the Bayside Roof and watched the tall candles burning shorter and shorter, while the music went on and her guests smoked their after-dinner cigarettes. Ahnoud consulted his wrist-watch then turned to Reana regretfully.

"My train leaves at the inconvenient hour of quarter to eleven," he said. "May I go alone? I do not wish to break up the party." A great relief came over Reana.

"Of course not!" she said. "We're going down to see you off." Then to the guests, "Mr. Bey's train leaves in twenty minutes, friends.

"Yes, isn't it an absurd hour? I hate to cut the party short, but . . . Oh yes, I want all of you to see him off—the more the merrier. . . . Yes, we should leave now . . . of course, no time to lose, and you're being so nice about it. Thanks, everyone!"

From the glamour of dance music, lilac fragrance, and colors shot with laughter, Reana's party went to the sooty ugliness of the railroad yards.

The crowd clattered down a short flight of iron steps, then the high heels of evening sandals clicked on the gray length of a concrete platform.

White floodlights fell upon the sophisticated sixteen with unflattering illumination. Sylvia, running along, confided to Johnny, "I've never set foot in a private car. Tell the little Arkansas gal how to act."

"After the third drink," informed Johnny, "you won't know it from any other place."

Ahnoud Bey's car was at the train's end and he stood beside its steps exhibiting a hospitality he hardly felt. Holding up the skirts of their airy dresses, the girls climbed into Bey's car. One of them gushed, "Oh there's the Golden Keys!"

"It's only an imitation," Sylvia corrected. "The real one lives at Villa Robinson and has for lo these several years."

Now the men came in, and last of all Ahnoud with Reana. Bey motioned to the waiting Yussef for drinks, then he whispered to Reana, "Follow me in a moment. I must see you alone." To his guests, he said aloud, "Excuse me, and make yourselves at home."

He had not been gone ten seconds when Reana left the crowd round the piano and passed into the next compartment of the private car. It was a tasteful and comfortable room. A small shaded light burned on a table by the bed. On that table the Golden Lady saw her own photo, framed in tiny blue mirrors.

"Darling," Ahnoud said, taking both Reana's hands, "you give me no chance to say goodbye." He stood there, lithe and dark in the glow from the lamp, his face a study in suppressed desire.

Reana steadied herself against the door. Her face was very pale under the curly bangs that fluffed over her forehead, under the purple hood of her velvet monk's cape.

Ahnoud tenderly pushed back the hood, until all of the golden head was visible, then he drew the slender figure into his arms, kissing Reana slowly.

"You do not feel this thing of parting as I do," he said at last, "but you are mine, nonetheless. No one else shall have you. I am jealous of every strand of your shimmering hair, of every smile that is not meant for me." He held her off and took her face between his hands, entreating, "Look at me and say that you love me."

"Oh I *am* looking at you," Reana replied, gradually weakening. "That's my mistake, I suppose. I am seeing your hair, like a glossy raven's wing, your face so tanned by our sun and those eyes in which I can see my own face, and—" She rested her own eyes on his mouth, then finished, "I am looking, too, at your lips that Venus kissed when you were a very small boy."

Reana put her arms up around Ahnoud's neck. Her velvet cape fell back, showing the white dress and bare arms.

"When I look at you," she cried, "I am

helpless! Don't talk of love, Ahnoud, don't ask me about that, but—" She dropped her face under his chin and sighed, "*You have me—I don't know why—nor how—*"

From outside there came a shrill and interrupting train whistle. Bey held Reana tightly, asking in that impulsive half whisper, "Reana, come with me this time my darling! We can be married at any town along the way, or in New York, as you prefer. Come with me! Do not tear my heart out by saying I must leave you here!"

She only shook her head and her fair hair was a silky illusion against his cheek. Now she drew away from his arms as the whistle sounded again.

"No, Ahnoud, not this time. Let me return to my guests," she implored. "The train is ready to leave! Hurry! Come and tell them goodbye!"

There was confusion in the drawing room as Bey and Reana reentered, for a brusque conductor was calling outside, "*All a-bo—ard —a-l-l a-bo-ard—*" and the engine was puffing like a great angry giant.

Through the bedlam, Ahnoud gazed over their heads at Reana. She waved to him from the vestibule door, then all at once vanished.

The engine began to move, yanking the cars into a noisy *clack-clack.*

Reana and her friends jumped off the moving steps of Bey's private car. In silks, jewels, and dinner suits, they stood grouped on the runway, waving the famous mystic a jolly farewell.

From his vestibule door Ahnoud also waved a friendly hand until the train gathered momentum. The stucco station was soon obscured from Bey's view by the closing in of night.

As Ahnoud Bey stepped back into the drawing room of his car, he was astonished to see, curled up in his best armchair, a sequin-coated and mischievous-eyed Sylvia.

LVI

"Well," said Ahnoud, stopping and bowing slightly, "this *is* a surprise."

"I didn't ask you if I could stay," Sylvia replied, rising from the chair. "You're sure you don't mind?" Her eyes held some apprehension in their dark depths. She took the gold cigarette case from her jacket pocket and shifted the shining favor from one hand to the other.

"Of course not," replied Ahnoud, "I am delighted to have you remain as my guest. Are you going with me all the way to New York?"

"Oh no," Sylvia laughed shakily. "I'm getting off at the next station. I told my friends—Johnny and the others—to drive up and meet the train."

"Too short a visit," said Ahnoud, shaking his head, then, his eyes falling on the empty cigarette case that Sylvia was now opening and shutting. "Allow me, my dear," he offered.

Bey slipped the case from her hand. He stepped to an occasional table that stood beside one of the curtained windows. Here was a cigarette box made of carved jade. Ahnoud lifted the top and filled the gold case with his favorite brand of cigarettes.

"Thanks a lot," Sylvia said as she took the filled receptacle, then added, "for both, I mean." They laughed while Ahnoud said, "Sit down and make yourself at home. It is all of thirty miles to our next stop. I know, because I've made this run so often."

More at ease now, Sylvia returned to the depths of her armchair. Ahnoud lighted her smoke and his. He settled in another chair facing hers.

"This was the only way," she finally said, "that I could see you alone. I wanted to ask you something. They say you have a way of knowing things, that you can tell—" She paused in a baffled search for words, but Ahnoud cut in, "Chérie, I do not do this sort of thing professionally."

"But just for a friend?" Sylvia asked. Bey laid down his smoke.

"Certainly—and you are one, I hope. Go ahead."

"Well," said Sylvia, "it's about Phil and me. Of course you've heard the talk." Ahnoud shook his head.

"Perhaps someone spoke of it once," he admitted, "but if so, only briefly. I can honestly say I know nothing."

Sylvia dropped her eyes to her hands that

were locked in her lap. "It's a mess all right," she went on frowning. "I have the best husband in the world. He's given me everything. I owe all the good things I've enjoyed the last four years to J. L. Sometimes I wish I had never met Phil Pelham. You see, we've known it a long time—that we love each other—*and today*—"

Sylvia saw Bey hold up a quieting hand. As she ceased talking she regarded him curiously. He had sunk back into the big armchair, his hands very still on the chair arms.

"Do not tell me any more," he directed. His voice, now a monotone, had a faraway quality Sylvia had never heard before. Ahnoud did not look at her as he spoke but stared across the room above her head. His attitude was one of day dreaming, or concentration heightened to such a point that physical objects were unseen by those strange blue eyes.

"You are concerned," Bey said calmly, "because you and your friend quarreled this afternoon. It was a bitter dispute and in a high place, with water below. A dark woman was the cause of this disagreement."

Sylvia's eyes grew very large and she bent forward anxiously. No one could have told Ahnoud Bey, she thought. Phil never talked about his affairs. She herself had not mentioned the incident to anyone but Trudy and then with no details. Trudy hadn't said a private word to Ahnoud since dinner.

"But about the dark woman," Sylvia asked, "was I wrong or right?"

"Quite wrong," Ahnoud answered. "There is nothing in that direction for you to fear. You are merely the focal point of this triangle. You think that this affair is ended, but it is not. It will go on indefinitely. Your husband, who loves you, will not give you up."

"But it's not going on," Sylvia said firmly. "Phil and I are through. It is better that way." Ahnoud shook his head. His eyes, still averted from Sylvia, were opaque.

"No, my friend," he said again in that deep dictatorial voice, far removed from the suave tones of Ahnoud Bey, the socialite, "this thing is not ended, as you now believe. You and your lover are drawn together by a power too great for either of you to resist. With this force comes a menace for one or both of you—not death, but another kind of destruction, more subtle and deadly."

"Oh don't—*don't!*" cried Sylvia. She was standing now above the mystic. The black of her full skirt moved with her protesting hands. The sequins on her coat threw back the light from a thousand golden facets.

"I know all you say is true!" she rushed on. "Only isn't there some escape for us? We're not bad people. Our fault is that each one cares for the wrong person—J. L. loves me, I love Phil. I don't mind for myself, but I can't see those two hurt. What can I do? *Oh Ahnoud Bey,* tell me, isn't there a way out?"

Now, with the entreaties of this girl's voice cutting into his thoughts, Bey came out of the daze into which he had gone. Once more his eyes saw ordinary objects, chairs, curtains, the piano.

Again his ears heard the rumble of train wheels and the engine's long, thin whistle. Before him too, in the flesh, was Sylvia, the girl he had just been viewing mentally. In this vision she had been a thoughtless child, racing on to her doom. Now Bey saw that she was a woman fully aware of her own danger. She knew her struggle against the situation was in vain.

"Ahnoud Bey," she cried again, "tell me the way out of this muddle. Oh you are so wise. You know everything! Surely there's some way other than hurting those I love? Isn't there—oh isn't there?"

Sylvia was pouring out her heart. She was speaking long-accumulated thoughts, which so far she had not dared voice to anyone. She bent over and clutched Bey's wrists. She searched his face with frightened eyes—dark eyes, like those of a hunted fawn.

Ahnoud Bey looked into those interrogating eyes. In his own there was sympathy but no ray of hope for a lessening of Fate's verdict which he had so recently read out of the ether. He did not say a word, only lowered his lashes and drew his brows together ever so slightly.

"Oh." Sylvia breathed. She released his wrists and dropped down on the piano bench in a lifeless sort of way.

She crooked one arm on the gold and white piano and rested her head on the arm. In one hand she held a trifling, lace-trimmed kerchief. Her hair, falling on all that gold, was like brown bells whose chime was hushed.

Ahnoud could not bear to see the tremor of that dimpled chin and those red lips wordless. Sylvia's lips had always been ready with a neat *bon mot.*

Bey gripped the chair with his fingers. He

felt as though he had wounded some young and trusting thing. He condemned himself for telling this child what he actually saw and knew. Better, he thought, had he lied than told the truth where it would hurt so deeply.

The silence was heavy upon them. Outside night was cut in two by the speeding train. Out there lights were beginning to dot the darkness. They grew brighter and signaled the approach to a town, which marked the first important stop north of Sun City.

The engine was whistling in a more expectant tone than when only jungles were ahead. In the next coach could be heard the conductor calling, "Orange Park—three miles! Orange Park—three miles!"

Sylvia seemed deaf to this, but Ahnoud was sure he must offer some solution without delay. One thing was certain. She could not go back to Sun City tonight. Bey rose and came near her, lifting the dark head with his hands.

"Come on to New York with me," he said softly. "Maybe if you get away for awhile things will straighten out at home. And," he managed a smile and his eyes twinkled as they looked down on the pathetic little face, "do not believe my predictions too much. I'm really not so good at things of that sort. I make mistakes very often."

Sylvia brightened. This thought cheered her and the concern of a famous mentalist was flattering. She forgot her problem and drew herself up, smiling at Ahnoud Bey. In that tone of high anticipation, which was part of her individuality, she came back with, "Your invitation, sir, accepted. *What a thrill!* To New

York in a private car, with Ahnoud Bey and his magic piano!"

"And with a girl who is even cuter when she is blue," Ahnoud finished.

Again the conductor's voice called from the next coach. This time Sylvia jumped up, peering through the window.

"It's Orange Park!" she cried. "My goodness, we got here quickly!" The train slowed to a stop and with all the noise of arrested locomotion, voices without were hard to distinguish.

Sylvia parted the curtains and saw the stucco station, where a group of parked cars waited to meet the Special.

"Sylvia! Sylvia!" came the call from outside, while young Mrs. Adams powdered her nose evenly.

Hastily she reached the vestibule of the private car through a narrow door. She stood at the top of three iron steps. Down there were Johnny, Trudy, and the others—some in Johnny's roadster, some in the big maroon sedan.

"Come on, Sylvia!" they urged. They were running up to the steps now.

"Hurry baby, are you nuts?" yelled Johnny.

The engine began to puff convulsively and the conductor called his "All aboard!" but Sylvia still stood on the top step of the car. As the train moved off she called back loudly, "Look Johnny, I'm going on to New York. Goodbye—sorry—"

Johnny, thunderstruck, stared after the departing train, after the shimmer of gold sequins in all that darkness. As he watched Sylvia, he saw that she waved to him with one hand while the other was taken and held by a handsome man, who had just stepped into the vestibule of his private car.

LVII

To Reana Robinson the night was cold and lonely after the pleasant evening she had just enjoyed. The Bayside Roof had been colorful and the glow of friendship inspiring. Her guests had said goodbye to each other and departed. She was alone once more, this time without even Ahnoud.

Reana was missing him already, for the Egyptian was good company. He was intellectual and well informed. They had both traveled extensively. Ahnoud had never bored her one second. He had disturbed her at times, but his personality never palled.

That scene, for instance, when she had been with him in his bedroom for a short while, Reana could not understand now. She had longed to go on with him to New York and had torn herself away.

There was a sense of relief that he had gone. Reana could not account for her own reactions during that interval in the private car. She huddled into one corner of her sedan's rear seat, drawing the velvet cape around her.

"Drive through town and down Bayside Boulevard," she told the chauffeur. He swung the car in the opposite direction from which it was headed. They covered Sun City's wide avenues, almost deserted now at midnight.

From one street the car passed to another that intersected, and in doing so went down a winding cross lane. Here a spring bubbled from a rock grotto, where a narrow park began. It ran along the middle of the road, parting the street into two drives.

From the spring a stream tumbled over rocks and sand for a quarter mile or so, down to the sea. Around this stream was a wild garden of royal palms, banyan, and banana trees. They clustered so thickly that the benches at their trunks were hidden from sight of streets on either side.

As they drove by the park and those long banana leaves swayed in the night wind, Reana's heart was heavy. Jules had loved the seclusion of this place, declaring it to be the only thing left of natural beauty.

Courtney had been so interested in the banana trees, wondering if they bore fruit and when. He and Reana drank, now and then, from the spring. Jules remarked how rare it was to find fresh water bubbling up so close to the sea.

Tonight in the darkness Reana heard water rippling its way over the rocks. She recalled a mild afternoon when they sat on the bank and watched the busy crystal brook. There had not been many words to say that afternoon. Their contentment was too great. Jules had held her hand in his. They were both speechless, because happiness was about them like a spell they feared to break.

There had also been a moonlit night when they walked beside the stream. Moonbeams sifted through green foliage and tropical bushes talked in the breeze.

The path they followed was a rough one. In her high-heeled slippers, Reana stumbled and as they both laughed, Jules caught her in his arms. He kissed her again and again. Joy was still around them like a spangled web.

Now the night was raw and the wind from seaward disagreeable as Reana's car swept into Bayside Boulevard. She rolled up her open window and pulled the purple hood over her head. Perhaps it wasn't really cold, she thought, only winter in her heart. A great weariness, a sense of futility, came over her spirit like a fog, yet there was no fog on the Bay.

The moon shone hazily through a thin veiling of clouds but the night was fairly clear. Lights of the city advanced with a knife edged brilliance, as Reana's car entered the more crowded section of the shore Boulevard. The Bayside Hotel, which could be seen for blocks away, was now rising, an exotic, lighted monolith amid delicate bracery of palms and blooming vines.

"Stop at the Yacht Club," Reana told her

chauffeur. She left the car and tipped around one side of the Club, then across the pier. Boards were wet under her fragile slipper soles. She held up her cape and skirt to keep them from the dampness.

Reana walked as though she were feeling for her footing. She was preoccupied.

At the pier's end, she stopped and looked about her. On the left was her own yacht, the Robinson craft, sleek and distinguished, brasses gleaming and flags flying. The crew, she thought, must have retired early, as the ship's portholes were dark.

At her right, Reana saw the white masts and hold, adventurous lines of a schooner, the only one of its kind in the whole harbor.

For weeks the boat had ridden there on its moorings—a gallant thing tethered, an argosy awaiting the word to sail—but no word came. Through the long, balmy days only Chris sat on deck, smoking a pipe, his chair tilted against the cabin wall, his feet on the rail. Even his hands dared not swing the big pilot wheel.

Reana knew that wheel so well. The first day her hands had grasped it, Jules' strong ones were over hers. His head bent close to hers, his voice directing her every move. The wind had blown nicely and she had known the thrill of piloting a ship. Now, with Jules away, what a dead thing his schooner was—like a body without a soul, the laughter, vitality, joy of living, all gone.

How like his ship she was too—left here—moored to memories. As Jules had brought life to her the first time, many years ago so he had brought it once more—*and now—?*

Reana caught at her velvet hood with one hand, for the wind was blowing it back from her head and billowing the purple cape behind her.

She hesitated there, lonesome in the dim light that hung over her as the glow from a lamp behind gray silk. She skimmed the bay with her eyes and wished she could forget how there used to be diamonds on this same water every morning.

LVIII

Reana walked toward the schooner, gathering up the flowing purple, and, as one seeking some lost and precious thing, boarded Jules' ship. She stopped on the deck before Chris.

"May I go below, Chris?" Reana asked, indicating the nearby cabin door. Chris, taken aback, scrambled for words. He nearly fell over his chair, as he reached the door, held it open and responded. "A course, Miss—*a course*—"

Without a word, Reana caught her skirts closer, lowered her head and went down the companionway. Chris followed at a safe distance, his eyes open in wonderment, fastened upon her.

He snapped on another light in the cabin.

Reana glided about, absorbed in her own thoughts. In this strictly masculine room, she was femininity personified. The gold and purple of her illumined the plain furnishings.

While Chris stood at a distance, Reana went over to Courtney's reading corner, where a brass lamp burned beside books and a much worn arm chair. With one hand she touched the leather back of the chair, her fingers smoothing a place where Jules' head had rested many times. With a sigh, Reana stepped to the shelf, where a dozen books stood between bronze ends.

On those ends, the Golden Lady placed her hand. She laid her soft cheek on the volumes Jules loved and had read so often. Standing there, her eyes fell on a framed picture of Courtney.

Reana moved over to the desk, taking the leather frame in her hands. Holding it thus, she bent to it as one would to a child—lovingly—bent to that vivid likeness, with the twinkling brown eyes, flippant moustache, and disclaimed dimples. She said nothing, only drawing in her breath and setting the frame down gently on the desk.

Jules' smoking stand stood beside his easy chair. There was his favorite pipe, just as he had left it. Reana picked up the pipe, cupping her fingers around its weathered bowl. She held it a moment, then replaced it on the stand.

As she crossed to the cabin's large, center table, Chris saw that the light did queer things to that face in the velvet hood. Was it just the light, he pondered, that made Miss Robinson's eyes so big and tired looking—her cheeks sort of thin and drawn over her face bones?

She didn't see him—*she didn't*—an' blasted if there was a way to tell what she was thinkin'—the way she never spoke nor smiled.

Her shoulders were bent, too, as she sat down at the table, like it was almost a comfort to sit there, where Mr. Courtney, he always ate his meals. Chris fingered his own pipe and his brass jacket buttons, perplexed. He didn't know whether to go or stay.

She was a lady—oh yep, she was a lady all through—and he wanted to do the right thing, but what to say to ladies so sad they couldn't talk was past the sailor's knowing. The words got tangled—like that—comin' up from a guy's talking box.

"Miss," ventured Chris, at last, in a squeaky voice, "kin I—kin I—get you anything—mebbe a cup a coffee?"

Before he could finish, there was a loud "Meow" and Chris cursed under his breath. The black cat had spoken, and was now approaching the visitor in that sociable way that was the reason for the little vagabond's rise in life.

"Scat! *Scram!*" cried the sailor, clapping his hand behind the animal, but Reana dropped a hand to "Emerald Eyes," calling, "Kitty—"

"Miss, I'll take it." Chris offered, coming forward, but the kitten had jumped into Reana's lap. Finding the purple velvet to its liking, the cat went round and round, purring, until it curled into a black, furry ball.

Chris' thick hands fell uselessly at his sides. Reana smiled now—just a little—up into the rough, dumbfounded countenance and Chris thought, No wonder they got bad luck—*her* a likin' that black spook *too!*

However, the sailor did not betray his thoughts, but drew back into the shadows of the cabin, respectful of the lady's likes, unfortunate though they might be. As he did so another contretemps occurred.

Heretofore, the parrot had been marching up and down his perch, sharpening his bill and rolling his eyes, but not offering any samples of his risque vocabulary. Now, to Chris' keen dismay, Bobo began to sing in his cracked, uncanny tones—and of all songs:

Oh she was the queen of the Lime-
house nights
An' he an' ol' devil whut rode th' deep
Ol' black hearted devil he was—he
was—

"Shut up! *Shut up—you!*" yelled Chris. With the parrot angry but squenched, the sailor glanced at Reana. He meant to say, "Miss, excuse him, he's a roughneck!" but when he saw Reana laughing, the words died on his lips.

"He's never sung for me before," she said, "much as Jules tried to make him!"

Her delight was contagious, there was no doubt about it. The sharp-eyed Bobo seemed to know that a stage and an audience were his. He ruffled his green feathers defiantly in Chris' direction. With a throaty curse at the sailor, Bobo continued his song.

Oh he wasn't afraid of nuthin'—of
  nuthin'
But th' queen of Liverpool
An' he pawned his ship an' his ol' peg
  leg
To buy her jools—to buy th' queen
  jools—

"Shut up!" yelled Chris. This time he crossed the room and picked up a protesting Bobo, perch and all. The sailor carried both to the seclusion of the kitchen, where the bird might finish his ribald song without offending a lady.

When Chris returned, he stared hard at Reana. The velvet hood had fallen back from her head and her laugh was like pieces of silver falling all through the room.

Chris laughed too. He couldn't help it. Somehow, a fella caught fun like that and he was that glad to see her come to life. A while back, he thought she was going to die, or had already croaked and was a ghost. Either way she would have haunted the boat. No haunts now—this was a lot better.

Reana took out her kerchief and wiped tears of amusement from her eyes. At last she was relieved of that strain in her heart. She had a conviction that things would straighten out nicely once more. Sobering now, she asked the sailor in a low voice, "Chris, do you hear from him? Is he all right?"

Chris beamed, showing his gold teeth. "Sure Miss," he replied proudly, "Mr. Courtney, he's—he's fine."

Hearing that, Reana put the cat from her

lap, rose to her feet, and went toward the steps, saying, "Oh Chris, I'm glad, truly, *oh, truly I am—*"

As she ascended the staircase in all her gold and purple, Chris meditated about ladies —if sometimes they laughed when they wanted, just the worst way in the world, to cry?

LIX

The next Monday was a strenuous day for Jules Courtney, a day for matters connected with his work and one of bleak, February cold. To shake off worries of the office, Jules walked home through crowded New York streets just as wintry dusk was coming in and Manhattan was lighting up for the evening.

In every window Courtney saw valentines, red hearts, frilled lace, and sentimental verses.

Oh yes, he thought to himself, I've a date with Gloria Valentine's night. We'll go to a nightclub or hotel roof, dance, and eat mint candy hearts. I must kick in with a Valentine present for Gloria, too, but none of your red satin boxes of candy, the kind that gave ladies of the gay nineties heart palpitation. Now it must be a gift with a good cash-in value, as solace when the day comes for lovers to part.

Well, that was life—modern life—all graft and no permanence. At least Gloria was fun. She was a swell chaser of blue moods that hung around on snowy days, when somehow a fellow remembered about Sun City and a dream of true love.

With these thoughts uppermost in his mind, Courtney opened his apartment door. As he entered the living room he saw his friend John Kingston waiting there.

"Well, hello, you old airplane tinker!" cried Jules, his face brightening.

"Hello yourself, playboy!" shot back John, then with mock ridicule, "Say—are they still screwy enough over at the office to let you hang around there?" Jules laughed and pummeled his friend's shoulders.

"If they weren't, they wouldn't let you fool them all the time too," Courtney replied. "Where've you been, anyway? When I got back from Sun City you were at Lake Placid letting that little blonde number talk you into breaking your shins."

"Since then we've been playing hide and seek. When you were in the office, I was out." Jules called to Martin for coffee, knowing well that Kingston never accepted anything stronger.

"Oh, I've been running out of town a lot," John explained, "up to Rochester to see the folks now and then. When I'm in town, you know how it is—home at six, bathe, dress, out again at seven-thirty for an evening with the blonde fluff." Jules shook his head as Martin brought the coffee.

"At your age—" Courtney admonished John. "You should have been married long ago. You're the husband type."

"What about you?" Kingston asked. Jules merely shrugged and said bluntly; "Let's skip me, I'm poor copy."

They settled into wide armchairs near the large fireplace. John gulped his coffee with much enjoyment. Presently he set his cup down and took a trade paper from his pocket.

"Read about a ship you designed," he advised. "I'll hand it to you, Jules. I tested it. The smoothest job I've ever seen."

Courtney opened the paper and seemed flattered, but it was obvious to John that since they had been separated something had dulled his friend's keenness for planes. However, Jules read the article.

After that he and John entered into a discussion of altitudes, parts, and other things concerning the design of this particular ship and ships of the future. While Jules spoke with great knowledge and some spirit, John sensed an apathy behind Courtney's words.

"Maybe I shouldn't tell you, Jules," Kingston said, "but you don't look well. Aren't you a bit underweight?" John scanned Jules' face with critical eyes, then growing more personal "What happened to you in Sun City?"

"Plenty," Courtney replied. "I went down there and fell in love with my ex-wife."

"*What?*" John was astounded. "Not *Claire?* I saw someone in Sun City who resembled her, two years ago, but I thought she was dead."

Jules frowned and his mouth grew very grim. "So did I," he echoed moodily. "You see, she calls herself *Reana Robinson* and I didn't recognize her as Claire. Several times I thought she looked like Claire. Each time I dismissed the idea as impossible. Lord, what a jackass I was. But honestly, John, she has changed like anything."

"As pretty as ever?" Kingston queried. "You know she was just a kid when you married her. Very few women stay the same for seventeen years."

Courtney took a deep breath. "She has a graceful maturity, a worldy wisdom, of which Claire knew nothing. No woman in Sun City is more attractive."

"Well, what was the trouble? Why did you come back here—and alone?"

"Revenge, my dear John, as I told you. She still counts me an enemy because of my youthful jealousies."

"Well," John scolded, "you were crazy to disbelieve that child's love and loyalty. You know I took her part at the time. So she has lived to take you for a ride?"

Jules stood up and put a log on the fire. He buffed his hands one on the other and bowed to Kingston. "Yours—with a sufficiently red face," he admitted, then resuming his seat and reaching for a cigarette, "but honestly, John, what am I to do?"

"Still love her?" Kingston asked laconically.

"Do you think I'd be telling you all this if I didn't?" Jules words were sharp, his voice rasping.

"Then," John elevated his feet to a tapestry-covered stool and centered his gaze on an orginal Reynolds above the fireplace, "go back and tell her you're sorry. Ask her to forget and forgive. Women love to do it—makes them feel so charitable."

Jules scowled over this advice. "That's very simple, but listen, she's under the spell of the famous mentalist Ahnoud Bey. I know that sounds like the wildest flight of fancy, but it's true. Bey gave Reana a gilded piano he had used so long in his act."

John sat up, his eyes on Jules. "Oh, *he did?* I was in Sun City a couple of years ago and saw Bey do his stuff at the Palm Club. That must have been the night Claire met him. I saw her as I have told you, but wasn't sure it was she. You know, it was all so long ago—your marriage to her in France. Bey was a knockout this night and she went for him in a big way. So he gave her that piano. *Well I'll be—*"

"See here," Jules interrupted, "this isn't a bit of gossip for you to roll under your tongue. It's about the woman I love and have loved, as you know, for more than seventeen years.

"She's controlled by this Egyptian wizard. She moves at his command, says what he'd have her say. I know, *believe me!* Her very soul's not her own. I'm convinced she sent me away because he told her to do it."

John stood up and baked himself in front of the fire. "Okay," he hinted, "Ahnoud Bey opens at a club five blocks from here tonight. If I were you, I'd go over and punch him in the nose."

Before Jules could reply, the phone at his

elbow rang and he answered it absently with a curt, "Yes—this is Courtney."

"Mr. Courtney," said the operator, "please hold the line. Mr. Adams of Sun City is calling you."

"What in the world does J. L. Adams want with me?" asked Jules, turning to Kingston.

"He's got a pretty wife, Sylvia, hasn't he?" John reminded.

"Yeah," Courtney nodded, "a pretty big handful," then into the phone, "yes, this is he—yes, Jim, this is Jules. "What can I do for you?"

James L. Adams of Sun City Rotarians and Chamber of Commerce, he who built causeways and promoted subdivisions, old J. L., who was worth much in money and more in prestige, was greatly disturbed.

His voice held a tension—a repressed scream—that was seldom in the confident tones of Sun City's most popular citizen. J. L. was cluthing at Courtney over the wire, grabbing at a friend with the frenzy of a drowning man. Jules knit his brows deeper and tried to get in a word.

"So she's here now, with Ahnoud Bey?" Courtney repeated. "Is that it? Are you sure?"

"Mmm," John speculated," Sylvia trouble. I thought so."

"And you want me," Jules continued, "To go over to Bey's place and get her? Well, good heavens, Adams, you've got your nerve—asking me of all people, when you *must know*—"

Again through the receiver came the pleadings of a doting husband. Sylvia was just a child! Of course she didn't go of her won accord! She was hypnotized! It was his, Jim

Adams' fault, always taken up with business, neglecting her. If Jules could only help J. L. He was nearly ill—and wasn't Jules a friend? It was just the thing to ask of a pal.

"Please—*please*—get her and send her home," Adams implored. "Put her on a plane." Courtney groaned, held his head, and made a motion of despair to John.

"Listen here," Jules argued, "you're asking a helluva lot of me, but if I can find the kid and send her home, I will. But just a minute," as J. L. began offering Courtney the Sun City Bank and Desdena's choicest lots as compensation, "I'm not going a foot toward Bey's place till you confirm this talk with a telegram and *have it delivered.*

"I'm not going to rescue anyone's wife unless I have something authorizing me as rescuer. Time? Oh can't you wait? She'll keep, you know. The 'gram'll be here in half an hour and I have to eat my dinner. All right, take it or leave it. Okay, just send the wire and I'll do all I can. Don't mention it."

Jules sat back in his chair and set the phone on its rest. He gave his watch a swift glance and looked around for Martin.

"Hurry dinner," he called. "We have to leave here in an hour."

"Yes sir," replied the valet from the dining room, "it will be ready in a few minutes.

"*We?*" asked John. "Who said I was going?"

"Want to?" queried Jules, his brows uplifted.

"You know darn well I do. That kid's a

friend of mine—she and her old man, J. L. What's the lowdown on this thing, anyhow? Why doesn't Jim fly here and get her himself?"

Jules laughed shortly. "He's so crazy he couldn't find the way to the airport right now. He didn't know till this afternoon where she was. Her crowd knew but wouldn't tell. Today Sylvia sent J. L. a wire from New York. At last her gang of young friends talked, told what they had seen, that Sylvia left Sun City in Bey's private car last Saturday night.

"Jim sounded like a lunatic," Courtney went on, "but from what I gather, Sylvia, the little fool, just went to Ahnoud Bey's train with a party to see him off. When Jim came home from one of his trips down state, she was gone. He couldn't find out a thing until tonight when Sylvia's wire came, telling J. L., quite naively, that she had gone on a trip to New York with Bey."

John whistled softly. "That fellow!" he ejaculated. "What the devil does he do to women? Poor old J. L. I bet he turned Sun City upside down, wiring and phoning to find his Baby. But Jules, this isn't like Sylvia. I know she has her boy friends and all that, right under Jim's nose, but to slap him in the face with anything this open is strange."

"Damned strange," cut in Jules, "if you didn't know Ahnoud Bey. Sylvia no doubt just went skylarking into his private car, on a dare maybe. Bey decided he wanted her to stay, to go with him. He made up her mind for her."

"Aw baloney!" hooted John. "Do you really believe that sassafras?"

"I'm telling you," Jules snapped out, then sat staring into the fire, a mean expression around his mouth.

Reana was down there, with Bey's piano in her house. Bey was a mental white slaver and had Reana in his power! It was true! Everyone in Sun City knew it. That was why she hadn't married. She wouldn't marry this Egyptian, so of course no other man on earth could get to first base with her!

Jules had seen it all. He had heard with his own ears, Bey speaking to Reana while he was on the Bayside Hotel balcony and she at Villa Robinson. It was no coincidence, Courtney knew now, that Claire had gone out to the lighthouse that same day, when the "sun was high."

There was a spell on her piano, too Jules was certain of that. Three times since returning to New York he had heard the music of the Golden Keys.

The first time was the morning after he arrived. On the second occasion, at the office, his head suddenly grew dizzy. He staggered over to open a window and listened to the Golden Keys again, this time as though at a great distance.

Last of all, he had been waiting for a friend, in the lobby of a Park Avenue apartment hotel, the evening before. As Jules sat there, a strange faintness had seized him. A cold sweat had come out on his forehead as he heard that music—insinuating and in a minor key.

"You know where Bey's apartment is, don't

you, Jules?" Kingston was asking, and Courtney sat up in horror as John continued, "It's a twelve-room duplex at——Park Avenue. The paper says the mystic arrived there last evening."

LX

White was the motif of Ahnoud Bey's metropolitan apartment—if not of his life—a white in exciting simplicity, modern as a Gershwin rhapsody.

In the large living room one would feel dull and drab unless polished to a hard, bright gloss—a little slow, unless geared to the orchidaceous crowd that slid easily into such a setting.

Sylvia was from such a crowd, self-fashioned to fit such interiors. Because this apartment represented some sort of goal for which she had been striving, young Mrs. Adams was happy over her attainment. While Ahnoud had been intriguing in his private car at the Sun City railroad yards, she now considered him a person with perfect taste. Four stars to Sylvia —for achievement.

"And now, the world shut out," Bey said pointedly. Friends had come and gone. They laughed over cocktails, swapped a few taut lines of wisecracks, wondered secretly about Sylvia, and trailed out. The women held Bey's hands as they said goodbye, mentioning dates of teas and dinners.

Sylvia reclined on a chaise longue in a corner near the piano. Her eyes rested on the baby grand, a model of classic ivory, nothing black but the small keys. Ahnoud's fingers were going over those keys as he viewed her with half-closed eyes. His playing was soft and sweet, but to Sylvia a nameless melody. In that, as Bey knew, lay its power. It was merely a subtle background.

Under frosted lights Sylvia saw the room in all its angles, squares, and triangles of eggshells against black, eggshell against silver. The rugs alone were worth a fortune, white fur, eight of them on a shiny midnight floor.

Complementary to all this was Ahnoud at the piano, his tall figure bending slightly over the keyboard. His hair was black as his conservative tuxedo jacket, the gardenia in his lapel white as the piano. Through all this black and white came the lure of indigo eyes upon Sylvia, asking her without words.

She moved uncomfortably. Her mind was pulling back from Bey's request. After all, she had only come with him on a passing impulse. He had been a gentleman—for two nights—as there were extra bedrooms on his private car and here also.

The Egyptian had ushered her into one of the latter last night, kissed her hand, and left her to the attention of a French maid. Now, Sylvia thought uneasily, What about tonight?

Bey's music drifted off into silence. He puffed a cigarette and through its smoke regarded Sylvia's beauty—a dark beauty, accentuated by a dress the shade of yellow narcissus. Ahnoud's eyes dwelt on the jonquil frock, with its short swing skirt and sleeves, full like blossoms. Sylvia had thinned a little, he thought. Her hair was like waved jet against the white leather chair.

"Faker," Sylvia said at last, grasping at the light and half contemptuous as a safety first move, "why weren't you a concert pianist?"

"Indolence," Bey replied with a self-condemning grimace. He crossed over to light Sylvia's cigarette. As he did so, he sat down beside her on the chaise longue. "Suppose I had been?" he asked. "Would you have taken me seriously?"

"Oh, very," Sylvia answered rather bravely in the face of all that was so dangerously near. "I'd have worn my ermine coat to your concerts and listened with the greatest awe. If I had met you I'd have been tongue tied." Bey was amused at the picture she painted.

"And you would have carried away my autographed programme, *only*—" he said. Sylvia shook her head sadly.

"Only that—a slip of paper—and not the famous mystic in his private car. How lucky for me, Ahnoud, that you were lazy."

"Lucky for me too," Bey replied. "Imagine missing the pleasure I enjoy tonight, as I see you in that spring flower dress." Sylvia smoothed her hand over the yellow silk.

"Like it?" she asked. Then, confiding, "It was an awful price, but so new—just ahead of spring."

"You went shopping today, without money?" Bey inquired.

"Of course," she answered. "Your car took me to the stores where I have accounts. I got a lot of ribbing for wearing an evening dress and sequin coat—just blowing in that way from Sun City. I told them I had come from a party on the private car of New York's most eligible bachelor."

Ahnoud bowed his head in response to this bouquet, then asked; "And are you coming over to hear that bachelor play his piano in public tonight?"

"Certainly," Sylvia replied. "You don't go on until late, do you?"

"Just before midnight."

"Then I can rest longer before I dress," Sylvia said. "I shopped all day, Ahnoud, and I'm worn out."

"But happy," he added. "I see those lights back in your eyes. They were not dancing two nights ago in Sun City."

Sylvia smiled on Bey gratefully now. "It was good of you to bring me," she murmured. "I feel so much better. New York is wonderful! I can close my eyes now and think of all the lovely things I saw today!"

"And what of the two you left in Sun City?" Bey asked ever so gently.

"I sent Daddy a wire. It'll be all right with him. And as for Phil—" Sylvia knit her brows as though trying to call to mind a face, a voice. After the whirl of today Pelham seemed a dim figure, way back somewhere. Ahnoud grasped this thought and caught her up at once, "You might be able to forget Phil, if you stay here awhile. There is so much to see, *and do*—"

Before Bey could finish speaking, the doorbell rang three times. Sylvia and Ahnoud heard the butler's steps in the apartment foyer, then his voice stating, "But Mr. Bey cannot see anyone tonight."

Another voice brought Ahnoud to his feet. "Sorry, but we're going to see Bey if he's here!" Again came the protesting voice of the butler. Ahnoud stood very still in the center of his living room. He heard that strong step—the one that Reana had claimed haunted her house—then the white-panelled door was flung open and Jules Courtney walked in.

"I know you and you know me," he said to Bey, "and it isn't pleasant to meet each other. I'm only here tonight because a friend begged me to come."

Sylvia too had risen from the chaise longue. Wondering what Jules could want here, she went forward to greet him.

"Hello Mr. Courtney—hello John," she said, and Kingston replied; "Hello honey—we've come to take you home."

"Yep," agreed Jules, "get your things, you're going with us."

Ahnoud was quick to object. "Mrs. Adams is my guest," he said flatly. "Who has given you authority to take her away?"

"The best authority in he world—" Jules shot back "her husband, only of course you wouldn't understand that."

He turned to Sylvia and went on. "J. L. phoned me, baby. He's losing his mind over your running away. Read this wire if you want proof he's worried."

Sylvia reached for the sheet in Courtney's hand. She read the delirious message, but as she glanced up at John and Jules, Ahnoud stepped to her side. He slipped an arm round the flowerlike waist.

"Chérie," he asked, very low, "do you *want* to go home?" The girl seemed in a quandary, but Courtney stood firm, drew in his breath, then said in a voice that was iron on granite, "*Sylvia*, get your things—we're not going without you." Young Mrs. Adams snapped from her irresolution. She stepped away from Bey's encircling arm, handing the wire back to Jules.

"Thanks, Mr. Courtney," she said. "I'll be ready to go in a few minutes." Jules' frown melted a bit. He patted Sylvia's hand as he took the telegram.

"That's right, kid," he encouraged. "Make it snappy. Jim wants you home." Sylvia skipped across the living room, her heels tapping the floor and sinking into the white fur of soft rugs, her dress a spring jonquil amid all the severity of modernistic black and white.

LXI

With Sylvia gone, a strained silence fell about the three men. Ahnoud Bey believed Jules' visit was inspired by a motive other than the rescue of the errant Mrs. Adams. Bey measured Jules Courtney with his eyes and then said. "Won't you gentleman have seats while you're waiting?"

"No thanks," replied Courtney. "I don't think she'll be long." Then, an aside to John, "How about going in there and helping Sylvia get her things together?"

"Okay—and delighted," Kingston answered. Courtney stood there with a thousand thoughts going through his mind. The words now scorching his tongue he felt could no longer remain unspoken.

As the two men faced each other alone for

the first time, there was fear, one of the other. Ahnoud knew that here was the one he dreaded most of all the world. Here was the man who held a place that no one else could fill in Reana's heart and life. Bey knew there was a hidden part of Reana's soul in which she lived to love only Jules Courtney. She cherished that youthful devotion of yesterday and matched it with the loyalty of today's love.

Ahnoud Bey might never be allowed into this secluded world. All his mental power and personal appeal had failed, so far, to break through. Therefore he feared Jules and in fearing hated him too. Now Bey's words were spiked with sarcasm as he remarked. "You seem anxious to take Mrs. Adams away, and who can question your altruistic motives? It is a bit strange, though, that a man must come, a knight in armor as it were, to save another man's wife from my clutches, when *his own is*—"

"Be careful you leave Claire out of this!" Jules cut in angrily. At this, Ahnoud seemed puzzled. He feigned a blank stare.

"Claire?" he asked, and Courtney said hastily,

"You know who she is, as well as I do. Now they call her *Reana Robinson!*" Ahnoud summoned a smile, but it was a faint one.

"Oh, of course," he assured, "the most beautiful woman in Sun City—the *Golden Lady!*" Somehow, there was a tone of ownership lurking under that brief observation. This made Jules clench his hands, square his shoulders, and rush on rudely, "The most unfortunate woman in Sun City! May God have mercy on her soul! She's dominated by the damnedest wizard that ever crawled up from the Black Hole of Calcutta!"

That was the gauntlet in Bey's face. The words that Jules uttered so clearly seemed to fling mud across the swank of white chairs, rugs, and divans. Ahnoud's eyes flashed with cold fury.

"You're merely excusing your own failure, Mr. Courtney," he replied. "Twice you have been unable to hold Reana's love."

"That's a lie," Jules shot back, and you know it. Claire's loved me all through the years. I found that out this winter. Why, I hold a heart you'd give this joint, your private car, and all your fame to possess. You'll never get that heart—that love—not while there's a star in the sky! No, women aren't made that way!

"You control her mind, all right, Ahnoud Bey—I'll grant you that—else why did she pull that 'Black Farewell' on me? She obeyed, poor kid, but she didn't *want* to tell me goodbye! It broke her heart! You can't do anything about *that!*"

There was a moment of suspense, broken only by the tinkle of Sylvia's laughter and the interweaving of her voice with John's as they came from the bedroom. Sylvia was handing Kingston several suit boxes, but Ahnoud Bey saw no one except the man before him. The mystic's aplomb was badly punctured and he thrashed out recklessly, "Perhaps I have used every power I know! Perhaps I have held Reana in the only way I can, but the fact remains—she is mine! I will stop at nothing to keep her for myself." The Egyptian was so transported by his own emotion that he gazed off, beyond Jules, forgetting for the time that Courtney was there.

"This madness about her is not a new thing," Bey continued. "I have loved Reana for years—seventeen years—since the first day I saw her, as Claire, in France."

Sylvia and John came across the room now. Kingston saw Jules start forward, calling out, "What are you talking about? She was married to me seventeen years ago in France!"

Kingston came closer and whispered, "Give him an uppercut, buddy!" Sylvia stood without a word, her eyes scarcely blinking as she listened.

"Of course you were married to her," Ahnoud was saying in a scatching sort of revelation, "but I was your neighbor at Faubourg St. André, where I had a summer villa. I was only a twenty-two-year-old neighbor, to be sure, but wise enough to know when I saw a woman and loved her. Reana was that woman!"

"Damn you!" cried Jules. "Damn you—for the thief you are! And you were the kindly neighbor who started talk of Claire's disloyalty to me? You filthy-minded Moslem, with that pile of dough left you by a cutthroat Turk, you created the doubt that grew into something worse, that destroyed my home?"

Ahnoud was more collected now. He disregarded these heaped insults, for his confession seemed to have relieved a pressure under which he had lived for some time. He answered coolly. "Yes, I used influence, money, everything at my command to gain my end.

With the news of your divorce, I knew I had been successful." Sylvia gasped.

Courtney stood with murder in his heart and eyes fixed on Bey. By tremendous self-control alone, Jules refrained from grabbing at Ahnoud's throat as Bey added further details.

"I followed Reana around the world for many years. I was near her, though she did not know it. Until her sorrow was lessened and she came to me voluntarily, I never met her—nor did I care to do so. Now there is no one living who can take her from me."

"Oh gee!" cried Sylvia, taking Kingston's arm. "Let's go, John, I'm scared! This is awful!"

"Wait baby," said John, "we're going to fight this thing out."

Jules heard this but stood by quietly. The thought of murder had already left his sane, law-abiding mind, but he felt stunned with the weight of a world falling upon him.

"No," he said at last decisively, "there's not going to be any fight." Courtney looked into that handsome face before him and the fact of Ahnoud Bey's mystical ability was now impressed on Jules.

Ahnoud's blue eyes seemed to dilate as Jules stared into them. That magnetic and powerful mind behind the eyes appeared to rise like a huge and indomitable monster, filling the whole room.

Sylvia, John, and Jules, all were as dwarfs before this mind, but Courtney was not afraid. He was badly baffled but he could not fear this demon. Courage came to Jules from somewhere and he spoke with calm deliberation.

"No, John, it's useless to knock Ahnoud Bey down, black his eye, or put him out for half an hour. Fists are no good here, John, nor are words. We must find another power—*a greater power*—to fight this monster of the mind!"

LXII

When Jules Courtney left Bey's apartment, his one desire was for solitude. The events of the past that Ahnoud had disclosed weighed upon Jules' heart so heavily he could not share his feeling even with John, the faithful friend.

"Take Sylvia to the apartment, will you?" Jules requested as he and John stood under the sidewalk canopy. Sylvia was already inside the Courtney Cadillac. John was slow in joining her. He scanned his friend's face, watching keenly the distracted eyes and bloodless lips.

"Come on with us," Kingston urged, taking Jules' arm, "we'll talk it all over at your place." Courtney buttoned his overcoat and pulled on his gloves, but made no move toward the car.

"I want to be alone for awhile," he replied huskily, then after a pause, in a clearer tone,

"Take care of Sylvia until I can see her back South. Phone for reservations on the next plane or train to Sun City. If you can, come along too. I will join you in about half an hour. Okay?"

"Okay," said John, dropping his hand reluctantly from Jules' arm. As Kingston took a seat beside Sylvia and the car door banged, shutting them into warm comfort, Jules went down the cold street.

Courtney walked along Park Avenue toward town. From the corners of his eyes he saw snow, banked at the sidewalk's edge—a snow which had fallen that morning. Of its frozen grayness and the knife like wind from East River, he was only half aware.

The lights ahead were brilliant against a stormy night. Buildings were pyramidal checkerboards of illumination. They rose into the sky, losing tower after tower in the murky clouds, lowering hourly.

Jules cut through to Fifth Avenue and, heading south, plunged into the theater crowd, Broadway bound. The packed busses, that mass of polished cars, crawling cautiously stopping at the red light, a cop's shrill whistle and upflung hand at street intersections, all made Courtney feel better somehow.

There was a good humored crowd of folks hurrying by. He was alone, yet, not in solitude, for he was one with the heart of New York's millions. How many troubles—riddles—are behind the faces passing him? Even the countless advantages, which this greatest of cities offered, might not solve those stubborn riddles.

Everything was here—everything the

modern world needed; yet in the Metropolis people died, spirits were broken, and love was lost. Walking the Avenue tonight Jules felt that there were those who sought, as he did, a power to straighten out that which the material world had sadly tangled.

No, he was not alone, for as he met oncoming faces—hundreds of them—Jules Courtney heard the echo of his own heart's voice, "How? Why? How—why—*if only*—but how—"

Jules walked on, crossing streets in the thirties, still on the Avenue but now deaf to its staccato scream of auto horns, its hurrying feet, and medley of voices. For the first time the import of Ahnoud Bey's admissions was coming to Jules with extreme clarity.

That monster of the mind! How it had filled the living room! He, Courtney, was as powerless against it tonight as he had been seventeen years ago! Returning to Sun City was all very well, even talking it out with Claire, but could Jules hope for anything more?

It was hard to believe Bey's recent statements. Jules recalled that villa in Faubourg St. André. Its grounds adjoined the place he and Claire called home. At that nearby villa were two foreign cars and turbanned servants. It was generally known as the summer house of an Egyptian lad whose grandfather was wealthy. A woman's dream comes true and a man's becomes his nightmares in the land of enchantment.

At the time Jules seldom saw his young neighbor, nor was Courtney curious about the boy. Never would Jules have linked Ahnoud

Bey, the famous mystic, with that foliage-hidden villa in Faubourg St. André.

Courtney's memory brought up an evening long ago, an evening before he and Claire parted. Things were going badly and she said to him, "Jules, someday you will know that I am true, that you have misjudged me." It was all so clear to him now.

He could see her face as it was then—a pure face, framed in curls that came to her shoulders. He had been blind with unreasoning jealousy, a jealousy he had never understood, as it was alien to his nature. At last he knew that he and little Claire had been helpless when the mind of a mystic drove them apart.

Jules sighed, frowned, and stuffed his hands into his overcoat pockets as he picked his way through the crowd. Seventeen years were lost—the best years of all—when he and Claire could have been together. That chance at happiness was gone forever.

Ahead of him Courtney seemed to see the children they might have had, a boy of twelve, a girl of ten, and another tiny tot. If Claire ever forgave, what then? What about the black magic that governed her every move?

It was for Jules Courtney to find a weapon stronger than that fiendish influence, but where, in the matter-of-fact city of New York, among people who scoffed at such things—where, in a world that cured tangibles only with tangibles?

Jules stopped in the crowd at an intersection, for the green light was on. As he stood with half a hundred other pedestrians, Courtney's thoughts still ran in the same channel.

He was sure that Claire loved him. It was his job to reclaim her, but how? What power was greater than that of Ahnoud Bey's mind?

With his brain aching, Jules turned his face from the wind. In doing so his eyes rested on the sign across the Avenue—the sign that read, "29th, St." Then there came to Jules Courtney's mind, as clearly as though spoken, the words, "And around the corner there is a Little Church."

"Oh," he said as though in answer, "of course." Courtney pushed through the mass of people and swung to the left into 29th Street. He walked rapidly until he reached an iron fence, enclosing a quaint churchyard of old New York.

Jules slowed his pace and paused on the walkway, looking about him. The yard glistened with deep, untouched snow. Across this white serenity oblongs of varicolored light lay—the holy light from strained-glass windows.

Courtney felt that he had dropped back almost a century. This stillness, this gracious atmosphere, was not of his day and time. Modern New York had gone off to roar its mad vortex in some distant sphere. Little old New York was here, in the shadow of Gothic arches, under ornamented cupola, and within the confines of an elaborate iron fence.

Jules felt himself to be a rude interloper. He stood viewing that era when carriages stopped at the gate and ladies in hoopskirts alighted to enter the church that was theirs.

He removed his hat and remained a bit longer. After all, he thought, the Little Church Around The Corner was ageless. It stood as a symbol of both happiness and consolation. It was not merely a landmark of yesterday, but a living and vital part of New York's life today. The great and the near great had come here—thousands to be married, many for that last of all services.

Jules crossed himself and entered on tiptoe, walking down the middle aisle.

He went almost to the altar. In the echoing silence he could hear his own breathing. Those stained-glass panels, he reflected, were memorials—not to saints of another age but erring mortals like himself. The windows were dedicated to people who had attended the Little Church, maybe not regularly, but when very happy or, more likely, when life was handing out deals too hard to take without help.

As they had loved the Church Around The Corner, so Courtney loved it. As they had come to it, seeking a real friend, so Jules had come tonight. As they had believed with simple faith in a good and infinite Power, so Jules Courtney at last believed.

He slipped into the nearest pew and knelt, his head humbly bowed, his hand on a closed prayer book. No use to open it, he thought. Those formal words were not Jules' solace now. The petition in his heart was one of desperate appeal. He was asking aid to overcome the powers of darkness—asking that a marriage be saved, here in a church where so many marriages were made.

How must he word that prayer? What could he say that would be just right? Fragments of the early Mass ritual he had known as a boy came back to Courtney, then lines from the Litany—lines he had heard sweetly chanted when this church was filled with people. Many times he had sung them in unison with the congregation. Now they were on his lips with a newer, deeper meaning, "*'Oh Lord, have mercy upon us—'*"

Jules locked his fingers around the prayer book and, the sacred silence of the church about him, finished with all the passion of a sorrowing heart in his voice; "*'And from this evil deliver us'—deliver Claire and me—*"

LXIII

They were letting down the awnings in front of Nick's café against the glare of afternoon sunshine when James L. Adams entered the restaurant. He stopped at the cigar counter behind which the portly Nick sat, straightening and replenishing his supply of "Garcias," "Havana Queens," and "Port Tampas."

"Hello," greeted the Greek, waving a hand to Adams, "you look happy."

"I am, Nick," J. L. returned. "My Baby's coming home this afternoon."

"Oh—you find out where she go," asked Nick as he flirted a handful of cigars in midair. Adams laughed till his bay window shook.

"You bet I did. I turned this town upside down and nearly drove the girls at the phone exchange crazy. I've sent them wristwatches for working so hard."

"What train she comin' on?" Nicholas asked again.

"From New York—bad weather held up the planes," J. L. replied, and the Greek added, looking at the big Western Union clock on the wall, "In forty minutes it be here."

"Yeah," acknowledged Jim, "and I haven't had any lunch. Rustle up some food for me, Nick, will you—and hurry?"

Nick left the cigar boxes in disarray and waddled from behind the counter. "Sure," he promised, starting for the kitchen, "I get it for you myself."

Adams left the cigar counter, moving toward the empty tables. At one of them in a far corner he saw Phil Pelham.

"Well hello," called J. L., crossing the room in his "greeter" manner. "I won't have to eat by myself, after all." Phil trumped up a smile and motioned Jim to the chair opposite him.

"Join me," he said, "in a cup of coffee." Adams sat down and centered his eyes on the boy.

"How's the automobile business? Working you too hard?" Phil shrugged and drank his Java.

"That's what I think sometimes. How's the Point Crystal job?"

"Fine!" J. L. spoke with pride and enthusiasm. "That's going to be the swellest hotel south of the Bayside. This crew has worked like Trojans. *And hot?* Look at the way I'm burned!" Pelham smiled at the florid face before him.

"Indian red," he observed, "but why stay down there, Jim?"

"To see the job done right," Adams confided under his breath.

"Can't Wallace, your crew manager, do that?" Phil asked again.

"Phooey!" J. L. waved a fat hand disdainfully. "Wallace is just a boy. He comes to me with everything. If I'm not there, why it's just *too bad.*"

Nick came with Adams' dinner and Jim hungrily eyed the man-sized plate of roast beef and mashed potatoes set before him.

"Thanks, Nick," he said. "That's real food!" As the Greek went back to his cigar counter, J. L. began to demolish the hunks of beef, talking, as he did so, between mouthfuls.

"By the way," he said at last. "I'm meeting Baby's train in half an hour. She's coming home from New York. Mr. Courtney's bringing her." Phil felt a stab through his heart and he was seized with self-consciousness.

"Oh," he answered, "the prodigal daughter returns?" The jibe completely went over Adams' half-bald cranium, however. J. L. continued obtusely, "Coming down to the train?"

"No," Phil responded, "I fancy she might not care to see me." Jim deposited a forkful of mashed potatoes in his wide mouth, clamped his lips shut, and, staring at Phil, questioned him with upraised eyebrows.

"We had a quarrel the day she went away," Pelham said, his eyes on the coffee cup.

J. L. swallowed his food, washed it down with a quick gulp of coffee, then advised in a "Now this settles it" tone, "Make it up, *make it up!* You kids are always fussing."

As his words burst forth in that blunt way, Phil's eyes arrested J. L. Adams. Pelham's face was haggard and Jim saw for the first time those tightly compressed young lips, holding back words of fire Phil didn't wish to speak. J. L. knew boys—he knew human nature, for that matter. Now his round face sobered as he laid down the active fork, asking, "Anything wrong, Phil?"

Pelham was quick to reply, but he frowned and fingered his spoon uncertainly. "It's about Sylvia, J. L. She and I aren't kids anymore. We're two people who love each other. That's why we quarrel, I suppose. That's why she went away. I won't see her again, I promise you that."

J. L. was speechless for a second or two, then he laughed harshly.

"See here, Phil," he said, "what sort of cockeyed double talk is this you're handing me?"

Pelham shook his head. "I wish it were only a gag," he answered. "Anyone else would have seen it all long ago, J. L. What about the many times you've come home and found me at your house, the rides Sylvia and I have taken alone in the Duesy, and all those nights we danced for hours at the Palm Club? Such things don't happen, they are planned. And you? Maybe you just pretended not to see, to *know*.

Jim placed his knife beside the fork. He

knew that this was one lunch he would not finish. Adams could not doubt the truth back of Pelham's words.

J. L.'s first sensation was one of anger—a primitive rage that had its roots in the burn of an inferiority complex. His face turned a deeper red and he sat glowering at Pelham. Sylvia *would* love Phil. He was young, curly headed, and a swell dancer. Pelham was made even more glamorous by taking the wheel of a car Jim Adams' money had bought.

Phil had found time to play around with Sylvia, too. He kept up with popular songs and styles. Of course she liked all that—young girls always did.

As he continued to think, his fury cooled and another viewpoint came to him. He was in his late forties and Sylvia was not far past twenty. He was fat and partially bald—just a businessman. Beyond telling her how pretty she was as he pinched her chin, what line had he, J. L., ever talked to Sylvia? Nothing but stuff about his own business!

He needn't have worked so hard, nor stayed away on jobs so long. He had always given Sylvia gobs of money. If she bought Pelham because she was lonely, whose fault was it?

"I guess I've been a dumb egg, Phil," Adams said at last. "Sylvia's young and you're young. I trusted you two—like a fool." Phil bent his head, covering his eyes with one hand.

"That's the worst of it, J. L. You didn't see what was going on. That made us miserable. We felt like thieves in the night. *Now—*" He stopped short, pressing his fingertips in the fair hair just above his forehead. Finally he managed, "I think I'll sell my business and leave town. Staying here would be too hard. I can't take Sylvia from you, although I love her more than anything on earth." Jim swallowed hard and the furrows in his sunburned brow deepened as he asked in a whisper, "And what about *Sylvia*—does she love you that way?"

Phil raised his head, looked Adams straight in the eye, and nodded. J. L. sat back in his chair. All at once his rotund person seemed to go slack and age. The sparkle left his small blue eyes and the spirit left him too.

"Oh, I see," he remarked, looking at Phil awhile, then beyond him.

As Jim Adams sank into a wordless sort of lethargy and Phil wandered in a dismal swamp of depression, there was the diverting sound of voices up front. Mrs. Nicholas, topped by a petal-pink hat, had come bustling in and was making her presence noisily known. J. L. at once came back to earth. Pulling himself together, he consulted the clock.

"*Gollee!*" he cried. "I've only ten minutes to meet that train!" With a great effort he rose from his chair, scraping it on the tiles. Phil rose also and they walked up to the cigar counter as though nothing had happened.

"Hello Nella!" J. L. addressed Mrs. Nicholas in his friendly boom. "You look sweet as a picture, under that pink cartwheel!" Adams paid his check and Nella, eyeing Phil, asked, "Mr. Adams, your wife—the dear little girl—she has gone away?" J. L. hastened toward the door.

"She's due back from New York in ten

minutes," he called. "I gotta rush to meet the train. So long!" As he banged the screen door behind him, Nella turned to Phil.

"And you too—are in a hurry?"

"I'm in no mood for work," Pelham commented. "I think I'll let the agency run itself this afternoon." Nick, behind the counter, shook his head, drew his black beetle brows close, and spoke to his wife.

"He work too hard, Nella," he shouted, as though he thought that by talking louder his English would be more intelligible.

"Yes," Mrs. Nicholas replied, looking at Pelham meaningly, "he need more play—get out in sunshine more."

Phil, with as much politeness as he could summon, which was not enough to make Nick suspicious, made his farewells and left the restaurant.

He took the opposite direction from that in which J. L. had gone. Pelham had not walked two blocks before a panting Mrs. Nicholas came running up beside him.

"Wait," she begged, her hand catching the dove gray of his polo shirt. Phil jumped, then laughed. As he stood still, Nella's face flushed and one hand, heavy with ten carats of diamonds, was pressed against her ample bosom.

"For so long I do not see you," she complained. "Couldn't we—*couldn't we*—take a ride? Round the corner in a parking lot I have left the Cord." Nella's dark eyes glowed as Phil met them, asserting, "Why not? It's a lovely afternoon."

As they rounded the corner, Nella clutching his hard, brown forearm and talking with a funny arrangement of English words, Phil, thinking of Sylvia, only heard one thing Mrs. Nicholas said, "I see you—last time—at the lighthouse. With you was Mrs. Adams and I hear—from good source—of the quarrel and I am the cause innocent?"

The afternoon sun was baking down on the parking lot. It threw reflections from Phil's light hair. He was tall and lordly in well-cut linen slacks, his broad shoulders under the cotton mesh of a polo shirt.

They stood waiting for the car to come and Pelham, meeting Nella's last question, drew his mouth into that one-sided smile. "As Shakespeare says, '*Trifles light as air,*' " this with an amused glance at Nella's generous dimensions, " '*are to the jealous, confirmation strong as proofs of holy writ—*' " Phil slid under the wheel of the Cord and shifted gear with a familiar hand.

"Oh!" cried Nella, clasping her hands, "say something from *Romeo and Juliet*. Something romantic—*please!*"

Pelham only smiled in response as he swung the car out the cross street and into a wide avenue that ran down to the Bay. Royal palms lined the street here and buildings were colored stucco with gay tiled roofs.

Bougainvillea and oleander bloomed in the Municipal Park, and ahead the street ended in a blue band of sea and sky. All this was lost on Phil, for as he piloted the Cord he heard only one thing—a whistle of the New York train, ten minutes late.

LXIV

That hour was kaleidoscopic for Jim Adams. Later he could only remember scenes, faces, swiftly working together and apart—hot sunlight, jewels, to buy back Sylvia's love. In the pattern was J. L. himself, his heart in a hundred jagged parts.

There was the café, Nick's white-tiled café, and Phil's harried face. Who could doubt his suffering? After this came the golden Boulevard—miles of pavement to J. L., though really but two blocks, and well-known faces he met with a forced smile.

Again the glittering pieces moved. His own words rang on his ears like echoes from a sounding board.

"Something for Baby. Yes—jewelry—perfume—*Sylvia loves them.*"

More street scenes seemingly unrolled before J. L. for miles, as space one might seek to cover in a nightmare. At last there was a railroad station, and into the kaleidoscope came Sylvia's face.

She opened the box J. L. handed her and squealed over Corday's eighty-dollar perfume wardrobe. She opened the small box inside and raved over a barrel cocktail ring with myriad and expensive stones for her little finger.

Jules Courtney laughed, quoting, "These Foolish Things," and tossed off Jim's fervent thanks with a casual "Oh don't mention it."

In bewilderment, J. L. saw his own chauffeur waiting. Adams had walked while the black boy had driven the Duesenberg down to meet "Miss Sylvia."

Again there was a whirl and shift, as scintillating pieces met and fell away. The Bayside Hotel, where they dropped Jules, merged into the Boulevard out to Desdena. Sylvia's face came in once more, her eyes dancing over the barrel ring on her left tiny finger. She removed a smart hat and Phil would have noticed that the sun played badminton in her curls. J. L. merely mopped perspiration from his red brow, assuring, "It's swell to have you home, Baby!"

That sounded so hollow and silly to Adams. He had said it a dozen times since Sylvia stepped from the train.

And now they were in the cool of their own living room. Sylvia sent her boxes up by Carrie Lou. She smoked a cigarette and chattered about New York.

Jim sat heavily in a deep chair. He had never felt so bald and gauche, so lacking in fine phrases with which to garnish Sylvia's beauty. His easy manner, ready quips, and loud laugh were gone. The thick shoulders were bent. Strong, short fingers clasped and unclasped restlessly.

Finally Sylvia noticed this constraint, this unaccustomed brooding. She jammed her smoke in the ashtray and focused keen eyes on her husband.

"What's the matter, J. L.?" she asked, and he answered slowly, "Phil Pelham, Baby. We just had a talk in Nick's café. I've been an old fool, kid, not to see that you and he—" Sylvia's face paled and her voice became toneless.

"Oh," she gasped, "so he told you." Her inflection fell, making it a sort of announcement rather than a question. J. L. lowered his eyes to the deeply piled oriental rug.

"It's natural, honey," he went on, "that you love someone closer to your own age. You never had much of a good time, I guess. You were so young when we married. I—I've always wanted you to be happy, and I still do." He glanced up at her and tried to smile.

"If you want a divorce, Baby, why I'll still count myself lucky. I've had you for four grand years—"

"Daddy!" cried Sylvia and she was across the room, standing by her husband's chair. "You couldn't let me go, could you? Don't you love me any more than that?" Her dark eyes were too much for J. L. He lost himself in them. They were a brown velvet sea and he foundered helplessly. His hands were shaking as he grasped Sylvia's slim flingers.

"Of course I love you and I can't let you

go! I don't care about Phil—" he cried, "—only don't leave me. Stay here, Sylvia, in the home I built for you. I don't want it without you. Just give me, maybe, a little of your love—what you can spare." Sylvia dropped down on J. L.'s knees and put her arms round his neck.

"Daddy," she cried again, "I couldn't leave you. I love you for all you've done for me, all you've given me. No one but you would have loved me when I was a poor little beauty contest winner, with one nice dress and a bathing suit."

Her eyes fell on the large divan opposite. She could envision Phil now as he slept there so late that afternoon. Had all that passed between them occurred just because she was rich enough to buy a Duesenberg?

"I'll bet Phil wouldn't have even seen me when you picked me up," she declared. "*He* wouldn't have taken me out of a ten-cent store and a hell of a home. Oh Daddy, I'm grateful! You're all I've got that's real! *I'm not leaving you—ever!*"

Sylvia hugged the strong, sun-ridged neck in her arm's crook and her curls were gentle against J. L.'s bald head. That softness was sweet to him, like the perfume she wore—some of the prettily bottled Corday—sweet like the firmly curved warmth of her body that his arm encircled.

"Okay Baby," he said. "That's settled and now let's be happy and forget it. And as to Phil—" Sylvia's eyes sobered and her heart did a flip-flop.

"That's all washed up, Pop." She cut in.

J. L. caught the feeling in her words. This was not indifference but a sort of anger that could blaze to love again at any opportunity.

They sat there quietly for a while. Outside the pines were standing tall and stenciled on a red-gold western sky. J. L. didn't see the flaming sunset, though he was gazing out nearby windows. The kaleidoscope of the afternoon had stopped turning. Before him there was now a fixed but unlovely pattern. It was called "Compromise."

Jim Adams knew the meaning of good sportsmanship, how to shake hands with the man who had defeated him. He also knew how to make terms with a competitor who sought to ruin him.

"Can't we talk it all over," J. L. always asked, "like two friends. Let's not get sore—but give and take and arrive at some sort of compromise."

Life often asked a man to make concessions, Jim knew that too. Sylvia was his and he was not going to give her up. At the same time he could not stop the love affair between her and Phil. It was just one of those things that might pass with time. Nobody was to blame—and nobody must suffer.

"Baby," Adams said, cutting into quiet, "Phil will still be our friend." After another pause, J. L. went on in a brisker tone, "Did you know Buena Vista was going to have a dance casino? We have the order for concrete and iron work. I've got to run down there tomorrow evening and see the job started right.

"I'm lucky—business is good, *so good*—"

He laughed shortly, "that I won't be home much—" He stroked his chin, then concluded significantly, "Just weekends, I guess, are about all I'll have to spend in Sun City from now on—yep, Baby—*just weekends.*"

LXV

That same twilight came imperceptibly upon Villa Robinson. Reana walked in her garden where sweet peas grew higher than her head. This was one of those still hours when the Bay lay very shallow at ebbtide. Palms were motionless in the rosy afterglow of western skies and cars whipped down the highway with an odd infrequency.

The air might have been that of June, not February, sometimes chilly in Sun City. The atmosphere was down soft and feather light. Sifting through was a dainty fragrance of sweet peas.

"Enchantment," sighed Reana as she walked over the thick green of her lawn. Stately and white gowned, she moved before the wall of giant sweet peas.

The climbing flowers had covered a seven-foot fence and their owner viewed them proudly. For Reana they grew, as did the slick-leaved jasmine bushes, yellow roses, butterfly lilies, and oleander trees bordering the estate. By unfailing patience and undying love for her adopted home that had brought her health and pleasure, Reana created beauty around her.

Because she appreciated this life in the southland, peace, more permanent than this hour, was sure to be hers. Today, she thought as she strolled along, had brought more of that peace—that long-lost joy—than she had known for many years. Perhaps it was just spring at her fingertips and the sweet peas in full bloom.

"Enchantment?" she asked herself, then shook her head. No—that meant Ahnoud Bey—and where was he? Not until this moment had she thought of him, today—nor yesterday. For months he had been forever in her mind, and now Ahnoud had suddenly been whisked off into a never-never land. Somehow the magnet of his attraction was removed. Indeed he might never have existed, so utterly was he gone from her mind.

Silly, Reana decided, then laughing went on a step or two. There she stopped abruptly and her heart went wild. Swinging round, she cried out, "Oh darling, oh Jules, I'm here—in the garden!"

She had answered before she knew—answered that one voice for her in the world—that strong, forthright voice!

"Claire!" he had called, and Claire had replied, for Reana was the girl of 1920 who loved a soldier boy. Now she was lifting her white and filmy skirts and running across the lawn to meet him.

Jules came toward her, his arms outflung. Instantly she was in them, her own arms around him, her cheek on his shoulder. This was so spontaneous, not what they had planned—clever speeches, the light manner. There were no words, in fact, but Jules' husky, "My sweetheart!"

There was the cascading ripple of golden curls and Claire against him in certain surrender, certain forgiveness. The wall of sweet peas became chestnut trees. It was "April in Paris" and they were young again. No years came between—no futile searching—for Claire was his once more and the power of a wizard broken. Thank God!

They walked through the garden until darkness brought out stars. The Golden Lady's laugh was tinkling crystal, her hair fallen moonlight. They walked hand in hand, Jules and Reana, and the misunderstanding of nearly twenty years was completely cleared.

As Jules told of his meeting with Ahnoud Bey, a light dawned upon Reana. She was serious momentarily. Her laughter stilled and hatred filled her heart.

"Had I known what Ahnoud was," she said, "I should never have called him my friend. To think that he was the neighbor in Faubourg St. André who caused all our misery! Oh Jules, it's incredible that he trailed me all those years, that he didn't care I was broken hearted, and found me here, in Sun City. It's cruel, fantastic, and yet—"

"And yet, is right," cut in Courtney. "Bey is nothing but a black Arab. He's had you under one of the most sinister mental influences anyone ever ran across. See here, Claire—" Jules turned her face to his own "—didn't Ahnoud Bey force you to send me away? When you went to the lighthouse that morning, had you planned to give me that 'Black Farewell'?" Reana looked him full in the eyes.

"No, Jules, the last thing I wanted was to have you go," she admitted. "I loved you, sweetheart, as I did seventeen years ago—" She dropped her voice to that low level, "and —as I do now. Trust me, Jules, *oh trust me—*"

"Of course I do!" Jules replied. "Only forgive me for the past, dear. Perhaps a mystic had me nutty—anyway, I was a blind young cad and I'm sorry for it." He closed his arms round Reana, his fingers gone gentle under her chin. He kissed her many times, as though making up for all the wasted years.

Shadows of banyan trees were upon them and stardust was drifting down. That Southern Night, feared of Ahnoud Bey, had opened again to engulf Reana.

There was dinner for two that night at Villa Robinson on the blue mirror-top table with pink candles and a center bowl of roses, as Jules observed, "to make it really summer."

"It seems a miracle," he went on, "leaving snow and ice in New York, and waking to find—" He gestured indefinitely, for Jules was never one to use hyperbole. He may have felt the lift and wonder of it all, but conversation beyond the commonplace was difficult.

"Shall we call it lost April?" asked Reana

softly, leaning forward, a cut-glass goblet between her fingers. Jules' eyes took in the loveliness of that face. There was the smooth gold of hair under a band of sapphires. The light in those violet eyes was half veiled by sweeping lashes.

The delicate lines of Reana's features were finer than a sculptor's alabaster model. Jules dwelt on the picture of beauty before him in the candlelight. Thankfully he raised his glass and said, "Let's call it April regained."

At nine the next morning, in the pretentious county court house, Jules Courtney bought, for the second time in his life, a marriage license. The names were still the same, only this time the text was in English, where previously it had been in French. With that, the news was out in Sun City and Reana's phone began ringing without cessation until noon.

"Yes, we're marrying at twelve," she said a hundred times, and, "No, not in a church but at the Mayor's office. You remember I promised Tommy to let him perform the ceremony."

To one who knew, she added, "We're marrying at the City Hall and then going down to see Father Couperin, who has the mission church at San Rafael. He married us the first time. In our faith, you know, Jules and I are still man and wife."

The majority, Reana cordially invited, "Yes—come down and see us off. We're going on the yacht to San Rafael for a short honeymoon. Yes, *do come.*"

Here, Reana dropped the phone. "*Made-*

leine!" she called. "Madeleine—I'm going mad! I can't get dressed! Take the calls and I'll pack my bags. If I try to speak to one more person I shall have hysterics!"

"Yes, Madame," consoled the flustered maid. "Your suitcases I have already packed. They are in the car." Again the phone buzzed. Reana asked from the next room, "Madeleine, has Mr. Courtney come?" When the maid replied in the affirmative, Reana murmured incoherently. Tearing off her negligée, she slipped into the blue dress and slippers, half crying aloud, "Oh, it's worse the second time—oh it *is* worse, *really!*"

The man-about-town mayor, Tommy Quinn, thought he had never seen Reana Robinson more beautiful than in the broad noonday light.

"This is a pleasure," he said, beaming upon the couple and trying to be dignified. "Yes—this is a pleasure, a great honor, and a promise fulfilled." He paused beside his mahogany desk. Sunshine came through the long windows and in this golden light Reana stood again to take her vows with Jules.

The ceremony was soon over and Courtney was kissing his bride. Tommy kissed Reana too and laughed to hide his feelings, for Quinn's hopeless devotion to the Golden Lady was well-known in Sun City.

The mayor followed Reana and Jules out to the City Hall's marble steps. Tommy patted the groom on his back, saying, "God bless you," as they went away.

The town looked particularly colorful as the Courtneys drove down to the Yacht Club.

The sunshine had never seemed so glorious, the sky so deep a turquoise.

"It will be swell," Jules said with an effort at composure, "seeing Father Couperin again. I'm sure he won't know me—a middle-aged man. I was only twenty, *before*—"

"And I only sixteen, but Father Couperin has an extraordinary memory. He has not forgotten us, *I* know that."

As Reana spoke, she and Jules neared the Yacht Club, left their car, and met friends who came down to congratulate the couple. Sylvia was the first one to reach Reana, to take her hand and say, "I'm so happy for you." Proffering a small but costly present, Sylvia stepped back into the waiting Duesenberg, thus avoiding Phil, who hovered in the background.

"I'm heart broken," mourned Ted Maxime, taking Jules and Reana by the hands, "but even so, I offer my very best wishes!"

"I knew you'd come back," Phil said to Jules. "Some things have to be. I do hope you both have every blessing." Pelham, like Sylvia, gave Reana a tiny but precious gift.

The Golden Lady's arms were filled with presents as she and Courtney walked the length of the dock, as folks gathered and went along with them. There was a lot of joking and fun, until the band inside the Yacht Club began to play "Oh Promise Me."

The classic strains drifted through open windows, down to the end of the pier from which the Robinson yacht was leaving. Reana and Jules stood on deck, waving goodbye.

Reana was overcome by tears of happiness. Her day of joy had come so soon and so unexpectedly. Madeleine knew how she felt—of them all, Madeleine knew best. There was the maid now, close to the boat! She twisted a kerchief in her fingers, crying a little, while Chris offered crude consolation in her ear.

The yacht began to move. The motor throbbed as the band still played "Oh Promise Me." Reana was caught in the intoxication of it all—the wind from the south, changing colors and mingling voices, then she heard Jules saying, "Throw your bouquet, Claire." She found herself leaning over the rail, her fingers clasping the stems of orchids and lilies.

"Madeleine, catch!" Reana called and flung the corsage into the hands of her faithful maid.

Madeleine caught the flowers, then she cried and laughed by turns, as Chris put a brotherly arm about her.

The ship went out and out until "Oh Promise Me" was lost on the air and the well-wishers seemed to be more midgets. Jules circled Reana with one arm as they stood at the yacht's rail. They waved to Madeleine, to friends on the dock, and to Sun City, white and green against the world's bluest sky.

LXVI

A picture of happy people is not always good for the lonely heart. This picture of Jules and Reana lingered in Phil's mind for the balance of the day.

Pelham's thoughts were on anything but cars during the afternoon hours. When the secretary came in at five-thirty and found Phil idling over important papers, she knew something was wrong.

"Mr. Pelham," she asked, "you wanted these put in the mail this afternoon?" Phil looked up at the girl, then down at the papers, which he had not even seen.

"Oh, yes," he answered in a dazed way, "so I did." He glanced at his watch. "Too late now, though. This can wait until tomorrow." The secretary was somewhat taken aback by Phil's neglect of a big order.

"Is that all for today, Mr. Pelham?"

"Yes—you may go now, Miss Nelson."

When the girl had gone, Phil bent his head to his palms, elbows on the desk. There he sat for some time, his eyes closed and a tumult in his mind. The outer office was soon empty. Pelham heard his employees drive or walk off. The building grew very quiet, but Phil's heart was like a beating drum.

At last he lifted his head, running his fingers through his hair. He sat back, slumped in the chair, his eyes dull and red from many sleepless nights. Lances of sunset gold through Venetian blinds met those weary eyes but lent no optimism to the wearier brain behind them.

Pelham was worn out with treading, round and round, one circle of thought. He must leave Sun City, go to Connecticut or New York. It was better for him to be out of Sylvia's sight. How, though, could he leave this prosperity, this diverting life?

How could he leave his friends, the best in the world? No, running away was cowardly. He should be strong. He should stay in Sun City and give up Sylvia as a sweetheart, only passing a word with her now and then.

That was his resolution. He had been sure of it until today at noon when Sylvia deliberately shunned him at the Yacht Club. Now Pelham's plan was all smashed to smithereens. He was beginning that circle in his mind, again going round and round, only coming to one conclusion. He wanted to see Sylvia, to hold her in his arms while moonlight fell about them. Only, that couldn't be. It was all wet—now that J. L. knew.

Phil left his desk and his office, passing through the large showroom where a dozen new cars stood for all Sun City to admire. When he reached the street, it was seven o'clock and the witchery of a star-strewn night was over the town. A pencil of light, the Boulevard ran straight down to the waterfront.

Pelham drew his car up before the Yacht Club where he had some business to finish. He was out on the sidewalk before he saw Jim Adams approaching.

"Hello Phil," J. L. said, as though nothing had happened and he stopped as to talk.

"Hello Jim," Phil replied, regaining his poise, "where're you going with all those bundles of Patty's sandwichs?"

"Umm," he mused, "doesn't she make good ones? I'm going to Buena Vista on a job and you know about the eateries there. But Phil, I'm glad I have a chance to tell you this. Last night the new Eighty Club met and I put your name up for membership. It's been approved, all rightie, as the other fellows wanted you in, too."

"Well J. L.!" exclaimed Phil. "That was nice of you! Naturally I'm honored. Who doesn't want to be asked to join the exclusive Eighty?" Pelham was delighted and somewhat embarrassed. He stood smiling, but with the hot blood mounting his cheeks.

This was his first meeting with Adams since that terrible day in Nick's café. The memory of that afternoon rose before them now and there was a moment of strained silence. Finally with an effort Phil broke it.

"What are you building at Buena Vista, Jim?" he asked merely by way of courtesy.

"A dance hall on the Pier," J. L. advised, "and you know me—off to see the job done to a turn." He pointed toward his parked car, then started that way.

"I'm driving down tonight and won't be back till—oh—*Saturday afternoon* anyway. The next three days I'll be tied there tight and fast, getting the boys broken to a new job."

With that, Adams climbed into his car and drove away. Phil stood in the Club walkway, repeating only those words that, ironically enough, J. L. must have intended the boy to clutch and hold—"till—Saturday afternoon"!

Dinner at eight usually meant white or black tie with tails or tux for Phil, but tonight it was botany flannels, in a new shade of hydrangea blue. This was dressing for an evening of "not dressing," or rather it was the *dernier cri* in sports clothes, which graced Sun City's yacht decks on a moonlit night.

Phil's melancholy mood probably enhanced his charm, for he was the most popular man at the fish dinner on the harbor's biggest ship.

"He's a dream in that blue suit," one of the girls whispered to another on deck after dinner.

"And get a load of that smile," the other one came back through the haze of her cigarette smoke.

Much to their disappointment, however, Phil left the party early. It was hardly midnight when he entered his room at the Bayside Hotel. He dropped on the side of his bed without switching on the light.

A deadly fatigue was upon him and also an old suffering, though not physical pain. Pelham had tried to outwork and outplay his yearning for Sylvia. Now here he was, still wanting her more than anything on earth, still needing the sight, the touch of her. There was J. L., too, putting Phil's name up for membership in the Eighty Club

He had coveted such a distinction since a Sun City branch of the national organization had been formed some months before. An Eighty Club emblem on any office wall drew more business confidence. The Club stationery alone was a gilt-edged reference. Now, cad that Pelham felt himself to be, how could he join in good faith—how be a member, alongside the man whose wife he loved hopelessly?

Phil groaned and dropped face down on the bed, his arms hugging the pillow. As he lay there he thought how such attacks of utter weariness had tormented him lately.

The past few weeks had been hectic, for Pelham was trying to outrun the Sylvia fever. He was making plenty of money and spending it at a pretty swift rate. At that, his agency topped all others in the state for actual sales figures.

Within another ten years, barring drastic reverses, Phil could retire and live snugly the rest of his life. Why jeopardize this for the sake of a little Arkansas beauty contest winner who kept her husband, whether or no?

"Why the hell," Phil asked himself, "don't I stop this rush of work and play? I should go off to some quiet port for a vacation, catch up on sleep, eat wholesome meals, and get my mind out of this rut."

He couldn't reason clearly. Funny how one raced about and, when a quiet time like this came, the brain played numb and foggy. Pelham's only two thoughts now were how comfy the bed felt to tired bones and how, with admission to the Eighty Club, complete could be the conquest of Sun City.

Phil closed his eyes to the weird light of a waning moon, but a salt breeze drifted through the window near his bed and cooled his face.

He sighed deeply and hugged the pillow tighter, his fingers in its linen folds. Days of torture had passed since he left Sylvia at the lighthouse! She had taken her spiteful trip to New York with Ahnoud Bey. Now she and Pelham were not even friends, but dodged one another in every conceivable way!

What to do? Phil's head ached and that dance music from upstairs seemed to come and go—*come and go.* There might have been lead plates on his eyelids and cotton in his brain! Just rest was what he needed, and that smell of salt air.

Oh Sylvia, *Sylvia*, look at the moon! We date the moon every time, you and I. Forget Mrs. Nicholas. It was nothing, I swear! Oh Sylvia! *Sylvia!*

LXVII

Phil was calling that name aloud—calling it with a sob in his throat, agony in his heart—as he awoke, sitting bolt upright in bed. He was in a chill, a cold sweat. His staring eyes scarcely credited peaceful moonlight and a starlit sky.

Phil jumped to his feet and stood swaying by the window. That was better, although he was a little weak in the knees and cold along the spine. His hands touched the net curtain, billowing in salt breezes, then his fingers gripped the window sill, smooth and firm beneath his faltering grasp.

Who could live with such sorrow all through a lifetime? Not he, who loved Sylvia more than life itself! Nothing mattered without her. He had known that a long time but kept it from his thoughts.

The truth in his own heart had him at last. Phil was almost glad. With returning strength, he crossed to the dresser in the half darkness.

Pelham pulled out a small drawer and his fingers closed over a key. He weighed it up and down, his lips parted, blue eyes alight.

Phil reached for a doorknob, swung open the hall door, blinked at lights above him, and walked toward the elevator.

To Pelham, the moments that took him to Sylvia in actuality were excruciatingly slow. Never had the Boulevard to Desdena seemed so long. Never was the pink archway, entrance to the subdivision, so welcome.

Once under it, once down the avenue where lanterns shone, Phil's impatience cooled. Now he steered around the flower-bordered circle and up into a driveway that took him straight to Sylvia's sun parlor.

On the tiled steps Pelham stopped, for the stillness of the small hours was about him. Birds, wakened by the car, were chirping sleepily from hidden boughs of the magnolia tree. Perfume of jasmine drifted on the breeze across Phil's face. In that same breeze green leaves of bushes surrounding the sun parlor tapped a tune on the window panes.

"Paradise," whispered Pelham as he unlatched the outer door to the little sun room and stood there among Sylvia's blue and aluminum furnishings. Tonight it was a moon room, he thought, with thin streaks of light on table and chairs. Near them was the house door—to which he held a key.

Phil unlocked the door and stepped inside the hallway that seemed somehow empty. The steps were carpeted and his feet made no sound as he took them rapidly.

Gently Phil opened the door and as gently closed it behind him, standing as he did so in the loveliest of bedrooms. Orchid and yellow and the cut glass of perfume bottles were reflected in long mirrors. Moonbeams filtered in through two side windows.

"Phil!" cried Sylvia. He heard her voice and saw her as she sat up in the wide bed with her tangled curls, one hand outflung to him, a little bracelet on its wrist.

"Oh, darling," answered Phil, crossing the room and sitting on the side of Sylvia's bed, "darling girl!" The words died as he seemed to see Sylvia for the first time.

His hands touched her shoulders, then held them in a caressing grasp. They were so smooth under his touch. The white fullness of her breast, crossed by sheer lace and satin, lifted and fell with her quick breathing.

Her perfume was about him and her lips raised to his—Sylvia's lips, red and moist from sleep. Phil kissed them deeply, then turned Sylvia into his arms, holding her cradled there, dark curls on the blue flannel of his coat.

He held her closer as he looked off through a moonlit window. In passionate assurance that his fears were false, his hand slid down to feel Sylvia's heart beating.

"Oh Phil, I wanted to die with you gone."

"Never think of such a thing again," Phil warned. "Never misunderstand me again. We'll not let ourselves in for any more of this sort of suffering, Sylvia. J. L. knows that—else why does he go off and leave you this way?"

"He's doing it on purpose," Sylvia said. "He knows everything and—and—doesn't care, so long as I don't leave him."

"Nor do I care—anymore," Phil continued a bit grimly. "The militant New England conscience is laid, my dear, for all time. It was killed tonight by the stuff that dreams are made of. Connecticut is a dead word. I can never go back—*now*."

Phil had a great sense of peace as he sat there with Sylvia against his heart. The tumult was subdued, the pain of separation assuaged, and the cycle of indecision gone from his brain. His eyes, though, were strangely bleak as he stared out the window and up to the stars.

This was all that was real to him now, he thought rather wistfully. Lost were the snows of Connecticut—"the forest primeval"—lost those stern as bedrock ideals. Pelham saw things clearly when it was too late.

This was destruction, the Fate that had been at his heels for two years. It was the destruction of yielding to an unwise desire, the blight of stolen happiness, and betrayal of a friend.

With a sigh Phil turned from the window and lowered his eyes to Sylvia.

"I don't know what you are," he said, "perhaps you're a drug or wine—or the spirit of forbidden things. I only know that I love you and want you. My denials along that line, even to myself, are ended."

Sylvia did not speak. She put an arm around Phil's neck as he lifted her face to his and kissed her again.

They were in the shadows now. The moon had moved its narrow bars of light across the room. A breeze was still bringing the sad and heady perfume of jasmine from flowering bushes outside. A mockingbird waked and began the sleepy round of his song.

How inexpressibly sweet, Phil thought, was that love song of the southland! It made him feel more completely lost, until Sylvia reminded, "That's Peter—the dickey bird!"

"You call every one Peter—season after season," Phil corrected, as he listened to the night singer's melody. Sylvia listened too, as tropical magic hung about them. But for Pelham, favored of the gods, New England ideals and "the forest primeval" were very, very far away.

LXVIII

Sun City's winter season was closing with a skyrocket splendor that seldom marked its opening. An exodus from resorts farther south taxed the town's capacity during the fleeting weeks of early spring.

By the end of March, year-round residents knew, all would be quiet, with room for them aplenty. The hint ahead of summer's long term meant shekels to spare left in coffers of hotels, restaurants, and shops.

At the moment, however, the onrush was chaotic. Sun City was a riot of spring flowers in the most outrageous colors. Wind whipped up foam-edged waves in the Bay.

The chaos was entirely human. There was an endless shifting of faces—gay, suntanned ones and those walnut or lobster red. They came from planes, cars, and trains, giving Sun City the grand rush, then moving on northward dutifully, if reluctantly.

The crowding was profitable only from a money angle. Who in that jumble could form acquaintance with anyone else? Who could really get to know Sun City, in the dash of a two-day stopover?

Mad March, the natives called it. They laughed secretly, as they kept going on about that legend about bobcats living in the jungle. These cats, it was said, prowled out in late spring. They knew the year-rounders, as dogs know their masters, but woe to the hapless tourist who lingered into April. The first rambling bobcat would get him, natives solemnly warned.

This was a standing joke among those who lived permanently in Sun City. The story was not without foundation. There were bobcats in the jungle and tourists always left before April.

Now, for the latter, March was sifting away like precious sand in an hourglass. No one felt that last snatch at a passing season more than the phone girls at the Bayside Hotel.

An extra crew worked during March—a corps hand picked for efficiency. In their glass-enclosed room one side the registery desk, the girls plugged in and out the switchboard incessantly.

"Bayside Hotel. . . . He's checked out."

"Bayside Hotel. . . . He has not arrived yet. . . . Yes, we are expecting him."

Such statements were reiterated until they droned into a sort of sing song, intensified by the professional monotone of the girls' voices. Then came the unusual to liven a day's routine.

"Bayside Hotel . . . Just a minute, I will see if he has come . . . Yes, Mr. Maxime, Ahnoud Bey is here . . . Shall I connect you with his suite?"

Up in 423, the phone buzzed a couple of times before Deane answered it for Ahnoud.

"Hello Ted," he said and turned to Bey, who made a let-me-off, this-is-too-much gesture.

"What's that?" the Bayside manager asked. "Yes, Ahnoud's here—yep, but he's on a vacation. . . . Oh you want him to play tonight at the Club? Sure, I'll ask him." Bey scowled and shook his head.

"He says no," Deana continued. "Well, yes, you might persuade him if you come over here . . . Okay—we'll be looking for you."

Deane put down the phone.

"How did he know I was here?" Bey inquired. The manager shrugged.

"My dear boy, Ted has a sixth sense about celebrities. He travels hand in hand with reporters." Ahnoud sighed and reached for a cigarette.

"The last people I want to see in my frame of mind," he observed darkly. "I had anticipated at least a few days privacy." Deane sat down in a deep chair opposite the mystic.

"I'm sorry," he said, "but you can't travel in a private car, under your famous name, if you want to have peace." Bey's eyes were expressionless.

"Peace!" he echoed. "As if there could be

any for me—now! You cannot know how I felt when I heard the news of Reana Robinson's marriage."

"But you said you knew when it happened."

"I suppose," Ahnoud ventured, "I still hoped that what I knew was untrue. You dashed that hope but made me the better mentalist—as if that mattered."

"You remember, Ahnoud, when we talked one night in your room here, some weeks ago? I told you about Courtney and Reana and I felt the affair would end in marriage.

"Later I learned that it was quite a story. They had been married and divorced, about seventeen years ago. Evidently they never ceased to care for each other. Strange, isn't it—or do you know that too?"

Bey's face grew enigmatic. His eyes went back under the sweep of dark lashes. He flicked ashes into a tray with much deliberation. When he spoke, his voice was purposely toneless, his glance averted from Deane.

"Yes," he admitted, "I know—about that story."

LXIX

There was knock on the door. Deane opened it and chipper Ted pushed in with two reporters at his heels.

"Hello Deane, hello Ahnoud!" Maxime slapped the Bayside's dignified manager on the shoulder, then crossed the room to where Bey still sat.

"This—" Ted said to the others, "is the answer to a club owner's prayer. With the season slipping through my fingers and crowds sated with ordinary New York talent, here I find the greatest attraction in the entertainment world—player of the Golden Keys piano!" Pausing, Maxime took an arm of either reporter.

"Ahnoud," Ted explained, "here's Joe from

the *Chronicle* and Eddie from the *Times*. Boys, *do your stuff*." The reporters shot fast questions, with Maxime promoting a performance on the part of Ahnoud Bey. Deane unhappily tried to protect his guest.

"Ted, I'm here on a flying trip," Bey replied, rising as though in self-defense. "Mike didn't know I came."

"Nuts to Mike," Ted cut in, discounting Ahnoud's manager with a wave of the hand. "You don't have to sign a thing. Play for me one night, two, as many as you like."

"I've told you I cannot play *one night*," Bey reproved.

Again the reporters began; "Mr. Bey, who is your favorite modern composer? What type of woman do you prefer?"

"Mr. Bey, is it true that the original Golden Keys piano was destroyed by fire before you ever came to America?"

Mr. Bey, would you like to live year-round in Sun City?" Ahnoud was bewildered, his poise going fast, his nerves on edge from loss of sleep. He glanced at one man then the other, while Ted persisted in a loud voice, "Four thousand dollars, Ahnoud, for one night! That's what I'll give you. Didn't you bring your piano?"

"Yes," the disconcerted Egyptian replied, "but I shan't take it off the car."

"Mr. Bey, is it true you were a good friend of the Duke of Windsor and once gave a command performance for him when he was Prince of Wales?"

"Six thousand five hundred, Ahnoud,"

called Ted. "We'll get it in the afternoon papers. The place'll be jammed tonight!" Ahnoud again looked round in search of escape.

"No, *no*," he cried, "I can't play tonight—nor any night! I came here to rest, to get away from it all!"

"Please boys," admonished Deane, coming forward, a troubled expression on his brow. "Make your visit short. You see he's in no mood to talk." The reporters looked at their watches.

"Okay, Mr. Deane," they agreed. "We're rushing this story against a deadline. Just one more question." They returned to their persecuted celebrity.

"Mr. Bey, have you any statement to make regarding the recent marriage of your ex-fiancée, Reana Robinson?"

Ahnoud grew rigid, his face pale, as that name seemed to stun him visibly. He stared past the reporters as he replied in a subdued voice, "No—no statement." He swung on his heel, crossed the room, and entered his bedroom. He shut the door firmly and pointedly.

"Oh—so that's it!" Ted cried, setting his jaw and shaking his head. "How dumb I am! But wait, I'll fix everything, boys. You'll have your story."

With his strong, sure steps, Maxime reached Bey's bedroom door, opened it, and went into the room. Ahnoud was standing by a front window.

"I'm sorry kid," Ted said, closing the door and then grasping the mystic's hand. "Look here," Maxime added, "I forgot about you and Reana. It must slay you to have her married. I could spank those boys for asking that last question. I'm really sorry, kid."

Somehow this sympathy broke Ahnoud Bey up, so that he was unable to reply. Because he was world famous, few were able to come near him in this hour when his heart—or was it his pride—lay crushed. There were few, he thought, who failed to gape at the piano-playing wizard, blind to the unhappy man beyond.

Trying to conceal the anguish in his eyes, Ahnoud centered his gaze off through the window.

"I suppose," he said thoughtfully, "retribution is seldom unmerited."

Naturally this allusion was lost on Ted Maxime completely. How could he know of the events at Faubourg St. André seventeen years before? Nor was it Ted's idea to unravel the living tangle behind Ahnoud Bey's last remark.

Maxime only knew that he had here—or had he?—the biggest drawing name in the world of nightclubs. For those boys out in the other room a deadline was nearing with every tick of Bey's leather traveling clock on the table.

On the edge of that table one of Ahnoud's well-known hands was resting. His head was turned from Ted. That handsome profile was cast darkly in glaring sunshine. There was the crimson mouth and that long line from high cheekbone to chin. There was also the downward sweep of thick lashes, over eyes surprisingly blue. On the temple lay a delicate tracery of blood vessels—worry's signature—above which grew the gloss of black Egyptian hair.

Ted smiled to himself. Profiles like that didn't happen often. When they did, their destiny was fame. This particular one was the delight of New York's portrait photographers.

"Look," said Ted, "let's fix it up for you to be at my place tonight. Is it a go?" Now Ted watched the profile relax as Bey spoke once more, "There is a reason why I cannot play. For two years Reana has been with me at every performance. No, not as you think, in person, but in thought. She knew when I was to appear, each time and where. I played to her and she heard the Mystic Melody.

"Now," he continued, "she has gone. Our mental tie has been broken. I have lost her! Reana Robinson is dead to me, Ted. You ask me to play—with a corpse for audience?" Ahnoud lifted his eyes and fixed them upon Maxime.

"No, my friend, I shan't play tonight." Bey's voice fell to a stage whisper. "*I shall never play again . . .*"

"That's a lot of hooey, Ahnoud," Ted sneered. "You're too smart a man to let any woman throw you. See here—I'll guarantee you, tonight, one of the swellest audiences you ever faced. At my Palm Club will be millionaires, movies stars, and nearly every item of headline fodder from Broadway, Hollywood, and Newport.

"You don't know how jammed Sun City is now with all the crowd up from Havana, *everybody*—" Bey was unimpressed by this effusion.

"Everybody but Reana," he answered coldly.

"Everybody *and* Reana," Ted shot back, with an inflection that made Ahnoud sure Maxime was in earnest.

"What do you mean?" Bey asked. "She is out on her yacht, for days—"

"Her tub docks tonight at nine," Ted cut in, "and I happen to know there's a party planned for the Courtneys. Their friends are meeting the boat when it comes in and bringing the couple straight to my Club. Now see—" He waved triumphant hands but spoke more confidentially, "Get up there, kid and give that piano all you've got! Show her you don't care!"

Ahnoud's face was immobile, his lips compressed. The breath seemed to be arrested in his throat as he replied with difficulty, "Show her that I care. You mean—" Then with that compelling note creeping into his voice," Show her that I intend to hold her forever. Not two years has she been free—nor have I—and there were years before that—when I followed her—*willing her surrender.*"

"Aw forget it," Ted interrupted, but he saw now a changed Ahnoud Bey. Those queer eyes were illumined by an inner light. That moody Eastern face was transformed by the glory of great hope.

"Promise me I can speak to Reana," Bey implored, "and I will play for you tonight. Promise that you will bring her to the Jasmine Dining Room—where we first met—" Ted nodded jubilantly.

"Sure, why not? I'll ask her myself. Jules couldn't kick about Reana's just saying a few words to you. That's swell, Ahnoud!" Maxime slapped the mystic's broad shoulders, then flung open the door.

"Boys—*your story*!" he cried. "Bey's playing at the Palm Club tonight!" The reporters grabbed their hats and made for the hall door.

"Thanks, Mr. Maxime," they called, looking at their watches, "just in time to get it in!"

"And see to my ads," yelled Ted. 'They're made up, ready for the press. Tell Ben and Charlie to let it roll!"

"Okay, Mr. Maxime," the boys shouted from the hallway. As they left, Ted ran over to the phone, picking it up and calling his Club. At the same time he talked to Bey.

"Where's your car, Ahnoud—on track sixteen as usual?"

Ahnoud stood framed in the open bedroom door. He was himself again, his lips half smiling and blue diamonds in his eyes.

"Yes," he replied suavely, "and in the car, as usual, is a very good imitation of the Golden Keys."

"Hello—hello Chunky—" Ted spoke hastily into the phone. "Look Chunk—we've got Bey for tonight—*yeah!* Look—send down to get his piano—yeah—track sixteen—private car —*yeah!*"

The stridency of Ted's voice drummed off and through Ahnoud's ears without registering meaning, for Bey was revolving something in his mind.

Our love cannot end like this, he thought, for it has been too perfect—too remarkable! Our memories are finely interwoven and our minds practically one. Reana has the piano, also, to speak for me—"

Like hundreds before him who had loved only to lose, Ahnoud Bey, famed mystic, held fast to his new hope. Like the others, he refused to see the ending. He dared not face the truth yet knew that awaiting him was the actual and fearful "goodbye."

LXX

Chimes of the clock at Boulevard and Fourth were ringing ten when the Robinson yacht docked. The anchor chain rattled and a crowd of Reana's friends hastened to meet the returning ship, crying, "Surprise—surprise party!"

"We're taking you to Maxime's Palm Club," the leader stated, "to celebrate!"

Jules and Reana responded in the same manner of carnival spirit. They laughed a lot and were genuinely pleased, yet withal a bit abstracted. As two wandering in from some sort of dream world, they were taken to a waiting car, then up the Boulevard into the gaiety of a Sun City night.

"Isn't this on the thrilling side!" Reana murmured to Jules, and he whispered, "Definitely!"

However, they talked only as by rote. Their eyes blinked at the headlights coming toward them down the street. At the Palm Club's entranceway, Ted Maxime met the Courtneys, taking their hands in his own.

"Welcome home, Mr. and Mrs.," he said simply. "Here's a wish that this evening may start for you both the happiest of lifetimes!"

The Club gleamed with expectancy, and distinction marked a crowd with many noted names. The orchestra was pitched to an odd downbeat of tomorrow's timing. Across the stage, concealing red floor and French windows, had been drawn the mysterious velvet curtain.

Reana viewed the curtain casually, ignorant so far of what was behind it shining in the half darkness. Others watched the blue folds eagerly, knowing well its golden secret. That, and possibly that alone, had brought them in droves to the Palm Club. The very name of Ahnoud Bey was an unfailing magnet.

Two years before, when he had first appeared in Sun City, the act was one of small renown in America. It was mentioned as a novelty—"the fellow who plays a piano with his mind."

Tonight—and such can be the swiftness of fame—the huge crowd packing the Palm Club was there to see and hear Ahnoud Bey. They knew him well now as a clever young mentalist —game for autograph hunters—in short, a celebrity.

They had read of his black and white Park Avenue apartment, his private car, and his reputation for correct dressing. Running through the rumors about Bey, intangible as incense, was something about a blonde in Sun City to whom Ahnoud had given his original Golden Keys piano.

On the subject of Bey's mental prowess, the crowd was divided into three groups. There was the sharply cynical doubter, the nicely balanced scientist, and the complete convert.

Some came to scoff, others to analyze, and some, of feminine persuasion, to fall for six feet of Egyptian good looks. All were drawn by the figure that gossip, publicity, and countless deft performances had made of Ahnoud Bey. He was an unrivaled attraction, as Ted had known when he went through that morning's purgatorio. Victorious, Maxime had filled his Club to overflowing tonight.

"Hello, hello come right in!" he invited, shaking hands, calling first names, and never forgetting that ladies loved compliments.

"Welcome to Sun City! Here! I'll find you a table myself!" Presently there were no more tables to be found. Soon the private dining rooms were filling and Ted wished that Ahnoud were the useful sort to make walls expand and tables rise from the floor.

The ropes went up—the foyer was half packed.

"This makes the third time I've missed seeing this Bey fellow by a split second," someone complained. "In both London and New York, I arrived just in time for a rope across my middle."

"How about standing room inside, Ted?" another questioned, to which the ready Ted promised, "We're lining the walls with chairs. You folks go in before the curtain rises."

It was noticeable that the women were especially in evidence, their flowers and jewels having an edge of dash and luster over any other evening. Their dresses were of flamboyant color and metallic dazzle, the swinging skirt of flame chiffon or the sheath of sequins. Laughs were high keyed, eyes unnaturally bright, for Ahnoud Bey could be had. At least this was the general opinion.

"If only one were nervy enough, my dear, to play with fire," murmured a brunette in neon blue as she returned to her table.

In that vein they talked, as it happened, always just beyond Reana's hearing. Her own party was sworn to silence. She herself was deaf to blaring trumpets and the absurd antics on a packed dance floor. At a gay table for twelve, Reana was detached from her surroundings and heedless of those about her.

"You know," she said to Jules as his hand covered hers, "I keep thinking of that sunlight on the Church and of Father Couperin. It was all so dear—quaint San Rafael—and the nights with only the sea around us!"

"So do I," Courtney echoed tenderly. "We can't snap out of that sweet experience all at once."

"And it will last this time, Jules?" Reana asked in a shaky voice.

"Of course, honey," he answered, patting her hand, "just as in the fairy tales—*forever and ever.*"

There they were in the midst of that giddy crowd—two moderns gone romantic, perhaps the only two in all that throng who had found real peace at last.

Unmindful of the mounting excitement around them, Jules and Reana did not see Ted hovering about his tables.

Maxime felt the electrified ether of his room, catching the painful expectation that always prefaced one of Bey's performances. A crowd like this was inspiring, yet took the most tactful handling. The sensibilities of these folks were heightened by the near hypnotic influence Ahnoud Bey seemed to cast over his audiences.

What a show, Ted thought, but by what a thread it hung! He was as one on a tight rope. Now he saw how long a chance he had taken this morning in offering Reana's visit as bait to the stubborn Egyptian. If she should refuse to meet Bey in the Jasmine Room—what then?

If Maxime were to delay longer in approaching Reana, she would surely hear comments eddying about the room;

"Ahnoud Bey? Where is he? Will he play soon?" Ted knew his game would be up, should that happen.

Almost at once he was at the table for twelve and Reana's perfume near him like the halo of her hair. To make conversation, Maxime asked Courtney something about his schooner and they laughed together, man fashion. After this, Ted said to Reana, as though it were an after thought, "Say, honey—you know the private rooms are full tonight. Someone back there has asked to meet you. I think she's a well-known modiste from New York. With your reputation for stunning gowns, naturally—" Reana appeared perplexed but not prejudiced, replying, "Really? I wonder how she heard of me?" Ted's heart missed a beat. He placed his hand on the back of Reana's chair.

"Will you come now?" he asked. "I'll take you back and introduce you. I know Jules won't mind." Reana half-rose to go, resting eyes on Courtney as she did so.

"Okay, darling? Just a duty call."

"Okay," saluted Jules, "but don't forget to make it short."

Ted could have whistled aloud with relief, although he well knew as he escorted Reana out into the foyer that his suspense was not wholly ended.

Maxine led Reana down the foyer to a quiet corner, well removed from earshot of the curious mob. Here he rashly broke the bad news.

"Look, honey—I'm not bringing you to meet any gown designer, though there is one here who asked for an introduction. I wasn't lying when I told you that, but someone else is waiting for you in the Jasmine Room." Ted gulped hard and ran one forefinger inside his collar, grown suddenly very tight.

"It's Ahnoud Bey, Reana—and he's playing here tonight!" A cloud fell over her face. She stepped back, shocked.

"Ahnoud? Here—tonight?" she gasped. "And you ask me to see *him?* Ted, you must be crazy!"

"Now listen, child," Ted soothed in a dulcent voice, "you see this crowd? Well these people have come to see Bey do his stuff. Maybe I've played the fool. I got Ahnoud for tonight because I promised I'd bring you in for a few words. If you don't see him, he won't play and my show'll be ruined."

Reana was listening in that quiet way of hers, nor did her manner belie her real feelings. She knew what this great night and this crowd meant to Maxime.

Reana also thought just what a friend he had been in her lonely years now past. Never had he refused when she had asked any favor. At times she might have fared badly but for his shrewd advice and true blue devotion.

"Oh I see it all, Ted," she finally said, shaking her head as one might at a bad boy.

"Dear Ted—what a showman you are! How do you manage to get into such ridiculous corners? Well, of course I will see Ahnoud. Only please," her voice dropped, "don't tell Jules."

Ted's eager face lighted. His black eyes twinkled and he began to breathe easily again. Gosh—what a place! Now—still on the rope! Thank goodness for Reana's friendship, bless her heart!

"I can't thank you enough, Reana," Ted heard himself saying. "Bey's in the Jasmine Room now. Want me to go in with you? Are you afraid?"

The next moment was reassuring for a jittery Maxime. Reana smiled oddly, her eyes on on the private room door. With one hand she touched Ted's arm and with the other lifted her organza skirt as though to leave.

"Go back to your marvelous crowd, Ted," she said, "I'm not afraid, *now*."

With the grace of a queen, Reana stepped

to a door at her right. She entered and closed it softly behind her, saying with a coolness that cut a famous mystic to the quick, "Hello, Ahnoud, you wanted to see me?"

LXXI

Ahnoud stopped short in a line of floor pacing. He swung round, searching eyes on the visitor. In his right hand he held a burning cigarette. The smoke wisped up into a blue spiral, drifting across the somber lines of his face.

For a moment Bey had no words, because he knew instantly that Reana was lost to him. The contact between her mind and his was broken.

She was not the "Golden Lady" of old, keen, responsive to his every thought. She might have been a puppet or any pretty woman, polite, a bit hurried, with her thoughts wholly elsewhere.

"Reana Courtney," said Bey in a subdued voice, as in half question.

"Yes—hasn't it a charming sound?" Reana dropped into a chair as she spoke. Ahnoud sat down across from her, his back to the open window.

"I wanted you to tell me, yourself, that it is true," he went on in the same characteristic voice.

"It's very true, Ahnoud," Reana said. "Jules and I renewed our faith and our vows at the San Rafael Mission Church. We are so happy, as we could have been all through the years had not—" Ahnoud's eyes became dull.

"Had I not loved you at Faubourg St. André in postwar France," he supplied. "Had I not been a rotten young idiot, who considered nothing beyond his own selfish desires.

"Say it, my darling, if you wish! Jules must have told you how I caused your heartbreak. Condemn me—put your hate into words. What can it matter tonight?" Reana said nothing for awhile. Fragments of music and conversation penetrated the Jasmine Room, as Bey sat, eyes glued to the floor. When she spoke, Reana's voice was kind and compassionate.

"Ahnoud, I have forgiven you for that. Father Couperin asked me to do so."

Bey raised his eyes. Reana was indeed a lovely vision, he thought. She was proudly seated in her chair. This was a new Reana, an even more desirable one.

She wore white organza with puffed sleeves and a little round collar meeting in front at her throat with a tiny bouquet of violets. There was natural color in her cheeks and a lively glow in her eyes. This, clearly, was the woman a better love had made—Jules Courtney's love.

Ahnoud would have preferred that Reana scathe him with denunciation rather than dismiss him thus, as an erring Moslem. He was stung by this disregard, yet Bey was not one to lose without a hard fight. He rose and stood now, towering above her, almost majestic in his height, with the light glinting across his black hair.

"Do you think I can forget how you came here—to me—that night?" he queried. "You *asked* to see me then."

"And if I had known—" she came back, "I should have cut off my hand before writing that request."

Ahnoud took the insult standing. This was better. Surrender sometimes followed abuse, he thought. The mystic was still struggling to repeat his victory of two years before—or that victory, strange as it seemed, of only six weeks before.

Bey put a cigarette between his lips and tilted his head upward. His eyes were a blue fire in the room, the line of his chin insolent.

"You were a Golden Lady that night when I found you here, sophisticated in dress, challenge on your lips, tragedy in your eyes. I kissed you, and later gave you the piano." Unshaken by Ahnoud's musical baritone, Reana rose with a glance at her watch.

"That was two years ago, Ahnoud," she said. "This is tonight. The miracle for which I dared not hope has happened. Jules has returned. He is waiting for me now. I must go."

As she finished speaking, Ahnoud stepped

to her. His movement was smooth and noiseless as his hands on her shoulders were firm.

"You cannot go!" he cried, holding her eyes with his. "You cannot cut the past out with a knife! Look at me and tell me it is over. *Look at me* and say that our ties of two years are broken. When I love you so, how can I be cast out from your heart and life?"

Unstirred by the power of that mind she had learned to obey, Reana stood very straight and still in Bey's grasp. She looked him full in the eyes. Her own were clear and unwavering, her lips firm, her breathing steady. About her was a strength she herself could not comprehend.

"If you mean that I am free, Ahnoud," she said at last, "yes—and do you know why? *Because there is a Little Church Around The Corner, where men go to pray for lost souls.*"

Ahnoud must have sat there, his eyes on the floor, his fingers locked between his knees, for many minutes before he moved an inch. He went through it all again and again. Reana's words had struck him hard; that she had really escaped from his mental mandates stunned him even more. His hands had slipped from her shoulders, then she had said, "Goodbye, Ahnoud—won't you say goodbye to me?"

With the props falling from under him, with an abyss of blackness yawning before him, he had replied in his cryptic way, "You will *see* my goodbye."

After Reana was gone he had found this chair somehow. Here he stayed, with defeat turning his body to stone.

Self-reproach was upon him now, too. How useless his whole life had been. Too much money—too much indulgence—and a Turk for a grandfather! That was the trouble, he supposed. Turks rode over dead bodies to get what they wanted and were cordially despised for doing so.

Under his grandfather's code, Ahnoud had never recognized the rights of others. He had used a great mental power only for his own gain. This had caused him to break the heart of the one women he could ever love. Now he had lost her, body and soul. Bey had a numb sensation as though he could not move. When he heard Ted come in, his voice sounded far off.

Well, Ahnoud, high time you went on," Ted commented with exuberance. "They're asking—begging—for you, the swellest audience this side of New York! They've paid for chairs against the walls, even for standing room."

Bey dragged his eyes from the tile floor and stared up at Ted. Maxime seemed a half acre away—but Bey spoke with an intense effort at reaching him.

"May I have a cigarette?"

"Sure," Ted agreed. "We'll each have a puff or two."

The club owner regarded his prize narrowly through the smoke. Ted felt that the interview with Reana had been a disagreeable one for Ahnoud, but it was not Maxime's place to ask questions. That Bey was ready to go on—that he had what it took to satisfy the mob out there—was of prime importance to Ted Maxime, the showman.

Now he walked up and down the small room, taking quick puffs at his smoke then tossing the half-consumed stub into an ashtray.

"Ready to go?" Ted asked. Seconds were hours, danger signals, when playing with the temperament of such a crowd. Ahnoud mashed out his own smoke and stood up before Ted. Bey was taller than Maxime by all of five inches.

"Of course I'm ready," the Egyptian said. He now saw Ted for the first time. Ahnoud ran the fingers of his right hand through his hair, then adjusted cuffs and tie absently. Stepping to the door, he paused as his eyes met Ted's squarely.

In that white face—in that taut, tearless face—Bey's eyes were blue torches, flaming for a lost cause. Ted was seized by a premonition that chilled him to the bone. He saw, too late, the situation he had caused. *Too late?*

"Ahnoud," he cried, "maybe you'd better not—" But Bey held up a hand of caution, indicating the foyer outside.

"You forget they are waiting," he said, the ghost of a smile on his lips. "Tell Mike, when you see him, of this crowd, this evening. Tell him it was as I willed it to be. Can you remember that? *As I willed it to be!*" With that he opened the door, standing aside for Ted to go ahead, thus making a way through the crowd.

Maxime shed his fears and nobly bucked the mass of people that knotted about the famed performer. Crossing the foyer was difficult with Ahnoud Bey along. Women pushed and shoved crazily while Ted elbowed his way through it all, the mystic behind him. Their goal was a door that opened into a hallway leading around to backstage.

"Let us through, please, ladies—*please!*" begged Ted. "Let Ahnoud alone, he's gotta go on! He'll see you later—yes, *yes* he's going on *now!*" They made the door and locked it behind them.

Immediately the news ran through the supper club like a high voltage current.

"Ahnoud Bey's going on!"

"Yes—he'll be on any minute—" The orchestra stopped playing and every eye sought the stage. Lights went down and gradually the velvet curtains parted until the whole scene was revealed. There was the red floor, a long French window, and the Golden Keys.

When Ahnoud walked from the wings and stood beside his piano, the applause was deafening. Some were lifting wineglasses in mute toasts to Bey.

Presently all was quiet. Ahnoud was flooded by a yellow spotlight, for there was no moon tonight at the long French window.

The pulsing enthusiasm of the crowd, the splendor of this night, were as nothing to Bey. A memory he dreaded was here, trapping him by its vague loveliness. His eyes were on a certain table, favored of her then, favored of her now.

That night two years ago, moonbeams had fallen across that table and into the pale light she had risen—"A Golden Lady."

LXXII

Tonight it was Jules Courtney who rose from that table, a scowl on his face, a napkin gripped in one hand and eyes on the stage.

"It's time we left this place," he said to Reana.

"We can't go, darling," she murmured. "Sit down—everyone will be looking at us." Jules resumed his seat, still watching Ahnoud Bey.

"What the devil is he doing here?" Courtney asked, then as he met his bride's smiling eyes, he himself smiled. "As if it mattered," Jules concluded abruptly, covering Reana's hand with his.

He gazed upon her long and fondly, knowing she was his, reclaimed from a wizard's potent spell. Courtney was very thankful for it all.

He dismissed Bey from his mind as he heard Reana say, "I love you—*that's* what matters."

Ahnoud saw the little scene between those two. He caught their absorption and the tenor of their conversation, if not the words. Bey knew he would never again see Reana with her face close to his own as during those moments in the orange grove, the lighthouse, and the private car. Near her now was the dark head of Jules Courtney. His was a laughing face, with brief mustache and dimples. Reana had no eyes for any save him.

Ahnoud at last settled on the piano bench. His fingers struck the Golden Keys in that dynamic introduction, then came lingering measures of close harmony, runs that were like harp music and sparkling arpeggios.

A hush fell on the supper club as that melody swelled in wave on wave of sound. Its bell-clear tones spoke to minds that were already Bey's with the first few resounding bars. An undercurrent of beauty in the ensuing movement broke hearts with its appealing refrain.

No one moved. No one spoke. All eyes were on Ahnoud Bey. Hands were dropped on damask tablecloths and cigarettes burned themselves out untouched. The frost on wineglasses ran and dripped in the heavy atmosphere.

For Ahnoud, his audience was ceasing to exist in the world he now entered. He barely heard a slight stir in the room as he stopped playing. Bey pushed his bench away from the piano, though not as far tonight as usual. He measured the distance exactly with his eyes.

His hands were cold as he placed them at each end of the bench. He worked fast, locking his feet over the seat's low rung, then fastening his eyes on the piano—on keys that began to move.

Now Ahnoud heard again the melody he had just played in actuality. He summoned it from the immediate past, bringing it back to the piano keys, and his Mystic Melody filled the room.

Bar by bar, note by note, Ahnoud drew it all from what had been a moment before—what still was in his mind—for he had mastered time. His eyes were on fire with that blaze of the Golden Keys. He reached mentally for the music, and it came to him. There was the close harmony and lilt of harp strings, there were the dynamic chords brought forth as with his own touch. The audience was spellbound.

"Oh," whispered someone, "how can I believe what I see and hear?"

"You must," someone else said. "It's the Mystic Melody!"

Another averred decisively, "I've never heard it like this—*so magnificent!*"

Ahnoud felt a stupor creeping over him and his eyes were dimmed by the Golden Keys. That music he had called back was coursing through his mind almost mechanically now, something beyond his control. With it all, he reflected, this was an end of love tonight. No longer could he face the facts that made him the unfortunate third in a triangle.

He feared that strange paradox—the specter of reality. It waited for him in the shadows outside the spot. What if the circle of light should close in on him, or the glint of Golden Keys grow dark? That might be better than fleeing from a specter.

Long ago Bey had decided oblivion for him would be best should Reana's story conclude this way. He knew now his decision had been wise. He should finish it all—the futile years—the tragedy that had come from imposing his will on others.

In thought Ahnoud went back to where there was no time, no space. He lived once more his schooldays in England, when he strove to be an Anglo-Saxon, scorning Egypt and her mysteries, all the while using those mysteries for his own ends.

Again, he rode the swiftest Arabian stallion in Islam, playing the young lord over ignorant natives whom he ruled with a hard hand. Later came the flight from Eton to Cairo, where his grandfather lay dying. Then the boy Ahnoud, only seventeen, came into an enormous legacy. Now the young Bey was his own master and his first proud plans were for four years at Oxford.

Four years stretched into five, then six, with postgraduate music study. Now he was playing too hard, throwing a little too much Egyptian money to the distant corners of London town.

Once more Ahnoud drank with the top theatrical favorites of that day. He had thought himself passionately in love with an actress who eventually married a title.

Then there were the summers in postwar Paris, parties with Americans at the Ritz and revels on the Bohemian Left Bank. Last of all, that Villa at Faubourg St. André where the Reana cycle began.

Ahnoud came back to the piano, to the stage and the Mystic Melody. Only partially, however, could he return, for his feet and hands were growing numb. A deadly detachment was moving to his heart, his brain.

The Golden Keys were too bright for him and he turned from them to the darkness. There on the window sill Jado was dancing. He whirled in the blackness—whirled and fell—to the rhythm of the music.

Ahnoud shuddered and grew colder. With hollow eyes he sought the Golden Keys. Now they were golden sands—the desert at sunset. He was walking through it alone.

Night came on, but still he wandered over the sands and across hills—weary, lost. Someone was following him and Bey heard his grandfather's voice calling sadly. Ahnoud's mother, Zyra, appeared now, begging her son not to go further. Bey shook his head to their entreaties. Deaf to their pleas, he went his way into the night.

Before him was a pile of gray and broken stones—the fallen colonnades and archways of a desert temple.

"Lost in the ruins of what once was," Ahnoud thought, roaming still under the stars, among the shattered pieces. Soon there were no stars and black night came down and down—the velvet night—until it met the towers of those ruins. There was no spot of light! It had closed, closed . . .

The Mystic Melody suddenly stopped. Ahnoud Bey threw both hands to his forehead. Without a sound he fell forward on the piano. There was a discordant crash as his great shoulders and arms hit the Golden Keys, as his dark head lay motionless on the bright and magical piano.

LXXIII

As one person the audience rose in agonized alarm, then there was a rush to the stage. Ted was the first to reach Ahnoud—Ted and a doctor. Others, men and women, clustered about, offering aid.

The Palm Club was pandemonium until the blue curtain went down. The orchestra leader stepped in front of it, announcing in a loud but solemn voice, "Ahnoud Bey is dead!"

A woman screamed, "Oh he can't be! *He can't be!* Only a short while ago he was playing the Golden Keys!"

"He was so young, so handsome, to die now," sobbed another.

"Ahnoud Bey is dead. They don't know the cause," was the word muttered throughout the supper club, leaving everyone stricken and staring. They were frozen amid their diamonds that failed to flash and flame skirts dull and limp.

"A great moment in which to go," said a prominent psychologist who knew Bey and a friend asked, "Do you think he wished to die?"

"I have no doubt of it," was the reply. "Those of the East are wiser than we. They recognize, often decide, the end."

Jules and Reana heard these remarks as they were standing beside their table. Courtney put an arm round his bride, proposing, "Shall we go?" He saw that she was pale but dry eyed as she answered, "Yes, dear."

They excused themselves to the party of friends and moved among the tables through the crowd of notables, of cynics, scientists, and converts. The women were inconsolable. How could a figure of youth and romance go forever? The musicians bowed in silent requiem over the lost Mystic Melody.

The Courtneys had little to say on their ride home, but Jules kept his arm around Reana, stating at last, "I think it's for the best that Ahnoud died. We know him better than many others who saw him pass away."

"Yes," Reana said, "maybe he couldn't live with remorse in his heart."

"If he knew the meaning of that word, which I seriously doubt," Jules added.

"I think he did," Reana answered very slowly.

They soon rode into the yellow lights and fairyland shadows of Desdena. The coquina house seemed quiet and serene to Reana as she and Jules entered. He took her into his arms, there in the soft light of the entrance hall.

"This is our first night at home," he said, deep emotion in his voice. "There's nothing now between us and happiness." Reana's face was alight as she lifted her lips to Jules'.

"Nothing now, darling," she whispered, "no one—ever again."

Madeleine came down the hall and the Courtneys spoke to her. "Madeleine!" Reana cried, her face shadowing again, "Ahnoud Bey is dead! He fell on his piano while he was playing."

"Tonight, Madame?" inquired the maid, "and where?"

"Here, at the Palm Club," Jules answered.

Now Madeleine twisted her kerchief in her hands. She was half in tears.

"Oh Madame, I can't help being glad he's gone! Oh—*now* you are out of his power!" She hugged Reana impulsively, then drew back, saying as on second thought, "He must have willed his death, Madame. I can tell it now, *the vow he made.*" She was talking rapidly. Jules and Reana hung on her words.

"What vow?" they asked. Madeleine led them to the music salon door.

"The night he gave you the piano," she continued, awe in her tone, "the night after M'sieur Jado died over at the Hotel. I was listening, Madame—as I should not have been—only through concern for your safety. As Ahnoud Bey stood by the piano, he said something in a foreign language."

Reana recalled this only too well. She

caught her maid by the arm, asking, "What did he say? Do you speak Arabic?"

"Yes, Madame," Madeleine replied. "I once served the wife of a British attaché who was stationed in Egypt. It was necessary that I learn to talk with native servants, so I came to know Arabic, spoken, at least."

"And the vow?" Reana urged.

"Ahnoud swore, Madame," the maid said, "by all the gods of Egypt and by the Prophet in whom he did not believe. He made the sort of vow that he could not have broken, had he so desired.

"He said, Madame, that if the one you loved—*M'sieur Jules*—ever came back and he, Ahnoud Bey, lost you forever, he would die by his own will. Gone also would be the music of the piano—the Golden Keys—that he had just given to you."

Jules whistled and frowned. "What a vow!" he exclaimed. "And Bey kept that vow tonight, as surely as we saw him die!"

Reana did not reply but went forward into the music room. There was the low dais where two lights burned beneath high windows. The solution of it all was clear to her at last. Ahnoud had paused, just there, and spoken in a language she did not know. Tonight he had said to her, "*You will see my goodbye.*"

Reana stepped up on the dais, and there in all its glinting beauty was the piano. As Bey had taken his own life, could he snatch from her too the music of this, his gift to her?

Hardly daring to do so, Reana touched a key with one finger, then struck a chord.

Swinging round, she called, "Jules! Madeleine!"

Both crossed the salon to the dais. Reana, her breath coming faster, sat down on the piano bench and for the third time ran her fingers over the shining keyboard.

As Jules and Madeleine stood beside her, Reana dropped her hands in wordless sorrow, for Ahnoud Bey had taken with him the music of his piano.

The Golden Keys were stilled.

THE BEST OF ROMANCE FROM WARNER BOOKS

IO GENTLE LOVE
y Rebecca Brandewyne (91-183, $2.50)

;he was a beauty, besieged by passion, sailing from Regency :ngland to mysterious Macao on an uncharted voyage to love. ;he was also unready to accept the love in her heart for the lomineering, demanding man whose desire for her was jealous, 'iolent, engulfing, but enduring.

AKEHELL DYNASTY
y Michael William Scott (95-201, $2.75)

'rom the first time he saw the ship in full sail like a winged bird gainst the sky, Jonanthan Rakehell knew the clipper held his lestiny. This is his story of conquering the seas, challenging the vorld and discovering love in his dream—the clipper. His is the old, sweeping, passionate story of a great New England shipping amily caught up in the winds of change and of the one man vho would dare sail his ship to the frightening, beautiful land f China.

IER SHINING SPLENDOR
'alerie Sherwood (85-487, $2.75)

.enore and Lorena: their names are so alike, yet their beauties so issimilar. Yet each is bound to reap the rewards and the troubles f love. Here are the adventures of the exquisite Lenore and her eauteous daughter Lorena, each setting out upon her own dyssey of love, adventure, and fame.

WARNER BOOKS
P.O. BOX 690
New York, N.Y. 10019

Please send me the books I have selected.
Enclose check or money order only, no cash please. Plus 50¢ per order and 20¢ per copy to cover postage and handling. N.Y. State and California residents add applicable sales tax.

Please allow 4 weeks for delivery.

_____ Please send me your free mail order catalog

_____ Please send me your free Romance books catalog

Name_____

Address_____

City_____

State_____ Zip_____